The Promise of HOME

A *Hearthfire* ROMANCE

The Promise of
HOME

A *Hearthfire* ROMANCE

MICHELE
PAIGE
HOLMES

Mirror Press

Interior Design by Cora Johnson
Edited by Cassidy Wadsworth Sorenson and Lisa Shepherd
Cover design by Rachael Anderson
Cover Image Credit: Brekke Felt, Studio 15 Portraits
Cover Model: Halle Holt

Published by Mirror Press, LLC

ISBN-13: 978-1-947152-45-8

Dear Reader,

The book you hold in your hands (or view on your e-reader) is the third and final installment in the Hearthfire Historical Scottish series about brothers Collin and Ian MacDonald. While *The Promise of Home* it is an exciting and romantic read all on its own, it is the continuation of the stories of several characters whose lives intertwine in the previous two books. May I strongly suggest that if you have not done so already, you read the first two books in the series before beginning this one.

Yesterday's Promise is the story of how Collin MacDonald—a Scottish laird—and Katherine Mercer—daughter of an English soldier—meet and marry. Starting at the beginning of their story will make this series a more fulfilling read. *A Promise for Tomorrow* continues Katie and Collin's love story and their attempts to right the wrongs done to each of their clans and to preserve their way of life in the Highlands. *The Promise of Home* brings their greatest adventures yet and also their happy ending.

Originally I had hoped to keep this series to two books, but the Scottish Highlands, Colonial America, and Nova Scotia in the late 18th century provided backdrops rich in both historical significance and tragic events.

Many of the events in *The Promise of Home* are based in fact, including the turbulent events surrounding Katie and Collin's ocean voyage.

Leaving bodies on the gallows was common in London, especially at Execution Dock on the Thames, where pirates and others were hanged for their crimes, their bodies left in chains as a warning to other would-be criminals. The execution of one Captain James Lowry, that Katie and Collin stumble upon, really did occur there in March of 1762.

Sable Island off the coast of Nova Scotia was a real threat, particularly during a storm, and known as the Graveyard of the Atlantic, with some 350 vessels having shipwrecked there.

Highlanders who chose to leave their sacred homeland set sail for a new world that included cities and locales up and down the coast of North America, from Nova Scotia to the Carolinas. Those forced to leave arrived in the Colonies destitute and owing between seven to fourteen years of labor as payment for their passage or crimes.

In 1762 in North America, the French and Indian War, also known as The Seven Years' War, was in its final year. Just as the Highlanders were being forced from their homes on the other side of the Atlantic, some eleven thousand French Acadians had been driven from their homes and deported to the southern Colonies, the Caribbean, and even France during this time period.

In *The Promise of Home* Captain Shenk's description of the New World as a wild and dangerous place, along with his tales of scalping and a people with a savageness unknown to Europeans, were apt descriptions of the events during this war.

Captain James Cook was not yet a captain and not yet famous for his explorations in 1762, but he was in Nova Scotia during this time, working on detailed maps of the area. He was also called away to St. John's late that summer, to retake the land after the French victory there.

One final note of historical significance (to me, personally, at least) is the appearance of another Captain Cooke in *The Promise of Home*. Captain Nicholas Cooke of Rhode Island (later the governor of Rhode Island) is my ancestor. He and his vessel, *The Charming Sally* did sail to Nova Scotia, and a 1763 notice shows him attempting to collect payment for passengers transported to Nova Scotia the previous year.

It is my hope with this trilogy, to capture a small bit of this tragic and exciting time in history and particularly the story of a resilient people who did their best to hold onto the past while forging bravely into an unknown and vastly different future. Amidst the records of my own Scottish ancestors, I've read of tragedy and hardship, yet also seen glimpses of love and joy . . . Family. Katie, Collin, Ian, and Eliza have become like family to me, throughout the telling of their story. I hope you will feel the same and enjoy every page of their journey.

Happy reading.
Michele

Prologue

The Scottish Highlands, October 1747

Collin

"Do you hear them, Collin?" The small, frozen fingers grasping my arms tightened. "They've set dogs after us."

Five-year-old Katie's words and the baying of hounds startled me to full wakefulness. I shot from our latest hiding spot like a lead ball from the pistols Highlanders were no longer permitted. The leaves I'd used to both warm and conceal us in the hollow beneath the tree scattered and then landed on a fresh layer of snow.

No wonder Katie's so cold. How long had I slept? I berated myself for dozing off. After three days on the run, I was exhausted. Yet even a momentary lapse of awareness might cost our lives.

The barking dogs and shouting men grew closer. Reaching down, I lifted Katie into my arms. We'd done well staying hidden in the forest this long. But now there were dogs; the time for hiding was over.

"We've but one choice," I said. "If we can reach the kirk and plead sanctuary, it's possible the soldiers won't be able to take you." It was doubtful at best. The English had little regard for our places of worship or anything else. They went where they wanted and took what they wanted. But I had to offer the lass—and myself—a bit of hope.

Her legs wrapped tightly around my torso, her arms around my neck. "Run, Collin," she pled. "Don't let them find me."

"I won't." Against such odds my promise felt hollow. Somehow I found another reserve of strength to start us back toward the keep.

As I ran I plotted. We'd go around the back way, where I could hoist Katie through one of the kirk windows. Father William was a kindly old man and would surely help us. No doubt he had somewhere to hide a tiny lass. And if the soldiers took me . . . I'd lived a year longer than my brother or my father. Perhaps I'd evaded death at the hands of the English as long as possible. At least Katie would be safe.

Running soon warmed me, though the clouds of my labored breaths confirmed that the temperature had not changed. Occasionally a stray, slushy snowflake landed on my face. In the past Katie would have laughed and brushed it from my lashes or the tip of my nose; but now her head was down, buried firmly in my chest as she clung to me. My gaze swerved back and forth, behind and ahead, looking for signs that we were being followed, and doing my best to keep a sure footing on the slippery leaves.

It would have been easier to run with Katie on my back. But then I wouldn't be between her and the soldiers—and any guns they might fire.

Without pausing, I strained to listen for the baying hounds. It sounded as if they'd moved west of us now, as if we were running a parallel trajectory. I hoped our scent would lead them a merry chase through the forest, to the many spots we'd stopped to rest and hide the past days.

Katie had woken me a few nights previous, alerting me to the English soldiers that would shortly be arriving in the hall below. We'd barely made our escape through the kitchens before the very men she'd seen in vision filled the courtyard, dismounting their horses and heading up the front steps. We hadn't lingered to see what they were about. Katie had known for weeks they were coming for her.

We were nearing the edge of the wood now. I had two choices—stay within and add at least an hour to our journey, or take the road a distance then cut back into the forest until we came around closer to the kirk.

I hesitated only a second before choosing the road. We would be in plain sight for a time, but the dogs had our trail either way. The sooner we reached the kirk, the better.

I ran on, grimacing at the stitch in my side and the pinking sky. Dawn would be upon us soon. We would be even more exposed.

Shouting sounded behind us a few minutes later. We'd been spotted. Soldiers were across the road, riding along a ridge that rose behind the wood. It allowed them a good view of us, and would continue to unless I disappeared into the forest. But out of sight was no longer safe, not with the dogs. I stayed on the road.

My chest burned, and the back of my neck ached from Katie's fierce grip. Her legs and feet dug into my sides and back. We were both desperate for water, food, and sleep. I prayed as I ran, that I wouldn't stumble and fall. I didn't think I could pick myself back up.

At last we darted back into the wood. I imagined I could see the grey stone of the kirk. "Almost there," I panted.

Katie moved her head in acknowledgement but did not look up. She had been afraid for weeks, and likely trembled as much from that as from the freezing temperature and the snow falling heavily now.

The dogs' barking was louder, nearly at our heels. The ground trembled with pounding hoofbeats.

With a final surge of strength I broke from the forest once more and sprinted across the field toward the kirkyard. As we drew closer, my heart sank. The back of the building was much taller than I'd anticipated. I wasn't certain I could hoist Katie up through any of the windows.

No matter. They'd seen us now. There would be no hiding her, only the possibility of pleading sanctuary in a house of God.

I was running so hard when we reached the building that I nearly crashed into it. I veered to the side at the last second and almost smashed my shoulder and Katie's into the corner. "We're here," I told her. "Find Father Williams."

We rounded the front, and I came up short—at the feet of at least a dozen pairs of shiny English boots and the horses between them.

I stepped back, my arms still wrapped around Katie. More hoofbeats and the barking of dogs sounded behind us now. The hunting party from the forest had caught up, and these others had been lying in wait . . . almost as if they'd known where we might go.

"Good job, lad. You were right. They did come here." A black-haired soldier at the head of the group flipped a coin in the air. I watched it spin end over end until it landed in a dirty, outstretched palm. My eyes riveted to an ice-blue pair that glowered at me. *Brann.*

His familiar sneer reeked of victory as he clutched the coin then spun away.

Sold for a pittance. I forced my anger back. Laird Campbell would deal with Brann later. And if he didn't, I would.

"Hand her over," the same soldier said to me.

I shook my head and tightened my grip around Katie's waist. "Her home is here. See how you've frightened her already."

Katie's sobs filled the kirkyard. "Don't let go, Collin!"

I didn't intend to. "Why can't you leave us be? She's done nothing to you."

"English blood runs through her," the soldier said. "Reason enough to take her from this God-forsaken place."

"She doesn't know what's good for her now, or she'd never want to stay," the Redcoat beside him added.

The first soldier dismounted and motioned to those on either side of him to do the same. The three advanced on us.

I'd no place to go. If I took even one step back, the men behind me might snatch Katie away.

"Father William!" I shouted. "We plead sanctuary."

The kirk doors remained firmly shut. No one appeared.

"He's been detained on a matter at the castle," the black-haired soldier said smugly.

"It would not matter if he was here," a third man said. "She belongs with us." He stepped forward and placed a hand on Katie's shoulder. She screamed, her shrill voice echoing through the trees in the yard and beyond.

"She belongs with her mother's people." I longed to thrust his hand from her shoulder but dared not release my tight hold.

"Don't be a fool," the black-haired one hissed. He drew his sword, and the others followed suit. "Come with us, girl, and no one gets hurt."

"I won't." She lifted her tear-stained face to glare at them.

"You will." As a threesome they advanced, one prying his arm between Katie and me, grasping her around the middle. My neck bowed forward beneath her grip as they began pulling her away.

"Don't let go of me, Collin," she shrieked. "Don't let them take me."

"Leave her be!" I landed a kick on one's shin." He cursed and raised his sword.

Katie's grasp slipped from my neck as they tugged her. She grabbed my arm; then her fingers slid down the length of it. I barely clasped her hand before she was torn away entirely.

"Don't let go," she sobbed, lifting her tear-filled eyes to mine.

The Redcoat raised his sword above us. "She's only half English. If you want her that badly, we'll let you keep a piece. You can have her hand." The steel blade sliced the air.

No! I let go, but not before I'd realized his intent and felt a sharp sting. Blood spurted from my wrist, and a bright red trail spattered the snow, following Katie as they whisked her away.

Not her hand! I scanned the ground but could not find it. *Please God, no.*

"Collin!" Her hoarse cry roused me. Clutching my wrist, I staggered after them.

"Katie," I shouted. "Don't take her. Please don't—"

Beyond the horses I made out a carriage. The door swung open, and the men handed her inside. I ran faster, not caring if they cut me down entirely in my attempt to stop them. Laird Campbell would come. Surely he would come and stop this madness.

I ducked between and beneath the soldiers, pushing my way through the horses in time to see the door close and the carriage lurch forward. Katie's muffled cries came from inside. She beat on the window, trying to get out, and a thick smear of blood covered the glass.

Someone grasped at my shoulder, and I shrugged him off and ran, steps pounding in the tracks of the carriage.

"Shall I shoot him?" someone asked.

"Don't waste your shot. Look at that blood. Let him run as he will. He's not long for this world."

I awoke to cold rain peppering my face. An unearthly *whooshing* sounded in my ears as I opened my eyes and strained to see through a dense fog.

"Bind that wrist up tighter; get that bleeding stopped. He's lost too much already." Laird Campbell's voice was oddly comforting. The man who I'd believed an enemy a year before had become a man I trusted with my life. He'd spared it when he might have taken it several times over and had even protected me from others.

"Too much blood be the way of it," another man said.

"He'll never make it back to the keep. He's the death rattle even now."

I *am making that sound?* I shuddered but felt only a vague motion in my chest. It was as if I'd lost feeling there, and in my limbs too. I could feel neither legs nor arms, only panic aplenty at the prognosis of my death.

"You'll not die on me, Collin. Do you hear that?"

One of my eyelids was peeled back to reveal Laird Campbell's face hovering above mine, his long, grey beard folded onto my chin. "What were you thinking to run after the carriage like that, with such a wound?"

Katie! I tried to sit up, but his hand held me firm.

"They've taken—"

"I know," Laird Campbell answered, his expression grim. "There was no deterring her father. But I extracted a promise from him regarding your betrothal."

I squeezed my eyes shut, but not before tears leaked from their sides. "Failed you. Failed her," I whispered.

"You've failed no one, Collin." The laird's hand was warm on my shoulder. "She will be safe enough and even happy. I have seen that much. It's you who has me worried at present. You're not to speak again. Save your strength. You've a long road ahead. But recover you shall." His voice grew distant.

I opened my eyes to see him staring off into a future only he could see.

"You will be well," he said. "And live long to be reunited with and to marry Katie. But you will be parted more than once in the course of your future together." He looked at me again. "One day it shall be *she* who chases down a carriage in search of *you.*"

Part One

They that sow the wind shall reap the whirlwind.

Chapter One

Oxfordshire, England, February 1762

Katie

A footman waited just outside the carriage, his hand extended to welcome us into another world. It wasn't the one we were ultimately headed for, an ocean away, but my brother-in-law's estate in the Oxfordshire countryside.

I accepted the outstretched hand and stepped from the carriage, vastly relieved to be free of its confines. We had rented one, only for today, Collin insisting that we arrive in style. His brother's horse trailed behind it. Having a strong aversion to carriages, stemming from an incident in childhood, I would have preferred the horse.

"Are you all right?" Collin stepped out beside me and studied my face, his own anxious.

"Better now that we are out of that contraption." I suppressed a shudder as the door was closed and the coachman drove away. The past two hours spent inside of it were the longest I had managed in a carriage—one that had actual glass in the windows, at least. Months ago Collin had broken all of the glass out of his, so I might endure the ride from England to Scotland, where we had first made our home.

We had endured much more than unpleasant travel in the months that followed. That we had both survived the first six months of our marriage was miraculous. What we had yet to survive, the adventures we were very shortly to face together, would require even more courage and faith. But I had learned that with Collin at my side I could do many things I would have otherwise believed impossible.

He offered his arm, and I took it, holding the skirt of my new gown as we made our way up the drive to the wide, curved stairs leading to a set of overly high, ornately carved double doors.

"They have *eleven* chimneys," Collin whispered when we'd passed the last of the servants lining the walk.

My eyes flickered upward. "Did you count?"

"Aye. And those are the ones visible from here."

From what we could see, the main house formed a U, with the base being the front. In all probability there were more chimneys. I felt mildly curious to see the inside of such a grand estate but far more interested in seeing my sister, Anna, and little brother, Timothy.

Anna's invitation to visit had arrived shortly before Collin and I left Scotland for good. As Anna and I had not been on the best of terms when we last were together, before her marriage last spring, I felt more than a little nervous to see her again.

We reached the top of the steps, and two additional servants came forward to open the doors for us.

"Christina!"

Before they had finished, the doors pushed open, into their unsuspecting faces, and a boy came barreling through them, straight into my arms.

"Timothy." I dropped to hug him and found myself too low for a proper embrace. "You've grown," I exclaimed, laughing as his small arms wrapped around my neck.

"I've missed you so, Christina," he said, calling me again by my middle name, the one I had used growing up.

"And I you." I pulled back a little to better look at him. "My, but you're handsome in this fancy coat and smart breeches."

His mouth turned down. "And lace like a *girl.* Look at

this." His chin jutted out, revealing the frilly collar at his throat. "I hate all these clothes Anna makes me wear."

"I know what you mean, lad." Collin raised his own chin, showing off the cravat at his throat. "Such a lot of waste, all this fabric."

I rolled my eyes at him. *He* was the one who had insisted on not only the carriage but that we each purchase a new outfit for today's visit.

"Can't have you looking like a pauper before your sister," Collin had said. No matter that we were practically penniless, or soon would be, once we'd purchased our passage to the Colonies.

Timothy smiled at Collin, and I sensed a fast friendship.

"Come along, then." Timothy took my hand and Collin's, too, practically dragging us into the house.

I stepped into the grand foyer, resplendent with beautiful furniture, an elegant chandelier, and art. *Oh, the art.*

When I would have stopped to admire each of the paintings, Timothy kept us moving toward a room on the left, before the sweeping circular staircase.

"Anna, they're here! Christina is here." Timothy's shouting negated any need for a butler, but one made an appearance anyway, ushering us into a sitting room even more lavishly decorated than the foyer.

I paused just inside, eyes locking on my sister's across the room. She stood awkwardly, the bulge of her unborn child straining against the folds of her gown. I had known she was expecting but hadn't realized there would be such a change in her so soon.

"Oh, Anna. You look lovely." I meant it with all my heart. The pregnancy seemed to have softened the planes of her face as well as rounding her body. She appeared gentler, more approachable than the last time we were together.

I crossed the room and kissed her cheek.

She returned the gesture and favored me with a wistful

smile. "Christina. You are the one who has grown into a beauty. It would seem marriage agrees with you."

"Very much." I returned her smile and felt myself blush. Though Collin and I had been married seven months, it was only recently that some of the finer aspects of marriage had come into play. "This is my husband, Laird Collin MacDonald." I stepped aside so Collin might greet her. Though Collin's land and home had been taken from him, never had I felt him more deserving of that title. The way he had led both our people the past months, the many he had saved, had proved him a leader of men.

"It is a pleasure to meet you, Lady Hartley. Katie has told me much about you." He took her hand and pressed a kiss to it, as any gallant English lord might.

I waited a breath, watching to see what Anna might think of him, his scars. Though largely healed now, and hardly noticeable to me, they had altered his appearance, particularly that of his hands. But if she found them disconcerting, she did not let on.

"Oh dear. I can imagine what tales those might have been." Her brows rose as she glanced at me.

"Indeed." Collin released her hand and stepped back. "They were rather astonishing, for what one might believe of well-bred young ladies. Midnight escapades jumping on the bed, fits of giggles, and the like."

Anna laughed. "All Christina's doing, I assure you."

"No doubt," Collin agreed with a smirk in my direction. "She has been prone to both adventure and trouble since the beginning of our acquaintance."

"Won't you sit?" Anna indicated the sofa behind us. "I'll ring for tea."

"Not tea." Timothy flung himself backward over a chair. "Boring people come for tea. Christina came to visit, to play."

"She came because I asked her to," Anna said, sounding very much like her old, snobbish self.

"I'm with the lad," Collin admitted. "After hours in a carriage, I think a bit of play, or a walk in your gardens at least, is in order. Will you come with me, Timothy?"

"Yes!" Timothy jumped from the chair and made for the doorway.

Anna called him back—rather more sharply than necessary, I thought.

He stopped where he was, shoulders slumped, head down. "Yes, sister."

"You did not ask permission to go out."

He turned and faced her. "Please, may I take Lord MacDonald outside to show him the gardens?"

Anna gave a slight nod of her head. "You may."

Collin's mouth twitched as he turned to me. "May I go out as well, milady?"

"Please do," I said, giving him a playful shove.

He gave a polite nod, accompanied by a wink and a rather sultry look that made my knees feel weak. As he left with Timothy I sighed inwardly, counting the hours until Collin and I might be alone together again. Flirting was new to both of us, and I quite enjoyed it and all that came after.

"Your husband is charming." Anna seated herself on the end of the sofa opposite me. "His appearance might lead one to believe otherwise, but when he looks at you . . ."

"I love him."

"He feels the same for you," Anna observed. "You are fortunate."

"Yes," I said, marveling that I felt that way and so gloriously happy when but a few weeks earlier life had seemed anything but.

"You are fortunate as well," I said, pulling my thoughts from Collin. "You've this beautiful home, and a bairn—a baby—shortly to arrive."

"Let us hope it is shortly," Anna said, placing a hand over the top of her rounded stomach. "He was supposed to come last week. No doubt Mother is doing her best from the other side to delay his arrival and thus limit the wagging tongues and scandal. I am fair certain it was the shame of it all that killed her."

My lips parted, but no words came out. I shook my head a little as I looked at Anna. "Scandal? What do you mean?"

"Can you not count, Christina?" Anna snapped. "I have been married barely eight months. From conception it takes nearly ten for a child to grow."

"Perhaps he is simply a large baby," I suggested.

"Don't pretend to be dim-witted. Of course Mother told you everything. Why do you think she had you wed so suddenly, without even meeting your bridegroom before?"

"Mother told me nothing," I replied, struggling to keep my temper. This was not going as I had planned or hoped. "I was not introduced to Collin because he was coming from Scotland. But I had met him before. We were betrothed when I was only four years old."

Anna waved her hand. "Well, the circumstances were odd, nonetheless. Though I see you, at least, are not suffering under strain of an early pregnancy. Mother kept telling me that I must pray it stays in as long as possible. But I don't even care now. I just want it out."

"Anna." I looked at her reproachfully. "You are speaking of your *baby*. A life created by you and your husband." *It was his child, wasn't it?*

"A baby I don't want," she said bitterly. She looked down at the swell of her stomach. "Do you know what happens when you give a man what he asks for?"

"He loves you for it," I suggested.

Anna let out a puff of air as she shook her head. "No. He cares for it—for you—less and only wants what he cannot have even more."

I frowned, trying to follow her conversation and logic. "Are you speaking of Phillip?"

Anna nodded. "Last April I gave him what he asked for,

though it wasn't—or rather *I* wasn't what he really wanted." Her gaze flickered to mine, with a flash of jealousy. "You were."

"Me?" I shook my head, then laughed. "You are gravely mistaken, sister. Phillip never had any interest in me. Remember, I was the odd daughter, the one who preferred to stay home alone to paint, instead of taking carriage rides to attend social events in the city."

"That is why he fancied you," Anna said. "You weren't like all the other girls, and you shared his passion."

I thought suddenly of all the paintings hanging in the foyer.

Anna nodded, perhaps reading the revelation on my face. "Why do you think we spent our honeymoon in Paris admiring and acquiring artwork? It wasn't *my* idea," she said bitterly.

I sat speechless, unbelieving and uncertain what I might say to make this visit gone horribly wrong turn out better. "I'm sorry, Anna. I didn't know." Little wonder she had been so angry with me when I had taken a turn with Phillip at a dance we had both attended.

"No need to be sorry," she said with a false air of cheerfulness. "I gave him what he asked for, and we both got this." She rubbed her hand over her stomach. "I don't even care anymore what the gossipmongers make of it. The child is Phillip's, and Phillip is mine."

"I am—happy for you?"

"Excellent," Anna said. "Someone in this equation ought to be, and it certainly isn't Phillip or me. Now then, if you'll be so kind as to ring for the servants." She indicated a rope behind me.

I pulled the tassel, though my appetite for tea or anything else had fled. I didn't understand Anna but felt only miserable for her or perhaps with her at the moment, as her misery seemed to permeate the very air around us.

A maid appeared, not with tea but a small trunk, which she set at Anna's feet. "Master Timothy's belongings are packed." She curtsied.

"Thank you," Anna said. "You may go now. I don't think we are feeling up to tea after all."

"Where is Timothy going?" I demanded as soon as the maid had left. "You can't ship him off to a boarding school somewhere. Losing both Father and Mother has to have been hard enough on him."

"He's not going to school, silly, though that would have done as well, I suppose. But Phillip wouldn't have been pleased about the cost. This is much better. Timothy is going with you, of course."

My eyes widened. She couldn't be serious. "Anna, we have *no* home. We are preparing to sail to the Colonies."

"So? Take him with you." She smiled, then stood as if the matter was decided.

"I can't take him from his homeland. You're here, and so is his grandfather."

"Grandfather is old. He won't be around long, and I'm going to have enough to deal with when this child comes. I have no use for Timothy here, and he is an annoyance. I don't *want* Timothy around, and neither does Phillip."

"How can you say that?" I stood, feeling my temper rise as well. "Timothy is your *brother*. You have everything here. You can provide him with a home and family, an education and opportunity."

"Timothy doesn't care about any of those things. He only wants someone to love him, and I can't give him that," Anna said. "I can't even love myself right now." She turned away from me, head bent.

I felt both terrible for her and angry with her selfishness. But if this was to be the last time I ever saw my sister, I didn't want to leave on a bitter note. I moved closer and put my arm around her.

"I'll take him." It seemed both a wonderful surprise and

8

blessing. *Collin will understand—I hope.* "What can I do for you? I want you to be happy too, Anna. How can I help?"

"Oh, Christina." She turned in my arms, and I held her close, letting her weep on my shoulder. "I've made such a mess of things."

For the first time since I'd walked into the room it felt like the old Anna was back, the one who used to share secrets and fears and laughter.

"There's nothing that cannot be fixed," I said. "This baby is yours and Phillip's. He will love it as he will love you for giving him a child."

"I don't know."

I detected the faintest trace of hope in her voice.

"I do," I said vehemently. "A baby is a miracle. The most beautiful miracle that happens between a husband and wife."

"You sound like you've experience," Anna remarked drily as she wiped her eyes.

I do." I told her of Lydia and how Collin and I had loved her, though she was not even ours. "You'll see," I promised. "Phillip can love you both. He will."

"What if I cannot love him?" Anna asked, startling me once again.

"What do you mean? You loved him when you married, did you not?" I thought back to all of the preparations for Anna's wedding and realized very little had included anything to do with her fiancé.

"I wanted him, and wanted him to want me," Anna said. "I wanted this." She swept her hand before her, indicating the beautiful room. "Truly I have everything I ever wished for. So why am I not happy?"

Much later I sat in the carriage beside Timothy, with Collin across from us, and thought sorrowfully of my sister. With so much hardship in the world already, why did some people choose to make their own, to make even more? It occurred to me that what we want is not always what is best. I had wanted the life of an artist, to be wealthy and well received, or at least enough so to support Mother, Timothy, and myself.

I had not wanted a husband, particularly one who was a Scottish laird. I had not wanted children, nor an extended family who expected so much of me. I'd not wished for weeks of harsh travel by land and more to come by sea. I'd not wished to leave my homeland forever to build a life in a new one.

I had attained nothing of my girlhood dreams. Aside from not having achieved fame and fortune, I had not even a jar of paint or a canvas at present. I had no home and scarcely a material possession to my name. Yet I could not deny the happiness bursting within my soul. I had Collin and now Timothy. And not too many months from now I would hold the baby Collin and I had created. I pressed my hand against my flat stomach as I smiled. Collin glanced at me, his own mouth curved with a joy I'd not seen there in months past. We had very literally nothing but our love for each other and the promise of this child and a home in a new land. In that moment I was certainly the happiest woman alive.

Chapter Two

Aboard the *Ulysses*, Atlantic Ocean, February 1762

Ian

"Don't you dare die. I *forbid* it. Do you hear me?"

"Aye," Ian murmured, the rasping sound of his own voice strange to his ears. Fingers pried at his lips, parting them, and a foul liquid trickled into his mouth. He tried turning his head away and found it held fast.

"It's all we've got. I'm sorry." The woman's voice was gentler this time.

We? Ian tried to place the voice, tried to imagine a woman who would wish him alive instead of dead, and one who would willingly tend him. He couldn't even remember why he needed tending or where he was.

She was wiping his face now, dabbing at the sides of his mouth where the broth—or whatever it was she'd poured down his throat—had trickled out at the sides. He forced an eye open and met only darkness. A black so deep . . . *Have I gone blind?*

"Where—" His voice gave out, but she seemed to understand.

"We're in the hold of the ship. That's why it's so dark. The crew wanted to throw you to the sharks, but I snuck you down here before they could. They said you weren't long for the world and wouldn't survive the journey. The English have a terrible habit of sending men to their deaths before they have earned them."

Her voice slipped, and her hand trembled as she pressed a cool cloth to his forehead. Ian felt an inexplicable urge to comfort this stranger.

"My father—the man who you helped to walk, when the Redcoats would have beaten him for being slow— *wasn't* dead when they threw him into a burning barn. They barred the door so he couldn't escape." Her voice was barely a whisper now.

Ian summoned enough strength to grope through the dark until he found her hand. He clasped it, offering the only comfort he could. Not much of what she'd said made sense. He couldn't recall how he'd come to be here, let alone who she was or having helped her father. But he understood sorrow. And loss.

"Name?"

"Mine or yours?" She inhaled sharply. "You haven't forgotten who you are, have you?"

Have I? If so, it was probably better. Without trying to recall specifics, he seemed to know the past as a blur of misery. *And pain. Lots of pain.* Like he was in now. Everything hurt, from his head, to his chest, to his legs and feet.

"You're Collin MacDonald, laird of the MacDonald clan and husband to the heir of the Campbells. Your wife is a seer. You escaped an English patrol to return to her, but then for some reason . . . You came back. You allowed yourself to be taken."

Collin. Ian remembered. *My ruse worked.* Amidst everything that hurt, both inside and out, he felt a small morsel of joy. The Redcoats had believed he was Collin and put him on the ship for the Colonies. Which left his twin, the real Collin, free. God willing, he'd found his wife alive and well and had rescued her from her vile clansman.

"My name is Elizabeth Campbell," his unseen companion said.

Once, not long ago, that name would have repulsed him. But a Campbell loved his brother, and it was Campbells who had sheltered Collin and seen that he grew up well. Ian found he could feel no ill will toward one now, particularly one who had saved his life.

"Eliza—" Ian managed before his voice gave out.

"You may call me that if you'd like."

He heard the hint of a smile in her voice and grasped onto that. In the bleak existence he had awoken to, there was a bit of good. God had not left him wholly alone this time. Not like those other years with the Munros, when there had been no light in his life. He had survived then, and he would now. If for no other reason than to someday see the smile that went with her voice. *Eliza's.*

Chapter Three

London, March 1762

The noise of feet galloping up the stairs and down the hall roused me from fitful sleep. *The boys are back.*

A second later the door to our room flew open, and Timothy charged toward me, waving a piece of paper. "Christina, I have my ticket. My very own! I'm going with you to the Colonies."

"Of course you're going with us." I winced and pressed a hand to my queasy stomach as he bounded onto the bed beside me. "You didn't think we were going to leave you here in England, did you?"

"We won't leave him, but we might tie him up before we board." Arms outstretched, reaching toward Timothy as if to snatch him up, Collin entered the room. A playful smile lifted the corners of his mouth, even as his eyes—filled with concern—strayed to me. "Off that bed, ye whelp," Collin said. "Unless you're wanting to clean up after your sister when she vomits again."

"Ugh, no." Timothy screwed up his face as he jumped off the bed, sending another jolt through the old mattress.

I held my stomach and closed my eyes briefly.

"You're not going to be sick again, *are* you?" Timothy backed toward the door.

"No," I said firmly, willing my revolting insides to agree. "I'm not, so long as you don't jump on the bed." I laid my head back on the pillow once more and concentrated on staying still, though it felt like a battle was raging within.

"Now that you've shown Katie your ticket, let me hold it for safekeeping." Collin took the paper and pocketed it with the others he'd just purchased, then withdrew his hand and flipped a coin toward Timothy. "Go downstairs and ask Mrs. Gibbons for a cup of her ginger tea."

Timothy caught the coin and bolted from the room. I exchanged an amused look with Collin as we listened to Timothy clomping down the stairs.

"Pity the poor souls in the rooms below." Collin leaned over and kissed my forehead lightly.

"Is he bothering you?" I asked anxiously, lifting a hand to Collin's cheek.

"Not at all." Collin turned my hand over and kissed my palm. "Timothy is a delightful lad. I shall expect no less spirit from our child. And I've no worry at all that I'll be bored on our voyage, with your brother to chase about day and night."

"I'm not certain I'll be able to walk, let alone chase anyone during the crossing." I let my hand drop and tried not to think of the painting I'd left behind at my grandfather's castle in Scotland. In a few days the tempest-tossed ship I had painted was to become our lodging for the next several weeks. I could scarcely manage the motion of walking at present. The thought of being in a ship upon the waves was too much.

"You're going to have to walk on board, at least," Collin said gravely. "And I've heard the voyage goes better if you stroll about the deck each day. To that end, we must get you up and moving before-hand—this afternoon."

I groaned. "Impossible."

My stubborn husband shook his head. "Not so. With a bit of ginger to settle your stomach, and Timothy and me to walk on either side, you'll do just fine. I thought we might take you to see the ship we are to sail on. She's in the harbor now and quite fine to behold."

I've already beheld her. Normally the thought of a sea voyage would not have troubled me at all, but the child I carried had changed everything. I'd become a great disappointment to Timothy—*you used to be fun*, he complained—and I feared to Collin as well. My fondest desire was for sleep, and to not feel as if I was on the verge of turning my stomach inside out every second of the day.

"You said yourself, afternoons are when you feel the best," Collin cajoled as he pulled me into a sitting position and fluffed the pillows behind me.

"*Best* being a relative term," I grumbled. Not that the idea of being outside didn't hold appeal. After nearly two weeks of being shut up in this room, fresh air and a change of scenery did sound good. "Maybe the sea air will help," I admitted, trying to be optimistic.

"Let us hope." Collin's forehead creased with concern, causing the scar above his eye to look a bit menacing. "We're all going to have plenty of it soon enough, whether you wish it or not."

I lifted a hand and attempted to soothe away his worry. I had plenty of my own, enough for both of us. "Have we any funds at all remaining? Were you able to get a reduced price for Timothy's passage?"

"It was £7, the same as ours."

"That much for a child as well?" I sat up farther as my stomach turned over for an entirely different reason. We had stayed in London longer than we'd hoped, awaiting a ship to take us to Virginia, the Colony the *Ulysses*—the ship Ian had sailed on—had been bound for. We weren't certain where our new Scotland was to be in the New World but felt starting out together, with Ian to help lead the Mac-Donalds, our best possibility for success.

But the delay had meant extended lodgings and food. This, plus the added cost of Timothy's fare, had to have left us with mere shillings. "Whatever are we to do? Oh, Collin, I'm so sorry."

"I'm not." He rose from the bed and walked to the lone window in the room. "We'll be all right. I sold Ian's horse this morning."

"His horse—"

Collin turned back to me. "It isn't as if it was doing him much good an ocean away. We can't afford to bring the beast. I would have sold it anyway."

I heard the pain and guilt beneath Collin's casual words. He already felt bad enough that Ian had gone in his stead as a prisoner of the English, shipped off to the Colonies for a fourteen-year indenture.

"I suppose it's just one more thing Ian will have to forgive me for. With all else, what is one grievance more?" Collin cast a rueful smile at me as he sat down heavily on Timothy's small trunk.

"I'm so sorry," I said again and pushed the quilt covering me away. Collin's sorrow and his obvious need for reassurance propelled me from the bed as nothing else might have. Forgetting my own discomfort, I crossed the room and knelt on the floor in front of him, taking his scarred hands in mine.

"You have given much to help my brother. I promise that when we reach the Colonies, I will do whatever it takes to help yours. We *will* find Ian. I know it." I brought Collin's hands to my lips and held them there.

He bent his head to mine. "I trust you are right."

I nodded, praying that I was. In truth, I'd seen no vision and had no indication of a future that included Ian MacDonald. I knew only how much I loved my husband and that he needed to find his brother to truly be whole again.

"Slow down a bit, Timothy. Wait for your sister." Collin walked with one arm around me while I held onto his other for support.

How quickly I've become weak, I lamented, wishing I was able to skip down the cobbled streets like Timothy. Instead, each step required effort. It had been so long since I'd been able to eat properly and have anything I did consume stay down. Apparently the child growing within me did not care for my offerings overmuch and was wont to let me know his displeasure nearly every second of the day. *Who knew someone so tiny—barely even a someone yet—could wreak so much havoc?*

My foot landed between stones, and I wobbled. Collin's arm tightened, and he looked down on me, lines of worry etching his face.

"I'm fine," I hurried to assure him. He had concerns enough without me adding to them. The past few weeks it felt we had ceased being partners in our endeavor and instead he had cared for me, while it seemed my body fought against me—against us and the most precious gift we wished to take with us from our homeland. Our child might never know Scotland, but at least he had begun there.

In retrospect, given the voyage ahead of us, perhaps conceiving a child had not been the wisest decision. But at the time, two and a half months ago, it had been the balm each of us desperately needed, a morsel of joy after months of trial and heartache. I prayed daily to be well enough to hold onto that joy.

"There are certainly sights enough to distract me from my misery, at least," I said cheerfully, taking in the many carriages, shops, and people. *So many people.* Merchants, street vendors, sailors, beggars, and immigrants lined the wharf, the latter with their meager belongings clutched in their hands. A few days more and that would be us, entrusting our hope of a better future, and our very lives, to a great vessel and those who would guide her across the Atlantic.

"Look at all the ships, Christin—Katie," Timothy amended. He'd been trying to become accustomed to calling me that, as Collin did, though I could tell it was an adjustment for him, as was my current, less-than-amiable state. I knew he missed his sister as she used to be. I missed that girl as well and hoped she would soon return.

I won't be ill throughout my entire confinement, will I? It was a thought that didn't bear considering.

My eyes followed Timothy's gaze, past the swell of people to the crowded Thames. He was right to be excited. More ships than I'd imagined crowded the waterway, and I wondered how some of them would ever get out or past those others around them. Tall sails rippled in the breeze, and some of the lesser vessels bobbed with the tide.

"They're magnificent," I said, truly delighted. For the first time I felt a stir of excitement at the idea of boarding one. Perhaps I would be all right. Maybe strolling the deck in the fresh sea air would do me and the child good. London's air was not exactly an improvement from our stale room.

"Come on," Timothy called, racing ahead again. "Our ship is down here."

"Quite a ways down," Collin added. "Are you able to continue?"

"Yes," I said, keeping my focus on the sails. We would have to come this way again in a few days. Hiring a carriage to take us would be a waste of our precious funds. I needed to be well enough to not only walk this route, but walk it myself, as Collin would no doubt have his hands full of our belongings.

Still quite a bit ahead of us, Timothy came to a sudden stop, at the edge of a swelling crowd. My relief, thinking that we would catch up with him now, was short-lived when he ducked between two men and disappeared into the mass.

"Timothy!" I started forward.

"I see him. Wait here." Collin released me and dashed down the street after him while I continued on, one slow step in front of the other. I loved my brother but worried his precociousness might land him—and possibly us—in trouble.

A shout rose from the gathered crowd. *Signaling a ship's departure?* Or perhaps a long-awaited one was returning. Eager to see such an event and to catch up with my family, I hastened my steps, one hand still covering my ever-queasy stomach.

As I grew closer the unified shout turned to foul words and jeering. Fists rose in the air, and feet stomped. These were not happy cries, but more the sounds of an angry mob.

Timothy. Collin. I began to run and, much as Timothy had done, squeezed my way through the edge of the crowd toward the middle, no longer speculating on what the occasion might be, only wishing to have my loved ones safely at my side again.

I reached the front and came up short, my eyes drawn sharply upward to the horrifying sight of a man's body jerking violently as he hung by the neck from a short rope. He was not yet dead, but in the process of slowly suffocating, eyes bulging, bound hands clawing frantically as his body writhed in midair. All this I glimpsed in the second before I turned away, too late to mistake the horror or to replace the image with another. Bile rose in my throat as the memory of Edan Campbell's corpse, hanging from the rope fastened about his broken neck, swam before my blurry eyes. Hand over my mouth, I pushed my way back through the crowd and barely made it to an ash can where I threw up the ginger tea and what little else I'd managed to keep down that morning.

Behind me the shouting continued, and my panic swelled. Collin and Timothy were somewhere within that angry mob. But I was powerless to move, forced to stay bent over and heaving, though my stomach was long-since empty.

"Katie!" Collin's shout reached my ears seconds before his hand was at my back.

I turned my head to see his other hand clasped firmly around Timothy's wrist. For once my brother appeared subdued, his face as drained of color as mine likely was.

"Thank goodness." I sagged against Collin, relieved.

He withdrew a handkerchief and held it out to me. I wiped my mouth and tried to block out the cries behind us.

"I'm so sorry," Collin apologized. "Had I known there was to be a hanging, I'd never have brought either of you today."

"It's all right," I said weakly. It wasn't. Not at all. Edan's death and Liusaidh's were once more fresh in my mind. As was all else we had endured during our months in the Highlands. These past weeks, away from imminent danger, we had grown a little complacent perhaps. But with the sight of the man on the gallows came the swift reminder that we must not be, that Collin himself was still a wanted man. At present the crown believed him to be in the Colonies. If it was discovered that Collin was not there, or if he was found and believed to be his twin brother, Ian—also with a price on his head—our situation would be most dire.

"When you're able to walk, we'll return to the inn. Or I can hire a hack to take us."

"No." I straightened and inhaled a deep breath of wharf air—slightly better, or possibly worse, than the way the rest of London smelled. At least that promised to improve once we were at sea. "We've come to view the ship, and so we shall." It had been too far a walk to turn back, and I felt strangely compelled to see our vessel now—today. Perhaps it was the gruesomeness of the hanging that startled me into thinking about something other than my own misery. I needed to see the physical evidence of our escape from this place.

"Are you certain?" Collin brushed the hair back from my face to better look at me.

"Yes." I nodded, then reached down and took Timothy's other hand. "We both need something else to set our minds on. A grand sight to sweep away that one." With a shudder I inclined my head toward the dispersing mob behind us.

"Aye," Collin said. "We'll go another way, then. It will take a bit longer."

"Worth the detour," I assured him.

With each of us holding one of Timothy's hands, we left the wharf and walked beyond the buildings lining it.

"Why did they hang that man?" Timothy asked in a quavering voice when we had been walking several minutes.

My conscience seared, and my heart broke. What a terrible thing for a child to witness. I knew other children—my own Campbell relations included—grew up among such violence and kept fear as a bedfellow. But my brother had led a happy, if not perfect, life. Though he'd seen both parents laid to rest before his eighth year, it had not been violence that took them from him.

"I'm sorry," Collin said once more as our eyes met over Timothy's head. He led us off to the side of the street, into the shelter of a building.

Crouching down to Timothy's height, Collin first gathered him close, then spoke to him. "It is likely the man committed a crime. Whether he deserved such a terrible punishment, I cannot say. But what you must realize, what your father understood and fought against and even lost his post for, is that the laws are not always fair. Those in power are not always good. And while we might not agree with it or them, we do have to obey, or to be very careful in our actions."

Timothy nodded solemnly as I pressed a hand to my heart. Never before had Collin spoken so favorably of our father—one of the men who had killed his. I recognized the great concession this was and loved Collin all the more for it, and for the kindness he showed my little brother.

"Is that why we're sailing to the New World? Do they not hang people there?" Timothy asked, his face scrunched as if trying to reason it all out.

"I don't know whether they do or not, but I am certain there are laws there. The Colonies are still under England's rule and will have Redcoats as well, I assume." He muttered the last beneath his breath.

"We're going because there is no place here for us," I said. "In the New World we can begin again. We can have land and build a home. We can be farmers or shopkeepers or craftsmen—even artists." I forced a smile. "We will have more freedom to forge a good life."

"Well said." Collin gave Timothy's shoulder a reassuring squeeze, then stood. "Best be off if we want to see the ship and return to the inn by dark."

We took hands again, Timothy in the middle, and marched briskly up and across a few more blocks, then back down to the wharf, emerging well past the sight of the hanging.

Here the ships were even more plentiful, crowded together at points along the wharf, some so close they were nearly touching. I could not begin to imagine how any of them were supposed to move from the Thames to the ocean without accident.

"They've skilled men at their crews," Collin said, as if he'd read my mind.

"They must have," I agreed. "To guide such enormous vessels here in the first place."

We walked past a dozen before I saw her, the one that was to carry us safely across the ocean.

"She is smaller than I'd thought," I said, staring at the exact ship I had painted months earlier.

"I wouldn't exactly call that small," Collin said. "Have you ever seen such large sails? And so many. She's bound to make good time." He released my hand, bringing his to his brow, shading his face as he peered up at the sails on the ship directly in front of us.

"That one isn't ours." Still keeping hold of Timothy, I moved past it toward the one on the other side. "This one is. I recognize the mast-head from my painting." An Egyptian-looking princess graced the front of the ship, her long, straight, beaded hair hanging down either side of her face, held in place by the ornate headband carved over it. Her dress billowed behind as if blown by the wind, and her sandaled feet crossed one another at the bottom. *Cleopatra. Of course.* I'd not recognized her before nor realized the name of the ship; but there it was, scripted along the other side, opposite the view I had painted.

Collin had not followed us but still stood in front of the other ship. "You must be mistaken," he called. "*This* is the ship I have purchased passage on, the one that is to convey us to Virginia."

"I am not mistaken." My empty stomach clenched with new worry. Timothy's grip tightened on mine as he looked back and forth between Collin and me. "Every detail is the same, from the rail to the paint." The only difference was that at present the Cleopatra stood upright in the water. In my painting she'd been nearly on her side, bowed over by a swell of the sea.

"But—you just said yourself that one is smaller than you'd envisioned."

I nodded. "Yes, but all else is the same. I am certain this is the ship we are to sail on."

Collin thrust a hand through his hair in a gesture of agitation I'd not witnessed for some weeks. "I don't even know where she is sailing. We've already purchased tickets on the other. Does it matter which one takes us, so long as we arrive?"

I did not answer but let him resolve the conflict his own way, muttering to himself and pacing up and down the wharf between the two vessels.

"What's wrong with Collin?" Timothy asked. "Why can't we sail on the ship he chose? I like it better."

Comparing the two, I preferred it as well. But I had learned, and I believed Collin had as well, that following the clues afforded us by my gift of sight as well as the instructions my visionary grandfather had left for us allowed us the best opportunity for success—and in this instance, survival. No matter that the ship I'd foreseen and painted *was* a smaller vessel on which to cross such a vast ocean.

I only wished I'd considered this problem before. But I'd no idea there would be *so many* ships from which to choose. I'd not realized that many people were intent on sailing to the Colonies—or wherever else all these were bound.

"Perhaps it is also going to Virginia?" I suggested when Collin's pacing brought him near to us again.

"And if so, will we be able to simply exchange our tickets with but a few days remaining before we are to use them? I arranged for these almost a month past." Collin sounded both skeptical and frustrated, while the lines of his face appeared resigned.

"More unusual things *have* happened," I reminded him.

"Aye." He ran his hand through his hair again so that it stood on end. "With you as my wife, I suppose I ought to be used to them by now." A corner of his mouth quirked as he reached for my hand. "Come along. Let's see what can be done. I will endeavor *not* to be surprised when all works out just as you have predicted."

The emigration office was some distance down the wharf, and once more we walked blocks out of our way to reach it and avoid seeing the gallows. Once there, and having waited our turn in line, Collin presented our problem—as best he could without sounding ludicrous—to the agent.

"The *Cleopatra is* set to depart this week as well," the agent said. "The same day in fact, but she is not going to Virginia."

Collin glanced at me as disappointment surged between us.

"Another Colony, then?" I asked hopefully. There were many of them, all connected, were there not?

"She's sailing to Halifax," the man said.

"Which Colony is that in?" Collin asked. "Is it north or south of Virginia?"

"North. Quite far." The agent paused as he looked up from the schedule in front of him. "Halifax is the port for Nova Scotia."

Chapter Four

London, March 1762

"Nova Scotia?" Collin's unsteady voice mirrored the shock on his face. "There is such a place—a place named such?"

"Yes." The agent peered down his glasses at us, as if we were less than intelligent or unworthy of his time.

"And do Scots live there?" Collin asked.

"How should I know?" The agent frowned. "*I* live here."

I stepped forward, coming to Collin's aid, and in my perfect English accent inquired as to the availability and cost of tickets. Though the ship was smaller, the amount of passage was the same we had already paid to travel on the larger one. I glanced at Collin, my gaze questioning.

He nodded. "Aye. We had best do that."

"Are you certain? What about the others?" How would we ever find them in Virginia if we landed elsewhere, far north?

"I don't know how it will all work out once we arrive," Collin said, answering my unspoken question. "But this cannot be coincidence." He turned toward the agent once more. "We will require three tickets."

I watched as more of our precious funds drained away. *I hope you're right.* I spoke to my grandfather as much as to myself. I had painted the *Cleopatra*. Grandfather had directed us to Nova Scotia. But would a ship to Virginia not have done as well?

We left the office in a sort of daze. Timothy did not quite understand the gravity of what had just transpired, though he was still subdued, as was I, from the afternoon's earlier trauma. I was second guessing myself, and Collin's face was grim with this latest burden. I imagined he was thinking of his brother.

How will we ever find Ian?

As we walked away from the building and in the opposite direction of both ships, a man bumped into Timothy, nearly knocking him down. Collin caught him before he could fall.

"Take care," Collin reprimanded the passerby.

"My apologies," the poorly clad man said. "Is your boy all right?"

Timothy nodded but moved closer to Collin, who had his arm around him.

Another man and a woman, both dressed as raggedly, and generally haggard in appearance, joined the one who had jostled Timothy.

"Were you able to purchase tickets?" the woman asked the jostler.

"No," he answered. "They've nothing we can afford. Had you any luck speaking with the captains or crews?"

The second man, this one considerably younger, shook his head. "There is nothing, Da. They won't hire without experience."

Collin clasped my hand, keeping me from moving forward if I might have. I wasn't about to, and a quick glance between us told me we were of a same mind.

"Where are you seeking passage to?" Collin asked the older man.

"The Colonies," he said. "We have traveled far already and now learn that passage is more than we were led to believe. We cannot go, but neither can we afford to live here or have any hope of saving for our passage, without reliable work. I do not know what we are to do." He hung his head as if defeated.

"Take heart," I said, smiling at the woman and feeling fortune smiling upon each of us.

"Do you know of employment we might seek?" the son asked, straightening to the height of his father, as if to show he, too, was a man, and capable of hard work.

"Not here, no," Collin said. "But I might be able to provide the passage you seek. How much are you able to pay?"

"We've but fifteen pounds, and passage is twenty-one in total for the three of us."

"We can help you." The lines from Collin's face seemed to melt away with his broad smile. "It just so happens that we are in possession of three extra tickets." He hesitated, looking at me a second. "And the total for all three is only £12."

"I feel like such a fool." Collin put out the lamp and crawled into bed beside me. His cold feet touched my legs, and I gave a little jump.

"Isn't it your job to *warm* me?" I accused as he hauled me back beside him and purposely put both icy feet on my legs.

"Mmmhmm." Collin nuzzled his face in my neck. "A task I'm finding a bit difficult at present, with your brother sleeping an arm's distance away."

"That is what has you feeling a fool?" I turned my head toward him.

"No. Not having realized that Nova Scotia already exists is the cause of my regret. I can ill afford ignorance such as I exhibited today."

"How were you to know?" I asked. "It isn't as if either of us has ever sailed anywhere before."

"I thought the name only your grandfather's dream for us. I ought to have researched the ports in the New World more thoroughly. I'll not make that mistake again. When we arrive, I'll set about learning all I can of this New Scotland."

"Precisely. When we arrive." I closed my eyes, not wishing to think of our upcoming journey or what awaited beyond. For now being here in Collin's arms was enough to keep me content.

"Being uneducated made me feel the fool," Collin reiterated, whispering the words near my ear before nipping it. "While being unable to make love to my wife has me feeling a bit surly."

"So I've noticed." I rolled to face him and draped an arm over his shoulder. "It won't be forever. We will have privacy again someday."

"Someday," he grumped. "Not aboard the *Cleopatra,* we won't."

"No," I agreed. "Definitely not there, or on the other ship either, had we sailed on her." Part of me still wondered if we ought to be preparing to sail on that other ship. As certain as I was that the *Cleopatra* was the vessel I had painted, and as astonished as Collin and I had both been at the discovery of an actual place called Nova Scotia, I could not stop fretting about never meeting up with the others in our clans, and Collin's brother Ian, all who *would* be landing in Virginia.

"Don't doubt yourself." Collin kissed my forehead and pulled me tighter against him. "If ever I had reminding of your abilities it was today when that agent told us of Halifax, *Nova Scotia*. It was as if your grandfather sent a bolt of lightning to strike me personally."

"You were speechless a good several seconds." I smiled into the dark, remembering and recalling as well the miraculous episode that had followed—the desperate threesome that had literally run into us, seeking their own passage to the Colonies. They had gratefully purchased our tickets to Virginia at the deeply discounted price Collin had given them.

"How could I not?" he had said to me later when I'd questioned his generosity. "It would not do for them to arrive penniless or to have naught for provisions on their journey."

Always a laird. Collin's awareness of others and his concern for their well-being was one of the many qualities about him I admired. One of the many reasons I loved him.

We were not quite as well off as we had been before purchasing our new passage on the *Cleopatra,* but the events that had unfolded since I'd first spied the ship left little doubt that we were embarking on our voyage exactly as we were meant to. If all had worked out so well for us here, who was to say it would not in the New World as well?

"Who knows but that the others, too, found a ship headed to Nova Scotia," Collin said, placing a light kiss at the base of my throat. "And if not—Alistair, Finlay and Gordon have good sense about them. They'll do all right until we meet up again."

"Of course they will." I arched my head back, inviting Collin to continue exploring my neck with his lips. "Mmm." I sighed happily. "You've the uncanny ability to make me forget all else—that anyone besides the two of us exists."

"Uncanny, nothing." Collin lifted one of my arms and pinned it above my head. "I practiced this for years every night with my pillow, imagining the day I'd feel your warm body beneath me instead of a sack of feathers."

"You did not." I giggled, just thinking of it.

"Aye. I did not," he confessed. "I'd no pillow most of my years. But I dreamed of you always. And from the day we wed, I could not get out of my mind what I'd do once we could finally be together as man and wife."

"You mean this?" I wrapped my other arm around the back of his neck and pulled him close until his mouth met mine. We joined in a tangle of lips and limbs, discontented sighs and hungry moans. He was reaching for the hem of my nightgown when Timothy murmured in his sleep from the cot beside us.

I ceased kissing Collin and froze, the illusion that we were alone shattered.

Collin hung his head, his hair brushing my shoulder as a stream of low Gaelic rolled from his tongue. I couldn't help but laugh at his frustration, though it was mine as well.

"Think it's amusing, do you?" He pinned both hands

over my head and stared down at me, almost savage in his appearance the way moonlight spilled over his face and the scar above his eye wrinkled. For some reason this made me laugh louder, and Timothy stirred again.

"Tell me you're not as desperate as I am," Collin demanded in a hoarse, strained whisper.

"More so," I freely admitted. "Though only during these rare hours when the effect of our earlier union is not making itself so known to me."

Collin's expression sobered at once, changing from humorously murderous to gravely concerned. He rolled away. "What a beast I am. Have I hurt you?"

I shook my head and leaned up on my elbows to show that I was perfectly fine. "You'd know if you had—I'd have been sick all over you. Right now our child is blessedly quiet."

"Even the wee beastie needs a bit of sleep, aye?" Collin settled beside me, pulling me down with him. This time when his hand reached beneath my gown it was with different intent. His fingers splayed gently over my stomach. "It is hard to believe he's in there. You're so small."

"It's not even three months yet," I reminded him. "Don't worry. He'll be braw like his father."

"Or she'll be bonnie like her mother," Collin said. "You know I'll love the bairn regardless."

"I know." I rolled away from him, my back curled to his stomach, his hand still secure against me. The feeling of absolute happiness I'd experienced in the carriage returned. In spite of the horror we'd witnessed this afternoon and the reminder it was of the dangers here and awaiting us, in this moment I felt joy. I may not have spent years dreaming of Collin, but I would spend every day the rest of my life loving him and yearning to be with him my every waking and sleeping moment.

"I love you," I whispered, then turned my head to kiss his arm beneath me.

"And I you, Katie," he murmured. "I would move

31

Heaven and Earth for you, for you are both to me, my every reason for life."

Chapter Five

Aboard the *Ulysses*, Atlantic Ocean, March 1762

"Collin?"

Eliza's whisper penetrated the fog in his mind like a ray of hope. Ian swallowed twice, then answered with a whisper of his own. "Here."

He struggled to sit up. How long had he slept this time? With such thick darkness surrounding him and nothing else to do, sleep came frequently and for long stretches. He could tell it was helping him heal. His muscles protested less as he sat up this time.

"Here," he repeated, ears straining for her light steps along the hold's slippery floor. Who knew what the poor lass might be stepping over. Rats, at the least.

"Take care," he whispered, although Eliza didn't need the warning. "It's black as the Earl of Hell's waistcoat here." Ian's mouth twisted in a grim smile as he recalled the times his father had muttered the same, mostly on moonless nights when they had been hiding from the English.

Her steps grew closer until at last he thought he spied her outstretched hands groping blindly through the dark. He reached, touched one, and held on. Her slender fingers closed over his as she gave a relieved sigh and tumbled down onto the crate beside him.

His chest heaved with relief as he clung to her hand. One could easily go mad down here, in the darkness and silence—and the air so damp, heavy and oppressive. Eliza had been generous with her touch each time she came, allowing him to clasp her hand, and for that he was grateful. The nourishment she brought might be restoring his body, but her touch and her voice kept him from certain madness.

"You are well?" she asked.

"Better, now that you're here." He took the bundle she pressed into his free hand and set it aside. Right now he wished only for her company.

"Perhaps you will feel even better—or not so well at all— when I share the news." She sounded worried. "They say we'll be docking in two days, and early morning at that. The captain means to have all the cargo offloaded as quickly as possible. *All* cargo," she added. "They even mean to begin the sale of the indentured that very day."

"Cargo," Ian muttered. "As if we are a side of beef or tankard of ale."

"That is how they see us," Eliza said. "I have little hope that the Colonists will feel differently. We'll be presented as wares."

"I'll not be presented to anyone," Ian said. "I've no intention of leaving this ship."

"So you've said." Eliza's voice held regret and possibly something more. "You will have to use much caution if you wish to remain undetected. There are a great many barrels and crates to be unloaded from here—the very one upon which we sit included, no doubt—and when that has been moved there is a large shipment of Virginian tobacco that is to be taken back to England. No doubt the hold will be a busy place for the next few days."

"That's quite a lot of information for one considered cargo to know." Ian wondered how she'd been privy to such and was again curious as to how it was she'd been able to conceal him in the first place. That Eliza continued to find a way to bring him food and water at least once a day was also suspicious. He'd attempted to ask her about it a time or two during her previous visits, but always she was quick to change the subject or even quicker to insist she had to return to the deck before her absence was noticed. He hoped she could stay at least a few minutes today.

"They trust me," Eliza said simply. "They've needed my help this voyage. Scotland's shores were not long out of sight when the cook's assistant fell ill. One of the ship's officers saw me preparing a meal for several of those too bedridden to help themselves. He took me above and said I must help in the galley. The ship's cook was not pleased. But he tolerated me once he knew I'd cooked for an English patrol."

"So you spend your days assisting him, serving the entire crew?" Ian wondered if there was more to the story than she was telling him.

"Aye—and listening. The men are at ease when they are taking their meals. Their tongues move freely, and I pay attention."

He did, too, and felt certain there was more to this story. "And for your service, you were allowed to move me to the hold and nurse me back to health?"

"I've not done much other than to leave you to your rest and bring you food and water when I might."

It was more than anyone else, save Collin, had done for him as long as Ian could remember. "You stayed with me the whole of that first night—or day." Whichever it had been. Impossible to tell down here. "I was fevered, but I remember your voice and your touch. You didn't leave."

"It was just one night," Eliza said. "You were too ill to be left alone. I feared that you were dying."

"Not just yet," Ian said, a corner of his mouth rising, though she'd not be able to see it. "You must be an excellent cook, if you were able to convince an officer to spare my life."

"That is not exactly the way of it," Eliza confessed. "He does not know of you. He *must* not if you wish to remain, and if—" She broke off suddenly.

Hiding something. He did not press her. He'd secrets enough of his own. The poor lass still labored under the delusion that he was Collin. How aghast might she be to realize she'd helped the outlaw brother instead of the one bent on freeing her clan.

He still held her hand and twined his fingers through hers now, making their clasp stronger. Not that she could exactly rush off in this thick darkness. From what he'd been able to discern, she'd placed him in a remote corner of the hold, far from the stairs that descended from above and the pinprick of light he saw whenever the hatch was opened.

"I only hope that whatever bargain you made to see to my safety was not at too great a cost to you."

"No," she said, and he wasn't certain if that meant it had been a terrible cost or not. "He—this officer—agreed to look the other way the night the other prisoners and I took you below. He does not know that you're here, only that I asked he be distracted from his duty for a half hour that eve."

"Why would he agree to such a request?" Ian asked, his fingers tensing over hers. He could think of several possibilities, none of them good. "What did you promise in exchange? No Englishman I know of would do anything decent without a price." And a hefty one at that.

"Perhaps they are not all as bad as you believe," Eliza said, sounding defensive now.

Ian imagined a pert little nose stuck in the air defiantly. He wondered if he'd ever get to see her face. He'd love to know what she looked like, to have more to remember her by than her angelic voice.

"Supposing you found the one good one," Ian said, still not believing for a second that there was such a man, "how is it that he—and the other crew—allot you extra food to bring down each day?"

"Obtaining food has been the least of my difficulties," Eliza said. "After the evening meal has been served and I have cleaned the galley, I am free to pack up the leftovers and bring them to those prisoners suffering in their beds—those too ill to cook for themselves and who would otherwise starve. I am providing a service to both parties by doing this. A dead man or woman cannot be sold, and there are many sick who need assistance."

"So you're not just *my* angel." Ian felt strangely disappointed to realize this, though he knew he ought to be grateful she was helping him at all. And he was. But there was something more to this woman. She intrigued him.

"I'm no angel," Eliza said, tugging her hand from his.

"Oh?" The inkling of unease was back. She *had* done something more to ensure his safety. "Why would you say that?" He leaned forward, palms braced on his knees.

"They were going to throw you overboard," she said feebly. "I couldn't let them."

"Oh, Eliza." Blindly he reached for her, found her shoulders and turned her to him, only just making out the vague shape of her face through the dark. "What have you done?"

"Just allowed him a kiss. Not my virtue. I—I couldn't do that."

"*Him?*" Ian's stomach coiled. "The officer who agreed to look the other way?"

"Aye." Her hair brushed his hands as she lowered her head.

Ian imagined the man's hands on Eliza, holding her roughly, forcing his mouth upon hers. *And she allowed it—to save me.* He released her and stood abruptly, grazing his head on the low ceiling.

"Would you have rather I let them toss you overboard?" Eliza asked. "It seemed a kiss for your life was more than a fair trade. But now—you think less of me?"

"Not of you." Nor even of the officer, truth be told. He might have required much else and easily forced her to it. Ian worried the man still might and suspected Eliza did too. "I appreciate what you did for me, Eliza. But no more. Don't barter your virtue for me. I'm not worth that."

"I believe you are," she said with that nose-in-the-air attitude. "No doubt your wife would agree."

He needed to tell her he was not Collin. Especially now that he knew what she had done for him. "I'm not the man you think I am. I've done terrible things."

The ship rose suddenly, then pitched forward, as if nodding in agreement. Ian's hand shot to the ceiling to brace himself.

"We all have."

There was a quaver in her voice—whether from his admission or from the ship's lurching, he couldn't tell. He dropped down to sit beside her once more. "I find it difficult to believe a sweet lass such as yourself has ever done anything close to terrible."

"It's true." Eliza gave a little hiccupping sob, and Ian felt a queer tightening in his chest. This faceless woman he'd conversed with less than a dozen times was somehow getting to him like no other he'd ever known. *Not even Aileen.*

"If it's the kiss troubling you, don't let it," he said, wishing he could find the man responsible and rearrange his face so he could never kiss a woman again. "It was a noble sacrifice you made, and I owe a great debt to you." He reached out until his fingers skimmed her chin, and his thumb found her lips. He touched them gently. "I'm sorry you had to endure even that much. It's a known fact the English know nothing of the proper way to kiss a lady."

"That is certainly true," she agreed, sounding a bit steadier, though a tremor passed through her. "But it's not the kiss that has me worried for my soul. I've done much worse. I've—I've killed some-one."

Ian slowly lowered his hand from her face. He wasn't shocked, but possibly impressed that she'd had enough courage to do such a thing. No doubt it had been a life-or-death situation. "These are terrible times. Terrible, *hard* times. I've done many a thing I'm not proud of, yet faced with the same situation, I might do them all over again. I believe we've all an ingrained will to survive—no matter what the cost sometimes."

Eliza released a great, sorrowful sigh. "This wasn't survival. It was revenge."

Chapter Six

London, March 1762

Thick raindrops pattered the roof of the hackney as it made its way along the street beside the wharf. Timothy pressed his face to the window, taking in a final look at the city. I leaned my head back against the seat, fighting both my usual morning nausea and the feeling of entrapment that panicked me whenever I rode in a carriage. Though I hadn't wanted to spend the money to hire one and would have preferred to walk, yesterday it had become apparent one was necessary when Collin and Timothy—after taking Timothy's small trunk with them—had returned with a much larger trunk.

"Supplies for our voyage," Collin had told me, when I'd inquired as to what was within. I'd been too ill yesterday, and this morning, to care to know much more than that, but both Collin and Timothy had seemed quite pleased, if not a bit smug about whatever purchases or trading they had done.

Collin reached forward and pulled Timothy from the window. "Keep back a moment until we've passed Execution Dock. Seeing it the first time was more than enough."

"They're hanging another man today?" Timothy's question and goggling eyes matched my own, disturbed sentiments.

"I don't think so," Collin said. "But I've heard they usually keep the body up a good long time—hung in chains as a warning to other would-be pirates."

The word *pirate* brought to mind Collin's brother, Ian. I

had thought him one from the moment I first saw him, though his act of selflessness in taking Collin's place as a prisoner last year had more than proved my judgment of him wrong. Still, there had been something very pirate-like about Ian. He was clever and cunning, and I sensed he balanced rather precariously upon the line between good and evil. I hoped that tendency would not be to his detriment in the Colonies. *Keep your head and stay safe until Collin can find you.* If only I could send him that message, to alert him that we were coming for him.

"Was the man they hung a *real* pirate?" Timothy asked, a sort of awe to his voice.

"No." Collin shook his head solemnly. "One Captain James Lowry, hanged for brutally murdering one of his crew."

"I suppose that ought to make me feel better, but it doesn't," I said.

"There is no 'better' when it comes to something like a hanging." Collin adjusted the pouch at his waist that held our remaining funds, then picked up Timothy and set him on his lap. Extra insurance, I supposed, as we passed by the gallows.

The *Cleopatra* was soon in sight, and Timothy's eagerness and enthusiasm returned. He bounced on Collin's knee.

"Do you think the captain might let me try the wheel?"

"Not in this harbor," I said, still skeptical that we would even be able to make it from the crowded Thames to begin our voyage.

"Perhaps," Collin said. "But not today. You must not ask him or pester any of the crew, especially when there is much to be done for us to set sail."

"You are to be with one of us always." I reiterated the rule we had gone over with him several times already.

The rain seemed to increase from steady to a downpour as the carriage rolled to a stop.

Collin jumped from his seat and was out the door at once.

"Stay here while I get our trunk. No need to get wet before you have to."

"I don't care if I get wet." Timothy was already on the step behind Collin.

"Stay with your sister," he said, then disappeared from sight.

Timothy glanced back at me. "You don't mind, do you, Katie? We used to play in the rain together. You never cared about mussing you hair or dress the way Anna did."

"I do not mind in the least." The thought of being shut up in the carriage another few minutes was far more disturbing. I alighted behind Timothy and took his hand—he was already straining toward the *Cleopatra.*

I flipped the hood of my cloak up, over my head, more to keep rain from collecting in it than from any hope of it keeping me dry.

"Let's go." Timothy pulled me in the direction of our ship.

I tugged back. "We'll wait for Collin." The tickets were in my reticule, so Timothy and I could have boarded and perhaps found shelter sooner; but I was not about to do anything that might separate us from Collin.

At the rear of the carriage the men shouted instructions to one another above the unrelenting rain as they struggled to free the trunk from the wet ropes. Rivulets ran down the cobbled street, winding twisted paths through the stones to the edge of the wharf, where dozens of miniature waterfalls poured into the Thames.

I drew Timothy closer, parting the front of my cloak with the intent to protect him, but he shrugged me off with the same accusing look I'd received from him several times over the past weeks.

"It's just rain. We play in it—remember?" he asked in a plaintive tone that struck my core.

In response I threw my head back and stuck out my

tongue. "I can catch more raindrops than you can, because I'm taller."

"Cannot," Timothy cried, his own head thrown back and mouth opened. But there was happiness in his voice, and when he peeked at me it was with his old smile. It warmed my heart and reminded me that while I was grown now, and wife of a laird with many responsibilities, to Timothy I was simply still the sister he adored, his one link left to the life he had known. I must not cease to be that for him.

So it was that some minutes later Collin emerged from behind the carriage, one end of the trunk clasped firmly within his arms, to find Timothy and me turning circles and jumping purposely in the deepest puddles.

Instead of asking if I'd gone mad, Collin flashed me a wicked grin and leaned close as he passed. "I hope you'll save some of that playful mood for later," he whispered so only I could hear.

I grabbed his arm. "*Much* later, you mean? As in, weeks from now, when we've arrived in Halifax?"

Collin shook his head, drops flinging from his hair. "There must be somewhere on that ship for a husband and wife to have a bit of privacy."

"What have you—stones in here?" The coachman hefting the other side of the trunk grunted loudly.

"No stones," Collin said. "Timothy and I have packed every nook and cranny with provisions. Isn't that right, lad?"

Timothy nodded, and we fell into line behind Collin. At the edge of the wharf I paused, still hesitant for what lay ahead, though I knew we must go.

"Come on." Timothy tugged me forward, and I lifted my foot, trading the cobbled stone for the worn planks of the gangway.

"Per mare per terras." *By sea, by land.* We were quite literally following the MacDonald clan motto. Collin and I had covered a great deal of ground during our first eight

43

months of marriage. Given the pace at which our life together had unfolded, I supposed it was time we took to the sea.

Goodbye, England, home of my childhood. Another step. *Good-bye Scotland, my true home.* Two steps more. *Goodbye, Mother and Father—Anna. Goodbye, Lydia.*

My throat constricted, and I blinked back tears as I thought of the infant girl Collin and I had loved as our own. She had been cruelly taken from us just before we left Scotland, and our stepping on this ship assured there would be no chance of us ever seeing her again. The hurt of our loss was weeks old, but it felt fresh and painfully raw as I took the last steps from the gangway onto the ship itself.

We were really leaving—Lydia, our parents' graves, our homes, and all else we had known and loved.

Except each other. I glanced at Collin and saw that his eyes, too, were bright. Our thoughts so closely paralleled one another's these days that his obvious emotion neither surprised nor alarmed me.

I breathed in deeply, trying to draw strength for both of us. "Nova Scotia—ùr na h-alba." I'd not learned much Gaelic during my months in the Highlands, but this phrase I clung to. It was our promise and hope for a better future.

Just aboard the ship we encountered the queue of passengers. Collin was waved ahead with the trunk while Timothy and I were made to wait in the pouring rain. With care I retrieved our paperwork from my reticule.

"Oh, no." Ink bled onto my fingers before I'd even unfolded our tickets. During my play with Timothy the pouch must have gotten wet. I dared not open the papers now, for fear of ruining them completely. Instead I tucked them beneath my cloak, praying the writing was legible enough that we would be allowed passage.

"Next," the purser called.

As we moved forward a bell tolled loudly. I turned in the direction of the sound and saw at once the ringing came not from one of London's cathedrals but from the ship next to ours, the one we had originally planned to sail upon. Redcoats swarmed her deck and lined the gangway, as the pealing summoned all passengers above.

"Why are there so many soldiers?" Timothy asked.

"I don't know." Neither did I understand why the ship was still in the harbor. Our previous tickets had stated it was to leave before this one, yet here it still was. My eyes struggled to see what I might through the blinding rain. Though the two vessels were but a stone's throw apart, the rain obscured our view, and I could not discern the source of alarm.

It appeared that passengers were being made to line up on deck, and tickets were being checked—by the Redcoats instead of the crew. "I believe they are searching for someone," I said. "Perhaps a stowaway."

"What's that?" Timothy scrubbed the rain from his eyes as he peered up at me.

"Someone who steals away on a ship—or tries to—without paying for his passage." I winced as the soldiers began knocking around two of the passengers.

"Like a pirate?" Timothy asked.

"It could be a pirate. But often it is boys wishing for adventure at sea who stowaway." I turned my mouth down in a stern expression as I looked at Timothy. "Don't get any ideas."

"I won—"

A scream cut through the air over the sound of the rain, followed by more shouts as fighting broke out on the other ship. I was not the only passenger staring now, transfixed with an awful horror as the soldiers used the butts of their muskets to smash into the rioting passengers.

"Turn away." Collin joined us again, steering both Timothy and me from the disturbing scene. "Keep your heads down. Don't look over there again." He pulled the hood of my cloak farther over my face and nudged us forward, nearer the purser. Collin wore his hat low as well, covering most of the scars on his face.

Neither Timothy nor I questioned him. I had learned quickly, within the first weeks of our marriage, that listening to him could mean the difference between life and death. I couldn't see how that could be the circumstance here, yet he seemed serious enough that I sensed it was.

We were next in line when a gunshot sounded. Collin's grip on my arm tightened.

"Have they actually shot someone aboard that ship?"

"Likely a warning shot," Collin said. "Fired into the air. I don't doubt they would fire into a crowd, though." He wrapped his other arm around Timothy. "Maybe Nova Scotia will have fewer Redcoats."

The line moved again, and then our papers were being called for. I withdrew them from my cloak, unfolding them before the purser. Our names were smeared beyond recognition, but with great relief I noticed the name of the ship and the date of travel, both more central on the page, were clear enough to discern.

"Names," the purser asked, head bent over the ship's log, quill poised.

"Mercer," Collin replied quickly. "Collin, Christina, and Timothy."

I did not so much as arch my brow at this sudden change. On our previous tickets we had been listed as Ian and Katherine Campbell—somewhat different from the truth as well.

"Place of origin?"

"Alverton, England," I answered, lest Collin had forgotten—the village being far from the place of his birth and upbringing.

We gave our ages next, honest about those. When all had been recorded Collin ushered us swiftly to the stairway that led to the sleeping quarters below.

"What is it?" I asked as soon as we were out of the storm and out of sight of the record keeper. Timothy clomped ahead of us, peering excitedly in every direction.

"Last week I thought I saw Rab Murray. I believed I must have been mistaken until I caught sight of him again. He was following me. I don't know why or how he's come to be in London, but I don't doubt he knows of the price on my—or Ian's—head." Collin took my hand, and we walked behind Timothy.

"He couldn't have followed us all the way from the Highlands!" I well remembered Rab and how Collin and I had bested him, leaving him alone and wounded for his brothers to find—reason enough to seek revenge. But to follow us all the way here?

"He wouldn't have waited to make his move if he'd seen us then," Collin said. "I think it far more possible that he met up with Alistair and the others on their journey and learned of our plans to depart from London."

"And he somehow found you here and alerted the Redcoats?" Revenge was one thing, but traveling to London on the vague hope of finding us seemed a bit drastic, even for a vengeful Highlander.

Collin shrugged. "It's not impossible. All he had to do was watch the wharf area closely. There are a lot of ships, but not too many places at which to purchase one's passage. And £12 sterling is a considerable amount of money to a man such as Rab. The Murrays are not well off."

"You can't be certain those soldiers on the other ship were searching for you." I stood firm in my denial, not wanting to believe that the threats we'd faced in Scotland had possibly followed us here. "They could have been after a stowaway or someone else who had committed a crime. They could have been searching for anyone." I trailed behind Collin in our pursuit of Timothy, who careened around a corner.

"Not anyone—*me*." Collin spoke in a low tone. "You might not have seen, but the two men they'd detained on the ship were the men we sold our tickets to. The scream you heard came from the woman with them."

"Oh, no." What felt like my heart stopping coincided

with our abrupt stop behind Timothy, who'd nearly crashed into a member of the ship's crew.

"Is this where we sleep?" Timothy's mouth hung partly open as he gazed down the length of a long corridor lined with narrow beds, stacked three high, on either side. Several other passengers had arrived ahead of us, many making up their beds already.

"Men on the right, women on the left. Claim the berth you'd like." The sailor held his hands out, indicating either side of the room.

I glanced at Collin and felt oddly reassured at his frown of displeasure. We hadn't expected privacy but had hoped to at least sleep beside one another. Knowing he was as disappointed in this as I slightly lessened my own distress.

We will be close enough. He is still here. We had only narrowly avoided certain disaster and must be grateful.

"Never second-guess your intuition," Collin said quietly, his own thoughts no doubt mirroring mine. "It has likely saved at least my life this day."

I squeezed his hand. Too much of our lives we had spent separated from one another. I would not lose him now. My heart raced with the close call we had just had.

"Take this one, Katie." He led me to the end-most, middle berth not yet claimed.

"A bit colder there than farther into the room," the sailor said. "Air from above travels down, as does the rain if the hatches are not closed."

It wasn't the cold I was worried about. "Perhaps this is a better choice if one is likely to be frequently ill."

"*Everyone* will be frequently ill once we're underway," the man responded with a surly grin. "Barely got the stench from the last bunch mopped up."

"I can tell." The past month my sense of smell had become over-sensitive, with the slightest odor being enough to upset my stomach. Since descending the stairs the smells of vomit and lye had been competing with one another, neither pleasant. I tried to focus on the lye, remembering the happy afternoon Collin and I had spent with Eithne and Gavin Campbell, where I had learned to make soap. They were leaving Scotland, too, with Alistair and the others. I looked forward to additional lessons on soapmaking, as well as a great deal of other skills, once we'd reached our destination.

But we had to reach it first—all of us. "If I take this one, where will you and Timothy sleep?" I asked Collin.

"Directly across from you."

"I don't want to sleep on the floor." Timothy ran to the first set of beds and began climbing. "I want to be up top."

"A wiser choice," the crewman agreed. "The bottom berths always get wet, especially those on the end. If you're going to risk the cold, don't compound it with being wet as well."

Timothy finished scaling the beds and settled himself on the top, where he could sit up if he leaned forward and bent his head low.

"Don't be falling off," Collin said to him. "I've no patience for scraping a lad off the floor in the middle of the night."

"There'll be plenty else to scrape from the floor day and night," the crewman said, sounding thoroughly disgusted.

"The edges come up high." Timothy touched the raised sides of the berth. "I *can't* fall."

It was probable that he still could, but I felt more inclined to take our chances with him up top rather than risk the damp of a lower berth.

Collin pried my hand from his. "Our trunk is just over there." He pointed to rows of similar chests stowed and stacked behind us. "I'll move it closer."

I kept a close eye on him as other passengers filtered into the room, receiving similar instructions from the crewman.

Still keeping an eye on Timothy, I sidled nearer to Collin. I took up the trunk handle on the opposite side and did what I could to pull.

"Would it not be better for us," I whispered, "safer, for you in particular, if we were to be in the middle of the room and less noticeable to all who enter? What if they do learn that you're right here, a dozen steps away—on the *Cleopatra*?" I tried to remember exactly what explanation, if any, we'd given the couple to whom we'd sold our original tickets. I didn't wish them ill and felt terrible if—as seemed the case—we'd caused them trouble. But I didn't want that trouble boarding this ship.

"If that happens, I stay as far away from you and Timothy as possible. You've not a price on your head, so it is likely you could remain."

"*Without* you?" My voice rose as I tugged harder, my paltry efforts actually moving the trunk a bit this time. "If you are taken, Timothy and I will leave this ship as well. I believed an ocean separated us once. I'll not go through that again."

"You will if it will protect you—and our bairn." Collin leaned forward over the trunk so that his face was close to mine. "There is nothing for us here, Katie. What do you think would become of the two of you if you stayed?"

I met his determined gaze with one of my own. "I would enlist my sister's help."

"As if she would give it," Collin scoffed. "She wanted you and Timothy *out* of that house before her husband's return. I am sorry to say such of your sister, but she only cares about herself."

He was right, but that didn't change how I felt. "And I care for you more than my own life. Don't ask this of me, Collin. If they come for you, I'll not—"

"You will." He gripped my shoulders and pulled me closer yet. "It is not just your life you are caring for now. You've your brother and our child to think of." He released me abruptly as two other passengers came over to retrieve their trunks.

I shivered beneath my wet cloak, not cold or frightened by Collin's outburst or show of angry determination but by the knowledge that he was right and I could no longer think of the two of us alone. Overhead the rain still pounded the deck, and I willed it to fall harder—or perhaps to cease immediately so we might embark. Whichever would prevent the Redcoats from further searching and see us safely from here.

The tempests at sea no longer seemed threatening.

Chapter Seven

Aboard the *Ulysses,* March 1762

*R*evenge. His sweet angel in the darkness had killed someone. Ian pondered this, as he had since her hasty departure two nights ago, when a crewman in search of ale had interrupted their conversation. Apparently there had been a bit of celebrating that evening, on account of land being sighted.

After the man had left, and Eliza as well, Ian had searched the hold and secured a couple of bottles of ale for himself—not for celebrating but for survival, as his source of both drink and nourishment would soon be departing the ship.

He wasn't too worried about surviving without her, now that he wasn't as ill; but he mourned the loss of Eliza's company. He'd waited all of yesterday and last night, hoping she would come to see him again. That she had not both worried and saddened him. *Strange*, he mused, how quickly he had become attached to her. For a man insistent upon keeping to himself, or at least to his own, he'd been acting most peculiarly of late, allowing his thoughts to dwell on Elizabeth Campbell.

Her surname alone meant she ought to have been an enemy. Yet he could not think of her that way. Away from Scotland, clan names and boundaries didn't hold the importance they once had. Or possibly it was that Collin's situation, his Campbell wife, had softened Ian's past hatred.

Eliza was a stranger whose face he'd yet to see, who at the same time felt like an old friend. It seemed he'd known her forever, and he desired to continue that acquaintance.

Such was not to be, even had circumstances been different. For while he might not harbor the abhorrence toward the Campbells that he once had, Ian could not see that he would ever join with one as had Collin. But the feelings Ian had begun entertaining most regarding Eliza Campbell were the sort that would keep her at his side indefinitely.

In the past he'd never thought much on marriage. For many years it did not appear he would live long enough to enjoy the blessing. But if he was somehow to outrun and outlast both the demons of his past and the Redcoats of his present, marriage might not be an unpleasant path to take.

Collin had seemed happy enough with it. For the first time in a long time—since Aileen—Ian could imagine himself with a woman. He didn't know what she might look like; but she would be kind and gentle, as Eliza had been to him.

He hoped fervently that she would return later tonight, one last time. Ian knew he ought not to think about that— about her—worrying over how he would handle their parting, when he needed to focus on what it would take to remain hidden on the ship while it was docked and on the return trip to Scotland. He'd no intention of setting so much as a toe in the Colonies, let alone being a slave there for the next fourteen years.

He hated the thought of Eliza doing just that but could see no way to keep her with him. According to the ship records, he was dead, tossed overboard with the other deceased earlier in the voyage. But Eliza would be expected to report with the other prisoners. Even worse, one officer in particular would be looking for her. Ian suspected there was far more to that story than what she'd shared.

He tried putting it, and her, from his mind. She'd done him an extraordinarily good turn, but that didn't mean he owed her his chance at freedom. Instinctively, he knew she'd agree. She'd want him to return to Scotland. *To my wife.* At the least, he ought to set that record straight before they parted. She had a right to know the real name of the man whose life she'd saved.

Ian finished the last of the hard tack and cheese Eliza had brought him on her previous visit and wished fervently for a sporran of oats. A man could get by a long while on a pouch of oats and a flask of whisky. He hoped that at least some of the return cargo would be something edible. If not, he'd have to resort to killing and eating the rats in the hold. He'd lived off such before and cared not to again, especially without at least a fire to cook the wee beasts.

With these less-than-palatable thoughts in his mind and the rats in question scurrying about his feet, Ian lay across the crate that was his bed and dozed a while.

When he woke it was to feel breath on his cheek and a cool, gentle hand on his forehead.

"You're fevered again."

"Am I?" He lifted a hand to his forehead and realized Eliza was right. He was warmer than normal, though not dangerously so. What was dangerous was that he continued to sleep so soundly. It was as if his lifetime habit of being alert had gone.

"No matter," he said brusquely, and sat up too quickly. Dizziness swept through him.

"I've brought you a whole bucket of water," Eliza said. "And as much food as I could sneak away, and a candle as well. The shore is close now. It's near midnight, and we'll be docking soon."

"Thank you," Ian said, his emotions suddenly spinning more out of control than anything the fever had caused. He didn't want her to leave. "I'll miss you," he said feebly. Something he'd never said to anyone before, not even his brother.

"And I you." Her hand found his face and cupped his cheek. "Be so very careful. They'll be unloading soon. You'll have to take great care not to be found."

"I'm good at hiding," Ian assured her. "My father, brother, and I hid from the English, often right under their noses, for months after Culloden." He caught her hand as she lowered it from his face. *Must be all this touching,* he decided. He wasn't used to human contact, especially not from a female and given tenderly. It was addicting. Probably a good thing they'd soon be separated. He didn't need anything fogging his brain, distracting him from his goal. *Scotland.* He had to focus on that and returning to claim the MacDonald land and lead his people.

"I must go now," Eliza said. "Much of the crew is about tonight. It was a risk coming down here."

"*You* take care," Ian said. "Don't give away any more kisses to save scoundrels like me."

"I won't." There was a smile in her voice again. But when she spoke once more it was with a catch. "I don't believe I'll ever meet another scoundrel quite like you."

He hoped not. He hoped she'd end up in a good home with a kind mistress, maybe a widow who needed help with running her house. That wouldn't be such a bad life if Eliza had food enough and a roof over her head and people who treated her kindly. It was more than she'd come from, more than many Highlanders had in years past. *What are the odds she'll be so fortunate?*

She eased her hand from his grasp, and he heard the rustle of her skirts as she rose.

"Thank you, Eliza," he said once more, the last time he would say her name. His throat constricted strangely, as if he'd swallowed something too large to go down.

"You're welcome. God speed to you. I hope you find Lady Katherine well upon your return."

There is no Lady Katherine for me. She is my brother's wife. He didn't say the words, fearing that the truth between them would somehow make it harder to part.

Chapter Eight

River Thames, aboard the *Cleopatra,* March 1762

"Here, take this." Collin placed a folded quilt in my hands. It was soft and worn, obviously used.

"I'm afraid that will have to do for both comfort and warmth," he said with a rueful look at the crude, wooden berths. There were no mattresses to speak of, nothing at all save the wood that made them up.

"This is lovely." I traced the pattern with my finger while admiring the faded, though still colorful fabrics. "Where did you find it?"

"Mrs. Gibbons told me of a shop where I could barter for and purchase supplies." Collin tossed another blanket up to Timothy, sitting happily in the top bunk, his legs swinging over the edge. To him this was the beginning of a grand adventure. Even the swarm of Redcoats aboard the other ship had seemed exciting, to him.

I set the quilt on my bed and returned to Collin, arms outstretched for another, one to go on his bed. Instead he pulled a shirt from the trunk, then closed the lid.

"And what are you to sleep with?" I asked with a pointed look at the threadbare shirt, the same he had worn throughout our journey from Scotland to England. Were we not so destitute, I would have questioned bringing it at all.

"You, I'd hoped," Collin said regretfully. "I thought we would be sharing a bed."

"You'll freeze," I said, dismayed.

But Collin only shook his head. He tossed the shirt on his berth to claim it. "If I was going to freeze from sleeping in the cold it would have happened long ago, in the Highlands. I'll be well enough in a fine ship like this."

"Fine ship," I mumbled, grasping the side of the berth as the floor rocked beneath us. We were still at anchor, yet bobbing like a cork in this storm.

"I think they may be removing the gangplank," Collin said hopefully. "Perhaps we are about to get underway."

It had been a tense hour since we'd boarded, been divided into groups, and given a brief tour of what was to be our home for the next several weeks. Though the amenities aboard ship were lacking, they seemed sufficient that we would survive the voyage—if only it would begin. The rain had continued, possibly causing delay or difficulty for the crew. But the soldiers on the ship next to us were the bigger worry. I fervently wished both them and us gone from this place.

A series of shrill whistles sounded from the direction of the stairwell. The *Cleopatra* did not have a large ship's bell, so we had been told that passengers would be summoned and time marked by whistle instead. We'd been given a signal that meant it was our turn to cook, and another for when it was our turn to wash. We had one for our rotation up top and another that meant all passengers must stay below. But the series of whistles we heard now meant the opposite—some situation that required all crew and passengers to report to the deck.

My heart sank. Collin moved swiftly, lifting Timothy from his berth. "Take your sister's hand and hurry up the stairs."

"What about you?" Timothy asked.

"I'll be along," Collin said. "I've a few things to secure first." He placed one hand on Timothy's back and the other on mine and nudged us toward the other passengers heading to the closest stairwell, the one on our side of the long, hall-like room.

"What are you about?" I demanded of Collin in a terse

whisper as we walked, using a turn of phrase he'd oft spoken to me.

"Say not a word of me," Collin replied in his own whisper. He withdrew our paperwork from his pocket and handed it to me—minus his own ticket. He kissed me swiftly on the lips. "I love you, Katie. Never doubt." He gave us another, firmer nudge, and we found ourselves surrounded by passengers on either side.

I glanced back to see Collin once more, but he had vanished.

We moved around the short wall and up the steep staircase. I clutched Timothy's hand tightly and bent close to him for a second. "If we are asked questions, let me speak. Go along with whatever I say—even if it is a lie."

His eyes grew large, but he nodded and continued glancing about, appearing nonplussed by the entire situation. "Maybe they're only bringing us up top so we can wave goodbye to England."

"Perhaps." I bit my lip. My fears were confirmed when our heads reached the height of the topmost step, and rows of shiny black boots came into view. *Redcoats.*

I drew my hood up once more, under pretext of keeping the rain from my face. We were made to line up with the other passengers. For some minutes we waited, rumors being whispered back and forth amongst us.

A murderer had escaped from London and was believed to be in the wharf area, so all ships were being checked—to ensure the passengers' safety, of course.

A known criminal on his way to be hanged had broken free and was believed to be aboard one of the ships harbored at this end of the wharf.

The last story to reach my ears—that a wanted man had purchased a ticket on the other ship but had managed to escape that vessel onto ours and was even now among our ranks—nearly paralyzed me with fear.

Two soldiers and an officer—obvious by the insignia on his coat—made their way down the rows of passengers. When it was our turn we were told to step forward and state our names. Timothy was questioned first, and I said a silent prayer of thanks that he could answer honestly.

"Timothy Mercer," he said.

"And who is the pretty lady with you?" the officer asked with a patronizing smile.

"My sister Christina, but she's not a lady." Titters and laughter broke out from both the soldiers and passengers alike who were near us. "Only our other sister, Anna, is a lady, and she's boring and grumpy all the time."

"And who else are you traveling with?" The officer asked as he consulted the passenger records. "Your father?"

Timothy shook his head. "He's dead. Our mother too."

"But there is a man traveling with you. Where is he?"

Timothy shrugged and glanced at me. I placed a hand on his shoulder. "You speak of our brother." I nodded to the record in the officer's hand. "He planned to come and even boarded with us, before changing his mind at the last minute." My eyes filled with tears at the end of this unrehearsed speech. The last time I had stood before Redcoats and defended Collin it had not gone well.

"Why would a man do such a thing—abandon his family and waste the precious cost of passage?" His eyes roved over us, assessing our financial situation, I supposed.

I stood taller, grateful that both Timothy and I had worn our best. "Why does any man veer off course?" I asked. "Is it not usually because of his interest in a woman?" The lie I spun was growing more entangled, threads stretching out to directions I might not be able to recall.

"Let us hope you are telling the truth, Miss Mercer." The officer looked pointedly at my hand, resting on Timothy's shoulder, and the carved Gaelic wedding band on my third finger.

Foolish. Silently I chided myself for a mistake that could prove costly.

"Why wouldn't I be?" I said indignantly, all the while praying Timothy would keep silent.

"We are searching for a wanted man, Ian MacDonald, believed to have purchased passage on this ship only a few days ago. It's possible he is here now, using another name as an alias—and perhaps with another person to assist him in hiding. It would not go well for such a person, were that to be the case."

"I am hiding nothing," I said in my perfect English accent as I pulled the hood of my cape back, as if to prove my innocence.

"I did not think him in there," the officer said and moved on down the line.

We were made to wait in the rain at least another hour while every passenger was questioned. At the same time Redcoats, accompanied by the crew, searched the ship. Every time one returned to the deck, I held my breath, fearful that Collin would be with them. Three times men were pulled aside and detained by the soldiers. And twice the same officer returned down the line to look at me.

At last it was determined that Ian MacDonald was not aboard. The intruders began to withdraw. Had I still been standing I would have sagged with relief, but Timothy and I and many other passengers had long since found places to sit.

Not having slept much the night before, Timothy had succumbed some time ago. His head lay in my lap, and I leaned over him, doing my best to keep him as dry as possible. As the line of rain-slicked, black boots marched past us, I dared not look up. Even after they had all gone and the whistle had blown, releasing us to return to our quarters below, I waited—afraid of what I might or might not find below. Though it did not appear the soldiers had found Collin, I feared he had somehow left on his own to ensure Timothy and I were safe.

"The Redcoats could not find a man was he right in front of them," a crew member grumbled to another as he returned to his work.

"Look at this lot." His companion inclined his head toward the wet passengers still scattered about the deck. "Hellish way to start a voyage. No doubt half will end up with fever and have to be tossed overboard."

"At least they've paid in advance," the first said. "None indentured on this voyage to lose."

I'd heard enough. I prodded Timothy and half-pushed him from my lap. "Come along. We've got to get you below and into some dry clothes."

The same sounded good to me as well, though I could not think of that for myself until I had discovered what had become of Collin.

We descended the stairs once more and found the dormitory-like room bustling with activity as passengers settled in. Some had hung blankets about their berths for a bit of privacy. Others waited in a long line for the door to the privy. My eyes scanned the room, from Collin's bed to the long corridor beyond, but saw no sign of him.

"How come all this is up here?" Timothy perched on the middle berth—the one that was to be Collin's—while grasping the edge of his own and peering strangely at it. From my vantage point I could not see all that he saw, but enough to realize that the contents of our trunk were piled atop Timothy's bed.

The trunk. I whirled around, facing the area where much of the luggage was stowed. Our trunk was not close to our beds, as it had been, but farther back, with another, smaller, chest placed on top of it.

Heart pounding I hurried toward it, guessing that Collin might have squeezed inside. But who had moved it, and would he be trapped with the other on top?

With a little effort I moved the other chest then knelt to

open our own. A padlock I'd not noticed before hung closed over the metal clasp at front.

"Collin," I whispered and banged on the side. No answer came. My panic escalated, remembering the look of contempt the officer had given me the last time he passed. Horrible images flooded my mind—Collin bound and gagged within, left by the soldiers to suffocate. Or worse, what if he was dead already, and they had left his body for me to discover?

My trembling fingers jerked a pin from my hair, and I inserted it in the lock, twisting to no avail.

"*Collin.*" I bent my head to the trunk, offering an urgent prayer.

A tap on my shoulder made me jump. I would have fallen over save for the strong hands that caught me. *Collin's hands.*

I burst into tears as he gathered me close.

"Sshh." He steered us both to another trunk, facing the wall of the ship instead of the main part of the room. "This one is ours," he said. "We must still be careful. The danger is not yet passed. Nor will it be, I fear, until we are arrived in Halifax."

I nodded and took deep breaths to quell my emotion. "I thought—"

"I can see what you thought." Collin glanced at our trunk. "It is not far from the truth. I intended to hide in here, but there was a lad who needed the space more than I."

"*What?*" I turned to him. "What do you mean?"

Collin glanced behind us, at Timothy busily removing items from his bed, then leaned close to whisper in my ear. "A young thief had stowed away. If caught, he would have lost his hand—at the least."

"Where is he now?" I struggled to keep my voice low as my emotions swung wildly from a swell of love toward Collin for his tender heart and habit of always looking out for others, to wanting to strangle him for putting himself at even more risk.

"I don't know where he has gone," Collin said. "I suspect he is still on board. He was not in the trunk when I returned."

"Returned from where?"

"Above deck, of course," Collin said. "You and Timothy were within sight the entire time."

"You hid—in plain sight?"

Collin shrugged. "It was the only option left to me. The soldiers were already coming down the stairs. I made my way up with the last of the stragglers. An old woman required help getting up to the deck, and I was most grateful to oblige, and to stay at her side."

"Did they not question you?" I asked.

"They did," Collin affirmed. "She told them I was her son and gave a name they wrote down. Her papers were as ruined as ours."

I heaved a sigh of relief and said a silent prayer of gratitude. "Thank heavens for rain, and that what you sow, you reap." Again Collin had proved that looking out for others first served him well. I touched my forehead to his and brought a hand to his cheek. "Do you believe she meant to protect you?"

"I think it more likely she really thought me her son."

"Then her son you shall be," I proclaimed. "At least for the duration of our voyage."

"I just came back from tucking her into bed beneath a warm quilt." He stood. "Precisely the same treatment I intend for you."

He received no argument. I felt suddenly exhausted. Timothy, on the other hand, was apparently starving. He sat amidst our supplies stacked on his berth, happily eating a biscuit.

"Those were to be a treat," Collin said, but his voice was only half-scolding.

I allowed Collin to help me out of my wet cloak. "Let Timothy enjoy his biscuit. Today he has earned one."

Chapter Nine

Aboard the *Ulysses,* Portsmouth, Virginia Harbor, March 1762

The hatch door swung open, and the light from above nearly blinded Ian.

Here we go. The unloading of the hold was about to commence. He reduced the gap between his eyelids to slits and stared up from his hiding spot between the barrels stashed beneath the wide stairs. During his candlelight assessment of the hold just a few hours earlier he'd discovered these barrels all held grog—or had, at one time. Roughly three fourths were empty, and all were pushed aside, separate from the rest of the cargo. He reasoned that these were the crew's stores and would likely be left alone during the docking.

He was about to find out if his assumption was correct. The first set of boots, scuffed and brown, appeared on the topmost step, clomping down hurriedly, with no apparent concern over the possibility of falling down the steep staircase.

A muffled cry reached Ian's ears between the staccato of the boots, and a second set of shoes—considerably smaller but just as worn—appeared.

"Now we'll find out who you've been stealing away to see." The hatch thumped closed, but light remained, swinging precariously from a lantern clutched in a filthy hand outstretched above him.

"And if he happens to be gone, you can show me what the two of you been up to down here."

"Let go of me!"

Ian's eyes snapped fully open at Eliza's frightened voice. His body tensed as her scream was cut short.

"Doubtful anyone up there is going to hear you now or care if they do. They're all too busy."

Still crouched low, Ian craned his neck to see the man dragging Eliza down the stairs. The battered boots matched the rest of him, from his ragged coat and beat-up hat to the stench rolling off him. *Not an officer, then, but a lesser member of the crew.*

"Show yourself, coward." The man swung the lantern in a wide arc as he peered through the dark, while his other arm remained firmly around Eliza, his large, dirty hand clamped over her mouth.

Ian ducked before the lantern swung his direction. He picked up the bottles of ale and moved stealthily from his hiding spot.

"Ow!" the man shrieked suddenly and flung Eliza away from him as blood welled on his finger.

She clutched the rail and began climbing.

He grabbed her leg before she'd gone two steps.

"Let her go." Ian thrust the bottle's open end into the man's back. "Unless you've no care for your kidney, that is." He held the bottle so as not to spill the precious contents, while pressing firmly enough that it should feel like the tip of a pistol. Collin had pulled the same trick on him not too many years back.

The man released Eliza's leg.

"Hands in the air," Ian ordered. "Give her the lantern."

The man stretched it toward her, and Eliza reached a shaking hand out to grab it. In that second of distraction, Ian whipped his other hand up and brought the second and full bottle down heavily on the back of the man's skull. It shattered on contact, spraying glass and ale over all of them.

Ian swore, and Eliza shrieked and jumped as the crewman fell forward, striking the side of his head on the second rung. His body followed, crumpling in an unnatural and unmoving heap.

"Is he . . . dead?" Eliza's eyes were large as she looked at Ian. She clutched the lantern so tightly her knuckles were white.

Ian took it from her. "Shouldn't be," he muttered, holding it over the man. "A bottle to the back of the head isn't usually fatal. I didn't intend it to be—or to break the bottle." He'd tried to make contact on the edge, where the top met the circular bottom. "Shameful waste of ale."

Ian set the unbroken bottle aside, then stooped to remove a knife from the man's boot before nudging him with his foot. When he didn't move easily, Ian grabbed the man's shoulder and flopped him onto his back. A telltale trickle of blood flowed from behind his left ear, and his eyes were open, staring blankly upward.

"Oh, no." Eliza clapped a hand over her mouth. "I've killed another man."

"You haven't done anything," Ian said. "Though you're right, he is dead." *Bloody inconvenient.* "I'm the one who hit him. The stairs are what did it."

"Oh, no. Oh, no." Eliza clutched her middle and turned away. "They'll hang us for this."

"Only if they find out," Ian said, thinking fast. Using his boot and the blade of the knife, he swept broken glass out of the way. "Help me move him before anyone comes down here. Take his feet. I'll get his torso."

"All right." There was a rattle to her voice as she moved down the steps and crouched to pick up the man's feet.

Ian suddenly realized he was seeing her for the first time. Light brown hair swept back in a loose bun, much of which had come free during the tussle. Strands hung on either side of her face, framing its porcelain features. She was blessed with fair skin, expressive eyes of the deepest brown, a nose less pert than he'd imagined, and lips turned down in a worried expression Ian longed to kiss away. He stared a second more, willing her face to memory, wishing he had Collin's wife's talent for sketching and could capture Eliza's features on parchment to keep with him always.

The sound of feet clomping and something heavy being dragged across the floor above shook Ian from his trance.

"What are you doing here, girl? Get outta here," someone snarled above them. Footsteps skittered away.

Ian and Eliza exchanged a tense glance and stood frozen in place, expecting the door to open any second.

When, after a minute, it did not, and the sounds of feet moving away carried below, Ian set the lantern aside and stooped to pick up the man. "Be careful of any glass on his clothes."

Eliza nodded, then grappled with his boots. Together they half-carried, half-dragged the corpse behind the stairs.

"Put him down here." Ian dropped his end none too gently. He wiped his brow, feeling cold sweat and realizing he was in trouble if such meager exertion weakened him. A shiver rumbled through his ailing body, and silently he cursed the ongoing fever.

Trigger-happy Redcoat. There'd been no need for the soldier to shoot. Ian had clearly had his hands raised and was turning himself in. If the idiot hadn't shot him weeks ago, and if not for that still-festering wound, he might be himself again.

"Help me get his clothes off." Ian bent to strip the man of his jacket.

"*What?*" Eliza stared at him as if he'd gone mad. "What good will that do?"

"It's one thing to keep myself hidden. It's another entirely to hide myself *and* a corpse. The smell alone will give him away in a matter of days. Not to mention he'll probably be missed and someone will come looking for him." Ian tugged the first sleeve from the man's arm. "I'll not be able to stay here now. But perhaps with these borrowed clothes I can pass as crew, get myself off the ship during the unloading, and find my way onto another." Ian's fingers moved nimbly, freeing the man of both his jacket and the soiled shirt beneath.

"You've done this before," she said, not exactly accusing, but not sounding impressed either.

"Often." Ian's answer was muffled beneath the shirt he tugged over his own. "During the uprising. My brother and I went among the dead after battle. We were to remove anything of value from a body. The Redcoats were generally dressed better than the Highlanders, so we'd take every last item from them." He thrust his hand through a sleeve. "But our side always carried better spirits."

"And we wonder why we lost," Eliza muttered.

"We?" Ian glanced at her. "I wasn't aware that the Campbells sided with us." He tried not to sound bitter, but the truth was, had the Campbells—and the other clans they'd persuaded to their side—supported the Jacobites instead of aiding the English, Charles Stuart might now be sitting on the throne and life for the Highlanders could be vastly different. *Da might have been alive.*

"The Campbells didn't fight for Charles." Eliza met his gaze unflinchingly. "But that doesn't mean they are in favor of what the English have done."

Ian shook his head, feeling disgust at such logic. One was either for or against something. There was no middle ground when it came to England and Scotland. "You say that now, because the English are going after *all* the clans. But back in the day, your clan was all about gaining favor with the king— playing a part to reap rewards, even if that cost your own countrymen."

In the lantern light Ian saw her eyes narrow. But when she spoke it was not with anger but a calm conviction.

"Think what you like. I know differently. I thought you did, too, growing up under Liam Campbell's tutelage as you did."

Ian realized again that Eliza still believed him to be

Collin. And he knew Collin's view to be different from his own. Collin would have done just about anything for the old man.

"How old were you when you were sent onto the battlefields to search the dead?" Eliza crouched to remove a boot from the deceased.

Subject changed. Very well. "Twelve when it started," Ian said. "Mostly too young to fight, though we did sometimes."

"That must have been a terrible thing to see and do."

"War is unpleasant, from start to finish. Fighting and death, defeat and decimation." Ian paused before starting on the crewman's breeches. "You might want to turn around." He waited until she'd done so before continuing. "Much easier before they get stiff," he said as he donned the breeches. He remembered working alongside Collin and stiff bodies amidst the fog on the freezing moors, hours after a battle had ended.

"I'm not sure what good all this will do you," Eliza said, her back still turned. "His garments are scarcely better than your own."

Ian glanced down at himself and realized that while he had been admiring her beauty, she had likely been thinking the opposite of him. He had several week's growth along his face and was generally unkempt and uncleaned. He smelled of the stench in the hold, and his clothing was filthy and in tatters. Not a quality about him—appearance or otherwise—for a woman such as Eliza to admire. It was a wonder she hadn't fled.

Instead, her calm demeanor throughout the past several minutes increased his high opinion of her all the more. Though initially shaken, she'd not fallen apart but reacted with cool self-assurance. Not only was she was kind and gentle, she had a level head to boot. But then, she was a Highlander too, accustomed to hardship and tragedy, circumstances that bred empathy and resilience. Ruefully he lamented once more that she could not come with him.

Or, perhaps she could, now that he intended to sail on another vessel.

"You ought to come with me," he said, hit with sudden inspiration. "With your experience as a cook's assistant, you could find work."

"Not likely," Eliza said. "Women are considered ill luck on a ship. It was only desperation that led the crew to employ me. Besides, I should have to find a way off this ship first, without anyone taking notice."

Ian didn't have a response, other than swift disappointment to what was no doubt truth. He shouldn't have allowed himself to hope.

"If your situation was different, I would suggest that it is you who should consider staying here, in the Colonies." Eliza peeked over her shoulder, noted he was dressed, and turned to face him, careful to keep her gaze well above the corpse. "The past years have not been kind to the MacDonalds—to any Highlanders, as you said. It is doubtful that will improve." She handed the boots to Ian.

He took them from her. "I've no desire to make my home in the Colonies." No matter that the situation was different than she suspected, that he was not Collin and did not have a wife awaiting him in Scotland. "I'll disembark with the rest of the crew during the unloading, and at first opportunity I'll sneak off to find work on a vessel bound for Scotland."

"That sounds a rather risky plan."

"Aye," Ian agreed, tugging on the boots. The fit was snug, but they would have to do. When he'd awoken in the hold, his own shoes had been gone. "Let's go."

"We're just going to—leave him lying there?" Her eyes flickered briefly toward the floor, then back to Ian's face.

"Good point." Ian crouched awkwardly beneath the bulk of the added layers. Lifting the body beneath the shoulders, he hauled it to a sitting position, then braced it against a barrel. "Help me, please." He waved Eliza closer, and together they scooted the barrels in and around the man until he was scrunched in the middle of them, knees drawn up to his chest.

"That's better," Ian said, dusting his hands with satisfaction as Eliza looked on hers strangely, as if seeing them for the first time.

He clasped one between his two and found it icy cold. "There is nothing more we could have done," he said gently, sorry for his cross words earlier. "Had the outcome been any different it might have been you and I laid out here, with our throats slit and your dress up around your head. This was self-defense, plain and simple."

She gave a slow nod. "Self-defense. Not like the other I've to answer God for."

Ian's curiosity piqued again, as it had the first time she'd mentioned having killed someone. He wanted to ask her about it and felt that she wished to tell him, to relieve herself of the burden of secrecy if nothing else. But now was not the time.

He took her other hand and rubbed both between his. "You're freezing. We've got to get you out of here. But hear me first. Whatever else you have done, whatever crime is causing you distress, know that you have saved a life—mine—in exchange for the one taken. I promise to do good with that gift. Think of what you have done as this—the removal of evil and the rescue of good. Surely that will balance before God." As he ended the pretty little speech, he realized he could not share with her who he really was. His reputation in the Highlands preceded him. Ian MacDonald and good were not in the least synonymous.

Keeping hold of her, he led her toward the stairs, then stopped suddenly at the sound of someone above them. They exchanged another wary glance, held their breaths, and waited.

The hatch above clicked, or was that merely someone stepping on it? Ian's gaze strayed to the steps, and he watched to see if anyone would descend.

"I think we are still safe," he whispered at last, giving Eliza's hand a reassuring squeeze.

"We should leave this place," she said. "It is good the day is overcast. Your eyes will need some time to adjust."

"The lantern hurts them already," Ian admitted. He could not deny, though, that the prospect of being out of the hold appealed greatly. Instead of several more weeks in the dark, he might now have a sea voyage above deck. He was no sailor, but he knew how to work hard and was a quick learner. Surely he could be of some use.

"How did he—" he cast a last glance at the corpse— "come upon you at this time of morning, anyhow? You weren't coming to see me once more, were you?"

"I—I was," Eliza admitted quietly. "I shouldn't have, and I'm so sorry for the trouble I've caused."

It wasn't her apology, but something else that gave Ian pause. *Why* had she been coming to see him? "What was it that brought you here again?"

She pulled her hands from his and fidgeted as she turned to away. "I had to warn you. He gave me his word, but I felt to warn you anyway—in case he plays me false."

"He?" Ian's brows rose. "Who gave you his word? This man?" He nodded toward the corpse.

Eliza shook her head, causing more wisps to fall from her bun. "The officer, the one who brought me above deck to assist in the galley, the same who promised to look the other way the night I fetched you from the pile of dead to be tossed overboard."

"There was a *pile*?" Ian asked, momentarily distracted by the unpleasant image of her digging through bodies to retrieve his.

"Aye. All of them truly dead, excepting you. I wouldn't have known you were in it, but one of the other prisoners came to see me for food, and he was wearing your boots. I recognized them from that night in the forest when I helped you escape. They were worn, yet finer than most—fit for a laird. I asked the man where the boots had come from, and he told me he'd taken them off one of the men soon to be swimming with the sharks."

The night she helped me escape . . . Eliza was speaking of Collin again. Ian realized how fortunate it was that he had insisted that he and Collin trade boots. He'd told Collin to take his black ones, in far better condition and with more wear left, noting that as an indentured servant Collin might go years without any possibility of replacing them.

First time I've been rewarded for being deceitful, Ian thought with a strange satisfaction. Not only had he convinced the English patrol that he was Collin, but Eliza had remembered those boots, and now that very thing had saved his life.

"What did you do then?" Ian asked. He ought to have pressed her about the story sooner but had preferred to speak of other, more pleasant topics during their brief times together.

"I dragged the man with me, demanding he show me the body the boots came from. He took me to it—to you." She paused, a slight shudder rippling over her shoulders. "You were alive. You know the rest from there. I convinced him to help me bring you below while the officer agreed to look the other way for a short while. These past weeks I've believed he had no idea what I'd done that night, and that you'd still been counted among the dead."

"I wasn't?" Ian rubbed the back of his neck, pained at this latest obstacle.

"I'm not certain. But the officer—Second Officer Millet—told me last night that he knows I've been hiding someone. He has promised not to say anything, but . . ."

"He's English," Ian finished. His situation had just gone from precarious to nearly impossible. A dead man lay at his feet, and the ship's second officer knew about him.

"I'm so sorry." She began walking toward the stairs.

"The other prisoner kept my shoes?" Ian's mouth

crooked in a sardonic half smile. It was no more than what he would have done.

Eliza nodded. "It was how I agreed to get him to help me transport you. And he did not believe you were long for this world. I was not certain myself that first night."

Ian reached the stairs just behind her and took up the lantern. "It would seem you've made bargains all over this ship on my behalf. What did you promise this time for Officer Millet's silence?" He searched out her eyes in the flickering light.

She would not quite meet his gaze. "I agreed that I would remain with him after we dock. He appreciates a good meal, and as the cook is to be on leave, and Officer Millet is to be here for two weeks or more until he sails again and has need of—"

"I'll bet he has needs." Anger, quick and hot, ignited within Ian. He moved closer to her, so their faces were very near one another. "Don't do this, Eliza. Stay with the other indentured prisoners."

"And risk worse?" she hissed, not backing down, but moving even closer. "Would you have me sold to a brothel or to a man who would beat me?"

"No. Of course not." Ian felt as if she'd struck him. "But surely there are laws to protect those—"

"Can you be so naïve?" She gave a forced laugh. "There will be no more protection for us here than we had in Scotland. We are still a hated people—there or here." She tried to push past him, but he stepped to the side, blocking her.

"*I* am naïve?" he asked. "You have just agreed to warming much more than the man's supper. It's you in his bed he wants." Ian grabbed her arm when she made to move past him again.

"At least I know the man and there is only one," she spat.

"And what will happen when the two weeks are up?" Ian demanded. "When Officer Millet is to sail again? Where will he discard you? To the very brothels you fear?"

"I don't know," Eliza admitted. "But my chances are worse if I am sold." Tears shone in her eyes.

"Who told you that?" Ian asked. "Was it him?"

She didn't answer, but the first of her tears spilled over and trailed down her cheek, leaving a shimmering track reflected in the lantern's light.

Cool sweat broke out along Ian's forehead, and his insides clenched, as if he'd just been punched. A feeling of helplessness assaulted him, the likes of which he'd not experienced since that night his father had left him bleeding and broken at the bottom of a ravine—when the Munros had come, had stood over him, leering and poking at their prize. He'd felt an absolute panic and blinding terror at his vulnerability. He'd been entirely defenseless then. He felt the same now, though somehow this was much worse.

Over the years he'd grown callous, used to the reality that his life, pain inflicted upon him, his ultimate death was all out of his control. He'd not much to live for, so it hadn't mattered if it was taken from him. Being careless served him well when he put so little value on his life.

But this . . . This felt far different. *Eliza.* The internal ache intensified. Eliza mattered, and to send her—someone he cared for—to such a fate, to be unable to do a thing to change the suffering in store for her, cut a deeper wound than he'd previously known. She was young and had the possibility of a good life. And that was about to be taken from her.

She spoke at last, still not answering his question, but lifting her chin in the air, as he'd imagined previously, during their talks in the dark. "Life has never been fair. Nor has it been particularly kind. I should hardly expect that to change in the Colonies."

"Yet, you have shown kindness to me and many others."

"Little good that will have done if you are discovered. Let me go, before we both get caught." She pried his fingers from her arm and ran ahead of him up the stairs.

"Eliza, wait—"

She paused but did not look back.

"If you go with the others there's a chance—"

"Don't waste your freedom," she said before disappearing above.

Chapter Ten

Aboard the *Ulysses*, Portsmouth, Virginia, March 1762

Ian followed Eliza to the floor above, only to find her gone. He remained alone, wedging himself into a narrow gap between a wall and post. Once again he waited in the dark. Here, at least, light filtered from above through the open stairways, one on either side of the long passage.

He was grateful for it, and the promise of fresher air above. For while the hold had been dank and musty, the odors here were far worse. It smelled as if he'd stuck his face in a cesspool.

Berths crowded either side of the passage, three high and end to end, though not one of them looked long enough to accommodate a person of average height. Bodies lay in several of these, some sleeping fitfully, others moaning and yet others writhing in the agony of sickness or crying out their fears for what was to come.

Food, feces, blood, and vomit covered the floor, strewn amongst the few possessions those indentured had brought with them. Most, he suspected, had been forced to come and had little more than the clothing upon their backs. The scene was both foul and depressing, rousing in Ian no little yearning for the crystal lakes, mountains, and moors of the Highlands. *Home.*

Little wonder he had been near to death in this place. Eliza had spared not only his life but weeks of misery in a foul berth when she'd secreted him away below. All the more reason to thank her.

But the time for gratitude had come and gone. It was time to think of the future—*his* future . . . the only one he had a possibility of saving.

Twice men came from the other side but did not open the hatch to the stairs leading to what had been his sanctuary. Ian had no recollection of much that came before his time in the hold. He vaguely remembered being in prison in Scotland, though he'd been too ill to care whether he lived or died. He remembered being chained to the other prisoners and forced onto the ship. The men behind and in front of him had supported him the entire way. After that his next recollection was the day he'd awoken to find Eliza tending him.

It seemed wrong that there was nothing more he could do for her. Nothing he could have done to begin with. So why did he feel so guilty?

Sometime during his musings, Ian realized the sway of the ship had changed and the noises from the decks above had increased. Pulling the crewman's hat low and making sure his knife was within easy reach, Ian stepped from his hiding place. Better to begin his act before the full light of day, he reasoned, and made for the stairs above.

They led to another floor littered with crates, barrels, and coils of rope. The corridor was considerably narrower than that of the floor below, and numerous doors lined one end.

The officers' quarters. Bile rose in Ian's throat. Was it here Officer Millet would keep Eliza after the others had vacated the ship? Or had he chosen a tavern in town? Ian pounded his fist against the wall. *Don't care. Not one bit.*

Feeling suddenly desperate to be free of the stale air and surroundings, Ian hefted a coil of rope from a pile and lugged it up the next set of stairs with him, hoping to look as if he was busy.

He emerged onto the lower deck and paused a moment for his eyes to adjust to the early morning light and to drink in great gulps of salty air.

His squinting eyes assessed his surroundings, from the

worn deck to the crew engaged in various work upon it. Men pulled at the ropes commanding the sails that towered overhead, stretching almost beyond sight, reaching toward the heavy, gray sky. Ian had never seen anything quite so magnificent, and it held him in place, mesmerized by the sheer size of both ship and sails and the number of people moving to and fro, all with purpose and apparent knowledge of what must be done to manage her.

A gull cried overhead, and Ian followed it with his eyes to the land they were rapidly approaching. The magnitude of the task at hand struck him with awe as he realized the captain—standing at the helm on the upper deck, his back to Ian—intended to bring the enormous ship alongside the quay attached to the shore.

An anchor crew stood at the ready near a windlass, but Ian had little faith that an anchor could stop the vessel from her current course—bound straight for the dock and the buildings beyond. To his inexperienced eyes it appeared they would surely run aground.

"Heave to!" a voice cried from the upper deck, and the men surrounding the sails leapt into action, their movements quick, exact, and in unison.

Ian changed position so he might view the comings and goings on both levels. Two men manned the large ship's wheel, and another crewman cranked a winch near the front of the ship.

The sails flapped loudly, and Ian leaned his head back, peering up at the tall mast as the men maneuvered the canvases so that some filled with air and propelled the ship forward while the other sails somehow did the opposite and held it back.

Ian stepped over to the railing and looked down into the water, watching as the hull moved first forward then slightly backward, slowing the ship's progress, while still allowing it to move closer to shore.

Ian felt a new respect for the crew as he watched the men

work the ropes with precision. The ship began to turn—more sharply than he would have believed possible—and Ian stood awestruck at the ease at which the captain appeared to maneuver the large vessel.

"Strike the sails!" His commanding voice echoed across the deck.

"Going to stand about slack-jawed all day, are ye?" Another crewman shoved into Ian's shoulder as he passed. His nose wrinkled. "Smells as if you had more'n your share last night. None's my pity for ye, if you're fool enough to drink so much afore a full day of work." He shook his head. "Be smart now and get to the ropes."

Ian stared down at the rope in his hands. *Now what?*

"Give that to me and get o'er there, ye muckle." The crewman yanked the rope from Ian's hands and pointed toward mid-ship, where a line of men was hauling in the sails.

Ian turned away and ran to assist, then quickly realized that if he took his place at the end of the line he'd be expected to form the coil. One look at the loops of rope the end man shaped with ease upon the deck, and Ian knew his ruse would be over. There was a definite pattern to it—one he didn't know. Instead, he searched out the widest gap between the men and stepped in there, adding his weight to the pull, as if that was where he was supposed to have been all along.

A half dozen hauls and he felt both grateful for and miserable because of the extra layers of shirt and coat. It was good his own, wasted frame was hidden within the bulk of fabric, but the way it chafed was soon to make for more problems than he already had. Beads of sweat multiplied along his brow, dripping into his already-hurting eyes. Ian ignored his discomfort, particularly that of the sharp pain of the wound in his side, and concentrated on matching the rhythm of the muscled arms in front of him as they reeled in the heavy canvas.

"Make anchor!" The captain's next directive came just minutes later, and from the corner of his eye, Ian observed the crew near the windlass spring into action. The heavy clang of chain reverberated across the deck, and along with the "heave-ho" chant of the crews working the sails, those on the anchor began shouting their own instructions.

Had he not felt so miserable and worried over being discovered, he would have enjoyed the spectacle. The ship seemed almost a living, breathing thing, and the way she responded to those guiding her was nothing short of incredible. The analogy oft given between a ship and a woman made sense to him now. Ian thought suddenly of Eliza being commanded by the second officer. What had seemed glorious a minute before soured. Ian tugged even harder, determined to do his part so he could get away from this miserable place as soon as possible.

The Colonies. Virginia, to be exact, Eliza had told him. Ian wasn't sure what he had expected the New World to look like, but he thought it did a fair job of resembling the old.

He'd left the Highlands only three times in his life: as a boy, when marching with Bonnie Prince Charlie's men on their route to London; last summer, with Collin, when they'd traveled to fetch his bride; and then once more, before this wretched sea voyage, when the English patrol had taken him to Glasgow.

That city had not impressed him, nor did the row of buildings sprung up just beyond the shore that he stared at now. He'd take mountains and moors any day over a city crowded with people and animals and carriages—and boats.

No little number of ships and smaller vessels crowded the harbor. The docks were already lively with men, and the sun barely up. The air was chill and heavy, and Ian knew real cold for the first time in a while. He wondered how much of that was attributable to the fever and infection still fighting him, and how much was from being out of doors after so long being within. He wished he hadn't left behind the blanket Eliza had provided him.

He hoped he had enough stamina to make it through the day. The sails had long since been hauled in, the anchors sunk, and the gang planks laid out between shore and ship. The past two hours he had been part of a chain of men, passing goods from the hold to the front of the ship, where they were eventually to be unloaded.

Thus far no cry of alarm had sounded from below, and Ian hoped the regular stench of the ship would be enough to disguise the dead man several hours more.

Customs agents and ship's officers milled about the cargo that had been brought up, opening a crate or barrel here or there to inspect it and see that the contents matched that of the ship's records.

Ian didn't like the sight of the Redcoats any more than he'd cared for them in Scotland. *Some new world,* he thought bitterly, glimpsing already the injustices and inequality present near the docks. The poor still begged—or stole and were punished for it—and the wealthy still bought their way to power.

"Look lively, men. The taverns and wenches be just hours away." One of the officers who had been conversing with the customs agents turned to the line of crew still moving cargo. "Let's get this offloaded so the real valuables can be brought on deck." His smile curved into a sneer beneath his mustache. "Even Highland scum have some worth in Virginia," he muttered. Then louder, "To the warehouse with this lot. Follow me."

The sick feeling that had nothing to do with his poor health returned to Ian's stomach. *Officer Millet?* If so, why would Eliza agree to be in the man's presence for even a minute?

To save me.

MICHELE PAIGE HOLMES

Ian tripped, almost crashing into the man in front of him as they crossed the deck to the waiting cargo. He couldn't let her do this.

He didn't have a choice. Any more than he had a choice to risk further injuring himself if he wanted to get off this ship.

With a grunt Ian squatted, lifting the opposite end of a crate as the man across from him. Trying to ignore both the pain in his side and in his heart, he placed one weary step in front of the other and headed toward shore.

Chapter Eleven

The Thames, aboard the *Cleopatra,* March 1762

"Wake up, Katie. It's getting late, and you need to eat." Collin's whispered words against my cheek and his breath in my ear lulled me from a deep sleep.

I turned my head toward the sound of his voice and smashed my nose against the side of the berth. "Ouch." I leaned forward as if to sit up, but Collin's hand on my shoulder kept me down.

"Mind your head." He inclined his to the wood planking above me—the topmost berth in the stack of three.

"Thanks." I lay back but reached for his hand. "What time is it?" The cabin was dark, with only a faint light shining from the stairwell. Collin had been wise for more than one reason when selecting the outermost beds; we were close to the only source of natural light, and he was also able to sit beside me—an impossibility with any of the other berths, wedged close together, side-by-side as they were.

"About ten o'clock I think. They stop blowing the whistle at nine."

"Late," I murmured, snuggling deeper into the quilt. I could not claim comfort, exactly, with my only mattress being our clothes layered beneath me over the wood boards, but I felt cozy and had little desire to leave my nest.

"Forgive me waking you," Collin said. "But you should eat, or you'll feel even worse than usual in the morning."

This was true. Paradoxically, an empty stomach made me all the more likely to empty it again—or convulse painfully while attempting to. But right now, warm as I was and with sleep still hovering, I was willing to take my chances.

"There's something you should see."

"Can't it wait until tomorrow?" I asked drowsily, grasping for the pleasant dream I'd been having. It was still there, fuzzy at the edges of memory.

"The view will be different then." Collin squeezed my hand gently. "Just listen."

I closed my eyes and did as he instructed, hearing only numerous, muffled sounds of disquiet close by. There were several snorers among us. A child was crying. *Not Timothy.* Elsewhere in the room another, whispered, conversation was also taking place. Nothing I heard gave me any clue as to what Collin wished me to see. I gave a vague shake of my head. "What am I supposed to be hearing?"

"We're moving," he whispered. "There is an almost melodic creak to the ship if you listen carefully."

I tried blocking out the other sounds and thought I did hear something unusual—different—along with a slight swaying beneath us.

"If you don't get up now you'll have missed our entire departure," Collin said.

"I am a bit hungry," I admitted, even as my growling stomach proclaimed the same.

"Come, then," Collin said. He withdrew a parcel from his pocket and held it out to me—a last, precious and slightly squashed scone from the inn where we had stayed. "There's a moon out, the air smells fresh and clean, and London actually looks pretty from this view."

It was Collin's coaxing voice, the yearning I heard for my company, rather than the thought of any view or even food that persuaded me to rise from my warm cocoon. When I had done so I took the scone from him and nibbled as I shivered in the cool air. Instead of retrieving my cloak from the peg on the wall beside my bed, Collin took the quilt and wrapped it around my shoulders.

"It's chilly out. You'll stay warmer with this. Tomorrow when we're at sea and we've a good breeze, I'll dry your cloak."

"Thank you." I glanced up at Timothy's bed.

"He's been asleep about an hour," Collin said. "We stood at the rail and watched everything from the moment they weighed anchor. I'm sorry you missed his excitement."

"Me too." I frowned at Collin. "You should have woken me so I could stay with Timothy. I wonder that you took the risk of standing at the rail. What if you had been recognized?"

"I kept my hat low and head down until we were well away from the wharf," Collin said. "Besides, I was with Timothy and Mrs. Haddox, the woman who claimed me earlier. Those soldiers were searching for a single man, or possibly a couple, but not a man with his son and mother."

The way he said the word son so casually, as with the way he had so naturally assumed the responsibility of Timothy's care, warmed my heart. "You'll be a wonderful father." I raised up on tiptoe, leaned forward, and kissed his cheek, already scruffy now with a day's growth.

"Will? I am already." Collin wrapped his arms around me and placed a hand over my stomach. "And not just to this little one. I would never try to take the place of Timothy's father, but the lad is young and will yet need guidance for some years to come. I intend to do my best by him, as your grandfather did his best by me."

I sighed, partly with contentment from Collin's arms around me and part with disgust at my own lack of parental skill. Today I had pranced about in the rain, allowing and even encouraging Timothy in play that resulted in his only shoes becoming soaked. And then I had told an outright lie—a few of them—in front of him, all but begging him to go along with such. I'd no doubt of the displeasure our mother would have felt about both.

"Did he tell you how I lied earlier?" I asked as Collin released me and we left the room.

"No," Collin said. "He was too taken with all that was going on."

"That's good." I sighed again. "Though I very much doubt he'll forget. My dishonesty may come back to haunt me when I least expect it." We ascended the stairs.

"Nothing is going to haunt us for a good, long while I hope." Collin stepped out onto the deck ahead of me and held out his hand. I took it, and he pulled me close, into his arms. "I told you we'd find a place on this ship for a bit of privacy."

"This isn't it," I said, pressing my lips together to keep a smile, or perhaps a look of alarm, from my face. I nudged Collin sideways to make way for the rather burly sailor who'd come up behind him.

"Are you all right, miss?" he asked.

"Yes. But I thank you for asking. I couldn't sleep, so my husband and I thought to stroll the deck for a few minutes." I stepped back from Collin but linked my arm through his.

"Of course." The man gave a polite nod and returned to the shadows.

Collin and I strode away, only one of us smiling. Even without the man at guard, we wouldn't have been alone. We weren't the only ones out enjoying the fresh air after today's prolonged storm.

"What was it you wanted to show me?" I asked

"Over here." Collin led me to the rail. "Now turn around."

"Alrigh—oh." London, bathed in warm light from the three-quarter moon and the glow of lanterns shining through windows, was stunning. "It's beautiful."

"Aye," Collin agreed. He took the quilt from my shoulders, pulled it around us both, and wrapped his arms around me again. I leaned into him.

"I never thought I'd say such about London," he admitted. "But from here it does have a certain charm."

"I want to commit it to memory so that someday I may

paint it." My eyes sought to take in everything, my mind already mentally calculating which colors would work best for shades of the night.

The creak and sway of the ship was more noticeable on deck and, along with the gentle flapping of sails, lent a serenity to the scene.

"I shall call it *Farewell*," I decided, my fingers longing for brush and canvas. I stared harder, hoping I could somehow remember this when it was long past. "What do you suppose Nova Scotia will look like?"

"Scotland," Collin said assuredly. "The Highlands, to be exact, with lochs and moors, mountains, streams, wildflowers that I will pick for you and bring home to tuck in your hair." He nuzzled the side of my head with his face.

I wrapped my arms over his. "That sounds lovely. And what will our home be like there? Will you build us a grand castle with stones stacked high and battlements on top?"

"Is that what you'd like?" Collin sounded surprised.

"No," I exclaimed. "No more castles. I shall be happy with a plain and simple cottage."

"*I* am happy with you." Collin turned me in his arms to face him. "Do you realize at this time last year I had just finally learned of your whereabouts, had at last received word from your father?"

"If I had only known," I mused. "Had realized what was to come." A year ago I'd had no idea who Collin MacDonald was or what lay in store.

"You would have run far, far away?" Collin guessed, his brows raised and a slightly amused smile on his face.

"*No*." I placed my hand on his chest, then gathered the fabric of his shirt in my fist and pulled him close. "I would have rushed to the Highlands at first opportunity. I would not have wasted another minute without you."

"Is that so?" He bent his head so that our faces were but a whisper apart. "Prove it."

"I believe I have already, but since you seem to need reminding . . ." My lips touched his, and the flame between us ignited once more.

With the quilt gathered round us both, we had found a spot of privacy, enough for a few tender moments alone with our memories and dreams.

Chapter Twelve

Aboard the *Ulysses*, Portsmouth, Virginia, March 1762

"Men here. Women over there. Children at the end of the row."

"Excuse me, sir, are we not allowed to remain with our children?" A woman's panicked voice carried over the deck toward Ian, as he returned from yet another trip to the warehouse on shore, where the cargo was being transferred. He glanced at the line of those to be indentured and saw a woman clinging to a lass who could not have more than seven or eight years.

"I've no say whether you do or not," the officer directing them said. "Whoever buys your indenture will determine that, but I should not count on being sold together." With that he extracted the frightened child from her mother, who buried her face in her hands and wept. Similar scenes took place all across the deck as wives kissed their husbands one last time and children were wrenched from their parents' grasps. Redcoats stood guard over all of them, looking on with unfeeling expressions.

Ian's hands clenched around a rag he'd been using to mop the perspiration from his brow. With a vicious swipe he threw it to the ground then stepped away from the cargo and toward the officer who had just spoken.

"Don't." A hand on his shoulder stopped him.

Ian turned to look into the eyes of the crewman he'd worked with the past two hours.

"It will only bring trouble. Mind your own self and forget them."

Ian shrugged the man's hand from his shoulder and looked back at the pathetic line of those to be sold.

"Nothing you can do to help them," his companion said quietly. "Just plenty of ways to hurt yourself if you interfere." Ian's eyes flickered to the half dozen Redcoats standing on deck and then to the captain and officers also milling about. *I'd be shot before I could free anyone.*

He gave a curt nod as thanks for the warning, for the help keeping his head, then moved back to his work, trying to forget the little girl's frightened eyes and the woman's weeping. *If I was in Scotland . . .* He wouldn't have hesitated. His past was a series of one rash action after another, with little thought to the consequences.

He didn't see much purpose in changing ways now, except that he didn't want to die here. If he was going to be shot or hanged—the eventuality he'd resigned himself to long ago—it would at least be on the soil of his homeland.

And what of these people, taken from home as well? Ian told himself not to care. He was good at that, at not caring about anyone but himself, or he had been until Collin had come into his life again a few years ago. His brother was the opposite, and deep down Ian feared he was, too, that the instinct and concern and desire to protect that their father had instilled in them was still there, and, as of late, fighting to surface.

He'd grown up learning that he must always consider his people first and see to their care and well-being. It was the reason his father sent them to scavenge the fields of dead after each battle, a way to make use of what little they had while seeing to not only their own needs but the needs of all in the clan. Every man must have a coat; every man must have shoes. Every man must eat. Ian MacDonald, his father and name-sake, had seen to it that they did.

Until he couldn't anymore.

And then he had given the only thing he had left to give, to save his two sons. He'd given his life.

Ian swiped at his eyes with the back of his hand, wishing he hadn't been so quick to throw his rag aside, and angry that it wasn't sweat stinging his eyes and blurring his vision. *Don't care,* he told himself yet again. The woman wasn't a MacDonald. She and her child—all of these people—were not his concern. And even if they were, there was nothing he could do for any of them.

But I am a laird, he reminded himself. *It's my responsibility to care for those less fortunate. To lead when others cannot.* No matter that, at present, his own fortunes were not any better than that of the rest of the lot in front of him. He'd no keep to return home to, little land to work, no distilleries or animals or crops. He had nothing and was nothing. They all were, as subjects to the English crown. At least in the Highlands the English presence wasn't as constant. In the Colonies, he could tell already, that was not the case. Redcoats resided here and more were coming.

I will not stay. He could do nothing for those who would. Closing his eyes briefly, Ian turned away from their pitiful cries and closed his heart to even the thought of helping any of them.

Bending over another barrel, he rolled it toward the gangplank, eager to be away from the painful reminders of the past and the pitiful reality of the present.

A half dozen times more Ian returned with the other crew to retrieve cargo, each time unable to keep himself from looking to see if either the woman or her child had been sold. The line of those to be indentured had lessened considerably, though there were still a good number of people left standing in the chilly air, many with little to protect them from the elements.

Surprisingly, many of the women were gone. Those remaining, excepting the woman with the daughter, were all older and infirm. An older, well-dressed woman with the most ridiculous hat he'd ever seen perched upon her gray head, spoke with the mother, and Ian suspected she would soon be gone as well. Telling himself that he was merely curious as to what would be her fate, he stepped away from his work under pretense of getting a drink.

He withdrew the dipper from the barrel and brought it to his mouth, less thirsty for the tepid water than he was to hear what was being discussed between the two women. It became apparent soon enough when the older, well-dressed one, loosened the strings on her pouch and turned to the nearest officer.

"If this is all you've left, I suppose I'll take this one. I was hoping for someone younger, whom I might not be shamed to have working at the counter in my shop, but she'll have to do. I'm behind on orders as it is."

"My daughter is young and bonny." The mother reached to touch her would-be-purchaser's sleeve. "She would suit, and I could work in the back."

The older woman brushed her away as if she were a pesky insect. "Where is this young woman? Why haven't I seen her?"

"Because she is a *child.*" The officer cast a disparaging look at the mother before turning his attention to the older woman. "Ignore her. She's been at this all morning, trying to get someone to purchase not only her indenture but her child's as well."

"She's a good lass. Won't trouble you at all." The mother fell to her knees in front of the woman. "Please, miss."

"I'm no miss, and I've no need for a child in my shop," the older woman said with a note of finality.

"The price is £10. And you must agree to the terms of indenture." A second officer holding a sheaf of papers handed her the top one. "Look these over, sign them, and register your servant with Officer Millet." He nodded his head toward a man seated at a makeshift desk near the gangway, down which the cargo on the other side was being unloaded.

Ian choked on the water he was swallowing as his eyes narrowed in on Millet. Even seated, he appeared tall and lithe. Black hair speckled with gray swept over his crown and was tied with a ridiculously large bow, visible when he bent his head in greeting. Also ridiculous were his sideburns, easily covering half of each cheek. His uniform was trimmed out with braid and gold buttons, and when he lifted a quill, Ian glimpsed hands that were far too white and delicate to have done much of the real work on this ship.

Even had he not known of the arrangement between Millet and Eliza, Ian felt he would have taken an instant dislike to the man. Everything about him bespoke of privilege and power, and the knowledge that he was well in command of both—of anything and everything he wanted.

Including Eliza.

"I can't leave my daughter!" The woman about to be purchased fought against the officers as they dragged her toward the table.

Farther down the line her little girl had begun crying and was being restrained as well.

"Please," her mother begged. "She's a good lass."

"Cease this nonsense." The older woman waved her hand dismissively. "I will not take the girl. She'd only be underfoot. You agreed to these terms when you sailed."

"They agreed to nothing." Ian flung the dipper aside, and it clattered loudly on the deck as he strode toward them. "None of these people here chose to be indentured." He swept his hand along the line of those still under guard and awaiting purchase. "None committed crimes justifying being forced from their homes and sentenced to fourteen years of servitude. Their only crime was poverty." From the corner of his eye, Ian saw Officer Millet rise.

"Who are you to interfere—"

"I have nothing to do with what transpired before," the older woman said, cutting off Millet with her words, while the look she directed at Ian would have withered a man less stout

94

of heart. "I came today to purchase a servant. If it is to be so much trouble, I shall go elsewhere."

"No trouble at all." Millet reached for the £10 note in her hand. "Back to your station," he ordered Ian. "Before we decide to sell you too." He inclined his head toward the nearest pair of Redcoats, who moved toward Ian.

The mother began wailing in earnest. "She is all I've left. My husband is dead. My son as well. Can you not show mercy?"

"Silence." One of the officers shook her, and she would have crumpled, save for the other still holding her arm.

Ian took another step forward, only to feel himself pulled back. He turned sharply, fist ready to strike.

"Have you lost your mind?" The crewman who'd warned him earlier held the back of Ian's coat in a fierce grip. "Shut your mouth and get back to work."

Ian hesitated, the good sense to look out for himself warring with the desire to stand up for the woman and her daughter, even though it would come to naught.

"Leave her be," another voice cried.

Eliza? Ian's head snapped around.

"Elizabe—Miss Campbell?" Millet sounded as surprised as Ian.

"There is no need to force this woman to be separated from her child. *I* will come with you and work in your shop." Eliza placed a cup of tea, likely meant for Officer Millet, into the older woman's hands.

"I have no child to bother you with," Eliza continued. "I will be respectful and work hard."

"You cannot go. You are spoken for." Millet leaned forward, palms pressed to the crate substituting as a desk. "*Miss Campbell.*" He spoke to her through clenched teeth with a pointed look while the mother raised her head toward Eliza as if she was some sort of savior.

Ian understood the look. *Yes, go,* he echoed in his

thoughts. A swell of hope rose in him as he allowed himself to be pulled backward.

"No one has purchased my indenture," Elizabeth said loudly enough for both Redcoats and the other ship's officers nearby to hear. "I have been happy to assist with cooking responsibilities throughout our journey overland and while aboard this ship, but now that we have landed, I am bound by indenture, and I *do* agree to the terms." Her eyes flickered briefly to Ian. "I am prepared to work off my debt to the crown. Fourteen years in your service, ma'am."

In any other circumstances her pretty speech expressing loyalty or obligation to England and her king would have incited anger, but Ian felt like cheering instead. Eliza was a good actress. *Full of surprises.* She would be all right. She could take care of herself. *If she can just get away from Millet.*

"Where were you a minute ago?" the older woman huffed at Eliza. She took the same looking-down-her-nose stance with Millet. "Is it your practice to hide the better servants until last?"

"Not at all." He looked as if he wished to say more but remained silent after a glance at the other officers standing nearby.

Ian's companion released him suddenly. "Hold this, keep your head down, follow me, and you might get off this ship alive." He shoved a small barrel at his chest. Ian grasped it, wrapping his arms around it before it could drop. He fell in line with those carrying cargo. His view of Eliza was lost, but he strained to hear the conclusion of the conversation.

"I should hope you are not engaging in such illegalities," the older woman continued dressing down Millet. "Just as I should hope there shall be no trouble with substituting this servant for that other." She cast a glance over her shoulder at the beleaguered mother.

"No—trouble," Millet said.

Relief swept through Ian. In spite of the heavy barrel, his

step felt almost light as he kept pace with the man in front of him.

"*Unless,*" Millet's voice rose above the other noises around them. "Miss Campbell does not wish to go."

Ian stopped, moving aside before the man behind bumped into him. Ian mumbled an apology, then crossed behind coils of rope to join those unloading cargo down the other ramp. What did his life matter compared to Eliza's? She'd just made a brave bid for safety, if not complete freedom. He'd not let Millet take that and what else he would from her.

"I have already said that I wish to go," Eliza stated calmly as Ian and his barrel arrived at the side of Millet's crate desk.

"Think this through carefully, Miss Campbell," Millet's voice dropped to a terse whisper. "I remind you of our previous conversation. Giving yourself over to servitude may lead to great misfortune."

"Or it may not." Eliza reached behind her to untie her apron strings. She jerked the apron over her head and tossed it on the table, so close that one of the strings brushed Ian's hand, resting casually on the edge of the crate.

"I am at your service, ma'am." Eliza turned to her new mistress and curtsied.

"Move aside, so we may leave this vessel," the older woman ordered. Ian realized she was speaking to him. Squaring his shoulders, he slid his fingers from the desk, hefted the barrel and marched down the plank, resisting the urge to look over his shoulder at Eliza.

The sound of her steps behind him were enough. She was away. She would be safe. His work here was done.

Chapter Thirteen

Portsmouth, Virginia, March 1762

Ian staggered down the gangplank beneath the weight of a barrel that he once could have lifted with ease. A few steps onto the dock and he stopped, placed the barrel on its side, and began rolling it as he had most of the others today. Let them think him weak. He didn't care. All that mattered now was that he preserved enough strength to get away.

"Barrels near the back. Put her over there," barked a man standing at the entrance to one of the warehouses lining the wharf. He pointed a grubby finger toward the far side of the building.

Ian gave a curt nod and rolled the barrel through the open double doors, following the steady line of seaman moving, antlike, back and forth from ship to shore. Three quarters of the cargo from the *Ulysses* had been unloaded, and Ian knew the time for him to break free from the others was at hand. Trouble was, there was nowhere to do it. British customs officers were stationed all along the docks, checking both incoming and outgoing vessels to see that they carried the exact goods they had declared.

Captains and upper crewmen stood on deck, overseeing the unloading, and warehousemen awaited to direct their progress the minute they stepped on shore. Sneaking off was virtually impossible. There was simply no point in the line where he might slip away unnoticed. But if he didn't break away soon, he worried he might slip—into unconsciousness.

The heavy lifting had reopened his wound yet again, and

he could feel the blood seeping through both shirts. It wouldn't be long before a stain appeared on the stolen jacket, or before he succumbed to the dizziness washing over him in near constant waves.

"Almost time for your pay, men. Keep it moving."

A corner of Ian's mouth lifted. He'd already been paid. About £4 if he was correct, when he'd relieved Officer Millet of some of the coins stacked neatly on his makeshift desk.

Eliza's carelessly tossed apron had provided the perfect cover for Ian's practiced fingers to snatch the coins and be on his way before anyone noticed. He figured he'd earned them today, the way they'd worked him for hours on end. And now there was no reason to stay on longer.

It was time to revert back to his original idea and what was by far the safer plan—hiding.

Ian stopped his barrel near the back of the warehouse, then took a minute to right it and fiddle with the bands, making a pretense of adjusting one that had slipped near the bottom. *Poor workmanship.*

Once, a *long* time ago, he and Collin had crafted barrels like this for MacDonald whisky. Ian's fingers recalled those days now as they worked the band—that would never have come loose if it had been formed and attached correctly—back into place.

With one eye half on the men coming and going and the other on the barrel, he scooted slowly around until he was behind it and only a few paces from the back wall of the building. Still fiddling with the metal, he continued working and watching until at last one barrel was stacked onto another in front of him, partially blocking him from sight of the approaching men.

When the one who'd stacked it turned to go, and in the few seconds before the next reached his position and could spot Ian, he half-leapt, half-crawled from behind his barrel to a much larger one beside. From there he maneuvered again as he could, until he was safely ensconced behind an overly large crate which he and three other crew members had delivered earlier in the day.

He'd been fortunate throughout the day that no one questioned his identity overmuch. Most from the ship believed he was a shoreman, and those from the shore thought he was one of the ship's crew. A little more luck, and no one would notice he'd gone missing.

Settled as best he could on the dusty warehouse floor, Ian took the battered tricorn from his head and set it on the ground, wondering absently what the chances were that he'd get lice from its previous owner. By the smell of the man's garments, he hadn't believed in regular washing of any kind.

Ian thought again of Eliza—Elizabeth, as he must think of her now, if he thought of her at all. Which he shouldn't.

Let her be safe. Ian brought a fisted hand to his forehead, pressing heavily, as if that might somehow increase the earnestness of his prayer. That he considered praying at all was peculiar. God likely had neither use for nor interest in sinners like him. Even if he did—

What does she matter to me? Once, the plight of a woman wouldn't have concerned him. He'd proven that well enough when he'd left the Munros and not only broken Aileen's heart, but sentenced her to a lifetime—short though that proved to be—of cruelty at her father's hand because she had dared to love Ian.

His heart ached from the memory, and familiar self-loathing infused his being. Strange how he'd thought so little on his past during his days in that dark hold. Instead he had focused on the one light present whenever Elizabeth visited. Thoughts of her had consumed him, and not in the usual, aroused and lustful way a man felt when a woman interested him. Before, with the Munros, he had always seen them treated as something to command, to use, and to disregard when a man had no more need of them.

But then last year he'd gone with Collin to fetch his bride home, to use her for the sole purpose of monetary gain. Collin had convinced him that was the matter of it, but once Ian had seen them together, he had known differently.

His brother loved this Englishwoman. Truly loved her in a way that made all else of importance in Collin's life fall away, or possibly come together, depending upon how one looked at it.

It wasn't that Katherine was an incredible beauty, though her clan had fawned over her with absurd compliments and Collin had stared at her as if it was so. Perhaps Campbells were all long in the face like the old Campbell laird. That would explain their thinking so highly of Katherine's looks.

Collin's fascination had only seemed to grow when he discovered her quick wit, foolish bravery, and strange talent with charcoal and brush. Ian had discreetly watched them during those first few days of marriage. He'd seen what she was doing to Collin, and it worried him more than any English patrol did. He'd vowed never to be vulnerable, as he sensed Collin becoming in her presence.

He'd needed to protect his brother, in more ways than one. There was a plan among some of the MacDonalds, led by Niall, to murder Katherine and steal her dowry. They didn't hold with having Campbells in their midst, and particularly with their laird marrying one. Ian hadn't felt much different, except he'd known what it would do to Collin if Katherine was killed. Instead, Ian had hoped to scare her away. If she left, Collin might regain his head. Ian had known of at least one MacDonald woman who would willingly help with mending his heart.

So it was he'd found himself secretly fighting to be rid of Collin's wife, yet spare her from death.

Ian had known he couldn't cause his brother the same suffering he himself had known upon learning of Aileen's death. And though Ian had only the barest toleration for the Campbells, he did love Collin.

So instead of killing Katherine, he had set out to scare her witless and send her fleeing back to her English home. It had not gone as he planned.

Ian grimaced, as much from the memory of her terrified face as she fell backward into the river as from the stinging now as he peeled back the bloody fabric, exposing the wound on his side. The fool Redcoat hadn't shot him straight, but at an angle. Ian gently probed the reopened skin. The bullet had torn through his back, shredded muscle, and exited his side with an angry explosion. His back had mostly healed, but his side still festered, the layers of muscle, tissue, and skin never completely healing.

Ian dug in the pocket of the dead man's coat and withdrew the half-used bottle of ale. He lifted it to his mouth and tipped the bottle back, savoring the stale liquid and wishing fervently for some MacDonald whisky.

When he'd taken a good long drink, Ian pointed the bottle the other direction and poured the remainder over the bloody hole in his side. His lips pressed together, and moisture squeezed from his eyes, but he didn't utter a sound. The noises of the warehouse continued beyond him—scuffling boots, swearing sailors, shifting cargo. He kept his eyes closed and thought of Eliza.

Nightfall couldn't come fast enough. Ian was cold, tired, cramped. He found himself wishing for the privacy of the hold and the rocking ship that had lulled him to a relatively peaceful sleep the past week. *Soon enough.* As early as a few days from now he might be on a ship bound for Scotland, and this time maybe he'd have a hammock to sleep in.

When at last the warehouse doors had been closed and pad-locked, and the sounds of the day ceased, Ian rose stiffly from his hiding place and stood to survey his surroundings. Moonlight lit the warehouse nicely through the high windows. This was going to be easier than he'd thought.

Pulling the knife from his boot, Ian began his inspection of the crates and barrels surrounding him. Loosen the band, a stab or two between seams, a careful wedge, and he could judge liquid or dry goods if needed. Many had their contents marked on the outside, and he'd made a point earlier in the day, as they'd brought the stores into the warehouses, to do his best to learn what was in those he and others carried. It helped that the warehouse was arranged by type of goods, each with its own section, with everything from furniture to foodstuffs. He knew a few contained salt pork—most likely left over from the voyage—and others beans and raisins. There were also crates of tea, but he'd no use for that.

Those filled with bolts of cloth were of no interest to him, but the one that held firearms was. Having a pistol of his own would make for an excellent beginning in this new world.

The moon rose steadily over the next several hours as he worked, his stash of contraband slowly growing. His years among the Munros were serving him well now. No one taught thievery better than they did; no student of theirs had ever been more motivated, with his life constantly at stake if he failed.

The trick, then and now, was to not become greedy. He didn't need twelve firearms, just one, and the plainer the better. Ian wistfully admired a double-barreled pistol with brass fittings, knowing it would be foolish to take such a treasure. Anyone seeing him with it would know it was stolen, and whatever British officer it was intended for might just decide to use it on Ian when he was caught.

Still, he'd never held such a fine weapon and felt more than a little tempted. But at last, with a sigh, he set it aside, dug through the crate and found one less conspicuous.

With the tools he'd found at the front of the warehouse, he resealed the crates as thoroughly as if they had never been opened. If he did his job well, tomorrow morning, no one would be any the wiser to his presence here tonight.

Pity the man who gets called out for cheating his customer, Ian thought, with a smirk in the dark as he imagined the recipient taking issue with one James Barbor of London, who had apparently made the guns, for cheating the British army of one light dragoon pistol.

With his pockets spilling over and his acquisitions still piling up, Ian decided to break into the crate of cloth after all. He retrieved a bolt of wool and cut a length away for tying pouches for his other wares—mostly foodstuffs. He was tempted to take fabric from the bolt beneath as well, a silk that looked to be a deep blue and would make a particularly fine gown for Eliza. But of course he couldn't give it to her. She was gone. He'd never see her again. Even if he had known where she was, it wasn't as if he'd be stopping by to bring her gifts or court her. They'd never dance together in his father's hall. She'd never touch him again.

He needed to forget her. But for a few minutes Ian stopped to rest and indulge himself. With his eyes closed and the silk between his fingers, he could almost imagine them dancing, Eliza's raised hand in his, with his arm at her waist as they turned a circle.

Nonsense.

Ian opened his eyes to reality, shoved the bolt roughly back inside the crate and secured the lid, blocking it from his sight. He'd never thought of dancing before, and he'd no business thinking of it now. That sort of life might be for Collin, but it wasn't for him. When he returned to Scotland it would be to a clan both downtrodden and impoverished. It would take all he had, all everyone had, just to scrape a meager existence from the land. There would be no time or means for dancing. *No pipers.* Or anything else that had brought happiness to his people.

If Collin had found a bit of it with his Campbell bride, then God bless them both. But Ian was not about to fall prey to the same temptation, to a Campbell now foresworn to serve in the Colonies for fourteen years. No woman was worth waiting that long for. Not that she would have had him if he was inclined to such madness.

Among his spoils, Ian had acquired a bottle of French wine and opened it now, yanking the cork out almost savagely and tipping the bottle back for a long, soothing drink. It wasn't nearly enough alcohol to stanch this new longing within him, and he knew better than to attempt to get drunk—there was yet much work to be done tonight. But it eased his physical thirst, at least, so he could continue on, foraging what he could before the night was through.

Next to the crate containing fabric, Ian found one containing a stack of hats and helped himself to a new tricorn. As it was far too fine to match the rest of his clothing, he set it aside, using it as a holder for the smallest fabric and food bundles.

It was probably around two in the morning when Ian realized he needed to stop. It was difficult, with a literal treasure trove at his fingertips, but he needed to figure a way out of here, or his night's work would all be for naught.

The windows were too high to climb through, particularly with his injury. While he might stack boxes tall enough to reach the windows on this side, it would be a long drop—with risk of being seen once he was outside. *If the glass even opens.* Ian pulled his eyes from the high panes, pulled the stopper from the bottle, and took another drink. Whisky would have been preferable, but the wine was doing nicely.

Dropping to his knees, Ian began crawling toward the back corner of the warehouse where he had begun the evening, using first his fist, then the butt of his knife to tap on the floor as he went. The sound became distinctly less hollow as he moved nearer the back wall, confirming his suspicions that the building was set on a slope. Near the back it likely sat flush with the ground, while the front met the wharf, elevated with room below for the tide to flow in and out.

The only question now was whether the tide was high or low or somewhere between. *Whether I swim or walk out of here.* Ian looked ruefully at the shiny new pistol. It would be a shame to get that wet.

Choosing a spot about a third of the way back, Ian began working his knife and then a pry bar carefully back and forth, this time into the seams of the floor. He guessed he'd need the width of two boards to squeeze through. This work took him longer than opening crates had. The floor was well built, intended to stand up to years of shipments stored upon it. By the time Ian had pried the second board from the floor, perspiration streamed down his face, and his side burned like it was on fire.

With care and patience he was quickly losing, he straightened the last of the nails, then tested the boards to see that they would fit into place as they had before.

Ian peered down into the hole, wishing he had a light. The high moon wasn't as helpful as it had been earlier. But maybe that was for the better. Hopefully no one would see him when he finally made an appearance on the street.

He retrieved his cache of goods, bundled all except the gun within the deceased sailor's coat, and set it on the side of the opening in the floor.

"Fare thee well," he mumbled to the room that had blessed him so abundantly this night. Perhaps, if he could not find a ship to Scotland right away, he would return here again.

Then again, that was a sure way to get oneself caught and hanged. He'd seen it before many times. *Strike once, prosper well. Strike twice, hear the death knell.* If he did end up staying awhile, there were other ways to provide for himself. Ian put a hand into his pocket, wrapped his fist around metal, and heard the comforting jingle of Millet's coins.

With both feet now in the hole, he eased himself down, cursing savagely when his wounded side scraped against the floor.

But he'd judged well, and it was but a short drop to the

ground—not a drop at all, really, as the top of his head was still barely above the warehouse floor. His feet landed in mud, not water, though a second later a wave lapped his ankles.

Ian retrieved the bundle and pistol and sloshed through the mud and water until he'd reached the back of the warehouse, where the floor met dry ground. He placed his belongings there, then returned to reattach the floorboards. When those were in place as best they could be, Ian paused to allow his eyes to adjust to the darker surroundings and to consider what he must do next.

It appeared—though he couldn't be certain—that the area beneath the building stretched a considerable distance, following the length of the wharf. Ian wished he'd paid better attention to the details of the dock during the day, but his view had been largely hidden by the barrels he'd been hauling. On the trips back to the ship, his attention had ever been focused on the possibility of seeing Eliza. And after she had gone, he had searched out the widow and her daughter, feeling strangely relieved when both were still on the ship, not yet separated for good.

I'll be as soft as Collin if I'm not careful.

A wave lapped at his feet again, and Ian shivered. It was far cooler beneath the building than it had been inside. This was nowhere to shelter the remainder of the night. He would leave, walk the length of the buildings attached to the wharf, and find a way out at the end. That seemed a better solution than attempting to exit here, where he might be recognized.

And then . . . Ian fingered the coins in his pocket. Enough for a night's lodging and a decent meal, at least, with funds left over to begin making more the following night, provided there were gambling establishments to be had in Portsmouth.

But if he was to find lodging, he would have to look—or at least smell—better than he did now. Ian glanced down at the water with distaste. He'd never much cared for cold baths. But he'd never smelled quite so bad either. He decided it was a necessary evil. A quick salt-water bath would either kill him or make his stench bearable enough that he could rent a room somewhere.

Before he could talk himself out of such insanity, Ian stripped down to his closest layer and walked deeper into the water. The freezing temperature quickly doused the sleepy effects of the wine, jolting every nerve in his body to full wakefulness. His wounded side screamed in agony as the salt water encased it but soon became mercifully numb, along with the rest of him.

Ian scrubbed at his hair, hoping to remove any wee beasties that might have taken residence there. He'd no soap but grabbed a handful of sandy soil from beneath his feet and scrubbed it over every surface as hard and fast as he could.

Teeth chattering, Ian rinsed once more, then staggered out of the water, wondering if that wasn't the most foolish idea he'd ever had.

Not until three hours later when he closed and locked the door of his room at The Young Devil tavern and his head hit the pillow on the bed that was his for the next two nights, did he decide the timely dip in the Atlantic had been worth it.

Chapter Fourteen

Aboard the Cleopatra, the Atlantic Ocean, March 1762

With the wind blowing wisps of hair across my face, I watched Timothy trail along behind a boy I guessed to be a few years older. Collin stood at the rail—also battling the wind now that his hair had grown longer—one eye focused on my rambunctious brother, the other on me. I forced a smile as he glanced my way. If I didn't pretend to be well he would worry, and I saw no sense in both of us being concerned.

He seemed to have troubles enough the past couple of days, brooding silently over something that I guessed had little to do with me or my condition. I wanted to talk with him, to see if I might share in his burden; but a time when I wasn't ill or Timothy demanding of either one or both of us had not presented itself.

It was all I could do this past week to try not to add to Collin's burden—whatever it was. With great effort I attempted to conceal how ill I felt and weak I'd become. I stayed up on deck most days for the simple fact that the strength it would require to cross the deck and descend the stairs again was more than I found myself capable of alone.

Collin escorted me upstairs each morning, believing me to prefer the chilliness and sunshine above deck to our accommodations below, and so I might help him keep watch over Timothy. Every evening near sunset, Collin offered his arm and walked me to our berths, where it was all I could do to keep my eyes open long enough to take some broth. I hated the shell of my former self that I had become, yet felt powerless to be anything otherwise.

The two boys disappeared from my line of sight, but instead of following Timothy as he usually did, Collin came my direction instead.

Uh oh. I snatched the uneaten bowl of oatmeal from the bench beside me and forced a rather hurried bite down my throat, using every means within to resist gagging.

Collin's folded arms and frown as he stood over me a second later told me he wasn't fooled in the least.

"If you need me to feed you, just ask. I rather enjoyed that game when last we played it at your grandfather's castle."

"I didn't." I returned his scowl, the mention of that dark time when I believed Collin lost to me a memory I didn't care to revisit. "I am doing the best I can. If your stomach was constantly revolting you'd be cautious too."

"You're probably right." The lines of Collin's face softened, and he kissed the top of my head. "It's just that I fear you are slipping away from me. I think two of you would fit in your dress right now. This can't be good, Katie."

"In my present condition two of us *are* inside this dress." I held a hand to my head, shading my eyes from the sun as I smiled up at him. "Feeling this way is definitely not good, but there is little I can do about it. Mistress Parker says some women do become very ill when expecting. She said the baby will take what he needs. He will be well." I grasped Collin's hand and squeezed, even that simple action draining.

Collin returned the gesture, with considerably more strength. "I suppose I am to trust Mistress Parker." He did not sound as if he wished to.

I nodded. "She has attended over seventy births. We are blessed to sail on the same ship." Her bed was not far from mine, and she had sought me out the third day of our voyage, instinct alerting her to my plight. Though she had not been able to relieve my symptoms, I found her presence and knowledge comforting.

Collin withdrew a piece of salted meat from his pocket. "Might you chew on this, at least, if the oatmeal is not to your liking."

I took it from him. "My liking and my stomach's—or perhaps the child's—are not in accord at this time. Please don't take it personally."

"I'll try not to." It wasn't much of a promise, and his mood still seemed dark, but I could not help but feel my spirits buoyed as Collin sat beside me on the crate I'd claimed as my favorite spot on deck. It was midship, out of the way of much of the crew, and I could see Timothy most places quite well from here. *Timothy.*

"Can you see Timothy?" I grabbed Collin's sleeve. "Do you know the other boy he's with?" Terrible images flashed through my mind—everything from my little brother being subject to a spew of unsavory language to being ridiculed or even hurt by this older boy.

Collin moved so he was facing me. "Aye. I ken who he is." He appeared unconcerned as he drew one knee up to his chest and settled against the large coil of rope behind him. "The lad is the cabin boy. He's been given permission—by the captain himself—to allow Timothy to join him in his duties today."

"The captain—how is it *he* knows of Timothy?" The *Cleopatra,* while not one of the larger vessels to sail to the Colonies, still had more than one hundred passengers on board. Who were we that Captain Shenk should know us?

"*Timothy* made himself known to the captain," Collin said. "Wee beastie, that brother of yours."

"Oh, dear." I leaned forward, anxious to hear what had happened. Was this the cause of Collin's dark mood the past two days?

"The lad snuck away one morning when I was helping you wash after—" Collin broke off, politely sparing me a recount.

"After I'd been sick for the dozenth time in an hour."

That had been four days ago, the worst of our voyage thus far and the day I'd met Susan Parker. "Go on."

"Timothy made his way to the captain's quarters, told him he was an orphan, and offered to work for his passage."

I gasped. "He didn't!"

"Oh, he did." Collin nodded in affirmation. "He had Captain Shenk going, from what I hear. Thought he had himself a stowaway and was taking the crew to task for it."

I clapped a hand to my forehead, thinking very much that I'd like to apply that hand elsewhere on Timothy when I caught up with him again. "Why, he might have been punished! Telling the captain he's an orphan—"

"That much *is* true," Collin said. "In fact, everything the lad told the captain was true. When the whole mess was cleared up later the captain and I shared a drink and had a good laugh about it."

"So we are *well known* to him now." I pushed strands of flying hair back from my face.

"As well known as one can be using a false name," Collin whispered. "And it has worked in our favor—for today at least. By tomorrow Timothy may decide that the life of a cabin boy is not for him, and I'll be back to chasing him about."

"I'm sorry." I looked down at the bowl of oatmeal in my lap, feeling guilty for wasting it, guilty that Collin had to spend his days supervising my brother, guilty that we were such a burden.

"Don't be." Collin moved his leg to the side and patted the spot in front of him. "Come here."

"I can't eat—"

"I only want to be close to you for a while."

He wasn't the only one. I set the bowl on the deck, then scooted closer to Collin, moving awkwardly until my back was to his chest and his arms were around me.

"You're warm." I snuggled closer.

"And you're hairy," he complained, brushing my long strands from his face.

I laughed. "It's this wind."

"A favorable wind," Collin pointed out. "Captain Shenk says it's moving us along well. We'll make good time if this continues."

Collin did not sound pleased about this; rather, his gloom had returned.

My mind flashed to my painting of this voyage, and I wondered if Collin's worry was the same as mine. I did not know how long these favorable conditions would continue, only that at some point during our crossing the weather would turn treacherous. I tried not to think of that. Finlay, one of my Campbell relations and also a seer, had said the journey would be dangerous but survivable. I put my trust in that.

"When you and the captain were sharing drinks and having a good laugh did you talk about anything else?" I asked, both fishing for clues as to what Collin was brooding about and hoping to draw him from his melancholy.

The source of his apprehension hovered at the edge of my vision, much as my dream had the other night, my mind being tuned to Collin's in an otherworldly way. If he wouldn't tell me, it was probable that I would eventually discover it myself, most likely through a dream, as I had no materials— or ability at present—to paint. Whatever it was, I felt it must be serious to trouble him so many days.

Instead of responding to my question, Collin tightened his arms around me as he nuzzled his face in my hair.

"So you did speak of other things, but you'll not share them with me?" I guessed when at least a minute had passed in which he had not uttered a single word. My voice sounded bitter, and I found that I was—not because Collin had enjoyed a few minutes of socialization, but because the thought of anything as simple as paying a visit to the captain was, at present, overwhelming for me. And now it appeared that Collin believed even hearing of that visit might be too much for me.

The feeling that we were a team, the two of us joined in

grand purpose, was slipping away. The past weeks my entire focus had become centered around providing nourishment for the child within me and keeping Timothy safe. Excepting Collin, little else seemed to matter, and managing those two required my every effort.

Being a mother was much harder than I had imagined, and I had not even met our child yet. At times being a wife was also difficult, particularly when the dark, brooding Collin took up residence. I did not think I could bear it if he chose to lock me out, to keep me from his thoughts, for the duration of our journey.

"The captain and I did speak of other things," Collin said at last. "He has made this voyage many times before. He is familiar with Nova Scotia."

"Oh." I turned my head to better see if Collin's expression was as grave as he had sounded. "What did you learn?"

"Not what I had hoped," Collin said.

"Is it not the land of moors and mountains, lakes and rivers that you had imagined?" The thought that our new home might not be as beautiful as Collin's beloved Highlands saddened me, but that didn't mean we couldn't find happiness there.

"Aye, it is," Collin affirmed. "Shenk says the land is stunning in both beauty and resources. The main piece is a peninsula, but there are islands as well."

"Just like Scotland." I smiled, recalling our journey from the Highlands to England. We had taken a rather circumspect route, given that Collin was a fugitive, and on our way had glimpsed some of Scotland's many islands firsthand.

"Aye. Similar in that," Collin agreed. "Shenk gave a description of numerous hills and low mountain ranges, a great many rivers and grand lakes leading to lush valleys and dense forests. But there are also windswept barrens and views of the Atlantic that steal a man's breath away. He said wild blueberries grow thick in the bushes hugging the cliffs."

I had a sudden vision of Collin and me, a small child

between us, walking along a bluff, carrying buckets laden with berries.

I smiled encouragingly. "That all sounds lovely."

"Indeed it does—to *many.*" Collin met my questioning gaze, his own sober, the shadows of worry returned. "We are sailing right into a war, Katie."

War? A familiar word, but it had never registered as a reality to me.

Not so for Collin. He had lived it during the Jacobite uprising, and it had cost him dearly—everything, from his land to his father. He knew the horrors of battle and its aftermath first hand.

"What do you mean?" My words were so quiet it was as if I merely breathed the question.

"The native peoples who have been there longest have sided with the French in fighting against the Colonists and British forces for the land and control of the rivers."

This made little sense to me. "What about the Scottish people? Are we not going to *Nova Scotia?*"

"We are." Collin's chin moved against the side of my face as he nodded. "Named so by King James I in 1621, when he granted the land to Scottish colonizer Sir William Alexander. But how long could that last—an English king granting land to a Scot?" Collin's tone sounded bitter. "You might imagine how ignorant I felt learning all of this from Captain Shenk. It would seem my education was not as well serving and complete as I'd believed."

"Our experience is in the Old World," I reminded Collin. The first I had heard of Nova Scotia was when reading it on the stone my grandfather had buried in the Campbell kirkyard. "Is it a British Colony, then?"

"The English say it is, but the French have other ideas."

"Who is winning?" *What does this all mean for us?* We were fleeing poverty, corruption, injustice, and cruelty caused by both the Crown and men within my own clan. It had never occurred to me we might be headed toward worse. I'd known we faced the difficulty of starting over with scarcely anything, but—until this sickness had consumed me—I'd relished the challenge. This would not be my home, England, or Collin's or my grandfather's home, the Scottish Highlands, but *our* home that we built together. Nova Scotia held the promise and appeal of more than a new Scotland to me. It was the place where we would find peace and truly begin our family. It was to be *our* place.

"Who do you think is winning?" Collin took my shoulders and turned me toward him once more, his expression dark.

"We—they are?" To count myself with the English was nothing less than treason to our marriage. Scotland might be under English law, but that did not mean the Crown had our loyalty. That English blood ran through my veins no longer seemed to matter. From the moment I had crossed the border last year, claiming my own Scottish heritage and declaring myself one with my husband, everything had changed.

The Scots were certainly not perfect, with their blazing tempers and penchant for taking care of things by violence, but after witnessing the oppression caused by the English, I could not blame my Campbell relations or my husband's MacDonald clan for their methods.

Collin nodded slowly. "Britain appears poised to conquer. Shenk told me that since 1755 the English have been rounding up the French Acadians in Nova Scotia—near eleven thousand men, women, and children thus far—forcing them from their homes, and shipping them off to various colonies or even back to France."

"1755—scarcely ten years after the rebellion in Scotland." Our eyes met.

"Rather than risk a people who might rise up against them, the English have taken to evicting those they consider different. They mistrust anyone unlike themselves."

"Have these people at least been compensated or—"

Collin laughed bitterly. He brushed aside a strand of my

hair that had blown in his face. "They have been *forced* from their homes, Katie—as much or more than we have been. Taken at gunpoint by soldiers who slaughtered their livestock and burnt their fields and homes."

"Even if the poor souls were to make their way back, they would have nothing to return to." I could imagine the scene all too well. It had been playing out all over the Highlands.

"Aye. That is the way of it. There—" Collin inclined his head behind him, the way we had come. "And there." He nodded in the direction we sailed.

It was difficult to imagine what could be worse than we had left. Collin was a wanted man. I had nearly died at my clan leader's hand, and many others had. We hadn't enough food to survive the winter. The reasons to fear for one's life and well-being were numerous and constant. I did not relish similar circumstances. But we had survived before and would again.

"We will be all right," I said. "If the war has been raging so long, perhaps it will be finished by the time we arrive. Or perhaps—"

"False hope I do not want either of us to have," Collin said. "We must be prepared, and aware of the dangers." He paused, as if considering carefully his next words.

"There is something else you should know as well. The natives have a long tradition of scalping their victims."

"Scalp—"

"Aye." Collin's expression turned from serious to grim as he brought a hand to his head. "It is what you think it is—to cut off the top skin of a person's head, with the hair attached."

I brought a hand to my mouth, fearing I might be sick. "That's—horrible." I'd heard such tales before, but I had never paid them much attention.

"The French pay the natives for the scalps of the English," Collin explained. "And now the English have taken up the practice as well. Shenk shared several stories with me. They were proof enough that the Dragoons stationed in the new world will be no less, and likely more, brutal than those we left in the old. I fear that the Highlands will seem most civilized to us compared to Nova Scotia. In Shenk's own words, 'The people have a savageness unknown to Europeans.' We are headed to a wild and dangerous place."

I closed my eyes and leaned against Collin, grateful my stomach was mostly empty as images of men being scalped swirled through my mind. Tension flooded my body, followed by tangible fear. How was I to keep Collin safe in such a place? And precocious Timothy? A newborn babe? For the first time I wondered how far into the future my grandfather's visions had extended. Had he known the hardships we were to face in the New World? Or had he only seen that we must go?

"Perhaps Virginia would have been the better choice," I mumbled.

"Don't say that," Collin said. "Chances are I would not be here with you now, had we sailed on that ship. You can't have forgotten already."

I hadn't. The sound of the soldiers' boots as they'd clomped down the stairs in search of Collin would likely remain with me the rest of my life. As would the memory of them dragging him away from me in Scotland. I suppressed a shudder and snuggled deeper into Collin's embrace. *He is here. We are well . . . but the danger is far from over.*

"I suppose this means there are likely to be a great deal of soldiers in Nova Scotia."

"Aye," Collin grumbled. "Halifax is primarily a military town and naval base. It is sure to be flooded with them."

"Rest assured I shall speak to my grandfather about this some-day," I said, doing a bit of my own grumbling. "When my spirit has departed this earth and joined his I shall ask him what he meant by having us leave one place of danger only to meet with worse trouble."

"Not anytime soon you won't be speaking with him." Collin threw one of his legs over mine, as if to hold me here with him. "And it may be that he didn't know what awaited us—only that we could not survive, did we stay."

"Or perhaps there is no place free of war in this world," I suggested, feeling sad resignation to the fate awaiting us.

"Either way," Collin said. "We've no choice but to face it now."

"Together." I placed my hand over his. "I am grateful you told me. I think I can endure anything with you, but when you lock me out—when you brood alone and do not allow me in to comfort you—life, grand as it may be, is awful."

"Will our life be grand?" Collin's question was sincere. He'd shared with me, and now he wished me to share with him, anything and all that I knew.

"I'm not certain," I said honestly. "I have given our future little thought, so focused were we on leaving, and then with Timothy's care—"

"You are to let me see to him from now on." Collin swung his leg from mine and sat up fully, nudging me away from him. "I know he is your brother and you love him and feel responsibility, but let me see to his needs these next weeks. I wish only two things from you during that time, both terribly important." He stood and retrieved my bowl of cold oatmeal from the deck.

"I need you to take any nourishment you possibly can. I beg you to force yourself to it." He glanced at the untouched piece of dried meat on my lap. "I need you strong when we arrive. If we have to journey far, it will most likely be on foot. When we wed you surprised me with your willingness and ability to ride or walk, to follow me anywhere, across loch and moor, and over mountain. I need you to be healthy enough to do the same again," Collin pled.

"Where do you think we will be going?" I'd assumed— wrongly, now that I realized Halifax was a naval base for the British—that we would settle somewhere close to the city. Living amongst Redcoats would not suffice, but neither did I relish the idea of being out in the wilderness and perhaps at the mercy of scalp-hungry natives.

"That is the second thing I need from you." Collin sat beside me once more. He placed the bowl in my hands, then covered those with his own. "Your grandfather is gone, Katie. His visions have taken us as far as we can go. You are the Campbell leader now, the one who has the gift and right to see what lies in store for us. I need you to use your gift. One misstep in this new world could cost our lives. We're going to need all the guidance we can get."

The burdensome cloak of responsibility for our future settled over my shoulders once more. Ironically, Collin's gloom seemed to have dissipated somewhat, while I felt mine just beginning. Yet again I wondered why we could not have sailed to Virginia, where there was not a war, to build the new life we sought. Instead, our families had sailed there and awaited our direction. Unless . . .

I leaned forward excitedly. "What if we were only meant to sail to Nova Scotia so you might avoid the soldiers in London? And from there we are really to travel directly to Virginia, to be reunited with your brother and the others of our party?"

Collin's mouth twisted skeptically. "That is what you've seen?"

My countenance fell. "No. It seems a reasonable possibility though. I'd prefer the Colonies."

"This can't be about what we want," Collin reminded me. "We both know that. I didn't want to buy passage on a second ship, but it was most fortunate that I did."

"Very well." I sighed deeply. "I shall ponder it. That is all I can do without—"

"Be right back." Collin had released my hands and run off before I could finish my sentence.

I set the offensive bowl of oats aside. Hunger gnawed at my stomach, but that feeling was far preferable to the other. I lifted the piece of dried meat and nibbled.

Collin was back at my side in record time, a smile transforming his face entirely from the one presented to me earlier.

The many moods of my husband, I mused.

"Here. For you," he said, a little breathless. He whipped his hand from behind his back and held a sketch pad out to me.

I stared at it a moment, hardly believing it was real.

"Go ahead. Touch it, take it." Collin practically laughed.

I reached out with both hands and brought the precious book to my chest, holding it close to my heart. My eyes stung as I turned to Collin, seated beside me once more. "There are so many other things you could have bought. A blanket for yourself, tools, clothing,   seeds—"

"I hope the paper is all right," Collin said. "I brought this with me to the shop to try to match the weight." He withdrew a folded parch-ment from his pocket. It was creased and dirty, smudged and worn, and not even a year old yet.

I took the paper from him and opened it, spreading it flat carefully over the new sketchbook. Collin's face stared up at me. He appeared different then—not just because he'd acquired new scars since—but because I understood him now. I'd known him but a day when I drew this, and the cares in his eyes, the worry in the lines of his face had been a mystery to me. But now I understood him, and them, well. We understood each other.

Collin withdrew a box of artist's charcoals from his other pocket and handed it to me.

"A whole box?" I stared at him, openmouthed. One would have been enough of an extravagance and might have lasted for quite some time.

"Open it," Collin urged.

I did, my eager fingers carefully unfolding the flap to preserve it. I tilted the box a little, and the contents, sticks of different thicknesses, slid into my waiting hand. I stared at them and felt the familiar stir of excitement and the desire to create take hold.

"I didn't know what sort of shops they'd have in Nova Scotia," Collin said. "I wanted to buy paints and canvas—and you'll have those again someday, I promise—but I hope these will suffice for now."

I leaned forward and threw my arms around him. "They'll more than suffice. You shouldn't have spent so much. You'll spoil me."

He pulled back to better look at me. "I hope I shall someday, Mrs. MacDonald." He kissed me swiftly. "Now get busy sketching, and this time draw something better than that sour-faced Scot."

Chapter Fifteen

Portsmouth, Virginia, April 1762

Two days more. With a last glance at the *Iris,* the ship that would carry him home to Scotland, Ian turned away from the wharf and headed back toward the tavern that had become his temporary home the past week. The Young Devil, appropriately called, with him in residence—not that he was particularly young anymore, having nearly thirty years—had provided far more than a bed three of the past six nights. He'd doubled his money each evening he'd spent in the tavern, and was contemplating whether or not he dared risk an additional night at the tables, or if it would be better for him to seek out one of the other establishments in town so as to avoid notice or suspicion.

He was expert in more ways than one at relieving others of their possessions, a fact evident by the new clothing he wore and the healthy pouch at his side. But his ways weren't necessarily honest—what about gambling was?—and he had no desire for anyone to become the wiser and cause a stir.

Get in, get rich, get out.

Some might not call £14—or about that many dollars, as they were sometimes called here—the pinnacle of wealth. But it was more money than Ian could recall having at once—ever. He would have had even more by now, had he not purchased new clothing, plentiful meals, and passage home as soon as he'd been able. It was almost a shame to leave, as America really did seem to be the land of opportunity.

With a satisfied smile, Ian turned onto Church Street just

as the bell in the high tower pealed noon and patrons began spilling out of the tall stone building. He hurried past, not wanting to get caught in the jam of the righteous on their way home for Sunday dinner.

Dinner . . . He wondered idly what the tavern fare would be tonight. His appetite had returned with vengeance this week, and between regular, mostly satisfying meals and the luxury of undisturbed sleep each night, he was feeling better than he had for a long time. *Good enough for another serving of—*

"Collin? Collin MacDonald?"

The female voice shocked Ian from his reverie about last night's shepherd's pie. He stopped, pivoted, and found himself staring into the face of Elizabeth Campbell.

She wore a new hat, adorned with pink ribbon, and a jacket and petticoat trimmed out to match. Her worn cape had been replaced as well, with a fine brown one that settled heavily over her shoulders. Her mouth was slightly open and her eyes alight with what he guessed to be surprise as she brought mittened hands up to her flushed cheeks.

"It *is* you. You're still here, and you look so different, so . . . well. Like a whole new man with your beard shaved off." She gave him a fleeting smile, which Ian returned whole-heartedly.

"It is you who looks fine." He took one of her hands and bent over it gallantly, ignoring the questioning glances of the parishioners making their way past. His lips brushed the tips of Eliza's fingers where they extended from her mittens, the slight contact searing his heart. He had worked so diligently to forget her these past days, only to discover he had failed miserably.

"*Why* are you here? Instead of on a ship to Scotland?" Seeming discomfited, she withdrew her hand when he would have kept it, then stepped sideways, out of the main throng, and stood so they were partially hidden behind a tree. "Why have you stayed?" she repeated. "Have you been forced to indenture?" Her eyes brushed over him quickly, admiringly, lingering a moment on the lips that had just been upon her hand.

Or was that his imagination?

"I am not indentured," he said, clearing a throat that suddenly felt hoarse. "I managed to break away from the crew of the *Ulysses* as we unloaded the ship. I hid in the back of the warehouse until it was dark, and then . . ." He paused to lower his voice, lest any of the passersby overhear him. "I made use of some of the wares I found there." He touched the brim of his new hat.

Her smile faltered, and she looked to either side, as if wary someone had heard him.

"Of course not everything I am wearing came from the ware-house." He fingered the lapel of his new coat. "I have been fortunate at the gaming tables the past several nights and have secured supplies and passage home." *I can provide for myself now. And you.*

"How fine," Eliza said brusquely. "I can see you have indeed used your freedom wisely, as I bade you." Her smile was gone now, vanished into lips mashed together in a thin line. "If I were you, I should take great care not to get caught and make all haste back to Scotland. Good day, Collin."

"I've upset you." Ian caught her arm.

She pulled back, and he let her.

"If you'll excuse me, I need to return to the shop before Mrs. Perkins becomes concerned. She has a headache and trusted me enough to let me go to church on my own. It would not serve well if she, or anyone else, discovered I had spoken with you."

"Why not?" Ian asked, wondering what it was exactly that had caused Eliza's sudden turn. He would have sworn she was pleased to see him a few moments ago. "Mrs. Perkins doesn't own you, Eliza. You're not a slave, but a servant. It should seem that Sundays, at least, are your own to command."

"Mistress Perkins treats me well," Eliza retorted, sounding as if her ire was up, along with the chin she'd thrust out and her nose that pointed upward. "I must not betray her trust." She made to move past him, but he blocked her way.

"Eliza—"

"Elizabeth, if you please." Her face softened slightly as he caught her eye.

He didn't please, but chose his next words with care, hoping to change the course of their conversation. "I only meant to say a proper thank you for all you've done for me." He thought he understood her sudden bitterness. She'd risked her life for him and ended up with fourteen years indenture as repayment, while he was free to go about his way. It *wasn't* fair.

But it *was* within his power to change.

"You're welcome." She looked away with a curt nod. "I wish you well, Collin. Godspeed back home to your wife. And please, be wary until you are safely gone."

He was tired of being wary, especially where Eliza was concerned. It was time she knew the truth. He took a deep breath, then exhaled. "I don't have a wife. My name isn't Collin."

It was Eliza who stopped mid-step this time. Instead of seeming surprised, her eyes narrowed in anger as she looked—no, stared—at him once more.

"Of course it is. I don't believe you. How else should you know my name? And if that was true—which it is not—what a dreadful trick to play upon a lady. You might have told me you were not the person I believed at the start of this conversation."

"But I *am* that person." Ian grasped her arm at the elbow when she would have left.

He pulled her farther off the main path and onto the grass nearer the church. "I *am* the man whose life you saved on that ship." He lowered his voice. "And the one whom you helped undress a corpse."

She gasped and jerked free of him. A couple passing by glanced their direction, and Ian smiled congenially and tipped his hat. They continued on their way, two small children trailing behind. Ian scowled at the young ones, so they would leave off staring at him. He waited and watched as their eyes widened and they hurried to catch up with their parents. Then he turned and saw that Eliza, too, was in a hurry, marching briskly across the lawn. He ran to catch up with her.

"I don't know what you mean by saying you're not Collin," she huffed.

"If you'd give me two seconds to explain, you would." Ian ran in front of her and blocked her path. "I'm Collin's twin brother, Ian. Back in Scotland after you helped Collin escape I switched places with him so the English would have a prisoner and leave the area and our clan alone while Collin returned to his wife."

Her eyes widened, and her hand flew to her mouth. "*Ian* MacDonald?" She shook her head and stepped backward, fear in her eyes.

"Aye." She wasn't reacting at all as he'd hoped. He could see there was to be no praise from her for his sacrifice. "It doesn't matter who I am. Listen, I've some money." He dug into his pocket and withdrew the pouch. "I could buy you passage home as well. I would like to."

"No." She turned on her heel and began running the way she'd come.

"Why not?" Ian followed, catching up easily. He trotted beside her as she headed for the church steps. "Consider it repayment for your kindness. I'll give you the money now, no strings attached."

At the bottom of the steps she whirled on him and thrust a hand out, palm forward as if to keep him away. "I won't go anywhere with you, or near you. I probably wouldn't have saved you had I realized—"

Ian winced.

"It's well known that Ian MacDonald murdered and

plundered his way across the Highlands. You even tried to kill your own brother's wife."

Ian opened his mouth to refute Eliza's claim, but no words came. She was right, except for the last. Of course the story of his actions at the river would have spread throughout her clan.

"Stay away from me," Eliza said. "I don't want your stolen money. I don't want anything to do with you." Tears blurred her eyes.

He held out the pouch. "It's not stolen." *Not really.* The other men at the table had known the risks. *Mostly.* She could take all of it. He didn't care. Anything to have her stop looking at him like that. "You can take a different ship," he said hoarsely. "Or buy your freedom and stay here. There's enough—"

"Buy my freedom with money earned illicitly? I don't think so." She shook her head angrily, curls tossing about. "I would rather be indentured. Who knows but that you've killed for some of it. You've done so before, and I saw the pistol at your side as you were showing off your hat to me." Her eyes riveted to his waist.

"I would rather be a slave here than go with you. Even being with Officer Millet would have been better. At least he told me the truth." She turned and fled up the stairs into the church, leaving Ian standing alone, staring after her, feeling as stung as if she'd just slapped him.

The bells had ceased pealing. The last stragglers exited the building and hurried toward their homes, cloaks pulled tight and heads bent against the wind just starting to whip up. The church doors closed behind Eliza with a solid clang. Ian supposed she'd find someone inside to escort her home. Or, at the least, she would watch from one of the many windows and wait until he had gone.

And why shouldn't she? He had lied to her. And yet . . . Ian wondered if that might have been forgivable, had the person he really was not been so abhorrent to her.

His own head bent for more reasons than the buffeting wind. He turned from the church and started back toward The Young Devil. His lodgings were as appropriately named for him, as had been the church the perfect place to find Eliza. He was not like her. *Not worthy of her.*

Ian picked up his pace, as if that might somehow help him outrun his self-loathing. It shouldn't have mattered what she thought of him. He hadn't much cared what anyone believed of him before—not even Collin.

He had his reasons for the things he'd done—even for the people he'd harmed or killed. Mostly it had been for survival. But for some reason Eliza's opinion of him mattered. Her rejection stung and soured the sweet memories he'd been reliving in his dreams the past week. And what of her timid, guilt-laden confession to him there in the darkness and safety of the hold? Had she not committed crimes of her own? Or had their conversation that night occurred only in his imagination? Had he imagined the perceived trust between them?

Trust. He'd broken hers. And hadn't Da always said that was not something easily or always mended?

Their friendship during the voyage had been an illusion, borne of his lie. His father had always taught them that the truth would set a man free. Ian realized he had discarded the truth until too late. And now he was on his former path, a person he was no longer certain he wanted to be.

Chapter Sixteen

Aboard the *Cleopatra*, the Atlantic Ocean, April 1762

I drew my knees up to my chest and closed my eyes in misery. "I swear if I survive this, I'll never again complain about riding in a carriage."

"I won't hold you to that," Collin said. "And you *will* survive."

"I'm not sure—" I began gagging and leaned over the side of the bed, stomach convulsing as it attempted to empty once again. Very little came up. Collin held my plaited hair out of the way and whispered words meant to soothe. But it all made me want to cry—cry and succumb to the violent illness tearing me apart inside.

"We'll have only one child, Katie. I promise," Collin was saying. "I'll not subject you to this again."

"I *may* hold you to that." I mustered a wan smile and lay back on the uncomfortable bed again. "Perhaps we can adopt a child in need . . ." My thoughts went at once to our precious Lydia. Collin's overbright eyes told me she was in his mind too.

"Do you suppose she is well?" I whispered. We'd hardly spoken of her since she'd been taken from us. It was a source of great pain to us both, a sort of haunting and traumatic memory with no relief. My best hope was the possibility that someday holding the child growing inside of me now, would ease the ache in our hearts so that the memory of the little girl we had loved would become bearable.

"I pray she is," Collin said. "I try very hard *not* to think of her."

"I like to think of the night you first brought her to me. I'd seen it in a dream and feared, yet when she came it was perfect. And all those nights after when you rocked her or we lay together in our bed with Lydia between."

"She softened your heart toward the beast I'd become," Collin mused.

"Not a beast." I reached a hand up to pat the scruff on his face. "Just a man trying to be many things to a lot of people and needing the one closest to him to realize what and who he really was."

"And who am I, Katie?" Collin leaned into my touch.

"My husband. First and foremost, beyond all else. I am rather selfish, you know." My smile grew and brought a surge of strength with the overpowering love I felt for Collin.

"It suits you well." He took my hand and kissed it.

"Kissing again? Ugh." Timothy had entered the room and stopped short of my bed, his face a perfect mask of disgust, from his pout to his crossed eyes.

I would have laughed had I not known how it would hurt my already aching insides.

"That's right," Collin said, keeping my hand as his lips worked their way up my arm. "It's a smart man who kisses his wife every chance he finds."

This time I did giggle. I couldn't help it.

"I'm not ever going to marry," Timothy declared. "I'm going to be a seaman like Captain Shenk."

"Being a seaman is all well and good," Collin said. "But even Captain Shenk is married. And between me and you, I'm the more fortunate one, able to kiss your sister whenever I wish."

"I can be a captain without being married, right?" Timothy's forehead furrowed with concern. "A man doesn't *have* to have a wife, does he?"

"That he does," Collin said solemnly, winking so that only I saw it. "It is a man's duty to find a lass he fancies—and she must fancy him as well." His look slid from Timothy to me, tender affection in his gaze.

"The thing to do," Collin continued, placing a hand on Timothy's shoulder as he stood, "is to find a woman who is kind and loving, brave and true. If you are so fortunate as I've been, she'll be bonny as well. You must find this woman and marry her. Take her to your heart for life. And excepting God, whom you thank daily for the blessing of this woman, you love none other more."

"Church *and* a wife *and* kissing?" Timothy shook his head dismally. "I don't ever want to grow up."

"Not now, you don't," Collin said, gazing fondly at him. "But someday . . . you'll feel differently."

"You seem filled with inspiration today." Collin sat beside me on the crate, careful not to disturb the charcoals I'd laid out or to jostle me as I sketched. My time with the sketchbook not only helped the hours pass and pulled me somewhat from sickness, but it enabled a new and fascinating world to unfold before my eyes.

Reluctantly I allowed my hand to stop and took the pencil from the page. Numerous times today I'd noted Collin's boots as he passed. I'd sensed his eagerness to see my drawings and the way he'd forced himself not to bother me.

Looking up, I realized the sun sat low on the western horizon. I'd been drawing for hours with little thought of anything else. I laid the book in my lap and set the charcoal aside until tomorrow, praying the images and inspiration would return again.

Collin handed me a cup, and I sipped slowly at the water while he waited, watching me curiously, his eyes straying to what had to appear to him to be strange drawings. They were strange to me as well. I'd never drawn anything like this before.

When my thirst was quenched I returned the cup to him and flipped the sketchbook back two pages. "Would you like to see what I've been drawing?"

"Does a MacDonald like his whisky?" he teased.

"Very well. But beware that the *new* MacDonald land shall not be known for its production of fine whisky. There are better crops to be grown, and if I'm right about what I'm seeing, it will be a labor to grow them in a shortened season."

"Sounds like the Highlands," Collin said. "Are you certain you've not been dreaming of home?"

"I've not." I shook my head, as positive as I'd ever been about anything my gift of sight had before shown me. "But a place very much like it, I believe."

"I want to see too." Timothy left the ropes he'd been braiding on the deck near me. This latest task Captain Shenk had set him to, telling him all good sailors must know how to braid and knot rope, had occupied both Timothy's hands and mind for several hours today.

He squeezed between us, with Collin's arm braced behind him, to keep him from toppling backward off the crate.

"These drawings won't ever lend themselves to paintings," I said. "They're more like . . . maps, I think."

A corner of Collin's mouth lifted. "Your talents continue to impress."

I shrugged. "I realize that one cannot draw a map without having traversed the land, but these past few days it has almost seemed as if I *am* there, walking it myself, or even seeing it from above, as if I were a bird flying overhead." I moved my hands, showing them the first page.

"I believe this is what the port of Halifax will look like— or what the shape of it is, anyway. It is here, in the middle of this longish strip of land."

"Is it an island, as England was?" Timothy asked.

"You mean as England *and* Scotland are?" Collin corrected him. "English are always forgetting about their top half," he grumbled good naturedly, ruffling Timothy's hair.

"It isn't an island. At least, I don't think so. I believe it connects to quite an enormous mainland like this." I flipped to the next page, showing Halifax as only the tiniest dot, on the edge of a land into which several Englands would have fit. "But there *are* islands. This one." I pointed to one quite a distance from and running almost perpendicular to the strip of land where Halifax was located. "And another that does not seem it would be as difficult to reach." I placed my finger on the odd shape I'd drawn to the east of the other island and north of Halifax. "It is this area that I keep returning to, this that I have spent the better part of today drawing."

I flipped to the third page of the sketchbook and held the detailed drawing out for Collin to better see. "The eastern and north side of this island interest me," I continued. "There would be a sea for fishing still, yet it would be sheltered from the greater storms of the Atlantic. And though I've not drawn any of this yet, I can see what it looks like in my mind. It is a wilderness of great beauty—a place with water aplenty, forests of trees, great rocks, mountain highlands and plateaus, animals—"

"What kind? Can you draw those too?" Timothy crowded closer, peering at the paper.

"I can try," I said. "I'm still just working at the shape of the land. I don't want to waste even one page, so I'm thinking and visualizing much more than actually sketching. But I do see *so* much more. It's beautiful, Collin." I turned to him, wishing there was some better way to share what I had seen. "Truly it's the Nova Scotia we've dreamed of."

"Can that be possible, so close to Halifax and the English presence and goings on there?" He gave me a pointed look, and I knew he was thinking of the war Captain Shenk had advised us of.

"I believe so." I nodded slowly. "This land that I picture, it is a wild, largely untamed wilderness." I was reminded again of the journey Collin and I had made from my home in England through the wilds of the Scottish Highlands.

"Like the Highlands," he said, echoing my thoughts.

"Aye." My brogue was still lacking, but the response elicited a smile from him all the same.

"Perhaps all is not as dismal as I'd been led to believe. Perhaps our hope of a home is yet alive."

"Very much so." I closed the sketchbook and placed a hand over my stomach, feeling a future that was alive and full of promise in more ways than one.

Chapter Seventeen

Portsmouth, Virginia, April 1762

Ian punched his pillow and turned away from the wall and the unmuted sounds coming from the other side. His mid-hall room on the second floor hadn't bothered him until tonight, when instead of joining in the ruckus below or cheating men out of their coins, he'd chosen to eat early and spend the night in.

He'd hoped—foolishly—that a Sunday evening meant a smaller, calmer crowd at The Young Devil. He couldn't have been more wrong. Earlier, from his window, Ian had watched the steady stream of men, and a few women, on horse and afoot as they converged at the crossroad where the tavern sat.

For a while he'd kept his door open, chair propped near the entrance to his tiny room, and observed the goings-on below. The experience was reminiscent of his childhood, when his father would send Collin and him upstairs where they might watch, but not participate in the events happening in the great hall.

Vague though those memories were, Ian felt certain that the goings on in the hall of his father's keep had been far better, more honorable, than those that took place in the room below—and now those beside—his.

He'd scrutinized those coming through the doors and noted that while a few appeared respectable men merely in search of refreshment or a short-lived relief from their burdens, the far larger number seemed to be the very dregs of humanity, the most lazy and dissolute. They were trouble even before a drop of alcohol tainted their veins, and they progressed to worse behavior as the evening wore on.

Ian had noted that drunkenness, cursing, cheating, and fighting were not only tolerated but seemed to be accepted without consequence. Bawdiness in both speech and action was the prevailing behavior of both men and women. Arguments were frequent and loud, with a few escalating beyond words.

Those gambling at the tables, as he had previously done, were perhaps the best of the lot, mostly idle while intent on their game as equally as with the spirits in their cups. Many were the unkempt, low-lived sort, risking what little they had in the hope of getting something for nothing, or very little effort.

These observations had done little to ease the burden he'd felt since his meeting with Eliza. At last, disgusted with the lewd behavior playing out in the barroom, Ian had moved the chair and closed the door. He had participated in it, been a part of it or similar scenarios numerous times before, but he had never before had this viewpoint on the whole affair. What he'd witnessed had been eye-opening in the worst sort of way. If he hadn't had cause to loathe himself before, he certainly did now.

The bed in the room next to his thumped loudly against the wall, followed by high-pitched laughter. *Too high to belong to the room's primary occupant,* Ian reflected darkly, having nodded to the man on several occasions as they passed in the hall or on the stairs.

What did you expect of a place called The Young Devil, his conscience accused. He hadn't thought much about it that first night he stumbled inside. He'd seen the sign and that there was a light on, in spite of the hour. He'd been half frozen from his sea-water bath, and stiff and sore and sick to boot. That the man had rented him a room without a second glance should, perhaps, have been his warning that the place wasn't one of prestige or even a modicum of standards. If he, any old scum off the street, could rent a room, what was to keep anyone else from doing the same and then doing whatever he wished inside those rooms?

Ian banged the wall above the headboard with his fist, willing the occupants on the other side to cease their merry-making, or at least to keep it quieter. He didn't want to think about what they were doing—didn't want to think about anything to do with women. Yet there it was again in his mind. There *she* was—Eliza.

He rose from the bed and went to stand at the window once more. The streets below were quiet now. With the moonlight bathing them in soft light, they appeared almost tranquil. If he didn't look too carefully he might imagine Portsmouth as any other Scottish village. The next man to appear might be wearing a kilt. He might even be the piper preparing to climb the hill to herald the sun in a few hours.

Those days are gone.

As were his days of gambling and thieving, Ian realized with a suddenness that was alarming. Having witnessed what he had tonight, from the perspective of one not involved, he felt repulsed by the life he had led and what he had become. He'd forsaken murder some time ago—excepting the necessity to be rid of Niall, and the accident with the crewman on the ship—but the other vices he had retained and even honed.

Da would not be proud. More likely, he would have pulled Ian over his knee for a sound thrashing, followed by a boot to his backside, with the order to get out.

No less than I deserve. Ian opened the window a crack, allowing the cool, misty air to wash over his face, as if that might somehow cleanse it.

For years, to stay alive, he had played the part of the Munros' lackey, doing what they told him when they told him. He'd hated the errands of thievery at first but had gradually allowed the thrill of the quest to surpass his fear of being caught—or worse, being tortured and killed by the Munros if he failed. With each subsequent success, there had grown within them a grudging respect for him, even if they tried not to show it. There was never reward nor praise, merely less harassment and perhaps better food. Never freedom nor trust. Never gratitude nor camaraderie.

Little by little he'd come to loathe both the Munros and their requests—stealing a half dozen cattle from the neighboring McNabs, raiding the Grants' distillery, or even kidnapping the Maclean's daughter—less as the years went by. He'd reasoned that the Munros had taught him the skills to survive. What he did for them was no more than anyone else in the Highlands was doing since the failed uprising. He'd become good at it, so good that one night he slipped into an English patrol camp alone, slit the throat of the soldier on watch, and made off with two horses, all on his own, with no repercussions to himself or the Munros who sheltered him.

As far as Ian still knew, no one had any idea who'd been responsible for the raid that night. Evidence had pointed to the Macraes, whose bottles of overly fermented whisky— stolen and placed strategically in the path of the patrol by Ian the day before—were found among the drunk soldiers of the camp. Only the watchman had remained sober, and had paid with his life.

Ian glanced at his hands pressing upon the windowsill, feeling the man's blood upon them once again. Regret flooded his senses, and a dozen other scenarios filled his mind—as they had several times previous. He hadn't needed to kill the man. A simple rock to the back of his skull would have left him unconscious, but alive and none the wiser to the horse thief's identity.

Of the many things he had done wrong, of the times he had killed, Ian regretted this incident perhaps most of all. It had been his first time taking a life, and it had been unneces-sary. There were not words for how he'd felt after and how he still felt, all these years later.

That deed had confirmed Ian's reputation as a first-rate

thief and marauder and not one to be trifled with. With bitterness Ian remembered the sense of pride he'd felt, returning to the Munros with the horses. The Munros hadn't seen him, alone in the forest, sick and shaking after he'd killed the soldier. They couldn't know the war he fought within himself, justifying his present actions while forever burying the lad he had been. Why fight against it, Ian remembered asking himself. His father and brother had abandoned him, leaving him to this cutthroat means of survival. And if he could make use of it to do more than survive, what was the harm in that?

By the time he'd strolled into the courtyard of the Munro keep, leading a horse on either side, Ian had made a sort of peace with his conscience, or at least chained it and submerged it in the deepest recesses of his soul. The inner demon had prevailed and would continue to.

Or so he had believed. Until the day he'd been reunited with Collin and faced the task of using the same blade that had ended the soldier's life to end his brother's.

Ian leaned forward, inhaling the cool air that did nothing to soothe his burning eyes and swollen throat.

With singular anguish he mused that perhaps he should have remained in bed and thought about Eliza. The meanderings of his mind had certainly not brought him anywhere better tonight.

He left the window and considered going downstairs for a drink or two after all. It might be the only thing that brought him any measure of relief or sleep. But Eliza's voice remained forefront in his mind. Her words had driven him to this room, and they held him here, in a web of self-loathing and recrimination.

I would rather be a slave here than go with you. Even Millet would have been better.

Would he? That statement, above all others she'd flung at him, bothered Ian the most. As far as Ian was concerned, there was no lower form of life than an officer, Redcoat or otherwise, who thought himself better than his fellow men. Ian's experience with them was that they plundered for amusement. He'd seen British officers give the command to slaughter livestock, burn fields, and rape women, for no other reason than that it seemed a diverting way to spend an afternoon.

Millet would have ruined Eliza, then left her alone or sold her off to the highest bidder. That she would compare Ian to such a man rankled, cut him to his core, and at long last released the conscience he'd buried that night long ago.

He left the window and began pacing the room, arguing with himself yet again.

Relying upon the luck of the gaming tables—and creating his own luck at them—as he had the past week was not necessarily evil, he reflected, though neither was it praise-worthy. Much like his years with the Munros, it had been necessary. He had to eat. He'd needed a place to shelter and decent clothing to wear. If not through gambling or stealing, how else was he to provide for himself? He hadn't killed or even hurt anyone in the process. He hadn't robbed a man and left him for dead, nor even robbed one so much as to hurt him financially.

True to form he'd been careful to steal a bit from many, striking here and there quickly. *Get in, get out.*

Still, Ian found himself wishing back those minutes with Eliza in front of the church. He oughtn't have mentioned how he had come upon his improved condition. He shouldn't have been surprised at her rejection, given his reputation in the Highlands and the proof of it he'd given her by all but bragging about his stolen goods.

How could he have imagined she might react otherwise and be eager to join with such a person as himself? She had called him out for what he was, a common thief, a cheating gambler, a liar.

A raucous scream echoed from the main room below, followed by another, more distinctly male shout and then the sounds of numerous glasses being clinked together. Someone had won the game and would soon be carrying his prize upstairs.

Fists clenched at his sides, Ian turned away from the sounds of sin. Last night he'd felt perfectly comfortable here; now he couldn't have felt more out of place. He didn't want to be here. It might have suited the man he had become, but it was a terrible fit for the man he had been raised to be.

Ian dropped to the bed and retrieved his boots. He thrust them on, then quickly retrieved his few belongings. He needn't stay any longer. He would leave tonight, return to the wharf, maybe partake in another midnight swim. It might cleanse more than the wound in his side this time.

Even as he had the thought, he knew it wouldn't work. There wasn't any preacher or baptism that might give him relief from the agony of soul he suffered. The pretty church that had welcomed Eliza would never welcome him. He belonged there even less than he belonged in the barroom below.

Trouble was, he didn't know where he was supposed to go. There wasn't any place Ian MacDonald would fit in.

Chapter Eighteen

Portsmouth, Virginia, April 1762

Ian decided against a dip in the ocean again almost as soon as he stepped out into the cool night air. He headed to the wharf anyway, intent on asking if he might board the ship a day early. He'd stay out of the way, or he'd even offer his help for free. Anything to hasten his return to Scotland's shores.

I'll take the high road, ye take the low.
Inverness for me, for thee Glasgow.
Meadow and Moor,
Towering mountains afore,
Loch Ness above to Loch Linnhe below,
she calls to us the same . . .

The words of the ballad stuck in his throat. It felt swollen again, and for a brief second Ian paused to close his eyes and remember. The Jacobite army had sung that upon its ill-fated return march from England, what was now considered to be the beginning of the end of the rebellion. *The beginning of the end to everything as we knew it.*

He'd been among those singing, believing with the others that they would soon be reunited with their families, and be returned to their homes, to the mostly peaceful, hard-working existences they'd enjoyed before.

Instead a great number of those men had been returned to the dust of the earth on the battlefield of Culloden. It was a memory and a place he would never forget, so long as he lived and breathed.

Many an unpleasant thing had happened to him, and many an unpleasant thing he had caused, in his beloved homeland. But it was still home, the land of his father and MacDonald ancestors going back centuries before. He would return and make them all proud.

His steps more resolute, Ian focused his gaze on the water at the town's edge. He walked the several blocks to the wharf, arriving just before the sun. Several members of the crew were already up and about their work, as seemed to be the case on most of the ships at dock. Ian noticed the *Ulysses* still in port, and he could only feel relief to know Eliza wasn't on board.

Millet was still about, though. *Up early for an officer.* Ian watched Millet roughly herding a group of two women, one man, and one child from the ship to shore. Something about the scene held Ian's attention, and instead of taking the ramp onto the *Iris*, he continued down the dock, following the group from a distance.

Turn away. There is nothing you can do to help them. The warning voice of the crewman from the day they'd unloaded the ship rang through Ian's mind. He should turn away. It was sound advice. And yet . . .

His eyes widened in recognition. The indentured mother and daughter were among the small group being taken from the ship. Ian ceased walking and instead hurried to catch up with them.

"Where are these people being taken?" he demanded in an authoritative voice as soon as he was close enough to be heard.

Millet started as if he was a child caught with his hand in a jar of biscuits. His back stiffened as he paused, then rotated a quarter turn. "Who are you, and what business is it of yours?" His eyes narrowed on Ian suspiciously, and for a terrible second Ian feared the man recognized him.

Reminding himself that he looked vastly different now,

Ian answered Millet with a question of his own, a lie forming quickly and sliding off his tongue. "Is this not where indentured servants are purchased? I have traveled some distance after being told I might find such aboard your ship."

The *Ulysses* is not my ship," Millet said, standing a little taller. "Not yet, anyway," he added beneath his breath.

"My apologies." Ian tipped his new hat, pleased that Millet was, as he had suspected, easily susceptible to flattery.

"We have been in port over a week," Millet said. "These— people—" he spat it out as if they were animals—"are all we have left."

"And are these off to market, then?" Ian asked, pretending to look them over as potential servants. He'd been correct. It was definitely the mother who had wanted to stay with her daughter. What good fortune they were still together.

"To the *slave* market," Millet drawled. "No one has bid for them. Law says that redemptioners can be sold as slaves if no one has claimed them after two weeks."

"I thought you said you'd been in port only a week," Ian replied, risking any favor he might have gained with the man.

"Yes, well we cannot be expected to linger here indefinitely," Millet said. "Particularly at this time. A man has been found dead on the *Ulysses*.

Ian took a step back and worked his face into a purposeful mask of concern. "Small pox? Scurvy? Just one man, or were there others at sea similarly afflicted?" He brought a hand to his face and looked askance at the indentured, as if he was suddenly repulsed by or afraid of them.

"No, no. Nothing like that," Millet assured him. "This man had been murdered. A few blows to the head, it looks like. We're following leads as to who might have done it. And with the ship under investigation, well . . . Taking these to the slave market a few days early is no great crime, especially since no one has come the past three. There has been absolutely no interest in any of them. They're only underfoot right now."

Ian felt the pouch beneath his coat and wondered how

far it would get him. He could not free all of these poor souls. That much was certain. But perhaps he had enough to release the mother and daughter.

"Not much to look at, are they?" he mused, stepping closer. He worried recognition might flicker in one of their eyes, but they barely noticed him. The hardships they'd left behind, the trying conditions of the voyage, and now the humiliation of being sold like cattle had likely become too much. He'd never seen such a downtrodden bunch.

"You're certain none of them are diseased?" Ian asked, continuing to play the part.

"They're fine." Millet waved a hand dismissively. "Don't be all day about it. I've other things to attend to."

Things or people? Ian worried what those leads Millet had referred to might be and fervently hoped one of them was not Eliza.

"If you'll guarantee their health—"

Millet nodded, looking annoyed.

"In that case, I'm in need of a laundress." Ian turned his head to and fro between the two women, as if trying to decide which would suit him better.

Millet gave a sorry shake of his head. "Not much to look at, and they're Scots Highlanders, probably lazy to boot."

"Probably not," Ian replied swiftly, meeting Millet's eye. "You must have noted from my accent that Scotland was the home of my birth as well. I'd heard the *Ulysses* was bringing Scots, and that is the reason I've come. They'll work hard. I'll take this one," he said, pointing to the mother. "And this small one as well," he added before the woman could begin wailing about her child. "We've need of a new ash girl."

"That will be £17 for the both," Millet said. "And a bargain at that. They'd fetch far more as slaves."

"I'm not purchasing them for life," Ian reminded him. "Only the normal period of indenture. Seven years, I believe."

"It was to be fourteen for this lot. Criminals, all of them," Millet said.

"Even the child?" Ian's brows rose in disbelief. "And what was her crime?" He shook his head and made a face of disgust. "No, I'll not be keeping any of them fourteen years. Don't hold with robbing a man—or woman—of half a lifetime."

"Keep them as long as you will, if you will," Millet said with an impatient glance down the street and a slightly worried one back toward the ship. If you want these two that's £17."

"You're mad to think these will command top price." Ian forced a critical frown to his face once more, hating that he had to participate in this charade at all. "You've said yourself what a sorry lot they are."

"And you have just told me that Scots work hard. " Millet flashed a toothy smile of victory at Ian. "Do you want them or not?"

Ian brought a hand to his chin, pretending to consider. "What say you to £12 for both? That's the going price for the woman, plus a bit more for the child."

"£15," Millet said.

"£14. My final offer." Ian reached into his coat but hesitated, waiting for Millet's move. "I am saving you the trouble of taking them to market—and being caught at your own game." Ian's eyes flickered toward the *Ulysses.* "I wonder, what would the captain say to know what you are about this morning?"

A look of discomfort flashed briefly across Millet's face, contorting his features. "Very well. I suppose it is two less for me to deal with. You're certain you don't want the whole lot?"

Ian did very much, and felt his heart break a little at abandoning them to a life of slavery. He thought briefly of the pistol at his side and what he could do with one, well-aimed shot. The others would be free to—what? To run and hide in a strange land, with no means or friend to assist?

While I would swing from the short end of the rope. And not even in my own country. The pistol would have to stay where it was, hidden out of sight.

Ian handed the entirety of his money over, counting out the pound notes first, then pouring the last of his coin into Millet's outstretched palm, feeling only slightly better that some of it had come from the officer in the first place.

"Good day to you." Ian tipped his hat once more. "Come along." He motioned to the woman and child. "Carriage is back at the inn. We'll have to walk a piece."

He felt Millet's eyes following them as they went. Ian practiced an unaffected stroll, pausing now and again to wait for his newly acquired servants to catch up while trying to figure out what he was supposed to do with them.

As soon as they'd covered a few blocks and were far from the wharf and free of Millet's view, Ian stopped and faced them. "I've no intention of owning you—have no need for any servants. You are free to go."

The woman stared at him blankly, as if she'd not understood a word he'd just spoken. Ian wasn't sure what he'd been expecting from her, but it wasn't this.

"Don't fall on your knees thanking me," he muttered. "Not when I've just spent my last shilling keeping you from that man and who knows what else."

"Thank you," the child said, her eyes on him as she rubbed her arms briskly and hopped from one foot to the other.

She has no cloak. At this realization Ian looked back to the woman, seeing that she *did* have a cloak about her shoulders, worn though it was, but had not offered it to her daughter. Bewildered at such a lack of motherly affection from the woman who had publicly begged to be allowed to stay with her child, Ian bent down and scooped the lass into his arms, settling her on the side opposite his wound and doing his best to wrap his own coat around her.

"Follow me," he said to the woman. He would take them back to his room at The Young Devil, where they could all get warm and sort out what was to be done.

He walked quickly, only glancing back once or twice to

see that the woman followed. Something was definitely wrong with her, Ian realized as he paused, after one such glance, to wait for her to catch up and again noticed her trance-like state. A sick feeling started in his gut. Perhaps Millet had taken his frustration at losing Eliza out upon the woman. In some measure, it *was* her fault that Eliza had fled.

For that alone I owe this woman. He would do right by her.

The more Ian studied her the more concerned he became. The spark of fight he'd witnessed last week was gone. Her head hung low, shoulders slumped in defeat. Something—or someone—had beaten the fight from her. Ian had seen similar behavior before, from those who'd suffered a grave trauma—most often at the hands of Redcoats.

If Millet had done the same—had forced himself upon this mother for attempting to keep her child—then Ian decided he *would* make use of his new pistol before leaving the Colonies. He'd exactly one shot, and he knew just where it would go.

Ian began walking again, almost smiling, thinking of the satisfaction shooting the man would bring him. He wouldn't kill Millet, but he'd make it so he could never force himself upon another woman again. Ian's mouth turned down once more, recalling the way his sister-in-law had almost done the same to him last year.

Ironically, that incident had been the turning point in the way he felt about Collin's wife. If the Englishwoman was willing to risk her own neck to save her husband's, then perhaps she really did care for him. Her shot had certainly demonstrated she harbored no such feelings for Ian. Later, when Ian had found her drawing of Collin, he'd realized his hunch—that she cared a great deal for Collin—was correct. She'd taken the time—who knows when, as they'd done nothing but spend grueling days of travel since the wedding— to sketch Collin's face in detail. Ian had tucked the drawing away until he'd been reunited with Collin and had given it to him.

And when will I be reunited with my brother this time? Ian shifted the lass to a more comfortable position and continued retracing the steps that had taken him to the water's edge this morning. He'd less than twenty-four hours until he was to sail for Scotland. That wasn't much time to see to the woman and her child. Somehow he had to make certain they would be all right when he left. Or he had to come up with the fare for them to travel as well. In purchasing their indentures, he'd taken responsibility for their well-being. And, at present, he had no way to provide much of anything in that direction.

He would have to spend time at the gaming tables tonight if he was to make any sort of money. But he'd nothing to gamble with now and would have to do a bit of thieving today if he intended to increase his fortunes tonight.

The road to hell is paved with good intentions. Here he'd intended to start anew, to leave off the life of dishonesty. And now he was to be forced to it again.

After what seemed a much longer walk than he'd taken this morning, Ian reached the doors of The Young Devil and pulled one open, allowing the woman to pass through first. He noted the few men still slumped in their chairs or over the tables, sleeping off their night of drinking.

The barkeep glanced up as Ian entered.

"No children—" he began.

"It's temporary," Ian responded. "I'll be down to see the owner shortly to explain." He hurried toward the stairs, this time not bothering to glance back at the woman. If she was smart she'd get out of that barroom as quickly as possible. Then again, she probably didn't deem it particularly wise to follow the likes of him upstairs either. Ian couldn't blame her.

But follow him she did, and it was with great relief that Ian shut the door behind them and bolted it. He set the lass down, drew back the covers of the bed, then lifted her again and tucked her within. "Snuggle in and get yourself warm," he said with a smile.

She returned it shyly, he thought, then did as he instructed, burrowing into the bed. Ian turned his attention to her mother.

She stood in the corner, arms dangling loosely at her sides, the same vacant expression upon her face that had been there all morning.

Moving slowly, so as not to startle her, Ian took a step in her direction. "I want to help you," he said. "It is the only reason I bought your indenture. You're free to go whenever you want."

Again, his words received no response, verbal or otherwise.

Ian turned back to her daughter, thinking he might have better luck if he began there.

"What is your name, lass?" He sat on the edge of the bed, so as to not tower over her.

"Aisla," she answered without hesitation.

"A fine name." He smiled at her again. This time his flattery was genuine. She was a bonny little thing with a head of brown curls and dark brown eyes to match. "And how many years have you, Aisla?"

"Seven—I think." She scrunched her face, as if considering.

"What is your mother's name?" Ian asked, hoping this personal information might be key to unlocking the poor woman from her trance-like state.

"Aisla," the child said. "Like me."

"Very good. Just like you." He pulled the covers up higher over her, then turned back to her mother.

"Aisla," he began, moving his head so as to catch the woman's eye. "We need to decide what must be done now— to provide for you and your daughter. Tomorrow I am to leave—"

"*She's* not Aisla."

Ian turned to face the lass again. "What do you mean? You just said—"

"My mother's name is Aisla." The child's eyes seemed to darken with sorrow. "*My* mother is dead."

Chapter Nineteen

Aboard *The Cleopatra*, the Atlantic Ocean, April 1762

"Make it stop, please." I thrashed about on the bed, clutching the sheet beneath me as what felt like the hundredth pain began.

"Would that I might," Susan Parker said beneath her breath, sounding worried. She turned from the basin and toward me once more, a wet cloth in her hands. She laid it against my burning fore-head. "You've passed the child and should be feeling better very soon. By this time tomorrow you may even be—"

My cry silenced her. My back arched as agony shot through me.

Tomorrow? The thought of enduring the seizing pains even another hour more was too much. I couldn't do it and feared the only way this would cease was if I was dead. "Collin," I begged her once more. "Please let me see him."

"Birthing is no place for a man," Mrs. Parker insisted. "He'd only be in the way."

"I'm *not* birthing." There would be no child at the end of this ordeal. I'd realized this hours ago with the flush of water and bright red blood that had caught me by surprise as I attempted to rise from my bed. The mass expelled from me an hour past had confirmed it. "What is there to get in the way of? There will be no child." I panted heavily as the pain finally ebbed.

"Not this time, no." Susan's voice was sympathetic.

"Don't trouble yourself over that. Something was wrong with the babe. This is God's way of taking care of it."

I didn't like to think so, but if it was true I was about to tell her what I thought of God's methods when another pain set in, hardly a second after the last, as if a knife were being twisted into my lower back, skewering me clear through. I cried out, hating that I'd no more control over myself to endure better.

"There, now." Susan adjusted the cloth on my fevered brow. I tried lifting a hand to swat it away but found I'd not even that much strength. "Collin," I begged. "Please. I want to see him before I die."

"You're not dy—Oh!" She jumped up, seizing a pan beside the bed, too late to catch the latest store of blood gushing from my womb.

I felt my eyes roll back in my head as the room spun. *An officer's quarters. So kind of Captain Shenk.* But they'd just throw my body in the sea when this was done.

"Stay with me, Katherine." Susan shook me a little and I felt more liquid spill between my legs.

"Collin," I managed once more, feebly. Though I thought my eyes were open, the room had gone dark. I wouldn't be able to see him if he came. But I could at least hear his voice and feel his hand take mine.

The covers were pulled back and my nightgown bunched up once more. Susan gasped, then dropped the gown and moved toward the door. She sounded far away.

"Get her husband, quick."

"Tell him—I'm sorry . . ."

Part Two

Today's Rain is Tomorrow's Whisky

Chapter Twenty

Portsmouth, Virginia, April 1762

With Aisla's hand firmly in his, Ian walked briskly along the streets of Portsmouth, reflecting that he needn't have worried about his last day in the Colonies dragging on. Instead of trying to fill the hours, he somehow needed to slow them. He was in a race against time, with very little of it left to see to the needs of Mrs. Jannet Campbell and her daughter Taye—not to mention seeing to the placement of the precocious child at his side.

It had been just his ill luck that the mother and daughter he had intended to save from separation had already been separated. Yet he could not regret his acquaintance, however brief it was to be, with the little lass at his side.

After a short nap this morning, eating the few biscuits he'd had left, and with Jannet Campbell's borrowed cloak doubled about her shoulders, Aisla had perked up considerably, almost skipping along at his side.

He'd tried to explain to her what he intended. He would speak to the mistress of the plantation, the one who had purchased Mrs. Campbell's daughter, about a trade. Aisla for Taye, one little girl for another. It sounded simple enough in practice, yet Ian felt misgivings gnawing at him as he listened to the child chatting happily.

She liked him better than the mean man who'd tried to sell them every day for the past week. She wished there was more to eat. She thought it wasn't very pretty here and wanted to go home.

Makes two of us, Ian thought with a glance toward the wharf.

Aisla's prattling continued. He half-listened, nodding his head and giving an occasional grunt of acknowledgment, his mind too preoccupied to listen fully.

She'd left behind a dog and a grumpy cow who didn't care much for milking. Had he ever had a dog or a cow?

"Two dogs," Ian said. Of course they'd had cows as well, but that was before the uprising. He'd never thought much about them—or any of the animals his da owned—until after, when there were none to provide for their needs.

Aisla chattered on. She missed her pets. She missed Scotland and was ever-so-glad to be off that cursed ship, the one that had claimed her mother.

Ian's heart dropped to his stomach. "Your mother died on the voyage from Scotland?"

"Aye." Aisla's cheerful babbling ceased. She looked at the ground. "They put her in a pile with other people who wouldn't get out of bed either. Then they tied them in a sheet and pushed them off the ship."

Ian's mind snapped from his own troubles and focused on the waif beside him. He stopped walking, knelt beside the lass, then scooped her into his arms and held her close, imagining how traumatic her mother's death must have been and the grief she was surely dealing with still.

Ian had been in that pile of the dead. Save for Eliza's goodness he'd be at the bottom of the sea with Aisla's mother. "Who looked after you when—after your mother was gone?" he asked gruffly.

She shrugged. "No one, really. But there was a kind lady who brought me food at night."

No doubt as to who that was. Ian remembered feeling jealous that Eliza was spending her time caring for others on their voyage as well. What a fool he was—a stupid, selfish fool.

"A kind lady cared for me as well," Ian said.

Aisla nodded. "I know."

Ian wondered if she'd seen Eliza extract him from among the dead. He stood, still keeping her in his arms. "I will care for you now," he promised. "I'll see that you end up in a good place." He prayed the Shurtley Hill Plantation was that place. He hoped Jannet Campbell had remembered the name correctly and that they found her daughter in good circumstances. If not, Ian didn't know what he'd do.

He already did not know what he was to do when he returned with Jannet's daughter. Where were they to stay? How were they to support themselves? How was he supposed to figure all of this out by the day's end? And the question that led to all others—

What had possessed him to purchase the servants in the first place?

That one act had the potential to complicate his life for days, or possibly weeks or months to come. He didn't have days or weeks or months. He had only today, and unless he was *very* lucky at the tables tonight, he feared it wasn't going to be enough.

So much for my reform, he lamented. What other choice did he have if he wished to leave Mrs. Campbell with some means to provide for herself and her daughter at least a short while? He would not be cheating others of their money for himself, but for the support of a woman and child.

And if I am not lucky tonight? Ian knew he would not be able to sail tomorrow. He hadn't saved Mrs. Campbell and the lasses only to abandon them to a potentially worse fate. The *Iris* might as well have been sailing away this very moment for all the hope Ian felt of being able to, in good conscience, board before it did.

Yet looking down at the child in his arms, he could feel no regret at his impetuous decision. Perhaps it was that he'd been motherless too. Or that he'd lost both his father and brother as a youth. He knew what it was to be alone in a place where he was unwanted, and he could not knowingly send a child to a similar fate.

Another mile, and Ian's side ached. He set Aisla on the ground once more but kept her small hand in his, talking to her as they walked. He asked what her life had been like, where she had come from in Scotland. It seemed she was not a Campbell, or at least that she could remember. She didn't recall her father and had lived on a small farm with her mother until one day the soldiers came and took them away.

She hadn't minded much at first, because the soldiers gave them better food and more of it. But the ship had frightened her, and her mother had taken ill almost at once.

Ian gave her hand a little squeeze. "Such a braw lass." *Such an unfair world.* Had the soldiers let them alone, Aisla would still be living in her homeland with her mother.

He told her about his life when he was a lad—some of the more humorous stories of the mischief he and Collin had caused. Aisla said she wished she'd a sister or brother to get into mischief with. Ian told her that she would likely be around other children her age at her new home, but then warned her that she must be obedient or would likely have a consequence as he and Collin used to.

Ian found the idea of anyone hurting her troublesome and hoped his conscience would soon be eased, that the plantation would be all he hoped and more.

They'd walked near two hours when they found it. They left the road and started up a long, impressive drive lined with stately trees, and ending at an enormous house. It wasn't as imposing or grand as the castles in Scotland, but it also wasn't centuries old and built to house entire clans during times of siege.

This belongs to one *family.* It was difficult to imagine why a single family would need so much. It was also easy to see how such wealth was attained. Beyond the trees lining the drive, and past the great house, Ian noted the barren fields being prepared for another season—by slaves. Free labor.

The unease in his gut multiplied. If the Shurtleys owned

so many slaves, what was to say they would treat an indentured girl with any regard? Nevertheless, he and Aisla continued up the drive and onto the wide porch.

He raised his hand to knock, but the door swung open before he could. A young black woman, scarcely older than a child herself, asked his name, then admitted them inside. They were told to wait in a tiny room just off the foyer. Aisla bounced nervously on a chair, while Ian stood stiffly, his eyes taking in every inch of the space, from the patterned paper covering the walls to the portrait of an older gentle-man hanging over the fireplace.

"That was Mr. Shurtley's grandfather," a voice behind him said.

Ian turned abruptly, disliking the feeling of being caught off guard. A woman who did not appear to be much younger than the man in the portrait stood before him, her shrewd eyes already busy taking in every detail of both his and Aisla's appearance.

He began his explanation immediately. "Mrs. Shurtley?" He extended his hand.

Hers remained clasped firmly in front of her gown. "Mrs. Thurston. Head housekeeper for the Shurtleys. How may I help you, Mr.—"

"MacDonald," Ian replied, removing his hat, as much for some-thing for his rejected hand to do as out of politeness. "I am here about one of your new indentured servants—a lass of about this age." He turned sideways, indicating Aisla, who now sat properly still on the chair.

Ian summarized the situation as best he could, as quickly as he could, noting the frown marking Mrs. Thurston's lips becoming more pronounced the longer he spoke. No sooner had he finished than she gave her response.

"A trade will not be possible. The girl you speak of has already been trained and is busy at her duties. This is a demanding household, and I've no time for training another. Furthermore, had Mrs. Shurtley wished this child to be in her employ, she would have purchased her to begin with. The mistress is most particular about the girls who work here—only wants those with the plainest features, so she has fewer problems when they grow older. This child is far too fair of face to meet those qualifications. Good day, Mr. MacDonald. Nellie will see you out." Mrs. Thurston turned and exited the room.

Ian followed her into the foyer. "Have you any children, Mrs. Thurston?" It was a gamble, but the only ploy Ian could think of.

"I don't see how that is any of your concern, Mr. MacDonald." Her frosty reply was given with her stiff back still turned to him.

"The Campbell lass's mother has lost her husband and two sons. Her daughter is all she's left, and it is through no fault of their own that they ended up here. They were—"

"Nellie, please show these people out." Mrs. Thurston's heels clicked sharply on the wood floor as she moved off into another part of the house, a door swinging shut behind her.

Ian looked down at the hat in his hand, wondering what he was to do now. He didn't think Jannet Campbell's heart could take this. The only way he'd coaxed her from her melancholic stupor this morning was the promise that he would find her daughter and bring her back. And now it appeared he was not going to be able to make good on that promise.

"Might we see the child, at least," he asked the young woman, Nellie, who stood near the door waiting to open it for them. "To reassure her that her mother is in the area and thinking of her."

Nellie shook her head. "Missus would thrash me if I did that."

"Please," Ian said. He stepped closer, caught her eye.

She bit her lip and glanced behind her. "Alright," she whispered. "But not here. Not now. Meet me at the south pasture fence tonight. Eleven o'clock. Don't let no one see you coming."

Eleven o'clock tonight. He'd planned to be at the tables by then, or at the very least at the warehouse near the dock, acquiring an item or two with which to begin the night's gambling. But that would all be for naught if Jannet Campbell returned to her previous distress.

Ian gave a curt nod of acknowledgment. He took Aisla's hand in his, and they left the house.

"That lady wasn't very nice," she said as soon as the door had closed behind them and they'd one foot on the drive.

"Aye," Ian agreed. "Think no more on her. You'll not be staying here."

"Where *will* I be staying?" Aisla asked. "What will you tell Mrs. Campbell?"

"I don't know," Ian said.

She lapsed into silence, leaving Ian to his thoughts and plans that were becoming more complicated by the hour.

Kidnapping wasn't a new crime for Ian. Years ago he'd abducted a considerably older lass at the direction of the Munros. At the time he'd feared for his life, both from her father and the Munros, if he failed to deliver the lass. But he hadn't worried over her safety. She was a valuable commodity to both clans, and Ian knew that neither would harm her.

This time it was different. His own life seemed paltry compared to that of the child staring up at him from the other side of the fence. She'd arrived just a minute ago with Nellie and wore only a thin sleeping gown, her feet bare and filthy. Her hair was matted, and either dirt or a bruise—Ian couldn't quite tell which, with only the moonlight to see by—marred the left side of her face.

He peered past the two, into the dark field beyond, worrying that, if caught, harm would come to the child, given the obviously careless manner in which she'd already been treated.

"Taye?" he whispered, crouching down to peer at her through the fence slats. "Your mother Jannet sent me. She misses you something fierce. She needs you. Will you come with me to see her?" Ian glanced uneasily at Nellie, hopeful he'd been correct in guessing she intended more than bringing Taye to the fence for a moonlight chat.

The child stared at him a moment, then nodded. Nellie, with tears in her eyes, helped Taye over the fence.

"It's not right, taking babies from their mamas," Nellie declared. "You go now. Quick."

"Thank you," Ian said, worrying for her safety and guessing there was personal experience behind Nellie's declaration and tears.

"Are they likely to notice Taye is not abed?" he asked, wondering how long they might have before being followed.

Nellie shook her head. "No, sir. The little girls all sleep in the attic, and no one likes to go up there unless they have to. There's mice, and it's terrible cold. But I got half the floor to scrub still tonight. And if they find me gone—"

Ian could guess easily enough the risk she'd taken helping them. If found out she might be beaten, or worse.

"Thank you," he said, wishing he might bring her along as well. But the repercussions for stealing a slave would be great, and Nellie would not be easy to hide. With a last nod to her, he clasped Taye tightly to him and moved off toward the road, keeping just beyond it, in the shelter of the trees. As he hurried through the cold night he wrapped Jannet's thin cloak around her daughter, and the girl twined her arms about his neck.

"This is my mama's," she said, burrowing her face into the cloth.

"Aye. She sent it to keep you warm," Ian whispered. "And now we must be very quiet. Sleep if you're able. We've a long walk and must take care not to be seen or heard."

The child nodded and settled herself better in his arms.

So trusting. Had she known of his reputation, as Eliza did, no doubt she'd not have been as eager to go with him. But he intended to deliver her safely and had no motive, beyond that which he had started with originally—to reunite mother and child. It was the fulfilling of the sincerest wish he'd had for years as a youth himself—to be restored to his family, to Da and Collin.

"Why didn't my mama come for me herself?" Taye whispered when they'd been walking several minutes.

"She wanted to," Ian said. "But I needed her to stay behind. It was safer for all of us."

He'd given Jannet Campbell his oath that he'd bring her daughter back, if only she'd stay at the tavern with Aisla tonight. He couldn't leave the lass there alone, and she wasn't up to another four-hour trek. Neither did he wish Mrs. Campbell and the lass here to complicate the situation. If he was going to remove Taye from the plantation, going alone was his best chance at success.

Taye grew quiet again, and Ian plodded on, doing his best to ignore the pain in his side where the old wound still bothered him. His empty stomach pained him as well, and he worried that if absolute quiet became necessity, its grumbling might give them away.

They reached the edge of the Shurtley plantation, then walked past another and another after that. Judging by the time it had taken him both coming and going on this route earlier, Ian knew he was a quarter of the way back. *Back to . . . what?* This was the last night he had the room at The Young Devil. He had no money to pay for additional nights—even if they had been allowed to stay. It seemed unlikely, given the way he'd all but ignored the barkeep's reminder that no children were allowed on the premises.

Ian had no means, save the pistol at his side, to barter. No collateral with which to bet. He'd gone a day without food, as had Jannet and Aisla. He found it difficult to believe that less than twenty-four hours ago, he'd had a full belly, a pocketful of coins and bills, and the enjoyable prospect of home to look forward to. In attempting to do something right, everything seemed to have gone horribly wrong.

With his mind still circling around the same problems without solutions, he trudged on through the chill night. The movement kept him warm, but he worried about Taye and paused time and again to pull the cloak tighter around her. She'd fallen asleep as he'd hoped, and that suited him fine. Any minute he expected to hear someone after them, despite Nellie's insistence that Taye would not be missed until tomorrow morning.

By then he had to have her safely stowed in the upstairs room at The Young Devil—assuming he made it back in time to figure out a way to pay for another night.

A low branch struck his cheek as he passed, cutting it. He had no hand to raise to quell the bleeding but felt the trickle of blood down to his chin. *Better me than the child.* Compared to his throbbing side, the pain was inconsequential. As was the cut. It wasn't as if he'd a woman he was trying to impress.

Eliza. The image of her standing before him in front of the church appeared in his mind, but this time her smile lingered. She was pleased with him, pleased that he was doing something good with his life.

Is she *why I've done this?*

The thought was more than a little alarming. It had been his sorry experience that when a man began doing things with a woman in mind, he found himself in trouble.

And here I am. His mind railed against the idea that Eliza had anything to do with his decision at the wharf this morning. He'd felt drawn to help those people, and Eliza had nothing to do with it—excepting maybe that she was the one who'd opened his eyes and heart to the possibility of thinking about someone other than himself.

It was after three in the morning when the outskirts of Portsmouth at last came into view. Weary from his march earlier in the day and again tonight, Ian kept to the shadows as he carried the sleeping child the last distance to the tavern. It wouldn't do to be spotted by a Redcoat or other officer now. Two were stationed on the corner near the pub, forcing Ian to walk an extra block and circle around from the other side to enter the back.

The rear door to The Young Devil sat slightly ajar, almost as if it had been left open for him. Ian pushed on it and staggered inside, a delighted cry from within stopping him at once.

"Taye! You've really brought her." Jannet Campbell ran toward him, practically jumping over the empty tables in her haste to reach his side and her daughter.

Ian gladly handed over his burden, asleep until she'd heard her mother's voice. He stepped back as mother and daughter wept and clung to one another.

"Mama," the child sobbed as she clung to her.

"Oh, my baby, what have they done to you?" Jannet's hand smoothed over the tangled mass of her daughter's hair as her eyes took in the bruise on the child's face. "It doesn't matter now. You're here with me. Safe."

This, Ian thought as he looked on the tender scene. This was why he'd acted as he had. It was what he was meant to do, to help and provide for those who needed it. It was what his father had tried to teach him those many years ago, and Ian felt an overwhelming gratitude to realize that he *had* learned. He'd remembered that there was more to life beyond his own pitiful existence—remembered what it was to give and feel—before it was too late.

A sensation of well-being and warmth, the likes of which he'd never felt before, flooded his senses. His eyes smarted suddenly, as if he was standing too near a smoky fire.

Time to leave. He cleared his throat. "I'm going to go up and fetch my things."

"Oh no, you mustn't." Mrs. Campbell's alarm was palpable as she stood abruptly, Taye still held close to her skirt with one arm. "Aisla is—sleeping. You wouldn't want to disturb her."

"I'll be quiet," Ian said, taking a step toward the stairs. Maybe he'd lie on the floor himself an hour or two until sunrise. He'd think better with a clear head. About the only thing clear right now was that he wasn't going to be able to sail tomorrow as planned. He couldn't leave a helpless woman and two children on their own to fend for them-selves.

"No." Mrs. Campbell grabbed his arm. "Don't disturb her. It would be better now if you just left. Isn't there a ship you're supposed to be on soon?" She added the last in a whisper.

"Aye. The *Iris*." Ian shrugged out of her grasp but kept his eye on the stairs. His suspicions aroused. "Where is Aisla?"

"Upstairs," Jannet said, straightening her back, as if affronted. "Where else would she be?"

"You tell me," Ian said. "What is going on?"

"Nothing." She pressed Taye closer to her. "Nothing at all. You should go."

He felt she was trying to tell him something with her eyes, but he could not fathom what it was. Didn't she understand that he could *not* leave now? What kind of man would abandon a woman in such circumstances?

"I'm to sail away, and just leave you here without purse or station? What will you do then? Continue to stay on at The Young Devil?"

"That's exactly what she'll do." Mr. Kent, the tavern owner said, as he came in through the front door.

Why had he been outside at this hour of the morning?

"Privy," Kent mumbled, as if he'd guessed Ian's thoughts. He closed the door behind him and barred it. "I've hired Mrs. Campbell to cook. Her work this evening proved she'll do nicely."

Again, Ian felt suspicious. The privy was out back. Why would Kent come in through the front door?

And moreover—*Jannet Campbell working at the The*

Young Devil? Ian could not imagine how that might have come about. He studied the woman still clutching her daughter in a tight embrace, the tears barely dry on her cheeks. He'd witnessed her enthusiasm at the reunion, but it was still difficult to believe Mrs. Campbell had taken the initiative to find employment on her own, given the trance-like soul he'd first spoken with this morning.

"We'll be all right," she said, as if answering his unspoken question regarding her change. "I thank you kindly, Mr. MacDonald, for returning my Taye to me. And now I've to see to her needs—and that of the other lass as well."

"Aye." Ian's gaze again drifted to the stairs. "The lasses will need to stay well out of sight. If even one man were to discover them it could lead to great trouble."

"Don't want no trouble," Mr. Kent said with a clap of his hands and a wary glance toward the door.

"Have a drink before you go, Mr. MacDonald." Jannet took a cup from the table and handed it to Ian.

He looked longingly at the amber liquid. If nothing else, it would warm him. "I can't pay for it."

Mr. Kent swatted the air in front of him. "It's on the house."

Ian's brows rose. He hadn't taken the man for the generous type, not with the way he'd callously dealt with several of the patrons the past week.

"One good turn deserves another." Mr. Kent broke off, a forced smile on his face.

"I'm tired, Mama," Taye said.

"Of course, dear. I'll take you up to bed."

Jannet started to turn away, then paused. "I am grateful to you, Mr. MacDonald." She stepped forward and touched his cheek gently where the branch had sliced it. "Take ye care." Her eyes flickered to his briefly; then she stepped back to her daughter's side.

"You, as well," Ian said, perplexed by her display of affection and many changing moods. Something about both

Jannet and Mr. Kent seemed off, but he couldn't say what. Or maybe it was just that he was exhausted, after two nights without sleep and a day with no sustenance.

He felt oddly dismissed, no longer needed here—if Mr. Kent and Mrs. Campbell had truly worked out on their own the problem he'd been mulling over all day and night, and merely wished him to go now.

Nothing left to do, then. Ian supposed he could sleep on the *Iris* as well as on the floor upstairs. He threw back the drink quickly, eager for the warmth it would start in his empty stomach. His eagerness was rewarded at once with a fire that started in his throat and burned its way down. His eyes watered, and it was all he could do not to choke as he placed his cup on the closest table.

"That's the good stuff," Kent said. "Save it for special occasions."

"Almost as good as MacDonald whisky," Ian lied. Tipping his hat, he bid a final farewell to The Young Devil and its occupants, then stepped outside into the cool air.

It was time to go home.

Chapter Twenty-one

Aboard *The Cleopatra*, the Atlantic Ocean, April 1762

Something brushed against my lips, partly covering my mouth. I tried to move my head away from it, only to find that it was cloth and continued along the sides of my face, then wound around my body as well. My fingers flexed, as if to move the offending fabric, and I discovered my arms bound at my sides within the sheet as well. I was lying flat, tipped back slightly, head angled down, causing the cloth to slip over my chin and lips.

Utterly confused, I forced my eyes open and saw the most brilliant blue sky above. I bounced a little as the floor beneath me moved and the stark white of an enormous sail swept into my line of view.

The *Cleopatra*. Memory slammed into me as roughly as the swinging sail had changed tack. *They're going to toss me overboard!*

"I'm not dead." My cry came out as little more than a whisper from a dry, scratchy throat. I moved both hands, fighting against my confinement.

"Collin, come quick!" Timothy shouted beside me. "Katie's awake."

He was there in seconds, bent over me, kissing my forehead, tears falling on my cheeks. "Thank the heavens. Timothy, go find Mrs. Parker. *Hurry.*"

Timothy scampered away, out of view.

"I'm not dead," I said once more.

"Of course not." Collin attempted a smile crossed with a

look of severity. "I'd be a poor sort of husband to allow any such thing. And in case you're still of a mind to try anything close to it again, know that I forbid it."

His words brought little relief to my panic. "You weren't intending to throw me in the sea?" My own tears started, leaking down the sides of my face.

"*No.*" Collin's fervent denial, along with the jerk of his head and his look of shocked horror, convinced me he spoke the truth. Realization of my thought process must have hit Collin, because he began frantically unwrapping me.

"It was my idea to bundle you so. Mrs. Parker had mentioned something about us having sorrow enough with no infant to swaddle, and I had the idea that we must do such for you. You'd lost so much blood. I wrapped you so you wouldn't move. You needed to be still until the bleeding had stopped. I lay you outside for the fresh sea air, and we tipped you slightly, to keep blood flowing to your head. You'd lost so much already, lost consciousness and—"

"It's all right." I placed my just-released hand upon his arm. The fear was palpable in his voice and words. My own fear still pulsed in my head, and I stared up at the blue sky, seeking calm.

It came slowly, in stages. *Collin won't let me die.* I breathed a little easier. *I'll not be thrown in the sea.* I willed my heartbeat to slow. *Our child is gone.* My tears began in earnest, silent sobs from a throat too swollen to do more. Gooseflesh sprang up along my arms as the last layer of blanket was removed and the cool air reached my skin.

"Have I hurt you?" Collin asked anxiously. "What is it, Katie? What do you need?"

"Our baby." My chest convulsed with sorrow.

"It's all right. It doesn't matter." Collin bent close, arms around me, gathering me to him without actually picking me up.

It did matter, though, and we both knew it. This pregnancy had nearly killed me, and I doubted either of us had the courage to risk another—if that were even possible after what I had been through. Lydia's loss was still fresh in my mind and heart, and in Collin's, too, I guessed.

"Will we never be blessed with a child?" I wailed, aching to hold the unseen babe we had lost as much as I still ached to hold Lydia.

"It doesn't matter if we are or are not," Collin reiterated. "What is important is that you are well, that you are alive, Katie. *You* are what I live for, the one I need. You frightened me so."

So he had thought I might die. I wondered how close I had come and if it might have been better, if Collin then might have had a chance for children with another wife, one of sturdier composition. *Someone like Mhairi.* That thought made me cry even harder.

"Don't cry," Collin begged. "Try not to. Don't think on it now. You must concentrate on getting better. I need you strong when we arrive in Nova Scotia. Think of your maps you've drawn and the distance we must travel. It will be like our wedding trip all over again. The two of us in the mountain glens, traveling together and discovering places of astounding beauty that not many have seen. Surviving on fish and oatmeal . . ." He held my face in his hands and smiled bravely.

I tried to do the same, for his sake. But inside I felt only loss. I had imagined us traipsing this new land together, but with my stomach heavy with our child, or perhaps with the babe carried in Collin's arms. I had envisioned the house we would build, and the cradle, like Lydia's left behind, that Collin would lay our child in to sleep.

I thought again of Mrs. Parker's explanation for our loss, that something was wrong with our child. I could not bring myself to believe that, but rather felt the blame lay with me.

Something is wrong with me. God is punishing me. It did not take long to realize why, or to feel the guilt begin to weigh me down along with grief.

The years I had been selfish, the times I had yearned for

the life of a spinster and an artist were returning to haunt me. I had shunned the idea of marriage and children, and God had not forgotten.

"I didn't know," I whispered. *I didn't mean it.* I hadn't really known what I wanted then.

"What is it?" Collin lifted his head from its place pressed close to mine. "What didn't you know?"

"How much I could hurt."

Chapter Twenty-two

Portsmouth, Virginia, April 1762

He was leaving. Really going home. *Back to Collin. To the MacDonalds. To Scotland.* For some reason those thoughts didn't garner the same excitement he'd felt just a day ago. Possibly because, rather suddenly, he wasn't feeling well at all.

Ian held a hand to his head and staggered slightly as he covered the blocks to the wharf. Kent's whisky might not have tasted good, but it had a punch. That, combined with his exhaustion and empty stomach, had Ian starting to feel like the village jakey. No doubt he looked like it as well, with two days' growth on his face and his clothes dirty from the day's travel. *Penniless and pathetic.* His fall from grace certainly hadn't taken long.

Scotland. He sought for the yearning for home that had been his just a day ago. But his eagerness to return was somehow tainted. Leaving felt almost wrong, as if he had unfinished business here. Even fuzzy as his head felt, Ian didn't have to think long to realize the source of his guilt.

He'd promised the lass, Aisla, that he would look out for her, had promised she would be safe. Yet he'd just walked away, without so much as seeing her again. He'd done the same to another lass, long ago, and his not returning had cost her life.

This is different. He'd not left Aisla with Munros, for one thing. She had Jannet Campbell to look after her as well. *And indefinite days or weeks—or longer—locked in a room in a tavern to look forward to.* What would the child think when she awoke and learned he had gone?

What if Mrs. Campbell did not truly look after her as she'd promised? What if something had already gone afoul, and that was why she had been against Ian's returning to the upstairs room?

Ian's recently returned conscience worked overtime now, assuaging him with arguments as to why he should remain in Portsmouth at least a few days more—a week or two at best, he reasoned—to see that the child was safe and truly cared for.

Ian brought a hand to his aching head, wishing—for the first time in his life—that he hadn't indulged in drink. His stomach was beginning to complain as well, with waves of nausea rolling over him.

Despite the cool temperature, sweat broke out along his brow. Ian clutched his stomach. He wasn't going to make it to the wharf. Maybe this was fate's way of forcing him to stay a little longer to keep his promise and see the lass truly safe.

I will. I swear. Ian gave the silent vow to whomever or whatever might be listening and inflicting such agony upon him. "I'll stay. I'll honor my promise. Only let me see about getting at least a portion of my passage refunded first." He'd no illusion about getting all £8 back, but perhaps a little of it might be returned to him, for the food he would not use.

The thought of any sort of food at all, and particularly the less-than-palpable fare offered at sea, was enough to push him over the edge into true sickness. With sloppy steps, Ian careened off the dark street and behind the bushes lining someone's property, where his stomach promptly and efficiently rid itself of the drink and all else he'd consumed in the past forty-eight hours.

Clutching his gut, he collapsed on the stiff grass, feeling only slightly better and utterly exhausted. He allowed his eyes to close, trying to gather his strength, while lamenting that the whisky had tasted even worse the second time around.

Voices and the marching of feet woke him suddenly. From behind the row of bushes, Ian watched as six sets of black polished boots passed. The tails of red coats were visible above the boots, and, when he raised his head just a little, their shouldered muskets were as well.

The cold sweat was back, and suddenly he was in Scotland again, body pressed into the grass on the edge of Culloden Moor. Any minute now it would begin. And then, less than an hour later—minutes that would seem like hours or even days—it would be over.

It is over. Pull yourself together, lad.

His father's voice. He heard it as clearly as if Da were right beside him. Ian found himself turning his head just to be sure. Against all logic, he felt keen disappointment at not seeing his father. Though that would have been an even surer sign of madness.

I cannot be far from it now. He blamed it on the drink he'd been given. Who knows how long Mr. Kent had owned that bottle or from whence it came.

Liquor may be the next vice I forswear. Ian scowled as he brought a hand to his pounding head and took in his surroundings. He still lay beneath the hedge. It was no longer full dark, yet neither had the dawn arrived. The small group of soldiers had moved on. It was time he did too, before the *Iris* set sail without him even having a chance to plead his case for a refund.

Moving slowly, so as not to split his throbbing head in two, Ian began to sit up, only to freeze as two more sets of boots came into view, this time with voices accompanying.

"The woman tipped him off. That's all there is to it."

Millet? Ian angled his gaze upward through the hedge

and glimpsed Millet's offensive sideburns, along with the rest of him, approaching.

"The tavern keeper swears she did not."

"Who's to say he was not an accomplice as well?" Millet said.

"Neither had any reason to aid MacDonald," the man beside him said. "Neither sought association with a murderer. Though I see now you were right. We should not have trusted them to detain him. We should have confronted him ourselves and would have done so if I'd believed we might without risking harm to the child."

"Little good your agreement does us now," Millet snapped. "The child does not matter. Another Highland waif—useless there *or* here. One less of that species would only be a good thing. And now your tender sensibilities have allowed a murderer to slip through your fingers."

"Rest assured that I feel tender no more, toward the child or anyone else involved with this criminal. We will have him yet."

"Let us hope so, Lieutenant. Or I fear you may find yourself serving in another, less-desirable position."

Ian's tongue felt thick in his dry throat. They had to be speaking of Mr. Kent and Jannet Campbell and her daughter. *Or Aisla.*

He shouldn't have left her there, a child all alone in a strange country, in a tavern, of all places, and with no one to look out for her. He'd seen exactly how much care Jannet Campbell was likely to give the lass. She'd hardly been aware of Aisla yesterday morning and had certainly not exhibited any motherly affection toward her.

Why *did I leave her?* Ian berated himself and fought rising panic. He'd not had a choice. Mrs. Campbell and Mr. Kent had practically forced him out of the building. *Why?* Had they been trying to help him or to see him captured?

Take care, Mrs. Campbell had said. Ian recalled the fleeting, but peculiar way she'd looked at him. *A warning?*

"I still say he's on that ship," Millet's companion said. "After all, he hid under *your* nose for how many weeks?"

"My *considerations* toward a certain female interfered with common sense," Millet said irritably. "I knew extra rations were being taken below, but I thought them only for the sick. Had I known a common criminal was being kept alive, I would have put a stop to it—to him—immediately. But as to MacDonald's already being on the *Iris,* I find that doubtful. And if he is, the captain has promised to hang MacDonald himself. There will be no merciful female to hide him this time."

Another reply was made to this, but the men had moved off too far down the street for Ian to hear any additional conversation, and he dared not follow.

Instead, he lay flat in the grass again, grateful for the sparse hedge that hid him, grateful even for the sour whisky that had curdled in his stomach and set him retching here, out of sight.

Or had it just been sour? Ian wondered uneasily if Mr. Kent had added something more. *Something that made me both unsteady and ill.* The more Ian thought on it, the more he felt certain that must be the case. He was a MacDonald. He'd been drinking whisky practically since he was a bairn and had never had a problem holding his own before.

It appeared that sometime since his meeting with Millet yesterday, his identity had been discovered. *Millet knew where I was staying. How? Eliza? Stay away from me,* she'd said, along with encouraging him to leave and to be careful. *Was that only because she was angry with me?* Or had she also been warning him about Millet? *When was the body discovered?* And when it was, had Millet sought Eliza out because of that? Ian rolled over and laid his head back against the damp grass, mind and vision spinning.

Aisla, Eliza, Jannet Campbell, and her daughter might all be in peril because of him. And there was not a blessed thing he could do, except to turn himself in. *For murder. I'll hang for certain.*

The irony was painful. He'd hang for killing a man while trying to defend a woman. *Even when I try to do good it turns out wrong.*

Chapter Twenty-three

Portsmouth, Virginia, April 1762

L et this be the right decision. Ian buried his pounding head in his hands as a sort of helpless prayer filled his mind. He couldn't turn himself in. He'd not trade his life for others' presumed safety. Not in this circumstance. He wasn't his father. He'd known that for years, but never more so than in this moment. But for the first time this didn't bother him.

In giving his life to spare his sons, Ian MacDonald had also left them alone in the world to survive and suffer through what may be. And while Collin had done fairly well with his lot . . . Ian's had been little short of hell.

He wouldn't do that to Aisla.

Neither could he turn himself in, knowing that would leave Millet unchecked in his pursuit of Eliza. Ian knew his plan was a gamble, but if his luck held and he played his hand right, he'd end up not only with his neck still intact, but having seen to Mrs. Campbell's and the lasses' safety—something he definitely could *not* do if he was dead. *As for Eliza's well-being . . .*

Ian hoped that for now her position as an indentured servant would offer a measure of protection from the likes of Millet.

And if not . . . Ian wasn't above abducting her himself if that's what it took to keep her safe. What was one more crime added to his already long list?

He struggled to a crouching position, silently cursing every move that intensified the throbbing in his skull. Even the slightest motion blurred his vision, and his stomach convulsed, though it was long since empty.

Fight it, he ordered himself. He was stronger than whatever ailed him. Keeping low, Ian made his way along the street, via the shrubbery growing there. The spring blossoms were in full bloom, offering more protection than he would have had a week or two past. At the end of the block he made a sharp turn, in the opposite direction of the wharf. There would be no refund from the captain of the *Iris* now, and certainly no passage to Scotland, even had he wished it.

Instead Ian returned to the church where he had last seen Eliza. He didn't know exactly where the millinery was, but he knew which direction she had been walking when she left the church, and that was as good a place to start as any.

Twelve hours later Ian wished he had not located Perkins Millinery quite so easily. Since early morning he'd been hiding beneath the small porch outside the back door—which he guessed led to a kitchen or private living quarters behind the shop. Multiple times throughout the day Mrs. Perkins had come out that door and visited the privy at the back corner of the small yard, but not once had Eliza come outside. Ian was cramped, and seeing no sign of Eliza had him worried. What if Millet had arrived earlier and taken her on the premise of questioning?

Dark covered the yard now. Ian pondered the benefits of knocking on the door versus confronting Mrs. Perkins outside when she next left the house. He didn't want to scare her or have her alert others to his presence, but Ian had to know where Eliza was.

Before he'd fully made his decision, the back door opened again. This time the step across the boards above him was light. A pale pink skirt swished briefly into view, and Ian made out the flicker of a candle as it bobbed across the yard.

Eliza?

He wasted no time scrambling from beneath the porch, then hiding around the corner of the house, so as to be able to step out and confront Eliza—if it was she—but not so close as to frighten her when she returned. Once situated, he waited. And waited. Minutes passed, and she did not reappear.

"Don't move." The barrel of a pistol rammed into his back, but the voice accompanying it made his heart leap for a different reason.

Heedless of the order and any weapon, he spun to face his assailant and grabbed the still-warm end of the candle Eliza had thrust at him.

"This way." She grabbed his hand and towed him toward a lean-to on the side of the house. Once there she opened the door and motioned him inside.

Ian hesitated, uncertain what—or who—might be waiting for him.

"I'm alone," she whispered, as if sensing his mistrust. She stepped through the doorway first, leaving him behind to follow if he would.

"Mind the steps and your head." Her warning came a few seconds too late—after Ian's still-aching head had grazed the top of the low doorway.

"Close the door behind you," Eliza ordered, and this time he did not hesitate.

The moonlight disappeared with the closed door, leaving them in complete darkness.

Just like on the ship. Ian hugged the wall and managed to keep his balance as he
descended a short set of steep stairs. He reached the floor, his foot tapping in front of him to make sure he was on solid ground.

"Eliza?" He held his hands out in front of him.

"*Ian* MacDonald." She spoke his name differently than the last time they'd met. The edge had gone from her voice and in its place he would have sworn he heard—admiration.

She bumped his outstretched arms. The candle clattered to the ground near their feet, and the next second her hands were on his face. Her lips pressed against his. Ian scarcely had time to register their warmth and softness or the surge of yearning and desire that spread like wildfire from his lips all the way to his toes, before she'd pulled away again.

He stood speechless, still trying to come to terms with the fact that she'd snuck up on him outside, and now that—*kiss.*

He could think of only one reason for such behavior— she must feel guilt for betraying him. *A trap.* Ian's back stiffened as the hairs behind his neck stood on end.

He reached blindly, grabbed her shoulders and thrust her aside, his pistol drawn as he peered through the dark.

"I'm alone," she said once more. He didn't believe it until he'd traversed the narrow space and discovered only barrels and shelves.

Behind him the candle flickered to life, its feeble flame illuminating the tiny storeroom and Eliza's face. Her eyes were alight with a curious mixture of anxiety and joy, and she smiled encouragingly.

"All alone, see."

Ian put the pistol away. "Then what was all that for? Why did you sneak up on me?" He'd thought the effects of whatever he'd had to drink in the wee hours of the morning had finally worn off, but maybe not, the way his head was spinning again.

"You don't think I've managed to keep my skirts down and my neck intact this long by being daft, do you?" The hand not holding the candle went to her hip, and her mouth turned down to scowl at him. "Or have you forgotten what my laird was like?"

"I've not," Ian said, recalling Collin's tales of Brann.

"I didn't know who you were, at first," Eliza continued. "Only that I was not alone in the yard—you made such a ruckus coming out from under the step. I crept round the side to see who or what it was."

"Oh," Ian said, abashed at his carelessness. He could ill afford such blunders. "I don't—seem to be myself today."

"Had a bit of drink from Jannet Campbell, did ye?" Eliza asked. "Don't worry. The effects will not be permanent."

"She *did* try to poison me," Ian whispered, furious, even as he wondered how Eliza had come upon this information. *After all I did to help her.*

"Did she mean to poison you, you'd be dead." Eliza thrust the candle at him. "Hold this."

Ian took it from her and watched as she extracted a long dipper from a barrel near the outside wall. "I expect you're thirsty." She took the candle back and handed him the dipper.

He eyed it warily but, at Eliza's exasperated expression, finally lifted it to his mouth and gulped the cool water gratefully. When it was empty, twice more he filled it and drank again, noting the pipe that ran from the barrel up through the roof.

"We've not much in the way of a meal in here." Eliza raised her eyes to the ceiling and the hanging braids of onion and garlic. "But there are apples in the bins behind you. You're welcome to those."

Ian didn't wait for a second invitation, but took three apples—one for each of his pockets, and one to eat now. He took a large bite, the crisp peel and juicy insides tasting better than anything he'd eaten in a long while.

Eliza's eyes widened as she watched him devour the apple. "Oh, and I've this too, if you'd like." She set the candle on a barrel, then withdrew a cloth from her pocket, unwrapped it, and handed Ian the piece of bread.

"You were expecting someone, or just saving a bite for later?" He bit into the stale bread, still wary and uncertain what had brought about this change in her behavior from the last time he'd seen her.

"Neither. There's a family of ducks at the stream just beyond the yard. Mrs. Perkins lets me take the end pieces to break off and feed to them. The shop was busy today, and I never got around to it."

Ian imagined Eliza, bent over a stream, casting bread at a baby duck. It was a pleasant image and, if she spoke the truth, gave him hope that her life here was somewhat pleasant. "I've robbed the ducks of their meal." He wiped the crumbs from his lips and took yet another dipperful of water.

"No matter," Eliza said. "I believe you needed it more."

"Aye." Though he still felt ravenous, the gnawing ache of hunger had dissipated somewhat. Conversing with Eliza again was as near to heaven as he was likely to ever get, but he feared lingering overlong. She might not have cooperated with Millet to lay a trap, but that didn't mean the man wasn't watching the house or likely to come around. The last thing Ian wanted to do was to cause her trouble. "Won't Mrs. Perkins wonder that you've not returned to the house yet?"

"Oh no." Eliza shook her head. "She's abed already, and she could sleep through anything—snores something fierce too."

This both comforted and worried Ian. Eliza might not be missed tonight, but if she was in trouble and needed help, who would be there to hear her cries?

"What you did just now was wise," he said. "Not returning to the house the way you'd come, when you suspected someone else was outside."

"A good thing one of us was using her mind," she scolded.

"You didn't let me finish," he said in a tone that matched hers. "Wise to beware, but what were you thinking being alone out here at night? And then sneaking up on a man like that. You could have been easily overcome by Millet or anyone else wishing to do you harm."

"I'd my Sgian Dubh." A swish of fabric, a flash of metal, and Ian felt the prick of a knife at his throat.

"You ought to have used that instead of the candle," he

said, angry at himself and his second act of carelessness in minutes.

"I didn't wish to harm you." Eliza's tone and the continued feel of the metal against his neck said otherwise. "You do enough of that yourself. It's a fine kettle of trouble you've brewed the past few days."

"Aye . . ." he agreed slowly. So she *was* still angry with him. "I mean to end thieving as soon as possible, but there are circumstances that—"

"I ken what you've done, *Ian* MacDonald."

There it was again, that peculiar way she was saying his name. *A signal to someone nearby?* They were mostly whispering, but that didn't mean that someone outside might not hear—or see light between the cracks in the chinking.

"You used your money to buy Jannet and Aisla their freedom." The knife moved away at last, tucked once more into Eliza's skirt. "It was noble—something like your brother, like Collin, would have done. When I heard—" Eliza broke off suddenly as if unable to speak. She took his hands and clutched them in hers.

Ian felt his world shift out of focus a little more. *Keep your head.* He spoke quietly. "How do you know this? Who told you? I wasn't aware that you knew Mrs. Campbell well." He wove his fingers through Eliza's, lest she had any ideas about getting away without answering his questions.

"We are both Campbells, both prisoners these many months," Eliza said. "Of course I know Jannet and her daughter. I had not known what became of them until yesterday evening, when Officer Millet paid me another visit."

"*Another?* How many times has he come to see you?" It was as Ian had feared. Eliza's indenture had not ceased Millet's harassment.

"It's a braw thing you did for Jannet and her daughter, and Aisla too," Eliza continued, ignoring Ian's question. "If only you hadn't tried to buy their freedom with Officer Millet's own money."

"What do you mean *his* money?" Ian asked. "I paid him £14, every last note and coin I had."

"The very *same* coin you stole from him the day you left the *Ulysses?*" Eliza's brows rose as she looked up at him, scolding again. "If you are going to steal from a man you shouldn't try to purchase something from him with his very own money."

"How was I to know Millet marks his coin?" Ian asked, perplexed and doubtful it was even true. He hadn't noticed anything unusual about any of the money he'd collected— only that it varied, with everything from British pound notes to Virginian printed money to both Spanish and English coins.

"Had you but studied the coins, you might have noticed," Eliza said. "Officer Millet's were Portuguese, instead of the more common Spanish dollar that circulates here. He'd acquired them on a recent voyage and had taken them out for only a short while, to show an acquaintance who had come aboard."

Once again Ian was astounded at how much Eliza knew of Millet's affairs. When and how she had discovered all of this alarmed him.

"The coins disappeared but minutes after he'd set them out—near the same time that Mrs. Perkins came looking for a woman to work in the millinery. Officer Millet had given up hope of retrieving them, until—"

"I placed them in his hand yesterday."

"Aye." Eliza sighed.

Ian closed his eyes and leaned his head forward, once more abashed at his carelessness. "It is good I've vowed to leave off thieving, as apparently I'm no good at it anymore." He opened his eyes to find Eliza's face directly in front of him, her forehead nearly touching his.

"*Why* have you vowed to leave that life behind?"

"You saved me for better, and it is not what I was raised to be."

Her mouth curved upward. "Ian." This time his name was but a whisper, carried on a sigh. Her gaze drifted to his lips, and the heat he'd felt at the unexpected kiss rose in him once more. A minute ago he might have said he imagined that the kiss had happened at all, but now . . .

"The other day at the church, when I was clean-shaven, dressed fine and, well—*clean*—you made it very clear what you thought of me, that you never wanted to see me again and even regretted saving me. You said even Millet was better."

She squeezed his hands. "I oughtn't ha—"

"Let me finish." He returned a light pressure with his fingertips. "Tonight, I crawl out of a vermin hole, disheveled and filthy, a wanted, a *hunted* man, not a shilling to my name, not a thing in the world to offer, and you . . . kiss me?" Maybe it was *because* of that, Ian realized. *She feels sorry for me.*

"It wasn't really a kiss," Eliza protested.

"No?" Ian asked. "Where I come from that's what we call it."

"I meant it as a thank you—for what you've done, for Jannet Campbell and her daughter."

"A thank you," Ian mused. "Where I come from that is done differently as well. Is this a long-standing tradition among Campbells? If so, I wonder how Collin has taken to his wife kissing other men when she sees fit to show gratitude for something." He was teasing now, but Eliza did not yet realize it.

"It was perhaps a bit more than gratitude." She tried to pull away, but he would not let her. "The other day when you told me you were Ian . . ."

"You were furious." The sting of her rebuke was still fresh in his mind, and again he thought to wonder at this turn of events, this conversation he was having with her.

Eliza nodded, and their heads touched. She kept hers looking down, so he could not see her face.

"I *was* angry, but I was also relieved."

That was the last thing he'd expected her to say. "How so?" Were all women this curious?

"I was relieved because . . ." She shrugged. "I realized that I hadn't—fallen in love with another woman's husband."

It was as if a cloak of silence descended upon them at her confession. Neither spoke for what had to be a full minute, though Ian's heart thudded so loudly he felt certain she must hear it.

Did she—had she meant? There was only one way to find out.

Withdrawing one of his hands from hers, he whispered her name. "Eliza?" It came out in that same, breathless sort of way she had spoken his, and now he understood.

With his free hand Ian tipped her chin up, then bent to touch his lips to hers in a kiss that was about much more than gratitude. Weeks of desire, his thirst for her, the affection he felt, his desire to protect, to never leave her side—all surged forth in the movement of his mouth upon hers.

And miracle of miracles, Eliza responded willingly. Her hand came up to touch the hair at the base of his neck. He held her other hand close to his pounding heart. She tilted her head sideways, allowing their kiss to deepen, and as it did her fingers grasped his shirt as if she, too, never wished to leave his side.

Her lips were warm and welcoming, her yearning and desire seeming to match his.

"Eliza."

"Ian."

They spoke at near the same time when at last they'd stopped for breath. She threw her arms about his neck. His went around her waist, holding her as close as possible. Her hair was soft against the side of his cheek. She smelled of flowers, and she was oh, so warm against him.

"Come away with me," he whispered. "We'll go somewhere far. I'll find honest employment and earn a wage. We'll save until we have enough to sail home again."

Her head moved against his shirt, and not in the direction he'd hoped.

"I can't, Ian. I gave my word that I would serve this indenture."

"You don't owe a life of slavery to anyone," he protested.

She leaned back to look up at him. "Perhaps not, but if I leave, what becomes of Jannet and Taye? Of Aisla?"

Aisla. How could he have forgotten so quickly? He couldn't leave them. It wasn't the kind of thing a man Eliza loved would do. It wasn't what *he* wanted to do.

"We'll bring them with us," he said, already scheming about what kind of disguise he might need to enter The Young Devil once more.

Eliza shook her head again. "Millet would find you. He's watching them closely now. He would have taken them back to the *Ulysses* had the owner of the tavern not paid Millet to let them stay."

"Mr. Kent?" Ian was surprised to learn this. Perhaps the man *was* on his side. *He didn't turn me in.* And those soldiers Ian had seen near the front of the tavern—perhaps they had something to do with Mr. Kent being outside in the middle of the night.

Eliza nodded, as if she was following Ian's thought process. "He helped you escape, and so did Jannet. It was all they could do to send the soldiers who were nearby after a false lead."

"And that drink they gave me?"

"Let's just say that the Campbell women carry other weapons aside from our wee blades. We're well versed in the use of various plants and herbs." Eliza sounded a bit smug. "Some of which can have a negative effect upon a person."

"Negative," Ian barked. "I thought my very insides were going to be pulled from within. And the pounding in my head—it was horrible."

"But you survived, and you did not make it to your ship, where Officer Millet and others lay in wait."

Ian thought on this a moment. If what Eliza said was true, he felt better for not having been betrayed by Jannet Campbell. "I suppose I must thank her for that, for poisoning me."

"Aye, but not with a kiss." Eliza tipped her face to his once more in invitation. Ian kissed her again, half certain this was some sort of incredible dream, a hallucination caused by whatever drug Mrs. Campbell had put in his drink. Perhaps he would thank her and ask her for more. Whatever he'd suffered before, it was worth it to so vividly imagine Eliza in his arms.

Chapter Twenty-four

Aboard the *Cleopatra,* Atlantic Ocean, April 1762

"Please, Timothy, no. I cannot possibly eat another date." I pushed the fruit away, still feeling the taste and texture of the previous one in my mouth.

"Mrs. Parker says they'll help," Collin said as he joined us. At Timothy's pleading look, Collin waved him away. "Stay close, and keep out of mischief."

"I will." Timothy scampered off, and I let him go, too weak and lethargic to do otherwise. His care and tending had fallen entirely to Collin.

"Now then, about this date." Collin placed one in his open palm. "Sweet and chewy, a veritable treat out here in the middle of the Atlantic."

"I've had one today." I made no move to take the fruit and instead turned my head away.

"I'm trying to see you well again," Collin said. "You needn't be so stubborn, Katie. Mrs. Parker is only trying to help as well. She promises the dates will aid in easing your bleeding. Weren't you the one telling me a few weeks ago how knowledgeable she is, how many babies she has delivered?"

"I was not delivered of a baby." My eyes welled with tears. I wasn't stubborn but sad. Couldn't he see that? What did it matter if I ate the fruit or not? My body had failed me, had failed *us.* I felt defeated.

I squeezed my eyes shut and breathed shallow little breaths, holding in my grief as best I could, when really I felt like keening loudly, as the MacDonalds had done some months past, at what they had believed to be Collin's burial.

Somehow I had recovered from that, and I told myself I must recover from this as well. But it felt different. Sorrow flowed through my veins as surely as the blood flowing there, and I had no notion how to rid myself of it.

It was as if my excitement for life, and my will to live it, had left with our child. The only things I seemed capable of were crying and sleeping. I couldn't seem to bring myself to care about anything more—even Collin or Timothy or my health.

Collin sighed, then removed the date from in front of me and took my hand in his. "You're freezing."

I shrugged. I didn't care about that either. It could have been pouring rain on my head, and I wouldn't have felt it mattered.

He adjusted the blanket that had slid below my shoulders and pulled it tighter around me, then held it in place with his arm supporting me. "Come back to me, Katie. Please."

I glanced up at his profile, strong jawline, dark tousled hair, straight nose. *Handsome,* I thought without emotion, though I tried to recall how looking at him used to make me feel. I struggled, searching for an emotion other than sadness until exhaustion over-whelmed me. I leaned into Collin and allowed my eyes to close and whatever feeling I'd been grasping for to slip away entirely.

He would be better off without me. The one coherent thought, the only thing that registered in my mind when I thought of Collin, returned again.

Without me... It was probably only a matter of time.

Chapter Twenty-five

Norfolk, Virginia, April 1762

Ian grasped the knob and pushed open the door to the cooper's shop, then stepped from the weathered planks of the wharf into what felt like his past, as the tangy smell of fresh-cut wood and shavings overtook the less pleasant aromas outside.

Overhead a bell tinkled, though the gray-haired, wiry-looking man seated at a stave horse had already looked up from his work and taken note of Ian.

"May I help you?" he asked.

"I am hopeful to be of some help to you," Ian said. "Though being employed would be a great benefit to me as well." Both memory and possibility stirred within him as he took in the metal hoops hanging on the walls and the boards stacked beneath.

"Come about the sign, have you?" The thin, middle-aged man inclined his head toward the window, where the notice for help wanted was posted.

"Aye," Ian said, forgetting to mask his brogue. "Are you Rogers?"

"I am. Where you from?" he asked, setting aside a stave and reaching for another.

"Scotland. The Highlands," Ian added. No point in lying about that. No shame in it either. What he wouldn't be sharing was that, in the town just across the river, he was a man wanted for murder.

"Hmm," Rogers said, sounding neither pleased nor put off. "Have you any experience?"

"Some," Ian said. "In my youth."

"Go on," Rogers said, continuing his work.

Ian stepped closer, watching as the curved blade moved over the wood, forming it to the shape of the metal band that would go around it. He remembered the feel of the tools, the sound of the hammer striking metal, the pungent aromas of oak and pine. "My father taught me how to make whisky barrels, and I spent a good three years at it." A corner of Ian's mouth lifted with the memory.

The summer his and Collin's mischief had ruined the barley, Da had deemed it appropriate punishment that they come to understand just what their foolishness had cost—what a labor-intensive and delicate process the business of whisky was, from start to finish. For the next twelve months they'd done everything from working along-side those planting and harvesting the barley, to helping with the steeping, germination, and drying of the grain. Both he and Collin had come to understand his father's fury after spending months laboring to make the malt. And just when they'd thought their labor was done, their father had set them to building the barrels the final product was to go in. Ian hadn't cared for the growing, harvesting or any of the rest. But he had enjoyed crafting the barrels, and he and Collin had kept at it, long after their punishment was past.

He might not have been much for farming, but he'd found using tools and working with his hands held some appeal. While Ian had enjoyed working with wood, Collin had been taken with the molding of metal and could soon produce more hoops than were needed. They'd been a good team, and the work had been a pleasant distraction from the other studies and responsibilities Da had heaped upon them.

"Three years in your youth isn't much to recommend you," Rogers said, stopping his work to appraise Ian nonetheless. "An apprenticeship for the trade takes seven."

"I'm a fast learner," Ian said. It was true. His father had

always said that of him. "In a household where there was much work to be done there was no time for anything less."

"No dry cooper experience then?" Rogers asked.

"No, sir. But I can promise a watertight barrel." *And a fine Scotch whisky to go in it.*

"Ever make a bucket?"

"A time or two," Ian said.

Rogers stood, brushing wood shavings from his legs and apron. He walked over to a set of pegs on the wall near the door and retrieved a second apron. "I've an order for twenty stout buckets. Needs to be filled by Friday, and I've but four complete. You'll finish that order for me. If you do well with it, I'll start you on making hogsheads for the tobacco that comes from the plantations around here. Hogsheads and fish barrels are my main business. Not much Highland whisky in these parts."

Ian thought he detected the slightest lift to Rogers' lips, but he couldn't be sure.

"My apprentice came of age last week and did not wish to stay on. His workmanship was good, and I'd have paid him a fair wage. I'll do the same for you, if you're able to perform the tasks at hand with as little instruction as you boast. I'm not much for explaining. You either see how to do something and do it, or you don't."

"Aye." Ian couldn't have agreed more. *See what is to be done and do it.* He'd earn himself a position here and then work at saving enough to see to the safety of Eliza, Aisla and the others he'd left behind. He pushed thoughts of Eliza from his mind and took the apron from Rogers. Now was not the time to be distracted by memory, sweet or otherwise.

He'd made his way here safely over the last few days, and without dishonesty or thieving of any kind. He'd even worked loading and unloading the ferry to pay for his fare across. It was that task—unloading barrels once again—that had given him the idea to try coopering.

And now he must do it and do it well if he wished to be with Eliza again and to assure her well-being.

Ian settled at the bench, then picked up a ring and the first stave. He'd see to making sixteen of the best buckets Virginia had ever known.

Chapter Twenty-six

Norfolk, Virginia, April 1762

Dearest Elizabeth,

It was with greatest joy that I learned of your safe arrival in the Colonies. I regret that we have as yet been unable to come to you. Rest assured I look forward to making your reacquaintance.

All is well here. Uncle Rogers has taken on a new employee at the cooperage. He, too, hails from our homeland, and he seems to greatly enjoy and be quite skilled at working with his hands. I believe the new arrangement to be quite agreeable to all. I shall write again next week to let you know how that situation progresses.

Until then, take care of yourself—and your little family of ducklings. Please remember what I said about not going out to feed them after dark. Please write to me soon and share with me the latest news and hat styles.

Yours, ever affectionately,
Aunt Ilona

Ian tucked the borrowed pencil carefully into his pocket, then folded his letter to Eliza. He leaned over from his makeshift chair—a stump—dabbed his thumb into the thick mud, and pressed it over the fold. It wasn't much for a seal, but it was the best he could do at present. Fortunately the letter wasn't going across the Atlantic but merely across the river, where his *niece* Elizabeth lived.

It had seemed a little silly at first, writing to Eliza this way, pretending to be both a woman and her relative, but it was the best idea they'd been able to come up with that night in the lean-to. And silly or not—anything that enabled him to keep in contact with her was worth doing.

He stood, then knocked the dirt from his pants with the back of his hat and shook his hair free of frost before plunking the tricorn atop his head. He rubbed a hand over his roughly shaved face—the best he could do with only his blade and cold water—and knew his appearance still lacked considerably on the scale of respectable. There wasn't much to be done about it. He hadn't yet been paid, and without the use of unlawful means to acquire coin, renting a room of any sort was out of the question. A grove near the river had to suffice as his lodgings at present.

Thankfully the week had seen little rain or snow, though the almost warm wind this morning promised the weather might soon change and his current sleeping arrangements would prove more unsatisfactory than they were at present.

Rolling his stiff shoulders, Ian considered the merits of securing a room for himself after receiving his week's pay this afternoon. Much of his life he'd spent sleeping outdoors, but a bed of boughs or a mattress of leaves or hay in Scotland was infinitely preferable to the hard-packed earth and frozen grass of Virginia. And a woolen plaid might actually keep a man warm, whereas his coat was quite insufficient in that regard.

He moved quietly off through the grove, exiting at a different place than he had previously. The distance he'd put between himself and Millet wasn't enough that Ian dared to let his guard down too much. Under other circumstances he'd have traveled much farther, but he felt the pull of those left behind, particularly Eliza and Aisla, and wanted to return to help them as soon as possible.

Once on the street he stomped his feet, attempting to restore circulation. The brisk walk to the wharf did him good, allowing him to fully wake and warming him enough that his hands would be able to work upon his arrival.

Doing his best to ignore his empty stomach, Ian waited outside the shop, as had become his custom, for Rogers and Ben—the other man employed there—to arrive. The air seemed to have cooled significantly during his walk. The April chill bit into his fingers through the thin pockets of his coat, and Ian again thought longingly of the days of the kilt, when a man had a decent garment of wool to keep him warm.

Foolish. He chided himself for thinking of the unreachable past. He felt similar sentiment—foolish—regarding the spun cotton breeches that hit just below his knees and did little to provide warmth.

"Morning to you," Ben said, keys jingling from the ring in his hand. "You're here early again, and when you stayed so late last night. Rogers doesn't require you to live here, you know."

Ian wished he did. "Aye. Well, I didn't want to fall short of time with my first order. I knew I'd remember coopering, but I'd no particular notion of how long it would take me to perform the labor." He followed Ben into the shop.

"Looks as if you'll have no trouble finishing." Ben glanced at the two-deep row of buckets lining the south wall. "I reckon Rogers will keep you on."

"Thanks." Ian grabbed an apron. He had one bucket left to complete and would have finished it last night, but the light had become too poor to work. No matter. He could finish this morning in time for Rogers to deliver the order this afternoon.

Ben lit the stove and a couple of lamps, and Ian allowed himself a minute to warm his hands.

"Tea?" Ben asked, setting a kettle on top of the stove. "It'll warm your insides as well."

"Whisky's the drink for that," Ian said before remembering he'd sworn that off, too, along with his other vices.

Ben chuckled. "I don't think old Rogers will go for that. Not during working hours, at least."

"Probably not," Ian agreed, studying the other man. Ian guessed Ben to be a few years older than himself. Of a medium height, he was fit and trim, with a wild mane of reddish-blond hair that looked a challenge for the boldest comb. In the few days Ian had worked here, he'd learned that Ben was quick with a joke and freely offered advice or assistance when Rogers would not have. Not that his employer was unkind, but he'd been true to his word, to be a man of very *few* words.

Ben's wife and two children had visited the shop midweek, bringing a basket of pastries for the three men to share. That alone was enough to earn Ian's gratitude and friendship, but—perhaps noticing the ravenous manner in which Ian had consumed the pastry—Ben had gone out of his way since then to offer Ian tea or an extra apple or biscuit throughout the day.

He is a good man, a good colonist. With some reluctance Ian left the stove to begin work. His years with the Munros had left him wary of people, mistrustful, and suspicious. But here in this place, these colonies so far removed from Scotland or England, he was beginning to notice a difference. Excepting the Redcoats milling about, there seemed a core of human decency about most he'd met thus far—less prejudice, more acceptance. In the Highlands, his clan and the Highland people in general had been looked down upon. His entire life he'd known that he was somehow less than others—less deserving, less fortunate, less qualified or able to do anything with his life.

Here, in Virginia, that wasn't the case.

Ian straddled the bench, then secured the bucket in front of him, pressed tight between his thighs. Leaning into his task, he moved the circular wedge around the inside, cutting the groove for the bottom. The tools felt familiar in his hands, now that he'd completed fifteen other buckets.

Rogers came in a short while later, the aroma of fishing boats with their morning haul accompanying him through the open door. He said not a word to either of his employees—as was his custom, Ian had learned—but went straight to his own work.

Ian applied linseed paste to the groove, then used the compass to measure a piece for the bottom. This he cut, then fitted inside. When that was done he spent another hour and a half smoothing the sides, molding and fitting the final hoops, and braiding the handles.

It seemed intuition, almost, knowing how much to shave off and how much to leave. His fingers moved nimbly over the wood, testing the surface, leveling, finessing. His mind might have forgotten some of the particulars of the trade, but it seemed his hands had remembered all these years, and for that he was grateful.

By nine o'clock all twenty buckets were complete. Ian set the last one in place and rose from the bench. He crossed the room to Rogers.

"The buckets are ready for delivery. Would you like me to load them?" Throughout the week Ian had taken notice of earlier orders. He knew Rogers and Ben always brought the barrels out the side door, to the wagon Rogers kept parked there. The horses were stabled farther down the street, away from the bustling harbor, and would be brought over once a delivery was ready and loaded.

"Not yet." Rogers left his work, walked over to the buckets, and picked up two. These he carried toward the front of the shop. Seeing his intention, Ian ran ahead and opened the door. Once outside, Rogers made for the pump and quickly filled the first bucket to the brim with water. Ian took it from him, returned to the shop, and began pouring a measure of water into each of the remaining buckets. Rogers followed and did the same with the water his carried, then proceeded to lift each bucket, checking for leaks.

Ian watched, unconcerned. With all but this last bucket, he'd performed the same test last night, after Rogers had already gone home. Every one of them was watertight.

When he'd finished checking the last, Rogers tipped his glasses down and peered at Ian over the top of them. "You work fast, *and* it appears you know what you're doing." He crossed the room to the front window and removed the "Help Wanted" sign.

Ian half-smiled at the half-compliment. Rogers' observations were about as close as his father had ever come to praise as well. No matter. The satisfaction had come in the crafting, in remembering that he was good at something besides thievery. It might take longer to make a wage this way, but it was more fulfilling. He could be proud of what he'd done.

"Empty these, then load the wagon." Rogers walked behind the short counter and retrieved a paper. He glanced across the room at Ben. "Do you mind—"

"Not at all," Ben said, waving a hand, as if he'd known at once the question Rogers was about to ask.

Rogers nodded and returned his attention to Ian. "The buckets are to be delivered to the Johnston Dairy, about seven miles from here. If you're gone within the hour, you should be able to make it back by late afternoon. Half was paid half up front, and you'll get the other half upon delivery."

"Right." Ian whipped off the apron and replaced it with his coat. *He wants* me *to go. He* trusts *me.* Plenty of times the Munros had sent him on errands—illicit, dangerous ones—and always there had been a consequence if he failed to find success or return by the appointed time.

For the first several years of his captivity—for he thought of his time with the Munros as just that, no matter that his father had willingly left him there—consequences or punishments had all been directed at him. He'd taken the whipping if he failed. He'd go without food for days if he came back empty-handed. He was made to suffer. He'd been a prisoner of the Munro clan, as surely as his father had been a prisoner of the English in his final minutes. The only difference was the Munros were postponing his execution, waiting to fulfill their bargain to see him raised. Until such time consequences were always harsh, but never quite fatal.

And then, when that day finally came that he was of age, and they were free of the bargain they'd made with his father, the Munros had decided Ian was worth something after all. There was no better cattle rustler in all the Highlands, no man better at smuggling whisky past the Redcoats, no one quite as sly as Ian MacDonald. So they'd made the stakes for him staying higher. It had been the biggest test yet. He was to steal from his own clan, from his brother who was the laird. And if things became complicated in the process, he was to end his brother's life.

Ian tugged at the last button, fastening it securely. *No worries today,* he reminded himself and tried to shake the memory. The only thing Rogers expected of him upon his return was an empty wagon and the payment for the buckets.

Working quickly, Ian had the wagon loaded and the team hitched before a half hour had passed. The directions to the dairy were straightforward, and he was pleased to see they led him deeper inland, farther away from Portsmouth.

The day was clear and cold now, with the wind from this morning having picked up considerably. But the weather didn't bother him, and his fingers soon recalled the feeling of reins in his hands so that he settled into a steady, comfortable pace.

The opportunity to be out of the crowded town lifted Ian's spirits from bitter memory. Even in its winter barrenness, Virginia was a beautiful colony, with an abundance of natural resources. He wondered if the other colonies were similarly blessed and was beginning to see there might be some merit to staying in such a place after all.

But not for me. He'd a people and land to return to. And pleasant though at least some of this land might be, it didn't compare to the Highlands in beauty. A melancholy homesickness crept into his mind and heart. As the miles passed and the temperature dropped, Ian's mood did as well, souring considerably.

What was he doing here, spending an entire day driving a cart full of buckets? No wonder Rogers had trusted him with the delivery. No doubt, the man had not wished to spend a day out in the miserable wind.

But the cold seemed the least of Ian's concerns. Why was he wasting time like this—making buckets for a fair, but still insignificant sum—when he could have tripled the amount with a night or two of gambling? By waiting until he'd enough money to help them to a better situation, he was still gambling, this time with Aisla's life and perhaps Mrs. Campbell's and her daughter's as well. *And what of Eliza?* She believed her position safe, but Ian did not trust Millet to leave her alone. *I should be there protecting her—or better, getting her out of there.*

With a little cunning might he not have obtained what he needed to see them safely on another ship back home? Or at least safely away from The Young Devil and Millet?

What was the use of trying to prove himself honest when lives might be at stake?

The answer appeared in his mind, standing before the church, wisps of light brown hair blowing about her face as she peeked up at him from beneath that fancy new bonnet.

A kissing bonnet, he'd privately dubbed it, because it seemed big enough a man could steal a kiss beneath such without anyone actually seeing either parties' lips. Fortunately for him, he hadn't had to steal any kisses. She'd given them willingly.

Eliza. He ached to see her again, to hold her.

Ian edged the wagon to the side of the narrow road to let another going the opposite direction pass. Would he ever stop thinking of her? He'd often wondered the same about another woman, and while time had healed that pain—somewhat—he hadn't forgotten her or particularly his role in her death.

Ian nodded to the other driver as he passed. He *didn't* think of Aileen as often now. And when he did it was with slightly less guilt. He had made his choice that day, and he would make the same again. *Collin's life for hers.*

Once more Ian guided the team to the middle of the well-traveled road. He snapped the reins, increasing the pace, eager to be done with this drive and back in the shop where there were more distractions and less ability to be lost in haunting memory.

At the time of his choice, Ian hadn't really believed the Munros would kill Aileen. She was the laird's daughter, after all, not simply some crofter's lass. It was Ian whom Bruce Munro had near killed on the spot when he'd found the two of them together in the field that day.

If Ian regretted anything it was involving Aileen in his life in the first place. But he'd been lonely, and she the first kind soul in ages. Of course he had fallen in love and then into her arms at the earliest opportunity. He'd fully expected he would be killed for his actions. And he hadn't much cared. Life had been miserable for so long, and he was weary of it.

But old Bruce had other plans—bigger ones. And Ian stood to benefit from them. All he needed to do was steal the MacDonalds' whisky casks—easy enough, if they were still stored the same as when Ian was a boy—and set fire to the distillery and any barley crop yet in the fields. In essence, he was to destroy the MacDonalds' livelihood and make way for the Munros to capture the Highland whisky market.

In return for such service, Ian was to be given Aileen's hand in marriage and henceforth to be treated as a full and accepted member of the Munro clan. For someone so long denied camaraderie, friend-ship, or mutual association of any sort, the offer had been more than tempting. Never mind that he loathed the Munros—every last one of them, excepting Aileen.

Ian hatched a plan to take her and leave as soon as they

were married. He'd have the last laugh, stealing from old Bruce himself.

With little doubt that he would succeed, he'd set out to accomplish the seemingly impossible—MacDonald whisky and all its secrets were well guarded.

Then, at the last minute—in case the offer in place wasn't reward enough—Bruce Munro had added a threat as Ian left that morning. He'd just soundly kissed a tearful Aileen, who stood beside her father to see him off. Bruce threw his arm around her, not in a comforting, fatherly way, but with a jerking grip that had caused her to cry out. He'd leveled his gaze on Ian, upping the stakes considerably.

Ian and his crew were to return with the casks and proof of the destruction, or—instead of marriage—Aileen would pay for his failure.

With Aileen's tear-stained face in his mind, Ian had ridden off, fully intent on returning to her. He needed no compulsion to steal from his own brother and former clan, neither of whom had done anything at all for him these many years. While Ian had been suffering with the Munros, Collin had prospered, taking Ian's place as laird. It would be a pleasure to take it all away from him. And then a pleasure to take Bruce Munro's daughter away from him as well.

The crossroad up ahead pulled Ian from these memories and the turbulent emotion they roused. He slowed the wagon to a halt, consulted the crude map Rogers had drawn for him, then turned the team right. The crisp smells of the forest soon gave way to the pungent aroma of a dairy, and he found himself looking forward to meeting the dairy owner and presenting the buckets to him. Anything—unpleasant smells and all—to get his mind off the past.

Meeting her, he amended several minutes later, after he'd arrived and been shown into the house. *Mistress* Johnston, as she'd introduced herself when she found him waiting in the front hall, greeted him enthusiastically, then ushered him outside toward a smaller, red brick building.

The mewling of cattle seemed to be coming from every direction, and Ian counted three large barns. He wondered how many cows Johnston's Dairy kept but didn't think it his place to ask.

Beyond the barn, dozens of workers labored in the barren fields, preparing them to be planted, Ian assumed. The men did not all appear to be of color, and this encouraged him for some reason. The plantation he'd visited just days ago had made obvious use of slave labor, and he had found those in charge to be unfeeling. He wanted this time to be different, to have provided a service for a family who at least appeared to be honest, hardworking, and fair.

Smoke rose from the chimney of what appeared to be a small blacksmith shop, and over the mewling the sound of a hammer striking an anvil could be heard. People too numerous to count, and whose responsibilities he could only guess at, hurried to and fro, carrying this and that, engaged in purposeful work.

Longing for home, for the MacDonald keep as he'd known it as a boy, stole over Ian. He needed to return to Scotland to right things there, to return the land and people to the productivity and hive of activity that had once been. Collin had tried but had never been able to restore the order and function and profit that had reigned in the days of their father's stewardship. Ian didn't fault Collin. The uprising had stripped them of so much. But perhaps now tides were turning and the time had come to rebuild what once was.

"Watch your step—and your head," Mrs. Johnston warned after he'd held the door to the little red brick building for her as she preceded him inside. Instead of going up or being at ground level, two stairs led down to a stone floor. Even so, Ian had to duck as he moved beneath the doorway. Clearly this building was not set up for an average-to-tall man.

Inside the cool room the walls and even the ceiling were white-washed, and the stench from the animals lessened considerably as the door closed behind them. Four butter churns sat on a platform to the left of the door. Beside those were four chairs. On the opposite side of the room a set of shelves held neatly organized butter molds. Beneath those was another, wider shelf or work bench lined with empty pans. And at the far end, another set of shelves, these just the right size for buckets, stood empty.

There wasn't a crumb on the floor or even a particle of dust to be seen in the light filtering in from the cutouts at the top of the wall beneath the overhanging eaves.

Ian almost doffed his hat, feeling as if he'd entered a church of some sort.

"Never been to a dairy, have you?" Mistress Johnston asked, smiling knowingly at his expression—bewildered, no doubt.

In the Highlands cows were milked in a barn, and then the pails of milk were taken straight to the kitchen.

"I've not," Ian confirmed, and again felt an absurd desire to remove his hat.

"It's the cleanest part of any farm or plantation," she explained. "This room, particularly, where the milk is brought after it's been strained. Has to set in here at least a day—no more than two—then my girls and I begin our work."

"Making butter?"

"Yes. And cream as well. The best to be had for miles around. We've so much business we're expanding," she said proudly. "This room is new, just built. We've another like it that's been in use for some time."

"And is it as pristine?" Ian asked. Perhaps the room appeared so perfect because it was unused as yet.

"Oh, yes. It has to be. We can't have anything spoiling the milk. The floor and walls are washed every third day, between batches."

"I hope our buckets meet your standards." Ian found himself returning her smile. Mrs. Johnston was everything one might imagine of the mistress of a dairy—plump and smiling, rosy-cheeked. A white apron covered her ample waistline, and a matching cap edged with lace topped her head.

"Let's just have a look at them," she said. "You see where they'll go, of course."

"Aye." Ian inclined his head toward the empty shelves.

"The secret to good cream lies partly with the bucket, you know."

"I didn't," Ian confessed. He'd never thought much about dairies.

"A tin pail works well enough for collecting the milk, but after that it's best to be done with metal, though there are those who would tell you otherwise." She shook her head, as if baffled by such an opinion. "Earthenware is used for the pans, then afterward buckets hold the cream. A good pine bucket preserves the purity of the flavor."

"In Scotland a good *oak* barrel is valued for its ability to add to the flavor of the liquid it holds."

"Don't you mean *liquor*?" She cast him a look that managed to be both amused and disapproving at the same time.

"Aye," Ian admitted freely. "The cream of the Highlands does not come from cows."

Mistress Johnston laughed heartily, much to his surprise. "Perhaps it would, if they had *my* cows and tasted *my* cream. Come along. Let's have a look at these buckets."

They made their way to Rogers' wagon.

"Your accent speaks of Scotland. How long have you been in these parts?" she asked.

"Only a few weeks," Ian said. It felt more like years. "Today's delivery is my first for Rogers. I've only been in his employ since Tuesday." As soon as he'd spoken Ian wondered if he ought not to have been quite so honest.

"Good man, he is." Mrs. Johnston looked sideways at Ian. "As must you be for him to trust you with his team and wagon, not to mention the material and labor he's put into our order."

Ian cleared his throat. "Actually, I made the buckets. Most of them, that is. Sixteen."

"Did you, now?" She reached over the side of the wagon and removed one before Ian could reach in to assist.

He waited as she hefted it in her arm, ran her finger around the rim, then along the smooth inside.

"Fine workmanship," she proclaimed at last. "Though a bit dusty from your ride. Don't put them on the shelves, but bring them up to the house. They'll all need to be washed before we use them."

"Of course." Ian wished he'd thought to throw a cover over the wagon bed, but neither Ben nor Rogers had mentioned it. Perhaps they'd assumed Ian would realize as much on his own. He grabbed the handles for three buckets in each hand and followed her once more.

"Would you like me to wash them for you?" He wasn't certain how far his duties extended beyond the cooper's shop, but he didn't want the first customer he'd worked with to be displeased in any way.

Mrs. Johnston waved away his offer. "No need. I've girls who can do that—which reminds me. I need to be getting a few more soon as well, as they'll be needed with the additional workload. Meant to ask Ben about that if he came today. But I suppose you can pass it along."

"Ben—finds servants for you?" Ian wasn't exactly sure that was what she meant, but if so—

"He does." Mrs. Johnston glanced back at him. "Ben is my younger brother. He checks at the docks for me. Many who come off the ships are looking for work—like you were," she added with a smile.

"How many women are you looking for?" Ian asked cautiously, telling himself not to get overly hopeful.

"Well, I've four chairs to fill with the churns. Of course they'd have other duties as well. Can't churn *all* day." She held the door for him this time, as his reach was cumbered by the buckets.

Ian entered a large room that was at ground level and with a doorway tall enough that he didn't have to duck.

"Put them on the table," Mrs. Johnston instructed, pointing to a long, butcher-block table in the middle of a work kitchen overflowing with pots and pans, barrels, sacks, rolling pins, all manner of utensils, and a half dozen women all at work—tending the stove, rolling dough, chopping vegetables. She placed the bucket she had carried down first.

Ian set his six beside hers, his innards grumbling as the aroma of fresh-baked bread collided with his empty stomach. Aside from Ben's tea, he hadn't had anything since the previous night. More than one meal a day was a luxury he couldn't afford at present.

"I know of a woman who is in need of employment," he blurted, knowing it was not his place to be suggesting servants, but hoping Mrs. Johnston wouldn't think him too uncouth.

She faced him, hands planted on her hips. "Is this woman a Highlander like yourself?"

"Aye. She came on the same ship as me and—" Here is where the story became tricky. "She wished to remain with her daughter, so I purchased her indenture that she might."

Mrs. Johnston's brows rose, one slightly above the other. "Is this woman your wife?"

"No, ma'am." Ian doffed his hat at last, placing it over his heart as a gesture of his truthfulness. "I am not married. I did not even know Mrs. Campbell until our ship had docked." He refrained from mentioning how he'd freed the woman and her daughter.

"One of our neighbors is a Scot," Mrs. Johnston said. "Fine man. Fine family." Her lips pursed. "I suppose you'll be wanting repayment for her indenture."

"No. Not at all." The thought hadn't even crossed his mind. "I would be indebted if she—and her daughters—might serve with you for their keep. I've no home or need of servants myself, and I do not make enough at the cooperage to sustain them in their current lodgings."

"Daughters? There is more than one?" Mrs. Johnston's hands were still planted on her hips, and now her eyes narrowed shrewdly.

Ian's stomach grumbled again. Ignoring it, he plunged ahead with an explanation while silently cursing his inability to be completely honest. He imagined Eliza's look of disappointment and in his mind saw her wagging a finger at him.

He hadn't meant to lie. He *wouldn't*. "One lass is Mrs. Campbell's daughter, but there is another as well. She—I—" His hope of finding a place for them began to unravel. "The child's indenture had not been purchased, and she was to become a slave if I did not intervene." He still felt neither regret nor remorse of any kind about that decision. The hours he'd spent in the lass's company had touched him. She was a bright, pleasant little bit, with her whole life ahead of her. *A life that slavery would snuff out.*

"How old are the girls?" Mistress Johnston asked without so much as a hint as to what she might be thinking.

"They've seven and eight years, I believe." Ian turned his hat in his hands, wishing, hoping . . .

"Hmm. Not old enough to churn properly, but I suppose they could take over the milking for two of the older girls, and perhaps those are of an age to churn now."

"One of them has milking experience," Ian said, remembering Aisla's description of their ornery cow.

"And all three are to come at no cost?"

"None at all," Ian confirmed eagerly. "They will serve their term faithfully and only require their basic needs met in return, including transport here."

"Ben can fetch them," Mrs. Johnston said with a wave of hand not dissimilar to the one Ian had seen from Ben earlier in the shop.

"Seven years and little wages to pay." Mrs. Johnston shrugged. "Lars couldn't have found a better deal himself. Pity he's not here to congratulate me." A wistful look crossed her face.

Seven? Ian couldn't bring himself to correct her. And why should he? Why should any of them be indentured for fourteen years? The only crime they'd committed was being Scottish and poor—not something that ought to require giving up fourteen years of one's life.

"All right." She gave a firm nod of her head. "We'll try it."

"You will?" Relief, swift and sure, swept over Ian. "Thank—"

"Tell Ben I'll just need him to find one more woman after that. Unless you know of anyone else?"

"I might," Ian said, thinking fast. If Eliza knew Jannet Campbell and the lasses were safe, might she not be persuaded to come too? Before her term was up?

"Sit yourself down and try a piece of that bread your eyes keep straying to." Mrs. Johnston turned her back to him and his gratitude as she bustled about the kitchen, taking up a knife and one of the cooling loaves. "Thin as you are, a stiff wind is liable to blow you into one of your own barrels, and you'd not have the strength to get out again. Maybe if you'd quit buying people off the ships and pay attention to your own welfare . . ." Her scolding rang false, and when she turned to hand him the generously buttered slice of bread, Ian noticed her eyes were bright.

"Thank you, ma'am." Ian lifted the bread to his mouth and managed to take a normal-sized bite instead of stuffing the entire thing into his mouth.

"My Lars would have liked you." Mrs. Johnston looked out the window toward the fields. "If ever you tire of coopering, come this way, and I'll set you to work here, in the fields or elsewhere. Good men like you are just what Virginia needs."

Chapter Twenty-seven

Aboard the *Cleopatra*, North Atlantic Ocean, May 1762

"Do you wish to draw or walk first today?" The sun was scarcely up before Collin pulled me from my berth with-out a shred of sympathy.

Why can't he just let me sleep? "We walked forty laps around the deck yesterday. I know—I counted. I should think that ought to be good for a day off."

"Drawing it is, then." With one hand still holding my arm, preventing me from slumping back into bed, Collin took my sketch-pad and charcoals from their place in the trunk. "Let's go up top. You too, Timothy. Sunshine and fresh air are good for the soul as well as the body."

With my usual sluggish movement, I allowed Collin to drag me from the room. There was no point arguing. He was stronger than I—in spite of his efforts to change that, forcing me to consume more oats than any person should have to in a lifetime, feeding me dates, giving me bits of dried meat to suck on throughout the day, and marching me around the deck for hours on end in an attempt to help me regain my strength and fortitude. If I refused to go with him he would simply pick me up and take me outside. And that was the last thing I wanted.

I'd heard enough of the whisperings around us, both at night in our berths and throughout the day, that I didn't want to incur any more gossip by creating a scene. Fueled by the talkative Mrs. Parker, several of the other women on board were critical of me, saying that I was spoiled, mourned overmuch, and did not appreciate my husband's valiant efforts to help me improve.

"Have you ever seen such a patient man," and "what a dear soul," were words oft spoken of Collin. While I was assigned a more critical view.

"See how lazy she is, to make him support her like that as they walk about the deck. It isn't as if she had a child to recover from."

"She must be touched in the head to cry all the time like that. Mrs. Parker said she thinks it happened during the incident . . ."

The loss of our child—our *children*, really, for I still mourned Lydia—felt like far more than an *incident* to me. My thoughts frequently harkened back to a moment but a few weeks into our marriage, shortly after Collin and I had arrived at my grandfather's castle. We had been alone in our room, Collin doing his best to explain why we must avoid, at all costs, the possibility of a child while we faced threats from both his brother and my own clansmen. There had been a few defining moments that evening, but the one I remembered most often now was when I had first felt the desire to be a mother.

The feeling had come seemingly out of nowhere and had surprised me with its intensity and deeply rooted yearning. It had been a moment from which point forth I was never quite the same. Something within me had changed, and I longed for motherhood and had been willing to risk much to bring a child into this world.

Losing our unborn baby on this voyage had been another such defining moment, only this time I did not think it had changed me for the better. I'd known loss before, with both my parents' deaths. I'd believed I'd lost Collin for those many months, and together we had lost Lydia. But this time it felt like I, alone, had suffered the tragedy. It had been my body the babe had fled, and Collin, though he sorrowed too, could not fully understand the grief and guilt that accompanied such loss. I didn't *know* how to recover.

Eating well and taking walks might help me heal physically, but I had no idea how to restore my mind and heart. I *couldn't* move on and forget. To do so would mean to forget that little one who had never been born. As his mother, it was to me to remember him, to grieve his loss. He could not be replaced. I had conceived and carried a child and then lost that child, and I would never be the same for it.

But after nearly a month I felt enough aware of my surroundings that I grew tired of the scorn of others. To that end I'd ceased crying, except when I was alone in bed late at night and everyone else slept. I rose without argument each morning. I spooned the oatmeal into my own mouth each day. And I walked, lap after lap, around the deck. Getting stronger, Collin insisted, for the overland journey that awaited us in Nova Scotia.

When Collin had helped me to get comfortable in my usual place outside and had seen that I was adequately provided for with water nearby and a blanket to cover me, he and Timothy left to prepare the dreaded oats for our breakfast.

I flipped through the sketchbook that had delighted me only weeks ago but now—like all else—held little appeal. I'd not drawn any additional details of our new home or the route we were to take to get there but had instead, secretly, taken to drawing a series of portraits at the back of the book, on a page I'd allowed no one else to see.

Finding it quickly now, I stared down at the scene. Collin and Timothy were recognizable, standing beside one another. And I'd drawn a baby in Collin's arms to look like Lydia. At first this had perplexed me. Then it had alarmed me as the faces of the other children in the drawing took shape, taking on the likenesses of Lydia's older siblings. In my mind I saw no woman with them, only Collin with a brood of children about him. For days I had wondered what it possibly meant. I did not usually draw the past, but the future, and Lydia was far behind in our past, as were her siblings.

Then, two nights ago, I'd had a dream of Mhairi, standing

on a shore, watching a ship in the harbor. She held Lydia in her arms, and the other children were clustered not far behind. For a brief moment it seemed I'd glimpsed Mhairi's heart. She regretted not having come with the rest of her clan. She regretted her choice to marry the children's father and stay behind. And she was reconsidering.

I closed my eyes and allowed the book to fall shut. Perhaps she was on her way already. Maybe she had joined Alistair and the others before they left. Maybe I would have one more problem to contend with when we arrived in Nova Scotia. *Maybe Collin will love her more than me, because I am unable to give him a child.*

I had not awakened happy but now found my mood as dark as the clouds on the horizon.

"You never want to be up on deck, and now, in *this* weather you do?" Collin ran a hand through his hair in frustration, making it stand on end even more than usual just as lightning struck off the bow of the ship.

Close. My hand tingled where it gripped the rail. I jumped as the accompanying thunder shook the deck. My own hair lifted from the back of my neck as all around us men shouted and ran, scrambling to haul in sails. Outrunning the storm had not worked.

Two at the wheel did their best to hold the helm steady against the onslaught of sheeting rain and a ferocious wind lifting the waves—and the *Cleopatra*—to great heights.

The storm that had been threatening all day had struck swiftly.

"Get below, Katie!" Collin grabbed my free hand and began pulling me across the slanting deck.

"No," I cried. "Wait." A wave crashed over the side and sent us pitching sideways, with only my firm grip on the rail keeping us from sliding with the water. My arms stretched painfully in either direction, and I feared rebreaking the one. But I kept hold of the bar, and Collin kept hold of me even as we fell to our knees. Collin swung his free hand around to grasp the side, and we bent our heads and hung on.

Frightening minutes passed before the ship finally righted herself and the water receded. We staggered to our feet and clung to one another.

"Now will you get inside?" he roared above the sound of the storm.

I shook my head. "We can't. We need to get the others out as well."

Collin opened his mouth as if to argue.

I placed a hand on his shoulder and caught his eye, forcing him to truly look at me. "I've seen this, remember?" Understanding passed between us, and something akin to relief broke out in the near smile on his face.

He crushed me to him, strong arms holding me close. "Thank you, God." Collin pulled back after a minute, then kissed me swiftly on the lips. "I would live through a dozen storms like this to see you look at me as you just did," he said. "I've missed you, Katie."

"The others," I reminded him. "*Timothy.* When we capsize we'll go down quickly, and not everyone will be able to get out."

"Aye." Collin released me. "How I'm to convince anyone to come up on deck in the midst of this—" He started toward the stairs, then paused, changing direction, making his way toward midship.

"Collin," I shouted, my cry lost in the gale. I glanced toward the stairs, then released my hold and took an unsteady step. *I must get Timothy.*

The wind and rain whipped my hair free of its pins and plastered strands to my face and across my eyes so that I could hardly see where I was going.

"What are you doing?"

I startled once more, this time from Collin's voice at my

side. He gripped my arm, pulling me back the direction I'd come.

"I'll go after Tim and the others," he said. We reached the side, where he lashed a short length of rope around the railing. The other he looped over my wrist—the one that had not previously been broken—showing me how to loosen it if need be.

"This will hold firm, but you can also get free of it." He kissed me again, even quicker than before. "Don't move until I get back! I love you, Katie!"

Collin slogged off in the direction of the stairs, the deck being awash in the water from another wave that had burst over the bow.

The rope chafed my skin, but I saw the wisdom of it when the ship pitched forward again and I was thrown to the deck. The wet, polished wood was slick, and I slid until the rope stopped me with a jerk. I tried but couldn't find my footing, so instead pulled my knees to my chest and huddled against the side, my hand wrapped around the rope to shorten my tether and the distance I traveled with each rise and fall of the vessel.

Lightning struck again, followed by thunder so terrifyingly loud it seemed the heavens above had to have opened and dropped a boulder the size of the Earth on top of us. The ship shuddered, and I feared that any second she would splinter into a thousand pieces.

Instead of splintering or sinking she rose—high, higher, higher yet, with her nose in the air this time. Behind me the blue swell of the ocean appeared far below. The rope dug into my wrist and arm as my feet tried to find purchase on the slippery deck. I braced myself for the bow's eventual downward plunge.

The crew's shouts mingled with the noise of the storm, frantic instructions that made little sense to me.

"Come to! Come to!"

"Impossib—"

"Dead ahead, she is. Come to, I say!"

The stern began to level out as the bow began its descent. I tensed, awaiting the feeling of my stomach dropping once more, but our freefall was cut short. The ship was in the middle of turning when she struck something with full force.

My body bounced on the hard deck as my head snapped back and struck the side. I cried out, but my voice was lost in the others'—the screams and shouts of both crew and passengers.

The ship listed sharply with the leeward wind. Ocean rushed to meet us over the side from behind me, spilling icy salt water down the back of my dress and over my shoulders. Clinging to the rope, I hauled myself up and squinted through rain and stinging wind to see what had become of us.

It was impossible to see more than an arm's length in front of me, but I peered over the side, as another wave came upon us, tipping the ship even more precariously toward the sea.

This time the water covered my head, and for a few frantic seconds I spluttered and gasped, panicking until my face uncovered enough to suck in great gulps of salty air.

"We're stuck! She's going down."

"Abandon ship!" The cry echoed from multiple directions all at once.

"Collin!" I cried, turning my back to the rail. With my free hand I brushed the hair from my eyes and squinted in the direction of the stairs. People were staggering from them, but none that I could make out resembled Collin or Timothy.

A deafening groan came from the ship herself. I was flung back-ward against the side, then caught up with the retreating wave and swept overboard. Panic ensued again as I thrust my face upward, seeking air. The rope bit into my wrist and hand excruciatingly.

Another swell mounted almost at once, slamming me against the outside of the ship and lifting me enough that I flung my free arm over the rail and clung there, certain that when the wave returned it would carry me off for good.

This was not what Grandfather saw for me.

Not an easy journey, but survivable.

Two seers. And I one of them. Had I not predicted that we were to face grave danger? *I stayed on deck to survive. I* will *survive.*

Collin. Timothy. The surge came again, in reverse, covering my face, filling my nose and mouth with salty water. I coughed and gasped for breath, and, against all probability and the forces of nature, hung on.

My head popped free of the water, my feet and ankles remaining submerged. The ship was no longer moving, but somehow trapped in place, being beaten ferociously, mercilessly by the storm.

Collin. The feelings I'd forgotten the past weeks flooded my senses as surely as the ocean did. The cold water washing over me had woken me to the dangers, and, it seemed, had roused my spirit, my will to live—and love. *Collin.*

Wrapping my hand around the rope once more, I pulled with all my strength. When the upsurge behind me came again, I pulled harder with both hands. My chest reached the rail, and I leaned forward, kicking at the air until I fell headlong onto the deck.

Every part of me hurt, but I ignored all as I knelt by the side and clawed at the rope with my free hand. Wet, it was harder to loosen, but I managed to wriggle two fingers of my free hand beneath, loosening the circle enough to slip free.

Blood ran down my stinging arm, but it wasn't broken. "Collin!" I shouted, rising to my feet. One of my shoes was missing. "Timothy!"

A man rushed past me, placed one hand on the *Cleopatra's* angled side, and vaulted overboard. Screams filled the air, barely heard over the continuing storm.

I started toward the stairwell closest to me, a nearly uphill climb the way the ship tilted. When walking became too difficult I crawled, making my way in the opposite direction of those fleeing.

"Mrs. Mercer. You need to get *off* this ship." Captain Shenk reached down to help me up. He stood at the top of the stairs, along-side another officer. Together they were pulling passengers from the stairwell as they emerged.

"My husband and brother are down there."

"We'll get—"

"Katie!" Timothy's hand appeared, waving wildly behind the person in front of him. Captain Shenk and the ship's officer helped them both to the deck.

"That way." Shenk gave us both a little shove in the direction I'd just come. I barely had time to grasp Timothy's hand before we were sliding, full speed, toward the side.

"Where's Collin?" I shouted, my free arm swinging wildly, trying to catch my balance.

"Helping," Timothy shouted back. He sounded frightened for the first time that I could remember. "The water's high down there. Up to your bed already. Collin swam me to the stairs."

Stubborn, heroic Scotsman. My eyes filled with tears.

A low wave broke over the side, softening our impact as we hit the rail. Still holding Timothy's hand, I turned around, intent on going back for Collin. But the officer who'd been assisting the captain was right behind us.

"I'm to go with you and the boy," he said. "We'll have to jump, but it's not far to the sea."

I followed his gaze and saw the water even higher against the listing ship than it had been just moments ago.

"Land's not far either. I'm to help you swim there. Captain's orders." He picked up Timothy and swung one leg over the side. "Come along."

I hesitated. Timothy's eyes, huge with terror, beseeched me to follow, even as I turned away, looking upward across the now steeply-slanted deck. I could barely make out Shenk, one foot braced on the deck, the other on the step below as water continued pouring down the stairwell. *Collin.*

"Katie, please!"

Finlay had not said *who* would survive.

"Wait," I begged the officer.

He shook his head and pushed off the rail. Timothy's scream followed them for the short plunge into the sea. I leaned over, watching as they surfaced. Timothy clawed at the officer's head, trying to get his own above the water.

"Leave off, brat!" The officer shoved Timothy away and began swimming toward shore.

"No!" I cried. *You were supposed to help.*

Timothy's head disappeared beneath a wave. I grabbed the side of the ship and thrust my stockinged foot onto the rail.

"Timothy!" I pushed off, jumping toward the spot where he had just been.

Chapter Twenty-eight

Sable Island, Nova Scotia, May 1762

"Breathe, Timothy. *Please*."

A wave lapped at Timothy's feet. I put my arms beneath his shoulders and dragged him higher up on the sandy shore, out of reach of the tide. I laid him on his side and pounded upon his back as I'd seen others along the shore doing to their loved ones. *Breathe.*

I pounded harder, desperate for any response from his limp form. I worried he'd been too long submerged by the time I reached him in the sea and turned him upon his back. I hadn't known what else to do, had barely been able to keep my own head above water, and had only known to turn on my back, from last year's near-drowning in the river. It was Providence that we'd had but a short distance before my feet had struck the bottom of that same sandbar that had caught and trapped the *Cleopatra*.

Dangerous, but survivable, Finlay had said. I prayed him right. *For all of us.*

"*Timothy*." I spoke sharply, as if that might somehow elicit a quicker response. "Wake this instant." I gave his back another firm whack with the palm of my hand.

The most disgusting spew of sea water and vomit erupted from his mouth, followed by ardent coughing.

"Timothy!" I scrambled to his other side. His eyes remained closed, but I placed my hand on his forehead, overwhelmed with relief and joy and gratitude as his coughing continued.

226

"Can you sit up?" I asked. "Would that help?"

"Water," he croaked.

I had none, though we were surrounded by it. "I haven't any," I said. "You'll have to open your mouth to catch some of the rain. Can you look at me, Timothy? Can you see?"

After a moment one eye opened slowly. It rolled around a bit, taking in me and our immediate surroundings. "You look a mess, Katie."

I laughed, then bent and hugged my brother to me. "Oh good-ness. Don't you *ever* frighten me like that again."

Collin. My joy fled. Had he not said similar to me only weeks ago? I turned back to the ship, now over halfway submerged in the water, her bow up in the air, but the stern—where the passenger berths were—lost beneath the sea.

Heads still bobbed in the water between us, most too low or too far for me to make out their identities. *Let one be Collin. Let him be safe.* After another quick check that Timothy was still recovering, I stood and scanned the ocean.

In either direction, as far as I could see, people were staggering up to the shore. The storm had lessened—the rain no longer sheeting but steady. The thunderclouds and lightning had moved beyond us. I tried to be thankful for such mercy as I wrapped my arms around my middle, holding back sobs of worry and regret. I'd been so ungrateful these past weeks. *So wretched.* If I might only have him back, I'd tell him how sorry I was. *Don't take my husband.*

"Katie?" Timothy held a hand out to me.

I returned to his side and helped him up, keeping an arm around him to steady us both.

"Where is Collin?" Timothy's eyes looked as frightened as I imagined mine must be.

I squeezed his shoulder. "I don't know."

We stood thus a moment, anchored together, water lapping at our feet and rain stinging our faces as we stared out toward the *Cleopatra.*

He was helping everyone else. And here I stand, doing nothing. The sea is full *of people.*

"Timothy, quick." I awoke from the stupor of my own anxiety to realize others around us needed help. I pointed to a girl struggling to reach the shore. Though she wasn't far off, each retreat of the tide seemed to pull her farther away. "We must help her." I started forward, herding Timothy with me, unwilling to allow him out of my sight.

"Stay here," I instructed when we were closer to a straight line from where she struggled.

"You're not going back out there?" Timothy's voice was shrill and panicked.

"Not far," I promised. "There's a ledge beneath the water here. I'll not go farther than I can safely walk. Don't move from this spot." Still holding his arm, I sat him down on the wet sand. "I'll be right back, I promise."

Lifting my skirt, I saw that both shoes were gone now, and one stocking as well. *No matter.* We'd had little and now had less. *Only let us have each other.*

I gathered the layers of sodden petticoat and bunched them around my waist as I waded into the water. Twice the girl slipped beneath the surface. The second time I feared she wouldn't return, but at last I saw a hand emerge and then her face barely above water as well.

"This way," I shouted, waving my free hand. I tried running toward her, with no success until the receding tide caught me and swept me off my feet. I grasped her arm at the same moment I realized I could no longer feel the sand beneath me. It was deeper here. And the pull of the ocean was strong.

Too exhausted to speak, she simply clung to me, her fingers digging into my arm.

"On your back," I ordered, even as I flipped onto mine. My legs refused to rise, weighed down by heavy layers of soaked wool. With my free hand I stroked, pulling us backward toward land. "Kick your feet," I shouted, and tried to do the same, with little effect.

The tide came in again, and I attempted to use it to our advantage. If we could just get close enough to touch the bottom before it washed out . . .

I pulled harder, and my hand struck something. I turned my head and saw the body of a man floating face down in the water. *Not Collin.* I felt relief and guilt at the same time. This man's shirt was different, his hair grey. I hadn't a free hand with which to turn him over. Tears stung my eyes along with the rain as I left the man behind and we fought our way toward the shore.

My calves burned from all that kicking that had done little to move us. I allowed my legs to drift down while still managing to keep my head above the water. My toes brushed sand.

Quickly I turned us around to face the shore. "Jump," I yelled and surged forward, on top of the wave that would bear us in the wrong direction. My feet landed, touching more land now. My relief was short-lived when I realized the girl had let go of my arm and lay unmoving.

"No," I cried, unwilling to lose her. She'd been alive a moment before. Grasping the shoulder of her dress, I pulled until she was floating in front of me. Crying in earnest now, I guided her lifeless body through the shallow sea until we reached the shore.

"You promised you wouldn't go so far," Timothy shouted as I stepped from the water.

"I didn't mean to. Help me move her." I glanced at him and saw that though he still appeared dazed, he appeared otherwise unharmed.

"What do you want me to do?" His voice was small and frightened again, as he looked at the unmoving girl.

"Pound on her back." I rolled her so she faced away from him. "Like this." I hit her hard as I'd done Timothy, and at once she began to cough. Water drooled from the side of her mouth.

"A few more times. Gentler," I instructed, then brushed the hair from her face.

All around us this same scene and others were playing out. I looked toward the ship again and saw that fewer people were swimming to shore, and I could see no more jumping from the sides.

"Thank ye," the girl sputtered between coughs.

"You're welcome." I held her hand. There were likely others I should try to help. *Collin would.* But I could hardly move. That last scare in the sea seemed to have taken what remaining strength I'd had.

Timothy stopped patting the girl's back and laid his head against my shoulder. I put my arm around him and continued my bleary-eyed search through the steady rain.

"Where are we, Katie?" Timothy asked.

"I don't know." Collin had told me we were getting close to Nova Scotia, but this didn't seem like anything I'd drawn or Captain Shenk had described. This might have been one time we wouldn't have complained to see English soldiers.

"I'm cold," Timothy said.

"Me too." I craned my neck behind me, searching for any sign of civilization or shelter. We would need to move to higher ground, but I didn't want to do that yet, not when there was still a possibility . . .

"I need to find my parents." The girl sat up, looking as dazed as I felt. "They jumped with me."

The grey-haired man? "My husband is missing too." I understood her fear.

Neither of us made any move to search for our loved ones. I'd not felt the cold before but now began shivering uncontrollably. We needed to get out of our wet clothes and near a fire. I thought once more of my unexpected trip downriver in the Highlands. It had been traumatic, but Collin had been there with blankets and a fire. I'd give up both now, if I could just have Collin.

After a while of sitting there in a half stupor Timothy fell asleep, his head in my lap. It was a struggle to keep my own eyes open and tempting to let them close and escape the cold and misery all around us. The sounds of wailing competed with the wind. The rain had let up a little more, but the tide continued washing in bodies, many of them unmoving.

Help them.

I lifted Timothy's head and laid him carefully back on the sand. I dared not go into the water again, but I could see what might be done for those who had made it this far—alive or dead.

Without my asking, the girl I'd saved rose with me. Together we began pulling bodies farther up the beach. Rolling them on their sides, pounding on their backs. Others joined us, including Mrs. Parker, and between us we managed to revive three souls.

Dark was upon us now, and I realized I needed to return to Timothy, to see what might be done to help us survive the coming night.

In a state of exhaustion I retraced my steps along the beach, my eyes still on the barely-visible remains of the *Cleopatra.*

It's been too long. He would have come. My throat swelled. Tears obscured what vision I had left. I brought a hand to my mouth and sank to the sand, sobbing.

"Katie! Katie, there you are!" Timothy plowed into me, nearly knocking me over and throwing his arms around me.

I returned his hug, clasping him tight against me, so grateful that he had been spared, that we still had each other.

Timothy pulled back to look at me. "I thought you'd gone back in the sea and drowned. I told Collin that's what—"

"Katie!"

I was plowed into once more, caught up in strong arms that encompassed Timothy as well.

"Collin?" My hands touched his face, brushing away sand, then holding him close and kissing him. "You're *alive.*"

"Aye. Else I've perished and am having a bonny dream." A corner of his mouth quirked in the familiar half-smile I adored.

"No dream." I shook my head. "It's too cold and miserable here for that." I laughed, grateful suddenly for the cold that meant we were alive.

The three of us bent our heads together, and I began a prayer before Collin could. Gratitude for God's mercy overflowed, warming my heart that had felt frozen, weighed down in grief for so long. He had spared us. We were alive. Collin and Timothy both returned to me.

Our family. It was just the three of us, and it was enough.

Chapter Twenty-nine

Sable Island, Nova Scotia, May 1762

Timothy held a hand to his face, shading his eyes against the afternoon sun as he watched some of the *Cleopatra's* crew row away. "Do you really think they'll come back for us?"

"Of course they will." I tucked Timothy against my side and wrapped an arm around him.

"They'll send help is what they'll do," Collin clarified. "A ship or larger boats that can take us to the mainland."

"I wish I could have gone with them," Timothy said, a pout forming on his lips. "I'm a strong rower."

I brought a hand to my mouth to conceal my amusement. "I'm glad to see you've no lasting fear of the ocean."

"Never," Timothy declared. "Someday I'll be a captain of my own ship. You'll see."

"So long as you learn to swim first." I wasn't soon to forget the sight of his head slipping below the water.

"Let me have a look at those arms, lad." Collin knelt beside Timothy and made a show of feeling his muscles. "I daresay you *could* have rowed the distance with the crew, but your sister needs braw men like us here to protect her."

"From what?" Timothy asked. "There's nothing but a couple of horses on this island."

"A few dozen horses—and those people who come to visit." Collin's look turned dark as he peered into the distance. Shading his own eyes with his hand, he rose, looking steadily at a ship approaching not far from where our own small rescue boat had just disappeared.

"Someone is coming for us already?" It would be wonderful to not have to spend another night here.

"I don't think so." Collin placed his free hand on Timothy's shoulder. "Looters, most likely. Captain Shenk warned me of them."

"What is there to loot?" I nearly laughed, finding such a notion completely absurd and not at all troubling. My spirits were astonishingly bright this morning after so many days spent in a fog of gloom. To have felt death so near and cheated it, and to have found Collin alive when I'd believed him lost had swept all other troubles from my mind. We were together. The sun was shining. And Nova Scotia wasn't far at all, now. Life seemed as bright and hopeful as the beautiful day before us. "What would looters possibly come here for?"

"You'd be surprised." Collin looked at me over the top of Timothy's head, then spoke in a low voice. "I'll need to speak to the captain about some men to guard the bodies. Will you help me gather the others? We'll do best if we're together in a tight group."

"Everyone?" After surviving a bitter night, passengers and crew were scattered up and down the island, some working at salvaging what they might from the stranded ship, others at work finding water. Still others attempted to catch enough fish to sustain us until we could be transported to the mainland.

"Gather as many as you can," Collin said. "This island is called the graveyard of the Atlantic for good reason. So many ships have met their end here that there are those who watch the island closely, then come to claim the spoils whenever there's a wreck."

"You mean pirates?" Timothy sounded excited rather than scared.

"Aye. But none likely to bother us." Collin ruffled the top of his hair, sending a spray of sand tumbling out. I brought a hand to my own hair self-consciously, knowing it wasn't any better. We were all a mess.

"What would they want with the bodies?" I asked Collin in a hushed voice.

"Anything that is to be had," he replied. "Jewelry, clothing, or shoes of any value. A gold tooth."

I shuddered. "Come along, Timothy. Let's go warn others." The words were hardly out of my mouth before Timothy was off, running down the beach ahead of me, shouting as loudly as he could.

"Pirates are coming! Pirates are coming!"

"That'll be effective," Collin said with a wry grin.

I grasped the front of his shirt and pulled him close. "No more heroics, Mr. MacDonald. Let the looters have what they will, so long as it isn't you."

"Says the lady who cannot swim and went back into the ocean." Collin wrapped his arms around me and pulled me close. "No more heroics from you either, lassy."

"I'm a lass now, am I?" I teased, touching my hair again. "Must be this new style making me look younger."

Collin shook his head. "I misspoke. You're a woman—*my* woman," he amended. "*All* woman. Especially the way you looked yesterday with your wet gown clinging to you in all the right places. I've half a mind to throw you in the water again just to get the same view." He kissed me swiftly, then turned me from him and, with a pat to my backside, sent me on my way after Timothy.

"Collin!" I looked back to frown at him. "I don't hold with men beating their wives." *And leave it to a man to notice what a woman looks like at a time like that.*

"Not to worry." Collin laughed heartily, proving his spirits were as light as mine. "If I haven't beaten you yet, with *all* you've put me through, I'm not likely to start now."

With my arm looped through Collin's and my head on his shoulder, I stared at the firelight dancing before us. The black of night and a starlit sky above were our backdrop, making the flames somehow more magical than the many we'd sat before in my grandfather's castle in Scotland. I dug my toes into the sand and snuggled closer to Collin, wishing we were alone here, instead of surrounded by our fellow, surviving passengers. It had been a long day filled with sorrow for many, and hunger and trepidation for all.

A ship had indeed come to shore—not with the intent to rescue, but searching for what treasure might be had among us. Fortunately our bedraggled state had convinced the looters to leave us largely alone, and they instead had concentrated their efforts on retrieving what they might from ship and shore.

They were gone now. We were alone again, for which I felt grateful. I would sleep better tonight, without the worry of strange men coming to take what they might from us. *My lone stocking?* I smiled, thinking of the dirty, balled-up piece of fabric tied at my waist. Fearing I dared not waste anything, I'd kept it but had found walking around barefoot much preferable today.

The bottom length of my petticoat had torn to rags as well, and my hair hung wild and free down my back—the way I'd oft worn it in Scotland. Only when we had returned to England, and then on the *Cleopatra*, had I attempted to behave as a proper lady, showing some measure of fashion and decorum. *Very little these past weeks.*

Collin leaned forward, adding another piece of partially dried driftwood to the fire. His bare back showed through his torn shirt, reminding me of the first time I had seen him without one, on another firelit night, this one in the wilds of the Highlands. I remembered how I'd wanted to kiss him that night, had been frightened by such new and unexpected feelings. I'd pushed him in the water instead. Thinking of his words to me this afternoon, his idle threat to toss me into the water, and remembering that I *had* done it to him, made me smile.

The driftwood hissed and smoked; then, after a minute or two, the end caught the flame and held.

"You seem rather happy tonight," Collin said. "All day, in fact."

"I am. It is strangely pleasant here."

"Hmph. Would be a might more pleasant with something to fill our bellies."

"I think . . . you are rather prone to grumpiness when you are hungry." My hand crept down to poke at his stomach.

"Aye." Collin didn't argue the fact. "How can you *not* be?"

I shrugged. "I'm used to it, I guess."

This soured his expression even more. "Since you've been in want of food practically every day since we married."

"That is not true at all." I pinched him this time. "What I meant was that my stomach has been so ill at ease these past months that the ache of hunger is naught comparatively."

Collin grunted once more, that comforting Scot's sound I'd come to adore. I supposed he was long overdue a surly mood, given that he'd had to be positive for both of us for so long. "What I wouldn't give for a sporran full of oats right now."

Privately, I could only feel grateful we were done with his endless supply of oats. *May they rest peacefully at the bottom of the sea—or in the belly of some fish.*

"I am rather glad of what you do have in your pouch," I whispered, my hand lingering at his waist, where our remaining funds were tucked safely away. Collin had worn them thus since we'd first set foot upon the *Cleopatra.*

"How can I not be both grateful and happy?" I stroked the hair back from Timothy's face as he slept. "We are so blessed—" My voice broke. I glanced around the wide circle, noting that many were asleep already, and others deep in their own conversations or thoughts. Not all had been as fortunate. The girl I had pulled from the sea had lost her father. At least a dozen others had lost loved ones.

"I'm so sorry for the past weeks," I whispered. "I'm sorry about our baby."

"Me too." Collin raised my hand to his lips and allowed them to linger there. "I'll not tell you it will be all right and we'll have another bairn. I cannot bear the thought of risking such again. You were so ill before, and then after . . ."

"I was ill of mind." It was strange to think that the storm I'd feared for months was what had wrested me from my melancholy. "I hope to never feel that way again."

"I intend to see that you don't."

No bairns, then. No son to carry on Collin's name. No daughter to bear mine. This made me more sorrowful than I could say; yet with the memory of my miseries so fresh, I could not disagree. "We've Timothy."

"Aye. And a fine lad he is."

"Thank you for caring for him, for treating him so well when I could not."

"I have been glad to do it. He's been a bright spot in the voyage."

When I had failed him. Beneath my happiness the guilt was still there. *No other bright spot—no children.*

Or might there be, for Collin at least? Unwittingly I recalled the sketch I'd made of him holding Lydia, and the dream I'd had of Mhairi.

I held Collin a little tighter, unsettled by the vision and worried over what exactly it might mean.

Chapter Thirty

Norfolk, Virginia, May 1762

earest Elizabeth,

D*It was with great joy that I received your letter. I was pleased to hear that you've been given an assistant at the millinery. The lass Aisla sounds like she is a great help to you. It is good of Mrs. Perkins to allow her to sit with you and trim out bonnets during the long summer days. One is never too young to begin learning a new skill.*

Uncle Rogers' new employee learned coopering as a youth, from his father in Scotland. Though it was a skill that had lain dormant many years, he was able to recall it quickly and has proven himself worthy to stay on as long as he likes.

I regret that the climate still renders it impossible for me to visit you. However, another of Rogers' employees will be making a trip to Portsmouth soon. He intends to stop in at the shop to deliver a little something I've set aside for you. I should be very grateful if you are able to receive him, even for a few minutes, and if possible send a letter with him in return.

Please continue to take care, never venturing out alone.

Yours, ever affectionately,
Aunt Ilona

Holding a piece of tinder, Ian reached inside the barrel and lit the wood shavings resting at the bottom. "You'll go to Portsmouth next week, then?"

Ben nodded. "As soon as this order is done. I can stop by for Mrs. Campbell and the two girls on my way home." He wedged a band driver on top of the metal ring and began pounding. "We don't travel that far usually, but Rogers has had this client many years."

"I am grateful," Ian said. A month had passed since he'd spoken with Ben's sister about Jannet Campbell and the lasses coming to work for her. There had been no opportunity to get them before now, and he felt increasingly anxious over their welfare.

Thinking on it now, with particular concern about Eliza, Ian worked in silence for several minutes, tending the fire carefully and bending the wet staves, waiting for Ben to finish with the hoop before he spoke again.

"It may not be as simple as stopping by for Mrs. Campbell and the lasses. I'm not entirely certain of their circumstances at present. It may be that you'll need to persuade them to come with you, or even sneak them away, should the tavern keeper have become attached."

"So you've warned me," Ben said. "And if they don't wish to come?"

Ian shrugged. "I—we—you can only try. I should think the idea of working at your sister's dairy would appeal far more than living and working in a tavern."

"I still think it should be you who goes," Ben said, as he had before. "You could take the order." He looked up from his work to meet Ian's uncomfortable gaze.

"I would like to, but I dare not," Ian said, out of excuses and left only with the truth as explanation. "I ran into a bit of trouble in Portsmouth—with the law. If I truly wish to help those I've left behind, it is best I don't return. It is best they do not associate themselves with me." He lowered his head once more, on pretense of checking the shavings inside the barrel, though they were near to burning them-selves out.

He wanted to go himself. Oh, how he wanted to go, and he felt the coward for turning the task over to Ben.

It's not that I'm afraid—for myself, anyway. He feared for the others, and what trouble he might bring to their doorstep.

"I've had a thought that might help with getting Mrs. Campbell and the girls away," he suggested casually when another minute or two had passed and Ben had made no comment about Ian's confession, vague though it had been.

"What's that?" Ben's tone was not as friendly as at the beginning of their conversation. Ian could not blame him. In Ben's place, he would have wanted to know the particulars of his difficulty in Portsmouth. But Ian did not yet feel he could tell him. Ben had been a good friend this past month, but that did not mean Ian was ready to trust him completely. His years with the Munros had taught him caution, that it was better to be slow to trust.

"There is a woman who works in a millinery not far from The Young Devil. She has a bonnet larger than most I have seen, and it covers her face quite well. If the lasses and Mrs. Campbell were to wear such as they leave, it could help to hide their identities."

"What is this woman's, the hat maker's, name?" Ben asked.

"Eliza—Elizabeth Campbell," Ian amended quickly, but not before receiving a curious look from Ben. "She sailed on the same ship as Mrs. Campbell, the lasses, and myself."

"Perhaps she would like to work in the dairy as well," Ben suggested.

Ian wished that were possible. "She is indentured to the milliner." *Fourteen years.* He would be an old man by the time she finished her period of servitude. Eliza herself would no longer be young either. He would have to persuade her to leave before then. If Mrs. Perkins' money was refunded, Ian saw no reason why Eliza would have to stay. He hoped what he was sending her was proof of his intentions to free her as soon as possible—within a year, if he saved every shilling and took extra odd jobs, as he had been.

"You seem to know a great many Campbells."

"My brother is married to one," Ian said. "And crossing an ocean together provides opportunity for passengers to become acquainted." It was all he felt he could say. He couldn't exactly explain that he and Eliza had developed a friendship when she'd hidden him from the ship's officers, or that their relationship had deepened to trust and more while working together to undress and hide a corpse.

Rogers' return saved Ian from the further questions he sensed Ben wished to ask.

"Horses need to be returned to the stable," Rogers said by way of greeting as he entered the shop.

"Right away." Ian stood and brushed the shavings from his lap. He would sweep up later before going home, back to the boarding-house. His room there wasn't much in the way of a home—smaller even than the one he'd had at The Young Devil—but the meals were decent and regular. It was a place to lay his head and bide his time. *Until . . .*

He wasn't sure anymore. He still wished to return to Scotland, but first he needed to keep his promise to Aisla and see that she and Mrs. Campbell and her daughter were safely settled. If all went well, that might soon be accomplished, leaving him to focus on freeing Eliza. His wage being what it was, it would be more than a year before they'd be able to think of purchasing passage home. It was a long time, much longer than he had hoped to be here.

He stepped outside and made his way to the team.

If he was thinking only of himself, he could return to Scotland sooner. But it wasn't longing for his homeland that weighed on his mind these days so much as longing for Eliza.

Ian tugged the straps and pulled the horses forward, away from the wagon.

What would Da have said? What would he have me do? Would he roll over in his grave to know that not just one, but both of his sons cared for Campbell women?

Chapter Thirty-one

Halifax, Nova Scotia, May 1762

I peered at my figure critically in the dressing room glass, surprised at how much I had changed since our marriage. To be certain, I'd grown thinner. But then, food had been scarce much of the time and life harder as well. Gone were the days of idle after-noons painting in the garden.

In other ways I had changed as well, my shape filling out to a more womanly form than I'd known before. I turned sideways, rather startled at my profile from that angle. Perhaps our lost trunk and clothing were not as big a loss as I'd believed. It seemed doubtful that the gown I'd purchased to wear to Anna's would have fit now. For while my frame might be trim, other parts of me had definitely developed, as of late.

"It is good?" the dressmaker returned to the room, pincushion in hand.

"It's lovely," I said, relishing the swishing of a petticoat with all its length and fabric intact as I turned before the mirror again. We'd gone a week in Halifax with little but our rags for wear. The coin Collin carried had been enough for room and board, our two most pressing needs. Captain Shenk's generous reward—given to Collin for the lives he had helped to spare during the storm and wreck—were purchasing this dress and Collin's and Timothy's clothing and shoes as well. At last we would be respectable citizens again. Perhaps being dressed better would allow Collin to find the employment he'd been seeking. And tonight I hoped Mrs. Hodges, who ran the boardinghouse we'd found, would allow us to eat with the others in the dining room, instead of in our room, as we now had proper clothing, and shoes on our feet.

When our purchases were paid for, Collin, Timothy, and I strolled arm in arm down the street.

"You should feel welcome here." Collin nodded to the street sign on the corner. "They've already a road named for your clan."

"Hmm." I followed his gaze. "Somehow I doubt *Campbell Road* was chosen for us. And I *don't* feel comfortable here. Not with all these soldiers about." I lowered my voice as we passed two, standing near the corner. Though my father had once worn the same coat, I now associated it with the terrible events of the past year, when Collin had been forcefully taken from me by a patrol stationed in the Highlands.

"Lobsterbacks," Collin said, his voice low as well. "That's what they're called here. Fitting, like the red beasties themselves with their pinchers ready to strike."

"The sooner we are gone from this place, the better." So many Redcoats made me uneasy, given that Collin was still somewhat a fugitive. We had given my maiden name again when registering for our lodging, and Captain Shenk and the others we had met still knew us only as such. I longed to be at a place where we were free of worry and the need for deception.

Collin had paid for our room and board through the end of June, and I dearly hoped we might be gone from Halifax before the time came to pay again. Though I didn't see how. We'd no supplies or income as yet, and worse, no way to get word to Alistair and the others. *Including Ian.* Wherever he might be in the Colonies now.

I could not forget my promise to Collin that we would find his brother. *But how?*

"May I go down to the shore?" Timothy asked as we reached the street running alongside the harbor.

"Haven't you had enough of the ocean?" I certainly had.

"I want to look at the ships," Timothy said. "New ones arrive every day. Please, Katie."

"I suppose," I said, reluctant to have him far from my side in this unfamiliar city. "Don't go in the water."

"I won't. Don't worry. I won't spoil my new clothes," Timothy called as he ran off.

"It isn't your clothes I'm worried about!" I shouted, but he was already too far away to hear.

"Let the lad enjoy the view while we have it. According to your drawings, we'll be leaving the ocean behind, for a while at least."

"And when will that be? We've no maps, no provisions for travel, no one to come with us."

"One problem at a time." Collin placed his hand over mine. "I believe I've a solution to our most pressing issue."

"You've found work?" Since the day we arrived Collin had tried, unsuccessfully, to find employment. I feared there was a definite prejudice against him as a Scotsman. That he'd not been trained specifically in one trade did not help either. He was a leader with experience in many things from blacksmithing to farming, yet not expert in any one area and never apprenticed for a specific skill.

"Not exactly, no." Collin gentled his voice, alerting me to worry for what he might say next.

"Shenk is headed south to collect another of his ships. He has invited me to sail with him—ongoing thanks for my assistance during the storm."

"He wants you to be one of his crew?" In contrast to Collin's voice, mine rose sharply. "You would consider that? Sailing across the ocean again, returning who knows when? What of our plans? What of your brother? You'll be able to find other work here, Collin. I'm sure of it."

"You didn't allow me to finish." Collin pulled us off to a side street, then stopped in the shadow of a building to face me. This time he took both my hands. "Shenk's ship is in

Virginia. I would sail only that far. Once there I can set about finding Alistair and the others, and then we can all return to Halifax together."

I considered a moment, trying to discern if my immediate unease was about my unwillingness to be separated from Collin, my dislike of ocean voyages, or something else altogether—a premonition of trouble to come. Though I closed my eyes and reached inward, seeking the guidance I was occasionally blessed with, I could see nothing.

"All right," I said finally, remembering my promise to do what we must to find Ian. "Perhaps this is Providence itself, leading us to be reunited with our families. We can all go. There is no reason for us to separate again." *Ever.*

A pained look creased Collin's brow and the scar above his eye. "I'm afraid that's not possible. Shenk told me that Captain Larkland does not hold with females on his ship. He believes them ill luck."

"What utter nonsense. Females travel all the time. Were we not just in a ship full of women?"

"Aye, and it wrecked."

"And that is my fault? Because I'm a woman." I wrested my hands from Collin's and placed them at my hips.

"Of course not." He caught my eye, his pleading. "I don't believe in any such thing, and neither does Shenk, but the man offering us free transport to Virginia does. If I am to go, I must go alone."

"Why can't I come? I'm not a girl."

"Timothy! What do you mean by eavesdropping?" I looked over my shoulder to find him hiding behind my skirt.

"I wasn't. I just came to find you again. Only ships down there right now belong to the lobsters, and they're grumpy if you get too close."

Collin went down on one knee beside Timothy. "You are a fine sailor already, and would do much good, no doubt. But I need someone to stay behind and watch out for your sister. She finds herself in trouble rather often, you ken." Collin winked, and they exchanged a conspiratorial look, as if I was not right there, hearing every word and able to disagree. But I did not. If I was to be parted from Collin, at least I would have Timothy for comfort—something I would need far more than any guarding from mischief.

I brought a hand to my head, which was beginning to pound. *Separated, again.* How many times would this have to be? How long before we could live together in peace? I didn't think it was asking too much to have a little home and a simple life with the man I loved. We had given up our homeland, and now the notion of children. We didn't long for riches, merely enough to eat and a roof over our heads. Was being together and safe, and able to see to our own needs, such an extravagant wish?

When we married, I had imagined traveling to my new home with my husband and settling into a life similar to my old. I couldn't have been more wrong. Once I'd accepted that reality, together Collin and I had hoped and planned and acted to end the threats against us and to find security at the Campbell keep. That had not gone the way we had believed it would, either.

At the start of our voyage across the ocean, I had looked forward to our arrival in this new land which would become our home with our new baby. Then we had realized we would not be lingering in Halifax, but traveling on to more remote parts of Nova Scotia, in the midst of a dangerous war, no less. Each of those disappointments I had accepted. But now, to risk separation from Collin again seemed too much.

"Why not wait for a ship that can take us all?" I asked. Timothy nodded his agreement.

Collin stood and faced me once more. "We can do that," he said. "But it will delay us that much longer and perhaps make it more difficult to find the others. Then there is the matter of paying for our passage."

I folded my arms and began pacing the narrow alleyway, a habit I'd picked up from Collin.

"It's nearly June already," Collin said. "We need to be reunited with the others as soon as possible. We can't begin to think of travel to the remote areas you sketched until we are together again.

"Even then . . ." It would be too late to plant crops this year. How would we feed ourselves? Where would we find shelter, even if we were to reach the beautiful land I'd envisioned? My happy mood of the last several days deflated quickly into hopelessness.

"One problem at a time, Katie," Collin said, as if he'd read my mind. "First, we must find the others."

"We? You mean *you*?"

"Aye. Free passage to Virginia seems a gift we ought not over-look."

"And what are we to do while you're gone?" I stopped pacing and pulled Timothy—as long in the face as I felt—against my side.

"Some learning for this lad." Collin looked pointedly at my brother. "If you wish to be a sea captain when you're grown you must learn to read well and do figures. You'll have to know astronomy and the geography of the world."

"I can read. And I add and subtract too," Timothy said.

"Aye, but can you read the charts you saw in Captain Shenk's quarters?"

When Timothy didn't answer, Collin softened his look. "Not yet, but you will someday, if you'll pay attention to your learning now. The house where we're staying has a small library you can make use of while I'm gone. See how many of the books you can study during that time."

"When would we expect your return?" I still had not agreed that he would go.

"That depends on how long it takes me to find the others."

And Ian. Neither of us spoke his brother's name, but I knew we were both thinking it. *I promised.* Collin had so tenderly cared for my brother these past months, and for that alone I could not deny him the chance to find his.

"When do you have to go?" I asked, a tiny catch in my voice.

"The day after tomorrow. I know that's soon, but it's also fortunate."

I nodded, feeling extremely *mis*fortunate about the whole affair and not caring overmuch for Captain Shenk at the moment.

"With the remainder of the reward I've enough to pay room and board through the end of July."

"Why is Shenk being so generous with us?"

"He likes me," Timothy said proudly. Then his face fell. "Not that much, or he would have invited me too."

"He likes you fine—both of you," Collin said. "And I think he feels badly about the crewman who lost his head during the wreck."

"Lost his head and nearly caused us to lose Timothy," I muttered, still angry about that, though the man had been dismissed from his position. The rational part of me knew that there was no way of knowing how a person might react in time of crisis—in spite of instruction and training—until such a crisis occurred. Men and ships alike could be fickle.

"And if you aren't back by the end of July?" *Two months without Collin.*

He took my hands again. "I should be. The Captain reckons about three weeks to sail down the coast. A little more if we hit storms. That would leave me almost a month in Virginia to search before I would need to begin the return voyage."

"If everything goes well." *When has that ever happened for us?*

"Aye," Collin agreed. "*If . . .* I know it's a risk, but we've come this far. Your grandfather's visions—and yours— haven't left us alone yet."

I will be alone. And so will you. I gave a single nod, not quite agreeing, yet giving my consent. It seemed I had no other choice.

Collin pulled me into his arms. I buried my face in his shoulder, not caring that my brimming tears would soon wet his new shirt. His arms wrapped around me, strong and protective, full of love. Timothy nuzzled in beside us, and Collin extended one arm, pulling him into our embrace as well.

"I'll take care of Katie," Timothy promised solemnly. "I won't let anything bad happen to her."

"Thank you, lad," Collin answered, his voice gruff. "Take care of each other."

"We will," I promised, feeling more unsettled. *But who will take care of you?*

Chapter Thirty-two

Halifax, Nova Scotia, June 1762

"Excuse me miss, are you this boy's sister?" Clothespin in hand, I turned from the line and my half-pinned, mended petticoat toward the unfamiliar male voice. A tall, uniformed man stood in the yard, a hand on Timothy's shoulder in a way I could not discern as friendly.

"I am," I said. "His sister and guardian." I rushed toward them, despite the fact that the man towered over me. "I am sorry if he has caused you any difficulty. He is very creative and clever, and some-times that leads to mischief. But never does he intend harm."

My eyes dropped to Timothy, who seemed not frightened but insolent as he shrugged out of the man's grasp and started toward me. I pulled him close, an arm around him as together we faced whatever trouble he had caused.

"Master Timothy and I happened to become acquainted when I discovered him admiring my ship."

Though the man did not exactly sound angry, I cringed inwardly, imagining the many and varied ways Timothy might have been *admiring*. Look, but don't touch was a concept I'd yet to sufficiently instill in him. But merely touching a ship couldn't harm it—could it?

"Haven't you had enough of ships?" I asked my brother, attempting to keep my voice light.

Timothy raised a hand and pointed at the man. "He's one of the looters from the island. He stole your drawings."

"My drawings—" I turned Timothy toward me, a sinking feeling in my stomach that this situation was about to get very bad. "My sketchbook was lost when the ship sank. And even had it not been—even had someone found it, the drawings wouldn't have survived being in the ocean."

"But—"

"And even if they somehow had," I continued, cutting off Timothy's argument. "They're not anything that someone would have stolen." With a sheepish smile, I turned to the man.

"My many apologies, sir."

He gave a curt nod. "Accepted. May I advise you to keep a sharper watch on your brother. It is fortunate I was the one to find him. Other men might not take so kindly to the boy trying to steal something from their ship."

"Steal something—Timothy, you were *on* a ship?" My stomach rolled over suddenly as I thought of Timothy alone on one of the great vessels at harbor—one that might have carried him away.

"I saw your drawings, Katie. I'm telling the truth. He took them off the *Cleopatra*. I saw them through a window, and I went in to take them back."

I pressed my lips together, beyond frustrated with and frightened for my little brother. "My *sincerest* apologies, sir. It shall not happen again." I took Timothy's arm, rather firmly, and steered him toward the house. Afternoon roaming privileges had just ceased.

"I'm not lying," Timothy insisted. "He has your drawings."

"Excuse me, miss." Behind us the man cleared his throat.

I paused and turned back to him, afraid he wanted some further retribution for Timothy's attempted thievery. "Yes?"

"The boy seems most insistent, and if he is not normally given to lying or deceit—"

"He is not usually given to either," I said. "Though I fear his curiosity may be the downfall of us both."

The man actually smiled. "Perhaps not." His brown eyes sparkled. "At present I find myself curious, as well, to see if your drawings do, indeed, prove a close match to my own. I was hoping you might indulge me in allowing me to view one."

"I would happily do so," I said. "Were all not truly lost in the wreck of the *Cleopatra* off Sable Island."

"I see," the man said, his disappointment evident in the sudden droop of his mouth. "Do you think—might it be possible for you to produce a replica of one or more of them?"

"Again, I would do so happily." It was my face falling with regret now. "But I have nothing to do it with." I was beginning to be discomfited by the man's interest. The drawings I had done had not been spectacular, in the least. I was far better at painting than the simple landscape and lines I had done would lead one to believe. I could see no reason for his supposed interest in my work unless he wished to commission a portrait.

Even then . . . As much as the income would have been helpful, I did not think it appropriate for me to spend time in another man's company without Collin.

"Good day to you, sir," I said curtly, ending further speculation about any possibility of my drawing or painting him or anything else. With my hand still latched around Timothy's arm, I marched him toward the front door of the boardinghouse.

"Good day to you, as well Miss—I don't even know your name."

I closed my eyes briefly and gave a small huff of indignation. "*Mrs.* Katherine Mercer." Good manners bade me turn around and curtsy briefly.

"Mr. James Cook," he said, doffing his hat to reveal a crown of rich, brown hair that complimented his piercing eyes. "Master of the *Northumberland*."

Chapter Thirty-three

Norfolk, Virginia, June 1762

Ian counted the pence notes, the sum of several days' work, as he placed them in Ben's hand. "And this as well." He hesitated a moment, then placed a folded parchment on top of the bills. "Give this to no one but Eliza. If she's not at the shop, please ask when she'll return. This letter will explain everything to her—about the bonnets for Mrs. Campbell and the lasses," he added hastily.

"Bonnets like the one Eliza wore to church the Sunday she chastised you." Ben recited back some of the details he'd managed to wheedle out of Ian over the past week. "I'm almost as good as the letter." He grinned.

Probably better. Ian was eager to speak with Aisla, in particular, as she had spent time recently in Eliza's company. Supposing Eliza still felt the same about him, Ben would be a welcome visitor.

Sheepishly, Ian smiled and stepped back. "I thank you kindly for doing this."

"Not a problem. Rogers has done business with the Bell's Hill plantation for a long time. It's well for you they're not too far from Portsmouth. You've been a patient man, biding your time until you might have news from your lady friend."

Ian rolled his eyes, then turned his back to Ben. "I've *told* you, Jannet Campbell is no particular friend of mine. I only wish to see that she and the two lasses are safe." *Tomorrow.* If all went well they would be here, and then at least a few of his worries would diminish.

Now that the day had finally come, it all seemed almost too perfect to Ian. *Too good for the way things go in my life.*

"Didn't say it was Mrs. Campbell you were pining for, did I?" Ben said.

"Who do you think I've feelings for?" Ian asked crossly. "And don't say the lasses, because that's just wrong. Neither of them have even ten years yet."

Ben chuckled. "I'm smarter than that—and so are you."

So smart I left two women and two lasses on their own.

With no way, other than the one vague, coded letter he'd received from Eliza, to hear news of Mrs. Campbell for the past month, Ian could only hope that she was still at The Young Devil and that no harm had come to her or the children. Without declaring himself an outright criminal—and one wanted for murder, at that—Ian had alluded to Ben that the less his name was mentioned while on this errand, the better.

After the delivery this afternoon, Ben was to stop by the tavern for a meal, where he would seek opportunity to speak with Mrs. Campbell.

"And *why* ought she be persuaded to leave with me, a complete stranger?" Ben had asked when first presented with this plan and again repeatedly in the weeks after.

It had taken Ian a while to answer, his mind searching all the while for something that might be said to the woman without giving himself away. At last he had struck upon it.

"Tell her that Liam Campbell saw this, that it was foretold she and the lasses would work and live at Johnston's Dairy in the colony of Virginia."

Ben had seemed even more bewildered at this suggestion, but Ian, surprisingly, felt rather strongly it would work. Hadn't his sister-in-law left her home in England, married a MacDonald, and traveled with strangers to a new country—all because Liam Campbell had foretold such? The Campbells were a superstitious lot, even more so than most Highlanders, and they put great stock in their seers. If anything was likely to persuade Jannet Campbell, prophetic words from a complete stranger were probably the thing.

Ben finished a last count of the hogsheads packed tightly in the wagon bed then came around to the front and climbed up on the seat.

Ian placed a hand on the wagon box, as if reluctant to let it go. "I'm most grateful to you for doing this, and for checking on Elizabeth Campbell at the millinery. I just need to know she is well."

"No shame in admitting that." Ben's voice was sober now. "I look forward to meeting her and hearing more about *you.*" His grin returned. "Maybe she'll tell me what mischief you're mixing me up in, Ian MacDonald. We'll just see."

For the next two days the hours crawled painfully. Ian found himself glancing at the clock so much the second day that even Rogers took notice.

"Don't worry," he said. "It'll be well. Ben's his head about him."

Ian dearly hoped so—hoped he hadn't steered a good man into trouble.

"I'm going to close up early," Rogers announced not ten minutes later. "Orders for Monday are filled already. No point in staying late. Care to join me for a drink?"

Surprised at the offer and at the idea that the silent, serious Rogers ever did anything after work except go straight home, eat his supper, and go to bed, Ian looked up, a question on his lips as well as in his expression. "Sir?"

Rogers shrugged. "I'm not much for the stuff, but you're wound so tight it's obvious you need something to calm you."

What he needed was to see little Aisla here and healthy, safe and well. *And some word of Eliza . . .*

"Thank you for the offer." Ian made no move to rise from the bench where he worked. "But if it's all the same, I'd prefer to stay a little later. And I don't think alcohol is the thing just now."

"Scottish whisky doesn't solve everything, eh?" Rogers paused by the door. "Well, then, lock up when you're done. I'll see you Monday."

Ian gave a nod and returned to smoothing the inside of a barrel. This one was a rare oak, not unlike those he'd made for his da in Scotland. Ian breathed in deeply, willing the scent to return him to his childhood, to happier times, before the world had become so complicated. Instead the pungent aroma transported him to another time—the MacDonald keep, to be sure, and the building where the casks of whisky were stored—but not a particularly pleasant memory.

"How many you think are in here?" Hugh Munro stood in the open doorway, moonlight spilling in behind him, illuminating Hugh's greedy expression and what they'd hoped to be their biggest haul yet.

"Enough." *A lot less than there used to be.* Ian walked deeper into the room, surprised at how empty it was. He thought they'd be doing well to get a half dozen—particularly if Hugh didn't shut up and get inside. "Close that door," he whispered. "Or do you *want* a fight?"

"With the MacDonald laird? No." Hugh shook his shaggy head.

I'm supposed to be the MacDonald laird. Somehow Collin had escaped the Campbells to take the position as leader of the MacDonalds before Ian could. *Probably what Da planned all along.*

The bitter thoughts fueled Ian's determination. "Have you the cloth?" he asked Hugh.

"Aye. The lads have spread it upon the ground as you instructed."

"Good. Help me tip these barrels." They lay six over on their sides; then Hugh and the others began the process of rolling them along the wool, muffling the sound as their contraband made its way to the wagons hidden in the woods nearby.

While they worked, Ian set about his own task, spreading out the dry hay and preparing the torches. Their timing had to be exact. The whisky and men had to be well away before he set the fires, else they'd be in for more fight than they were prepared for. Hugh was wise in not wanting a match with Collin. In the few years since he'd returned to be laird, his reputation as a great defender of his people had risen in legend.

Like their father, he wasn't one to go picking a fight, but if it was brought to his doorstep, woe to the one who started it.

Until now, Ian thought smugly. His confidence rose as the last of the barrels—two more than he'd thought—made it safely into the woods. Through a notch in the wall, he watched the moon and waited, giving the others a good lead before he started any fires. The guards they'd dispatched earlier would be no trouble and were safe enough until they were eventually found and untied and had their gags removed. Ian was pleased to have avoided the unnecessary spilling of his kinsmen's blood. He'd learned a thing or two since the raid on the English patrol years earlier.

But he wasn't safely away yet, and Ian didn't delude himself that other guards, elsewhere around the keep, wouldn't be aware of the fire within minutes of it being set. He wasn't afraid of facing them, but he did hope he wouldn't have to kill tonight.

At last, he deemed it time. On legs that felt stiff from squatting, Ian rose, then turned and nearly wet himself when he found a man facing him, not ten hands away. And not any man. *Collin.*

"Next time, you need only ask." Collin inclined his head toward the empty space where the barrels had been. "What's mine is yours."

"Don't you mean what's yours should actually *be* mine?" Ian recovered from his shock and allowed the hatred he'd spent years cultivating toward his brother and father break loose.

"I don't seem to recall you doing any of the work to make that whisky. Though I know you're aware of how much it requires." Collin's hands hung loosely at his sides, and Ian could make out no weapons in the dark.

He wouldn't be foolish enough to come alone. Ian knew he'd a reputation as well. "The Munros operate a little differently," he said with a smirk. "More profit, less work. A model you might want to try sometime. Doesn't appear the MacDonalds are doing so well these days."

"We're not," Collin admitted freely. "The English take what little we have, then come back and take more. It's not been pretty or popular being a MacDonald since the '45."

Ian grunted. He didn't want to talk about that time. He didn't want to hear that his father's clan was struggling.

"We could use a good man like you," Collin continued. "Too many were lost at Culloden or rounded up after. We've more widows and bairns than men to take care of them and the fields that feed them."

"That's your problem." Ian stepped to the side, toward an unlit torch lying on the ground.

"You'd like it to be yours." Collin's guess was close enough to Ian's earlier thoughts to discomfit. "You're older. You should be laird," Collin said. "You *could* be."

The offer hung in the air between them. *A trick.* Nevertheless, Ian's heartbeat escalated with an odd burst of hope. *Another life.* He might have one. Something other than the misery that he'd known these many years. Then he remembered Aileen, remembered that he had to burn this building down, had to return to her. And if it came to it, he had to kill Collin.

"Why would you give up your position of power to me?"

Ian nudged the torch with his foot, checking to see it was where he thought it was.

Collin laughed. "You think being laird is about having power?"

"Of course it is." Ian thought of Bruce Munro. He had power over every single member of his clan. *And me.*

"You're wrong," Collin said. "If done right, it's the opposite. It's about responsibility and caring for people. It's about giving up what you want for the good of others."

Now it was Ian who laughed. "No wonder you've hardly anything in your storehouse."

"But I've a storehouse, at least," Collin said evenly as he took a step closer. "I gave you what you came for tonight—*gave* it, remember that. If I hadn't wanted you to take it, I would have stopped you. But I'll not let you torch our buildings. We've precious little resources as it is, and harassment enough from the English without needing it from my own brother as well."

For the first time Collin sounded angry. This didn't worry Ian, but rather ignited his own temper.

"*Brother?* You dare to call yourself that when you've let me suffer all these years among the Munros? You and Da left me there, left me for dead, left me to endure—"

"We didn't want to," Collin said. "I tried to stop him . . ." His voice died out with the excuse. "Da told me you were dead. He wept that night."

Ian didn't believe it. He'd never seen their father cry. Never when they were growing up, never when speaking of their mother. Not after any battle, even Culloden.

"He *wept*," Collin repeated, nodding his head as if he could read Ian's disbelief. "And then he gave himself over to the English. Bound me by promise not to move from our hiding spot while he walked right into their camp. Left me behind to hear the shots that killed him."

Ian cringed, feeling something other than anger. His jaw clenched as he tried to block the images Collin had painted from his mind. He didn't want to hear this, didn't want to hear anything that might alter the view of his father and brother that he'd believed so many years.

"I dug his grave with my dirk and my bare hands," Collin said. "It was shallow. Da hardly fit. His clothes were ragged and bloody—full of holes. They'd shot him so many times." Collin's voice wavered. "I'd barely laid him in it when the Campbells took me."

"He *left* me," Ian spat bitterly.

"He *died* for you, for us," Collin said. "Made it so each of us went to a different clan—ones who'd sided with the English, so they'd leave us alone."

"Well, the *Munros* didn't leave me alone." Ian realized he was practically shouting and lowered his voice. He didn't need a swarm of MacDonalds. Dealing with Collin was already more than he'd bargained for.

"So I've heard," Collin said. "So I see," he added.

"What's that supposed to mean?"

"You've forgotten who you are," Collin accused. "You're a MacDonald, not a common thief. You care for people and provide for them—not take from them."

"I do what I must." Ian reached down and in a fluid movement scooped up the unlit torch and removed his dirk. "Get out while you can."

"Stop this madness while *you* can," Collin warned, taking a step toward him.

Hidden behind the torch, Ian's blade was clenched in his fist, ready to strike. *He left me.* They *left me. Collin is laird. I should be.* He felt the anger burning within him. *Kill him.* Kill *him.*

"What are you waiting for?" Collin asked calmly. "I see your knife. Use it." He placed his hands on his hips, practically begging Ian to strike.

Ian tried to judge the look in Collin's eyes but found it difficult in the dim light. It couldn't be this easy. Collin had always given him a good fight whenever they'd a tussle as lads.

Half and half, it was. Sometimes he won, sometimes Collin did. Sometimes Da caught them at it and thrashed them both.

He wept.

Ian tried to banish the image of his father crying over him. *Curse Collin for telling me.* He didn't want to imagine that, yet he couldn't seem to keep it from his mind.

"Put the torch down and come with me," Collin said.

"I can't." Ian thought of Aileen. If he returned with the whisky but without having done the rest, what would happen?

"Why not?" Collin asked. "I don't see Bruce Munro here to stop you. I don't see any Munros."

"I've got to kill you." It was foolish to admit something like that to an enemy. But Ian's logic was unraveling quickly.

"I guessed as much," Collin said. "Go ahead and try. You've your weapon ready, and you can see I've none." He held up empty hands.

Ian tossed the torch aside. No need for hiding his knife when Collin had somehow seen it.

"You're a fool." *Kill him.* Bruce Munro's voice pounded in his head.

Da wept. He died for you. Collin and the truth stood before him. Ian raised his arm. He'd throw the knife, straight at Collin's heart. He wouldn't even have to touch him.

Collin didn't move, didn't run.

If only he would. That was it, that was the problem. "I'll not fight an unarmed man." Ian lowered his arm, relieved. It wasn't a fair fight this way. He didn't always care about that, didn't usually, but with his brother it was different.

"Put your blade away, then," Collin said.

"If I put it away, I pick up the torch. It's one or the other, or they'll harm her," Ian said, suddenly anguished over this decision.

"I can't let you burn us out. There are other lives besides my own to consider. If it comes to that, I'd rather you kill me."

He would have to do both. Ian reached for the torch

again. Collin kicked it from him as he grabbed it. Ian managed to keep hold of his knife and thrust it beneath Collin's neck.

"You oughtn't have done that," Ian hissed.

Collin stood slowly. Ian followed his movements, keeping the dirk so close it touched Collin's skin.

"Go ahead," Collin urged again, his voice free of fear.

Ian's chest pounded. He had to work to keep his hand steady. Collin's eyes never left his.

Kill him. Bruce Munro's voice sounded far away. Collin's face was right before him. Collin, who'd been at his side in mischief and tragedy, infant to near adult. *And then he was gone.* The thought of never seeing his brother again, never having another conversation, even another fight, was too much.

Ian's hand dropped to his side. The knife clattered to the ground, and he stepped back, humiliated, defeated.

Relieved.

Collin stooped to pick up the dirk. He held out his other hand.

Ian hesitated, then took it.

Collin clasped it heartily, a smile on his face, then jerked Ian toward him and twisted his arm behind his back. Ian felt the prick of metal at his throat.

"Welcome home, brother."

Ian's head snapped up, and his hand instinctively went to his neck. There was no blade there. No one was behind him. He'd fallen asleep. Outside Rogers' Cooperage the sky was dark.

A glance at the clock on the wall showed it was well past closing. Ian stood stiffly, then wiped the shavings from his apron. He went to the side door and opened it, checking for the wagon. It had not returned.

Ian closed and locked the door, then took up the broom and began sweeping. *What's taking Ben so long?* Even with the drive to the plantation and stopping in Portsmouth for

Jannet Campbell and the lasses, he could have easily been back yesterday. Ian hadn't really expected that, as likely it would take some arranging to get them away. But they ought to have returned today. His insides twisted with worry—not only for the children and Mrs. Campbell, but for Ben. He'd a family to come home to.

I'd no right to get him involved with my problems. I should have gone. All through tidying the shop, Ian berated himself. When he'd finished cleaning, donned his coat, and stepped outside, locking the door behind him, he made the decision to visit Ben's home first thing in the morning. He would have gone now, but feared disturbing Ben's wife and children at this late hour. Besides, it wasn't as if he could do much tonight. No ferries would be crossing until tomorrow. But then, Ian vowed, he would return to Portsmouth and see for himself what had become of Ben and the others.

As he walked toward the boardinghouse where he lodged, Ian thought ruefully of that reunion with Collin. Ian had learned that night that his brother was no less a threat than he was. Liam Campbell had taught Collin a thing or two about cunning and deceit. The difference was, Collin only used those skills for the good of others. He never acted maliciously, never harmed another without just cause. He hadn't harmed Ian that night, but had taken him up to their father's keep, fed him well, given him their father's room, and made sure he was watched at all times—for the next year.

Collin was right in being slow to trust me. Perhaps Ben had been too quick, and Ian had been careless with their friendship. *If some-thing has happened to him . . .* Ian couldn't bear the thought. It was nearly as bad as the fear he'd had for Eliza, when she had told him she was to remain on the ship with Millet.

More troubled thoughts than his mind had room to hold haunted him as he walked, and later as he attempted sleep. *I tried,* he mumbled tossing in his bed, hovering in a state that rendered him half-asleep yet seemingly awake as he spoke with his father. *I tried to be a better man. To do honest work. To help others—It has all gone wrong.*

You will yet have a chance to make it right. You've not failed, son.

His father's imagined words finally brought comfort and hope. And at last, Ian slept.

Chapter Thirty-four

Norfolk, Virginia, June 1762

Ian forced himself to wait until eight o'clock Sunday morning before he knocked on the door to Ben's house. Almost instantly, from the other side, he heard laughter and the cries of little voices along with the pattering of small feet.

He knew a second of worry, fearing Ben's children would think he was their father returning. But when the door opened Ben himself stood on the other side.

"You're back." Ian sighed audibly as the tension expelled from his body. Ben, at least, was safely returned and appeared no worse for his journey—dressed in his Sunday best, looking as if he was about to step out the door to go to church.

"I am. Late last night." Instead of inviting Ian in, Ben came outside and closed the door behind him.

"How did it go?" Ian asked, fearing bad news, given the lines creasing Ben's brow.

"Somewhat worse than I had expected. But Mrs. Campbell and the girls are now safely delivered to my sister," Ben added. "She is much pleased to have her new servants in place."

"As am I." Ian allowed himself to smile. "I thank you, Ben."

"As well you should." Ben did not return his smile. "Here." He pulled the pound notes and the letter Ian had given him the day before yesterday from his pocket and handed them to Ian. "We'd no need of bonnets, as we traveled at night.

I wouldn't have been able to get them anyway. Mrs. Perkin's Millinery burned down two weeks ago."

Burned. The notes fluttered from Ian's fingers to the ground. "Eliza—"

"The shop owner next door informed me that the indentured woman, one Miss Elizabeth Campbell, had survived and was imprisoned and awaiting trial for the murder of Mrs. Perkins." Ben stooped to pick up the discarded bills.

"No!" Ian's fists clenched. "Not Eliza. She's no murderer." Never mind her confession in the hold that day—or had it been night? She'd never explained what she'd done. *Or believed she'd done.* But he *knew* Eliza. She wouldn't have killed the old lady, wouldn't have started a fire. "She was fond of her employer. She—"

"Calm yourself." Ben reached a hand out to steady Ian as he ran shaking fingers through his hair.

"I must go." He'd left her. *Like Aileen.* It was the same nightmare all over again.

"Exactly what I supposed you would say." Ben shook his head. "But no. That wouldn't help anyone. In fact, it would place you *right* in Millet's hands."

"What do *you* know of Millet?" Ian's gut twisted with worry for Eliza.

"What I *should* have known when I started this errand." Ben's brows rose in a look of reproach. He dropped his hand from Ian's arm and stepped back. "Mrs. Campbell was kind enough to fill me in on the details."

"I am sorry to have been vague," Ian said, caring little what Ben or anyone else thought of him. *Eliza imprisoned.* "Whatever she said—"

"—doesn't matter as much to me as what *you* say." Ben caught Ian's eye and held it. "Did you murder a member of the *Ulysses* crew?"

"Aye. I suppose I did," Ian said unrepentantly. "Hit him on the back of the head with a bottle when he tried to attack

Eliza. Fool fell forward and struck his head on the stairs. That's what finished him." *If I leave now . . .*

"What did you do with the body?"

"Hid it behind those same stairs." Ian paced before the fence. *Does the ferry run on Sunday?* "I did not intend to hang for accidentally killing the man. And I wasn't about to have Eliza mixed up with it." *Eliza. Eliza locked up—*

"Having her help you move and undress the dead man *wasn't* mixing her up in it?" Ben sounded incredulous.

"I don't expect you to understand," Ian said. "I'm just telling you what happened. Eliza had trouble enough already, with—"

"Millet," Ben finished.

"Is there anything you *don't* know?" Ian glanced around, half expecting a pair of Redcoats to appear and arrest him, now that he'd confessed.

"Probably, but I expect you'll tell me shortly." The severity of Ben's expression eased. He took a deep breath, then released it.

"How do you know all this, anyway?" Ian asked, suddenly suspicious and hopeful at the same time. "Eliza and I were the only two there—with the body."

"You, Eliza, and the little girl who had followed her," Ben clarified. "She peered through the crack in the door."

"A child saw—"

"Not just any child." Ben smiled sadly. "One of those I brought back from Portsmouth. The girl you purchased from Millet. She is quite a talkative little thing and told us all she'd seen and heard—all that you just told me."

"Why did you ask, then?" Ian said, irritated, not over Ben's questioning so much as he was about Aisla having witnessed the scene in the hold. *What a thing for a child to see.* It was a wonder she'd come with him at all and hadn't given him away to Millet. "We're wasting time. I'm going to Portsmouth. Tell Rogers what you will about me tomorrow."

"I would not call what you did murder, but defense."

"Officer Millet is not likely to agree."

"True," Ben said. "He seems particularly bent on having you in his clutches, to pay for that crime—and others."

"Then let him," Ian said. "Let him have me in exchange for Eliza."

"You give in too easily, friend." Ben placed a hand on Ian's shoulder and looked directly at him once more. "You ought to have trusted me with all of it before I went. Though I see why you did not. Rogers, perhaps, would not be quite so understanding."

"Tell him, if you wish." Ian shrugged Ben's hand away, wary of its potential for restraint. He needed to be away from here now. He'd figure out what to do while crossing the miles back to Eliza. "It is of little consequence now what my former employer thinks of me." He turned to go.

"He is not your *former* employer, and I don't think you want to be going anywhere just yet," Ben called.

Ian lifted a hand in farewell but did not turn back. "I thank you, Ben. You *have* been a friend. More than I deserved."

"You'll not find her there, Ian."

He paused, hand on the gate to Ben's yard. "What do you mean?"

"Elizabeth Campbell went missing three days ago."

Chapter Thirty-five

Norfolk, Virginia, June 1762

"Escaped?" Ian shook his head as he strode purposely down the street, not bothering to see if Ben kept up. "I think not. If that's what Millet told you, he's lying. He's taken Eliza somewhere." *Just as he wanted to all along.* "I'll wring the truth out of him with my bare hands if I have to. And if he's harmed her—"

"Will you listen just a minute?" Ben demanded, grabbing Ian's coat sleeve.

"There's no time for talk." Ian tried to shrug from his grasp, and when that didn't work, he swung his fist around. Ben ducked, narrowly avoiding being hit in the jaw.

"You fool," he muttered. "I ought to let you run off and get yourself captured and hung." He flung Ian's arm away.

Something in his voice gave Ian pause. "One minute. I'm listening."

"Mrs. Campbell, the girls, and I were halfway home by the time I'd pieced together the story and just who Eliza was. I felt I must do something—knowing what she meant to you." Ben gave Ian a pointed look, as if to say, *don't bother denying it now.*

"I left the others safely hidden outside of town and returned to Portsmouth, searching for the home where Eliza was said to be jailed. I found it and pretended to be Mrs. Perkins' brother, come as soon as I'd received word of the fire and her death. I demanded an audience with Elizabeth."

"You went back?" Ben was an even better friend than Ian had realized, more clever and devious as well.

"It seemed probable, from what Mrs. Campbell and Aisla had told me of Elizabeth—how she had cared for others throughout your voyage, and how she'd volunteered to go with Mrs. Perkins in Mrs. Campbell's stead—that she was not the sort of woman to be guilty of murder. And I thought of you," Ben admitted. "And what you would feel upon discovering her plight. I didn't want you to return to Portsmouth and put yourself in danger."

"I don't see that I've much choice. You're right. I do care for her—a great deal." Ian ran one hand through his hair and held the other up in a plea of remorse. "I'm sorry to have struck out at you."

"It's all right." Ben glanced back toward his house. "I would have reacted the same was it Bess in peril."

"Then you understand why I must return," Ian said. "Why I cannot leave her vulnerable to Millet—any longer than she has been already."

"I spoke with the maid at the residence where Eliza was being held," Ben said. "Some nights before I arrived, Officer Millet had come to see Eliza. He'd dismissed the other guards for the night and carried a bottle upstairs with him. The guards and servants suspected he'd other plans beyond simply watching the prisoner, but no one felt to question him about it."

"Cowards," Ian muttered, knowing he was the biggest one of all, for leaving Portsmouth in the first place without ensuring Eliza was safe. "What right had Millet—what had a ship's officer to do with her imprisonment at all?" Ian imagined Millet going up the stairs to a room where Eliza was being held and felt as ill as he had been the morning he'd retched in the bushes. Of course Millet had other plans. He'd had them for weeks. And alone now, with no one to protect her, Eliza would have been helpless against him.

"Millet's involved because Eliza has also been accused of the murder of one Mr. Rupert Star, member of the crew of the *Ulysses*."

"That's ludicrous!" Ian threw up his hands. "No way Millet can blame—"

"She's believed to have been an accomplice in the murder, having assisted *Collin* MacDonald with the deed."

"My brother." Ian brought a hand to his forehead. "They thought I was him when—" At Ben's confused look Ian broke off. "Never mind. Go on." Ian's teeth clenched as he steeled himself for what he would hear next.

"There is little more to tell," Ben said. "Except that Millet was found the following morning, lying in his own vomit, intoxicated to the point of being delusional, and without possession of either his clothing or pistol. The prisoner he was to have been guarding—Miss Elizabeth Campbell—was nowhere to be found." A slight smile curved Ben's lips. "Rather an amusing picture that paints. Not knowing the man myself, of course, I cannot imagine it entirely, but I can guess you find it particularly humorous."

"Why should I?" Ian snapped. "Who knows what he did to her? He might have committed murder himself and tossed her in the river for all we know." Ian hung his head, his stomach clenching and his breath short as he relived a past nightmare.

Aileen is dead. Bruce Munro's sinister laughter rang through Ian's head. How long he'd tried to block it, and now he would have Millet's face and voice competing to haunt him. *I killed her. Like a coward, you left, so I took Eliza and I killed her.*

"If that were the case, I should hardly think Millet would have been discovered bound and naked," Ben said. "The entire incident is said to have resulted in great humiliation for him."

"You didn't tell me he was bound." Ian looked up. "It might still be false. The maid you spoke with could have made the entire thing up."

"That is possible," Ben conceded. "Though I think it at least as likely that your friend was clever enough to get Millet soused and then make off with his weapon and clothing—which, I might add, could prove a beneficial disguise."

"Soused, of course," Ian said. *Had she wanted to poison you, you'd be dead . . .* Eliza had known exactly what Jannet Campbell had put in that drink to make him sick. Might she not have done the same to Millet? Ian recalled how quickly he'd become ill that fateful night.

He felt a ray of hope. "I've got to find Eliza. I appreciate you telling me all this, but it changes nothing. I must go to Portsmouth."

"*You* should not return," Ben said. "Wanted as you—or your brother—are, it is too risky. You should probably not linger overlong in Norfolk, either, near as it is to those searching for you."

"I stayed close because of those I was trying to help. I should never have left them to begin with."

Ben shook his head. "You were right in leaving. You're no good to anyone if you're dead, Ian. Least of all, Rogers—who just might murder me, should I cost him the best cooper he's yet to have."

"You discount yourself and Rogers both," Ian said, refusing to be distracted by the compliment. "I'm sorry to leave you the task of explaining my absence, but I'll not delay."

"It's not your feet that need moving right now," Ben argued. "But your mind. Think this through, I say. Don't walk right into a trap. Have you ever considered that Eliza might return to rescue *you,* was she in hiding nearby and to learn that you had been taken? Or . . . it is possible she might try to come here, looking for her dear *Aunt Ilona* and Uncle Rogers."

"You read my letter." Ian's accusation was flat. Ben's prying was the least of his worries.

"Only because I needed every clue I could find," Ben replied. "Think about it, Ian. She's likely to come here. But if you're in Portsmouth—and if you're in trouble . . ."

"So I am just to wait, to do nothing while she is out

there—somewhere—" Ian threw his arms wide. "Facing who knows what?"

"You'll not be idle." Ben slung his arm over Ian's shoulders and turned him around in the direction they'd come. "On the morrow *I* will return to Portsmouth to see what else can be discovered. I would have stayed yesterday but had Mrs. Campbell and the children to see safely here. While I am gone *you* will need to do both your work and mine at the cooperage. I would also suggest speaking with Mrs. Campbell and the girls, particularly Aisla, as she has spent time recently with Elizabeth. It is entirely possible they will tell you something I missed."

"Why should you do that for me?" Ian asked, as they neared Ben's house. "Why concern yourself with my troubles?"

"Because you are my friend." Ben paused to open the front gate. "And because more than ever you must stay alive so you can be an even better friend to your Eliza."

"What do you mean?" Ian asked. Of course he was her friend. He would do anything for her. "I am willing to turn myself in if it means her freedom. I have told you as much already."

Ben nodded sagely and dropped his hand. "It may come to that. Though I suspect it may come down to giving up *your* freedom another way."

"I agreed to fourteen years' indenture when I took my brother's place on the *Ulysses.*"

A look of surprise and then respect registered on Ben's face. "I did not realize—but that sounds like a good tale for another day." He smiled. "I wasn't thinking of a term of fourteen years for you. It would be much longer than that, God willing."

"Stop speaking riddles and be out with it," Ian said impatiently.

"If, as you fear, Millet has used her ill, Eliza may need more than a friend," Ben said. "She may need a husband."

Chapter Thirty-six

Halifax, Nova Scotia, June 1762

Timothy slumped against the back of his chair. "Captains don't need to know the proper tense or how to conjugate verbs. They don't even use sentences half the time. They just say things like, 'Weigh anchor, scuttlebutt', and 'Give me the grog.'"

"Lovely." I rolled my eyes. "If you go around demanding grog and saying words like 'scuttlebutt' we'll find ourselves uninvited from the dining room again. Captains *do* know a great deal more than that. They might use those terms sometimes, but they must also have a good command of the English language."

Timothy folded his arms, kicked his foot against the table leg, and scowled. I sighed wearily. We were in for another long day, one spent entirely in each other's company, as I dared not allow him out of my sight since the ship-boarding incident.

Mrs. Hodges' library was as limited as Timothy's attention span. Collin had been gone three weeks, and already I felt myself going mad with the same routine day after day. I wanted to be doing something to move us toward our future, instead of stuck here biding my time. No doubt Timothy felt the same.

"Come on." I closed the books and replaced them in their exact spots on the shelf behind me. "Let's go for a walk and see if any new ships have come in today."

Timothy bolted from his chair. "Thank you, Katie." He threw his arms around my middle as I stood, nearly knocking me backward and causing the disturbing sensation in my stomach again—the same one I'd been feeling periodically since the day Collin left. I'd thought it must be nerves or anxiety, but now I was beginning to fear something was physically wrong with me.

And we've no money for a physician. We had no money for anything, which was part of our problem. Though we'd the necessities of room and board met and two sets of clothes apiece—one old and one new—we had nothing extra, not even a few shillings, with which to amuse ourselves. I'd not minded this lack of funds while living in the Highlands, with all the work that was to be done there and with Collin and many others to keep me company. But here in Halifax our days were idle, and the temptation to visit stores or otherwise engage in activities that required money was great. The unoccupied hours crawled by, made for irritability from both of us, and gave me far too much time to worry about Collin.

I took Timothy's hand, swinging it gaily, and attempted to cheer us both. "Perhaps we'll see—"

"A package just arrived for you, Mrs. Mercer." Our landlady entered the room, a brown, paper-wrapped parcel in her hands.

"Who is it from?" Timothy asked, bouncing up and down on his toes to see it.

"I haven't any idea." It seemed too soon for Collin to have reached his destination and mailed a package to us. But I could think of no other possibility. "Thank you," I said, taking the parcel from Mrs. Hodges.

She lingered nearby as I set it on the table we had just vacated. "Careful with the string," I advised, as Timothy began untying it. "Don't tear the paper." I would have preferred something lighter, but the color and texture of this heavier paper could work for drawing. *If only I had a pencil.*

The string fell away, and I helped Timothy fold back the wrapping, revealing a sketchbook and a box of charcoal, similar to that which Collin had purchased for me in London.

"Goodness!" I clasped the sketchbook to my heart, and a sealed envelope fell away. "It must be from Collin. They must have made *very* good time to Virginia." I turned the envelope over and broke the wax, wondering when and where Collin had obtained the wax and a scripted C stamp. It seemed a rather frivolous purchase, given all we would have to acquire for the journey ahead of us. Perhaps he had borrowed it from one of the Campbells. *Yes, that must be it.* C for Campbell, which meant he had already found our relations in Virginia.

But it wasn't Collin's handwriting that met my eyes when I unfolded the letter.

Mrs. Mercer,

I hope this letter finds you and your brother well. Enclosed please find materials that I hope will suffice for the reproduction of some of your work that was lost on the Cleopatra. *If your drawings are truly as good as your brother claims, they are of great interest to me. I will tell you why when we visit next. Please send word when you have completed a sketch, and I shall arrange for us to meet.*

Sincerely,
Your humble servant,
Mr. James Cook

"I don't believe this." I dropped the sketchbook on the table as if it was on fire. "I can't accept these."

"Why not?" Timothy asked. "Collin bought you the same when we were in London."

"These aren't from Collin." I set the letter on top of the pile and brought a hand to my head. "What does he mean by sending these to me?"

"What does *who* mean?" Mrs. Hodges asked.

"The seaman we met a few days ago—a Mr. Cook." I waved a hand at the letter absently. "You may read it if you'd like. Timothy tried to take a drawing Mr. Cook had made, believing it to be mine. And now the man has gone and sent me supplies to recreate that drawing so I can show it to him. I won't. I can't. I'll just have to send these things back." Having made that decision I felt slightly better.

"*Why* must you return them?" Mrs. Hodges asked, surprising me. With her prim manners and exact habits, she, of all people, ought to see the folly in this.

"You are an artist, are you not?" she continued. "At dinner last week you told us as much. Perhaps the man wants to hire you."

"Yes, but—" Only a year ago I would have been thrilled with such possibility. And now, it wasn't as if we didn't need any income I might procure. It wasn't as if I didn't have the time or desire to draw. "It does not feel right to accept a gift that isn't from my husband."

"Don't think of it as a gift," Mrs. Hodges advised. "From this letter, I don't believe Mr. Cook intended it that way. These items are the tools with which you can produce the drawings he is interested in seeing. This could lead to employment, Mrs. Mercer. Employment that would pay your rent, should your husband be delayed."

Ah, there it is—the real reason for her approval. Mrs. Hodges had expressed her grave concern when Collin left us here, with no income or means with which to pay for our lodgings beyond what he had already paid through the end of July. "He won't be delayed." But I could not deny that I'd had similar fears. I did not relish the idea of being homeless.

"Make your sketches. Then invite this Mr. Cook here. I will gladly chaperone," Mrs. Hodges volunteered.

I inhaled deeply, then sighed, still wary of keeping his company. But perhaps I would not have to. Maybe there was another subject he wished me to draw. "Very well." I brushed a finger over the top of the sketchbook, allowing myself to feel the pull of its pages.

"Can we go outside now?" Timothy asked.

"Of course." I gathered the book and charcoals in my

arms. "We'll go to see the ships, and you can play while I draw."

"Look at this one, Katie." Timothy held his palm out, a polished, oval rock in its center.

"That's a perfect skipping rock," I said. "Though you wouldn't have it anymore if you threw it into the water."

"I'm no good at skipping rocks." Timothy tucked his latest treasure into his already bulging pouch—a remnant of the fancy English shirt he had so detested.

"It's all in the way you move your wrist. Come on. I'll show you." I stood and brushed the dirt and sand from my skirt, then followed him the short distance to the shore, picking up a few rocks as we went. They were plentiful here, on this more remote beach, removed from town, though shells were hard to come by. "I'll show you with these, but you'll need many more to practice with. I must have thrown hundreds of rocks when I was learning how to skip them."

"Did Father teach you?" Timothy asked, a hint of sorrow in his question.

"No." I placed my hand on his shoulder and looked at him. "Father wasn't much for that sort of play. Collin taught me, when I was younger than you are now." I placed the best of the three rocks I had selected in Timothy's hand. "Watch me, and do as I do."

I turned, so that I stood sideways to the water. "Place your first finger against the edge of the rock and curl it around so the rock is in the crook of that finger—that's why you want one that feels like it has an edge or a good side. You're fortunate. There are a lot of good stones here. "Next, put your thumb on the other side, so you're holding the rock with the flat side parallel to the ground."

Timothy scrunched his nose. "What's parallel?"

"If you'd listen at lessons you might know," I chided him.

279

"Certainly any good sea captain does. Parallel is when two things—in this case your rock and the ground—have the same distance between them. If you put both arms straight out, they are parallel to one another, but if I bend one arm—"

"*All right.* I understand." Timothy held his rock as I did mine.

"Good. You can tell me later why a ship's captain must under-stand this as well. Watch, and I'll show you this slowly. Arm behind, then bend your wrist back as far as you are able. Arm to the front now. I think I add a little step in there too." This was more difficult slowly, when I had to think about the process. "Very quickly snap your wrist forward. If you do it right, your rock will spin. Like this." I sped up the sequence and sent my stone spinning across the water, where it took three good bounces before sinking.

"It's more difficult here, because there is a tide. In a loch you don't have that to contend with. You try now."

Timothy did, his first attempt about as successful as mine had likely been. "Don't give up." I ruffled the top of his head. "It took me a very long time. You keep practicing while I search out the good rocks." I picked my way along the shore, collecting as many as I could carry in the fold of my skirt. When I had a good enough pile to keep him busy for several minutes I returned to my sketch pad.

I flipped over the page with the drawing I had made of Timothy playing at the shore, to the one behind it—the island landscape I was attempting to recreate from memory. It was not long before I was again lost in the picture, as much a vision of the future as a copy of what I had already drawn.

"You see."

My hand jumped, and the charcoal fell from it. I turned my head and found my face nearly touching the beaded skirt of a grey-haired, indigenous woman. She bent closer, a bony finger pointing at my drawing.

"Pitu'pok," she said, touching the lake I had sketched in the middle of the island. "You see."

I nodded. "Is that the name of the lake? I haven't seen it with my eyes, but with my imagination." I prattled on nervously and pointed to my head, as if that might somehow explain. "I have not actually been there—yet."

"You will go." The woman squatted beside me on the shore. Moccasins peeked out beneath her skirt. Perhaps this was why I had not heard her. Collin had told me the Mi'kmaq wore shoes that muffled the sound of their footsteps when they walked. This gave them added stealth in the forest, when stealing upon their food—or enemies.

The woman retrieved my fallen pencil and stretched her hand out for the book. Reluctantly I gave it to her, wary of what might happen if I did not. My eyes strayed to Timothy, still throwing rocks, but now joined by two Mi'kmaq children who looked to be near his own age. A quick glance around revealed no more of the natives, and I breathed an inward sigh of relief. Though we had seen nothing of the violence Captain Shenk had described to Collin on our journey here, it was still in the back of my mind. Silently I berated myself for going so far from Halifax. I had wanted an unspoiled beach on which to sketch Timothy and, in my eagerness and excitement to create, had forgotten my promise to Collin to stay in town.

My companion knelt, placed the sketchbook on her lap, flipped the page over, and began moving the pencil over the paper.

I watched, fascinated. *Of course she knows how to use it.* That I had assumed otherwise seemed at once foolish and unfair. No doubt there was much this woman could do that I could not—skills far more practical for survival.

Her pictures were different than mine, smaller, more separate clusters that moved across the page, almost as the text of a book. I hoped I was not to be expected to read or understand when she was done.

After a few minutes during which I sat idle, my eyes moving continually from Timothy to the woman, she pointed down the shoreline.

"You dig."

I smiled, nodded, and held my hand out for my book.

Instead of relinquishing it, she pointed again. When I still didn't move, in her native tongue she called to the children playing with Timothy. They came at once, then moved beyond us and began digging closer to the water's edge.

The woman waved me toward them, and I went, still reluctant to leave the sketchbook. How would I explain to Mr. Cook if I lost it the very first day?

It was not long before the children began pulling shellfish from the holes they had dug. Timothy joined them, excited with each find, and soon I found my own hands and arms buried in the wet sand, burrowing below it for such treasure.

The woman had brought a basket with her, and I helped the children fill it. About the time we were done, she joined me at the edge of the sea as I washed my hands. I stood, drying them on my skirt. She held the sketchbook and charcoal out to me.

"Thank you." I took them eagerly and studied the drawings she had made.

She pointed to one of the marks, then pointed to our basket of shellfish. "You eat," she said. "You live first year."

Her next drawing reminded me of an animal I had seen in my own mind. Enormous, odd-shaped antlers sprouted from either side of its head.

"Moose. You eat," she repeated, pointing to the creature. "You wear." She pointed to her clothing and shoes.

She repeated this process with each of her drawings, telling me as best she could what each was and what it was to be used for. An oblong, hollowed-out tree was to be used to move upon the water. Fish and smaller game could be found in abundance on either shore. The large, antlered moose would be more inland. Through her gesturing and broken English, I came to understand that we were to be wary of that creature, as well as other large and furred ones.

Time passed without my realizing it. I wasn't certain how

long we had stood there, deep in conversation as she imparted a wealth of knowledge to me. Our differences no longer seemed to matter. I forgot to be afraid or even wary; instead I felt overwhelmingly grateful to her when at last our interview concluded and she called to her children.

"Thank you." Impulsively I reached to take her hand. She allowed it, and gave me the first smile I had seen from her.

"You see," she repeated the first words she had said to me, once more pointing to my crude sketches of the island.

"*I* see." She pointed to herself. "I see you come—forced from your land."

"Yes." A shiver passed through me at her words. "We didn't want to leave. We had to."

Understanding and compassion darkened her eyes. "We do not want to leave either."

Chapter Thirty-seven

Norfolk, Virginia, June 1762

"Where would a woman in hiding go—in Portsmouth?" Ian spoke the question aloud, though it was more a musing of his own than anything he believed Ben could answer.

"Who says she'd stay there?" Ben used a champher knife to curve the stave in front of him. "I still say she's on her way here."

Ian shook his head. "If so, why isn't she here already?"

Last night, after three days, Ben had returned alone and with no news of Eliza, and Ian's fear for her had surged. "I can't just stay here and do nothing—and don't say work isn't nothing. You know what I mean. I *have* to find her."

"At least wait until Friday, when Rogers pays you," Ben suggested.

"Little good money will do me if something has happened to Eliza."

"If you need it to escape it'll do you plenty good. If I was wanted somewhere, I'd get as far away as possible," Ben said. "Once you find her, you two ought to be on the next boat home."

"Easier said than done." Ian worked a bilge hoop over the barrel he was making. He took up a hammer and band driver and began pounding. "I'll. Not. Wait. Another. Day." He struck hard, forcing the band into place. "I'll tell Rogers tonight."

Ben did not speak for some time. Then, "A horse will get you there faster. You should take mine."

Ian stopped his work to look over at him. "I might not be able to return it."

"I know." Ben, too, paused his task.

"Why?" Ian asked as he had before. "A friend you are, but that doesn't mean you have to give me your horse."

"Well, I am hoping it is but a loan," Ben admitted. "And reason enough to get you back here." He grinned; then a second later his face fell. "My sister's husband died two years ago—there was an accident. He was building another barn, and I'd said I'd be there to help him for a few days to get the roof on. I was late because I decided to get a ride halfway and then walk, so Bess could have the wagon to drive out and join us for Sunday supper. Then we'd all go home together." He paused, then blew out a breath of air, as if this was hard for him to say.

"Lars started without me. He was a big man, not clumsy, but not particularly agile either. He fell from the top of the barn. You can imagine the rest." Ben looked away and returned to his task with renewed vigor.

"So you agree that I shouldn't delay," Ian said, understanding Ben's generosity a little more.

"Yes." Ben nodded. "As much as I hate to see you go."

"I thought she would stick to those places most civilized, so I searched those first," Ben reached below the horse's belly to grasp the saddle strap. "I imagined Eliza might have a hide-in-plain-sight sort of strategy. A woman alone might not survive in the wild."

"There's where you likely went wrong," Ian tossed a blanket Bess had given him on top of the saddle. "You forget, this one has a gun. And Eliza Campbell is not just any woman. She's a Scot, a Highlander. She'll know how to survive in the forest probably better than she might in an unfamiliar town."

"It sounds like you know where to start looking." Ben patted his horse affectionately. "She's ready."

"Thank you, Ben." Ian thrust his hand out and shook Ben's heartily. "I hope to return her, but if not, I'll make it up to you, I promise."

"I know. You're a man of honor, Ian—"

"—MacDonald?"

Ian tensed at the sound of his name pronounced in a thick brogue. *That voice...* He felt like he'd been hurtled back in time. His hand dropped from Ben's as his name was spoken once more.

"Ian?"

Impossible. It can't be.

Ben was looking past him, a curious expression upon his face.

Almost certain he was losing his mind, that he had to be imagining *that* voice, Ian turned toward it.

"Fine work." Alistair Campbell slapped the arm of the man standing beside him, while never taking his eyes off Ian. "The MacDonald in the flesh—and here in the Colonies. It really *is* you." Alistair's auburn locks were longer than when last they'd met, and the man looked to have lost a bit of his girth in the months between. He sounded jolly, almost pleased to see Ian.

Definitely impossible.

"Alistair Campbell." Ian would have known the man anywhere. After spending weeks traveling with him, including one of the longest days of his life shut up in a carriage together, Ian knew more than he'd ever wanted to about Alistair—from the way the line of his mouth hardened, then twitched when he was displeased, to the way he could strip a bone clean, or eat an apple right down to the seeds, slurping it through his teeth, to the fierce loyalty and devotion he felt for Collin's wife.

Ian's eyes roamed over Alistair, recalling all this and the many other things he knew. The man beside Alistair appeared familiar as well, though Ian could not place his name.

"You remember me, I see." Alistair's grin faltered, as if unsure how Ian would receive him. He turned to his companion. "How did you know we'd find him here, Finlay?"

The poet.

"I did not see him, only that we must come. Now that we're here . . ." Finlay paused to look directly into Ian's eyes. "He is away from this place. On an errand—of the heart."

"Never mind what I'm doing," Ian said, even as he weighed the possibility that they might help him. "What are the two of you doing in the Colonies?" He kept his tone gruff to mask the odd emotion that had arisen with their arrival. The last time he'd been with these men he'd been in the Highlands.

It had not been a particularly pleasant day. He'd just been shot—by his sister-in-law, it turned out—and he and Collin had exchanged bitter words. Yet they had been at home. Or near to it, at least. The sound of Alistair's voice and his sudden appearance had thrust Ian back to that place. *Back home.* If he closed his eyes he could almost feel the whisper of the cool breeze and smell the damp of the forest.

"There's more than two of us here," Alistair said with a chuckle. "And we've been searching for you—just one of the charges given me by your brother. That we've happened upon you, when we've been here but a month, is most fortuitous." Alistair's beard twitched with his smile. "Why, I'd only just learned that the ship you crossed on, the *Ulysses,* did not dock here at all, but across the river in a place called—"

"Portsmouth," Ian finished. "Collin sent you to find me?" He found this rather difficult to believe. If it *was* true, he questioned Collin's choice, as he and Alistair had barely survived the last time they'd been forced to endure each other's company.

"Aye, among other things," Alistair said, sounding purposely vague as he cast a look Ben's direction.

"Ben Hastings." Ben stepped forward and stuck out his

hand. "Ian and I work together at the cooperage. You're from Scotland as well, I gather."

"Aye. Not a MacDonald, myself, but a loyal friend to Ian's brother."

"I've no time to hear of Collin's plans now." Ian pushed his curiosity and the sudden longing for home aside as he walked past an open-mouthed Ben to mount the horse. Once seated he looked down at them. "I've my own errand at present—saving a Campbell." *I hope.*

"What do you mean?" Alistair released Ben's hand, his eyes narrowing in that elfish way of his as they followed Ian. With his brows cinched up tight together, Alistair stepped forward, then clamped a hand on Ian's leg, as if to hold him in place.

Ian resisted the urge to kick the older man. "There were some Campbells on the ship with me. Taken by the Redcoats at the same time Collin was. One was a woman named Elizabeth Campbell. She needs help. Ben can explain."

"*You* can explain." Alistair tightened his grip. "If you've some-where to go, we'll be heading there with you. Now that you're found, I've no intention of letting you out of my sight again. Your brother meant us to free you from your indenture, and I mean to do that. And if it truly is Elizabeth Campbell you're going in search of, she is my niece. Her father is my brother. Have you news of him as well?" Alistair looked at Ian, question in his eyes.

His niece. Ian wasn't certain how he felt about that, but he could not deny the appeal of help in his search. Alistair was an excellent marksman, if nothing else. And the poet seemed a bit like Katherine. They both knew things without having to actually see them.

"Your brother is dead," Ian said.

Alistair's hand slid from Ian's leg.

"He died before they left Scotland," Ian added quietly, allowing that it was the right thing to offer comfort when a man had just learned of his brother's death.

Alistair appeared to swallow with some difficulty. "Angus had his leg crushed—run over by horse and cart—for refusing to give Elizabeth in marriage to our laird. If that wasn't enough, Brann had the two of them taken away by an English patrol to be shipped off and sold. You know of her whereabouts, you say?"

"At present I don't," Ian admitted. "I am headed to Portsmouth in search of her. If you wish to join me, we must go at once."

"We'll come," Alistair said. "We've a few horses of our own to ride—purchased only yesterday to aid in our search for you."

"Well, then," Ian said, feeling better by the minute about their assistance. "If you've one I may use, I'll leave my friend's here."

"Aye, we do." Alistair gave a snort and shook his head, ending with an odd look at Finlay.

"I suppose that is why you insisted we purchase three."

Chapter Thirty-eight

Halifax, Nova Scotia, June 1762

The knock at my door startled me. *He's not here yet!* I glanced toward the window and saw that the sky behind the lace curtains was still dark.

"Yes?" I said softly, so as not to wake Timothy, then left the desk to make my way to the door.

Mrs. Hodges' voice came from the other side. "Candles cost money, you know. If you burn through yours too quickly I'll have to charge you for it."

Holding in a frustrated sigh, I leaned my head back and looked at the ceiling, praying we could be gone from under her thumb sooner rather than later. Living here felt much like having a nagging mother looking over my shoulder.

"Yes, of course, Mrs. Hodges. I'll put it out right now. Good-night." I retraced my steps to the desk as hers continued down the hall. With a last glance at the drawing I'd been working on, I blew out the candle. Mr. Cook was coming tomorrow morning, and I had hoped to add a bit more detail to one of the sketches I had done for him.

Unsure exactly what he wished to see, I had drawn three. The first was mostly a landscape, with Timothy in the forefront, playing at the shore. The second was a nearly exact replica—as far as I could remember—of the western side of the island where I believed we were to make our home. And the third and last drawing was a portrait of Collin. It would be the one Mr. Cook viewed last, and a good reminder to him, I hoped, that I was a married woman. A woman could not be too careful. I'd my relative, Brann, to thank for that lesson.

With dark filling the room, I made my way to the bed and crawled beneath the covers. From the cot on the other side of the room Timothy's even breathing comforted me. I was not entirely alone, though at night and in this bed I had shared with Collin, I certainly felt that way. I'd never been afraid of the dark, but I dreaded it now, for the loneliness and worry that came with these hours. Sleep was often elusive, and I would toss and turn for hours, wondering where Collin was and what he was doing, worrying over his safety—and mine, almost certain as I was that I had contracted some ailment during our voyage.

I placed a hand on my stomach and felt it again, a foreign, fluttery feeling inside of me, prone to making itself known mostly at night. It was not painful, but neither was it natural. During the day I tried convincing myself that I had imagined the sensations, but then they came again—more frequently now.

I'd overheard the crew on the *Cleopatra* speaking of illnesses that might be contracted during a voyage. Scurvy, the pox, and something like a worm in one's stomach if the water in the scuttlebutt went bad were all common ailments. I'd no fear of the first two, thankfully, but I had a distinct unease regarding the third possibility. I'd kept a close eye on Timothy and noted no symptoms in him, and I reasoned I wouldn't be the only one ill if I'd caught something from the water we all shared. Perhaps it hadn't been that water at all, but something I'd swallowed during my two unplanned swims in the ocean. Maybe that was where the sickness was coming from.

I was in no pain, and in fact felt in much better health than I had for some months. Yet I *was* constantly hungry, in spite of having plenty to eat. I imagined a giant worm in my stomach, consuming my meals, and felt very frightened indeed. If Mr. Cook did hire me, perhaps I should use some of the money I earned to see a physician. Though if one came to call on me here—and something was indeed wrong with me—

Mrs. Hodges would probably evict us, on the grounds I might contaminate the whole house.

In addition to this concern, the thought of being bled or any other number of cures commonly prescribed was terrifying. I didn't know what to do and dearly wished Collin was here for me to confide in. It was almost one year to the day that we had been married, and I missed him every minute. *What a difference a year makes.*

I hadn't wanted to marry him then, but I couldn't live without him now.

Hands clasped behind my back, I stood a good distance from the table, awaiting Mr. Cook's critique. He had viewed the first picture, the landscape, rather hastily and with seeming disinterest. But the second sketch, the geography of our future home, had seemed to paralyze him for the past several seconds.

"Your memory must be incredible," he said at last. "This is most impressive, but I must know the source from which you first copied this."

I frowned. "There is no source. My husband asked me to draw what I believed our new home would look like, and I did."

"Mrs. Mercer—" Mr. Cook paused to set aside a small magnifier, set in a tortoise shell case. "What you have *drawn* is none other than a map of exquisite detail—and accuracy, I might add. It would be impossible to create something like this from your mind. One would have to physically see the land, in which case he would have to be both a surveyor and cartographer—as I am—or he would have to copy this from a previous cartographer's drawing."

"I have done neither, sir." I resisted the urge to step forward, snatch up my book, and dismiss him. "I regret that my husband is not here to confirm that truth. The sketches and paintings I create are really visions of the future, a gift passed down to me through generations of my Highland ancestors, the Campbells."

"Scottish Campbells?" Mr. Cook's brows rose.

I nodded. "Yes."

"I'm not familiar with the Scottish Campbells. I had assumed—from your name and accent—that you were a fellow countryman. English, that is."

"My father was English, and I was raised in Alverton. My mother, however, was from Scotland." I held my head proudly as I said this.

"I see." Mr. Cook bent his head slightly and brought his fist to his mouth. "Unfortunately none of that information is enough to convince me that you are truly able to draw such an accurate map of a place you have never seen."

"I have nothing else to convince you." I regretted that this was the case, as much or more for my honor as well as for the income we could have used from his commission.

"Perhaps this will convince *you* to the validity of my opinion." He withdrew a rolled parchment from within his coat. I stepped closer, waiting with baited breath—though I was unsure why—as he unrolled it and spread it across the table. "This is Cape Breton, or Ile Royale, as the French call it."

"Oh, my." I leaned closer, feeling that fluttering in my stomach again, along with a strong sense that I had seen all this before. *Because I have.* I'd seen this island in my dreams, and the portions I had drawn—right down to the last detail of mountain elevation, the shape of the large lake in the middle, the inlets and points and curves on the island's western shore—were exact.

I sat down hard in the chair across from Mr. Cook. "Where did you get this?"

"I drew it myself," he said. "After *months* of study and measurement, surveying and exploration. I have spent the last few years charting these northern islands and believed I was the first to do so seriously. You might imagine my surprise when your brother accused me of stealing *your* drawings."

"Yes." I forced my eyes from the paper to his face. "I know not what else to tell you, as I have already given you the truth. As sure as you've drawn this map, I've drawn the other."

"You swear you have never set foot on Cape Breton?"

"I have not."

"Neither have you copied your drawing from another."

"Correct."

Mr. Cook leaned back in his chair, his fist upon his chin this time. "I must admit to being much puzzled. If what you are telling me is true, it is extraordinary—*you* are extraordinary."

"No more so than my mother and grandfather before me. I see not why you need be puzzled, Mr. Cook."

"Because I am a man who values science and exploration. I work in logic and numbers and charts. That an artist might sketch in days what has taken me months of work to discover . . ." He broke off, his frustration evident as he pounded upon the table, making his magnifying glass jump.

I leaned forward and pointed at the northernmost part of the island. "This area is a land of great beauty, is it not? A high land that is much forested."

"I have not traversed all of it, but yes," he said grudgingly.

"Would you like to see drawings of it in greater detail?" I asked.

"Have you any? I thought all were lost when your ship wrecked."

"They were," I said. "But I could draw them again. You could even be present while I work, if you wish."

I saw at once, from the way his eyes widened and his lips tugged upward, that this idea appealed to him. "You would allow me to do such?"

"In proper company, of course. Mrs. Hodges would have to approve of our continued use of her sitting room."

"Or you would be welcome to make use of the large table and the plentiful light in my shipboard lodgings. I would see that another officer accompanied us at all times."

"Oh, please may we, Katie? Please let us see his ship." Timothy practically fell through the door, no doubt having been eavesdropping, along with our landlady, hovering in the hall beside him.

"We shall have to see, Timothy." I'd no desire to set foot upon another ship, yet I could not deny being intrigued by Mr. Cook and his maps. If nothing else, this was an opportunity for me to discover the best route we should take when traveling to our new home. I had seen where we were to go, but Mr. Cook had stood upon that land.

"Might you begin at once?" he asked.

"Of course." Only a bit nervous now, I reached beneath his map to retrieve my sketchbook. While on board the *Cleopatra* I had learned to draw with others around me—occasionally looking over my shoulder as I worked. I had learned to ignore both the chatter and song of seamen and the sway of the ocean and all else that might disturb. In the past months I had learned how to close my mind to all but my gift, and to allow my hand to follow where imagination led it. I'd no doubt I could do the same once more. "For today I prefer to remain here and draw."

Mr. Cook nodded and stood. "Come along over here, near the window, Timothy." He beckoned Timothy to the large seat across the room. "Let's give your sister a chance to begin while I show you my compass and a few other things I've brought. These are the tools of a seaman."

Timothy's beaming face as he followed was enough to convince me I'd made the right decision. Who knew what might come of this map drawing, but for a few hours at least, my brother would be entertained, and I would be able to learn more about our future.

Chapter Thirty-nine

Near Portsmouth, Virginia, June 1762

Ian crawled back into camp under cover of night. Finlay lay near the fire, snoring lightly, while Alistair stood watch.

"The *Ulysses* still isn't in port," Ian said before Alistair could ask.

Finlay had learned the ship was making a relatively short voyage to the Caribbean and was expected back soon, but in the meantime Millet wasn't around to question. Ian had combed the forests outside of Portsmouth for any sign of Eliza while Finlay and Alistair had made inquiries in town. All had turned up nothing. She had simply vanished, putting in question the tale about Millet Ben had brought home with him.

Without bothering with a blanket, Ian lay upon the ground. A rock dug into his back, but he didn't care. It wasn't as if he would sleep anyway.

"If we don't find her will you resume your work at the cooperage?" Alistair asked.

"*When* we find her it is likely that I will." Ian refused to succumb to his deepest fears . . . yet. "Eliza could come with me to Norfolk. She could live and work at the dairy with Jannet and the lasses."

"If they stay on," Alistair said gently.

"Aye," Ian agreed. "If." He still could not bring himself to believe what Alistair and Finlay had told him, that all—or most of, at least—Liam Campbell's clan, and the MacDonalds, had fled to the Colonies. Only Collin and Katie were yet lacking, and they were expected to arrive any day.

Ian was surprised at this, though he probably shouldn't have been. From the moment he wed—even before, really—Collin's first loyalty had been to his wife. Ian supposed that with marriage that loyalty included the Campbells as well. Years ago Liam had promised Collin that he would one day lead that clan.

Though where that leaves our own clan . . . Ian worried about the MacDonalds left on their own in a strange new land. How were they faring without either brother to lead them?

Alistair finished walking a circumference of the camp and returned to sit on the ground beside Ian. "You ready to tell me what really happened on that ship, how it is you came to care for my niece more than your own self?"

Instead of answering, Ian swatted at a swarming insect, then used his sleeve to wipe sweat from his brow. He'd never experienced anything like this before. The very air itself felt heavy, not with rain or snow, but heat. He felt constantly wet, as if he'd just taken a swim in a warm loch. "Such a miserable place," he grumbled.

"Can't say I'm fond of the weather, myself," Alistair said. "Right about now, feeling the breeze beneath my kilt would be very pleasant."

Ian grunted his agreement. "No kilts here."

"Not yet," Alistair said in a jovial voice. "But that doesn't mean never. Where we are going we'll be able to do as we please. Kilts, pipers, pistols and all."

"A foolish dream," Ian said. "I cannot believe Collin went along with it and that you're all here."

"If you had lived his life these past months you would under-stand." Alistair scooted back to lean against a tree.

"What do you think I've been doing?" Ian asked. "I took Collin's place on that ship." *Where are you, Eliza?*

It wasn't really Alistair he was upset with, though

something about the man did seem to grind upon Ian's nerves. If they could just find Eliza, or at least some word of her, some clue to her whereabouts, his tension would ease.

When we find her I'll apologize. I'll give the man a hug, if it will bring her safely to us. Ian thought the desperate promise. He would do much more than that if it meant her return.

"You don't have to do anything more," Alistair said quietly. "You can leave right now, return to Norfolk and your position there. It seemed pleasant enough."

"I'm not going anywhere," Ian practically growled. "Not until we find Eliza."

"Why is that?" Alistair leaned forward, one elbow braced on his knee. "What is my niece to you?"

Tired of the older man's pestering questions, Ian sat up and turned to Alistair. "She saved my life. And risked hers doing it."

"Ah." Alistair resumed his position, leaning against the tree. "You feel a debt to her."

"It's more than that." Ian thought of Eliza's face when he had first seen it and then again in front of the church, when she had been so disappointed in him. Mostly he thought of her that night in the lean-to, when she had kissed him so unexpectedly and had confessed that at least a part of her had been grateful to learn he was not Collin.

It does not matter that she is a Campbell, Ian told himself for perhaps the hundredth time. At least she was not also English, like his sister-in-law. A half smile lifted a corner of his mouth.

"What?" Alistair asked, ever attentive. "What do you find amusing?"

"Not you," Ian grumbled beneath his breath. He was remembering what it was that so annoyed him about Alistair. Not a detail slipped by without the old man's notice. He had an uncanny way of reading people's minds—more of that

Campbell witchery, no doubt. The day in England they had shared the carriage together, Alistair had been so bold as to tell Ian that he saw through his bluster, that he knew his heart and that love for Collin overrode any other feeling he might have, including those of dislike toward Collin's Campbell bride and her family.

Ian had not taken well to Alistair's prying, telling him what he was supposed to feel and predicting he didn't have it within him to do any harm. Ian had set out to prove the opposite, frightening Katie at the inn that evening and causing further mischief in the days to come.

Though Alistair *had* been one hundred percent right in his assessment. Nothing in the world mattered more than Collin.

Collin had taken him from the Munros, had helped him remember who he was and where he'd come from before those dark years. Collin had stood by him, forgiven him, accepted him. In return Ian must accept his bride.

He'd tried, proving his loyalty by taking Collin's place in Scotland and being put on that ship to the Colonies. And now his brother was who knows where, and Eliza was missing. The two people he cared about most in this world.

"I've a question for you," Ian said, turning the conversation from him. "How will you feel if we find Eliza and I make her my wife?" There, he'd said it out loud. "And then the two of us sail to Scotland, to lead the MacDonalds." *What few are left there.* That seemed only fair, especially with Collin choosing to lead the Campbells over his own clan.

Alistair nodded, though Ian could not make out the expression on his face. "I . . . would give my blessing to the first, to your union," he clarified. "As for returning to lead the MacDonalds . . ."

"There is nothing to return to," Finlay said, joining the conversation suddenly. He stretched and sat up. "We tried telling you as much the other day, but you would not listen."

"There is always something," Ian said. "So long as I've land to stand upon and a people who need me."

"The land you speak of is gone, forfeit to the crown." Alistair drew in a great breath as Ian looked at him sharply.

"But the MacDonalds *do* need you. Here."

Chapter Forty

Halifax, Nova Scotia, July 1762

The day was bright and breezy as I left Mr. Cook's ship, swinging the basket that held my drawings and pencils. Timothy was to stay another hour, with Mr. Cook's promise to see him safely home. Today was the first that I had set foot on his ship, vastly preferring to work in Mrs. Hodges' sitting room. But she'd been hosting a tea this morning, and Mr. Cook felt most anxious that we continue his work mapping out the island. To accommodate us both, I'd completed most of the day's work before boarding his ship, as I still felt somewhat uncomfortable in his presence, though he had been nothing but a perfect gentleman thus far.

More than that, really, I was grateful for the way he'd taken to Timothy, encouraging and even furthering his interest in a life at sea. I wasn't at all certain how I felt about that, but I could not deny that, at present, Mr. Cook's attentiveness, and his pay for my sketches, allowed me time today to do a bit of shopping. *A rare freedom from responsibility.* I loved Timothy dearly but had never before realized how exhausting little boys could be.

While Mr. Cook had been tutoring Timothy in the skills of compass-reading and star charts, Mrs. Hodges had been teaching me to sew, and under her tutelage I'd worked diligently on a shirt for Collin, using the money from my employ with Mr. Cook to purchase the cloth and thread. With her help the garment was turning out fine and was nearly complete. Today I wished to find fabric for a pair of breeches to go with it.

And if that goes well, perhaps I will come right out with it and ask her to teach me how to cook. I'd hinted at that possibility a time or two, but any offer of help I gave or question I asked in that regard was almost immediately quelled. Mrs. Hodges seemed rather possessive and particular about her house in general—especially so when it came to her kitchen. If she ever did allow me to help, I would probably have to begin with tasks like peeling carrots on the back porch.

At least I know how to grow those now. Mrs. Hodges *had* been keen for help in her garden, and while Timothy and I had worked there, she had imparted a wealth of information about growing every-thing from flowers to berries and vegetables. I'd copied her advice on the back pages of my sketchbook, and I had been collecting seeds, keeping them folded securely within the brown wrapping paper in which my drawing materials from Mr. Cook had been delivered.

By the time Collin returned I would have a new set of clothes for him, some money saved, and I would have learned at least a few things about surviving in our new home.

He had been gone seven weeks now and had hoped to return within the next two. I'd had no word from him but tried not to let this trouble me. He'd an enormous task to accomplish. Each day Timothy and I checked the ships at the wharf, certain that soon we would see not only Collin disembarking but our other relatives as well.

In the meantime we kept ourselves busy. The harder I worked during the day, the easier sleep came at night, though it was never truly easy. I blamed this on the long hours of summer light while trying to ignore the ever-increasing problem within. If Mary Campbell returned with Collin, I could ask her help. She'd healed my horribly broken arm once, and I trusted she could heal whatever was wrong with me now.

Until then . . . I glanced down at my stomach and was dismayed to see the small bulge of it visible, with the wind blowing my dress tight against me. I moved the basket from my side to my front, in an attempt at covering the abnormality, then smoothed my windblown hair and stepped into the shop.

I'd been here only once before, with Mrs. Hodges as my guide. I felt slightly nervous on my own but recalled her instructions for selecting good, stout cloth for men's breeches. I wouldn't be able to afford the buckskin, though that would have been best for where we were headed. Instead she had suggested I purchase a thick cotton weave, the coarser the better for wear, though not necessarily for comfort. I hoped I could choose well. What good were pants if the wearer felt miserable in them?

I considered the buttons beneath the glass case while I awaited my turn. The store was busy today. Two women examined bolts of fabric farther down the long counter, several others milled about the store, and behind me the bell jingled again.

"Mrs. Mercer?"

I turned toward the familiar voice as the image of a bowl full of dates came to mind.

Mrs. Parker came toward me, a pleasant smile upon her face, though I had not been particularly pleasant to her the last weeks of our voyage.

"Hello." I smiled and shifted the basket to extend my hand.

"It is good to see you," she said, taking it. "And looking so well."

"Yes." I nodded. "I am much recovered from the last time we saw each other." That had been the day we had both been bedraggled survivors upon the beach after the wreck.

"You have decided to settle in Halifax, after all?" she asked, taking a spot beside me at the counter.

"Only temporarily. We are awaiting the arrival of others in our family before we go any farther."

"Of course." She nodded. "Very wise of you to travel in a

group. You cannot be too careful. Word has it the French are very active up north at present."

"I've heard." Mr. Cook had told us of the unrest and that he expected to be called upon to restore order in a place called Newfoundland very soon. "Have you been reunited with your sister as planned?"

"Sister-in-law," she confirmed. "Though it is not as restful here as I had hoped. Between the two of us we are quite busy. A great many children being born . . ." She trailed off, as if only just recalling the tragedy and grief of my recent situation.

"It is quite all right." I patted her hand gently, appreciating more now how soft with age it was and what care she truly had taken with me. "When we washed up on the shore of Sable Island and I found myself blessed enough to be alive, and to have my husband and brother both alive as well, I realized how fortunate I am. I will always mourn the child we lost, but I find joy in life again now."

"And someday you *will* know the joy of children as well," Mrs. Parker said. "You are young yet and have many years in which—"

I shook my head, cutting her off. "I do not think that is to be our blessing. I've made my peace with that. It is enough to have my husband and my health—" *Ask her.* I stopped mid-sentence, my mouth open as the obvious struck me. Mrs. Parker was not a physician, but she did know quite a lot about the human body. Perhaps she might be of some help with the stomach ailment I was suffering. *Just so long as the cure does not involve eating large quantities of dates.*

I glanced to either side of us, noting the women still selecting their fabrics and the others in the store with their attention elsewhere. Stepping closer to Mrs. Parker, I lowered my voice.

"May I ask a question of you—about a possible illness?"

Her eyes widened with curiosity, and she nodded. "My

experience is mostly limited to expectant mothers, but I will answer you if I can. I have some knowledge of other—situations—that can affect the female body."

"I fear something is wrong with me," I confided. "While I am far better than I was during our voyage, I think I may have caught something during it—perhaps an ailment of the stomach from foul water."

She frowned, then scrunched up her forehead, looking rather intrigued instead of repulsed or alarmed, as I knew Mrs. Hodges would were she to find out.

"What are your symptoms? How long have you had them?"

"About a month. It feels as if—as if something is moving around inside of me. Mostly this happens at night when I am still. I am terribly hungry almost all the time, though we've plenty to eat at present. I overheard some of the crew talking about a sort of worm that can exist inside a person in the stomach. Do you think I might have—"

Mrs. Parker's forehead scrunched even tighter now. She stood back, as if to survey me.

"Yes," she mused. "I thought your dress looked a little tight across the chest, though you were so ill and so thin—turn to the side, dear."

I obeyed, wondering what that might possibly tell her.

Slowly the lines on her face eased, and her gentle smile returned—the same she had used with me the day I'd lost my child and been so very ill. "Come outside a minute, Mrs. Mercer. You can see about your purchases later." She put an arm around me and steered me from the shop as my mind raced with panicked thoughts.

Once outside we walked a short distance to a small park, my despair growing with each step.

It must be terrible. She hadn't wanted to tell me in the store for fear I'd scream or make a scene. *Or faint.*

She sat on a bench, pulling me down beside her.

"Now, then." Mrs. Parker leaned forward and patted my hands, clasped nervously in my lap. "I don't know about any worm, though if there is such a thing it would seem that I would have it, too, as would others from our voyage, and that hasn't happened, that I'm aware of."

I'd come to the same conclusion myself but had no other plausible explanation.

"What you have just described to me, and what your profile shows me, is that you—" She paused, then sat up straight, a smile blooming on her face. "You are with child, Mrs. Mercer."

It took a few seconds before her announcement registered. "That's impossible." I shook my head. "My husband and I both agreed not to try again. He has been gone some seven weeks, and before that we were—" I felt a blush creep up my face—"careful not to—"

"Oh, I don't think this is a *new* pregnancy," Mrs. Parker said, something akin to wonder in the twinkle of her eyes and her delighted expression. "I believe that, somehow, you are *still* expecting. You see, a woman begins to feel her child moving around the fifth month of her confinement. It is also a time of rapid growth for the child, and it is quite common for a woman's appetite to increase during this time."

"But my courses—"

"You've had them recently?"

I nodded. "Yes. I mean, I think I have. I bled so long afterward, and then a little here and there since. I thought . . ." I'd thought my body was simply taking its time healing, returning to the way it had been—before.

"Some women do bleed throughout their pregnancies," she said, much louder than I would have preferred.

I glanced around, relieved no one was nearby to hear us discussing such a delicate subject.

"Given what you went through, it does not seem unusual that you would."

"You really think—a baby?" I placed a hand over my stomach, feeling the mound that had troubled me so the past weeks.

"When did you first conceive?" Mrs. Parker asked.

I blushed again. Thank heavens she had directed us outside. "The beginning of January," I said. "Shortly after Hogmanay."

"That would make you . . . about six months along, then. You're really quite small for someone that far, but little wonder, you had such a rough go of it at the start."

"But it's impossible." My hand rested on my stomach, wishing it could be true. "You were there. I lost that baby. I nearly died myself."

"I've not forgotten," Mrs. Parker said. "Thank heavens we'd a ready supply of dates on board. You'll need to remember that for when you give birth. You're a bleeder, and dates help—"

"—stop the bleeding. I shall *always* remember that. I promise." It was also likely I would loathe dates to my dying day, but I did not share that with her. "If I lost that child, then how is it possible—"

"It is rare, to be sure," Mrs. Parker said. "But not impossible. I've known a few cases where the mother was carrying twins. One child miscarried early on—as did yours—but the other continued to grow and thrive and was born quite healthy some months later."

"Twins?" I said, a catch to my voice.

"Well, not now dear. Not anymore." Mrs. Parker patted my knee comfortingly. "But one healthy child, it appears."

Don't forget, I'm a twin. Collin had said to me teasingly that night in Scotland, in the old MacDonald keep. I looked up at Mrs. Parker, unsure if I was about to laugh or cry. "It's a baby in there—not a worm?" Crying won. Tears spilled over and began to slip down my cheeks.

Mrs. Parker clasped my hands. "It's a *miracle,* in there. And yes, a baby too."

I smiled through my tears and felt a great bubble of joy rise in me and surface as laughter. The idea of a worm inside of me seemed suddenly absurd. The knowledge of a growing child, on the other hand, seemed sure.

Our growing child. I couldn't wait to tell Collin.

Chapter Forty-one

Halifax, Nova Scotia, July 1762

"Here you'll find a waterfall flowing over a great deal of large stones and ending in this pool." My finger hovered over my latest drawing, a vellum overlay placed carefully on top of Mr. Cook's map, which was spread across Mrs. Hodges' table. "The surrounding area is densely forested, so I believe it will require no little effort to reach the falls."

Collin and I had hiked to a waterfall like this in the Highlands. *The Falls of Bruar.* I remembered Collin's gallant bow as he'd presented them, as if we were at court. He'd been courting *me,* I realized now—wooing his bride, taking me out of the way on our journey home, so I might see some of his beloved Highlands and so we might have a bit of time alone together. I sighed inwardly and with longing, remembering that lovely spot, how a picnic of stolen cheese and bread had seemed a feast, and the feeling as if I was just coming alive, with my budding feelings for Collin. What I would have given for an afternoon like that with him now. *An afternoon anywhere with him.*

"Add your waterfall to the map," Mr. Cook said, bringing me back to the present. He spoke almost absently, and without his usual concern for accuracy and attention to detail.

"Don't you wish to check—"

"I trust your work, Mrs. Mercer. Simply add the falls and all the other details you have gleaned the past few days." He waved his hand dismissively at the stack of vellum drawings.

I had shown him but two this morning. This was an extraordinary departure from our usual routine, during which Mr. Cook meticulously went over every drawing, checking it for scale and accuracy against his own, lesser-detailed maps.

"Add what you can today. I'll be along to pick them up this evening. That will have to conclude our work for the time being."

"Have I done something wrong?" Though Mr. Cook and I had merely a working relationship, he had been solicitous to both Timothy and myself, and even Mrs. Hodges, reimbursing her for the almost daily use of her sitting room the past weeks. I hated to think that my work was no longer to his satisfaction or that I had somehow offended him.

"On the contrary," he assured me. "I regret very much that our sessions must end. You have been most helpful in mapping out Cape Breton. I should have liked to continue with the other areas of Nova Scotia as well, but I will be leaving tomorrow. The French have taken St. John's, and I am among those summoned to take it back."

"The war . . ." It had been almost easy to forget about it of late, since meeting the peaceful Mi'kmaq woman, and with my mind so occupied in the week since I had spoken with Mrs. Parker. My days were consumed with caring for Timothy and producing drawings for Mr. Cook. Nights had become cherished times during which I dreamed of Collin and marveled at our growing child.

"The war continues." Mr. Cook sounded more annoyed than anything by this. I imagined that he was. His passion seemed to lie not in fighting but in discovering and exploring new places.

"See that you take care, Mrs. Mercer. Do not wander or allow Timothy to do so. The victory at St. John's has given the French confidence, and word has it they are sallying forth nearer Halifax as well—they and their native allies."

I remembered Captain Shenk's tales of scalping and

contrasted that with the Mi'kmaq woman's sad eyes as she told me they did not wish to leave their homeland either.

Are we not the ones driving them out? Was there not land here enough for both? For all?

"Mrs. Mercer?" Mr. Cook asked once more when I had not replied.

"Yes. Of course. We will stay right here in Halifax," I promised.

He took his leave of us, much to Timothy's disappointment, and I dedicated my afternoon to transferring the waterfall and my other discoveries to the master parchment. My abilities had grown in the past month, not only artistically, but even more so my aptitude for seeing the places of our future. Just as the layered vellum added to the drawing we had begun with, it seemed another lens was added to my mind each day, as if a telescope was trained on the island we were to inhabit, and each day its focus grew stronger.

I was thus laboring, adding detail to what I perceived to be a path around the northeast shore, when Mrs. Hodges appeared in the doorway, a letter in her hand.

My heart seemed to skip. I rose slowly as she crossed the room.

"From my husband?" I felt myself trembling as I took the envelope. It had to be from Collin. There was no one else who knew we were here.

None except Captain Shenk, whose signature caught my eye as soon as I'd broken the seal and unfolded the parchment. This time it felt as if my heart seized. I scanned the contents quickly.

Dear Mrs. Mercer or MacDonald (as the case may be),
It is with a sense of urgency that I write this letter.

MacDonald? Captain Shenk did not know us as such, unless—Collin had confided in him? I continued reading.

Upon our arrival in Portsmouth, it soon came to our attention that your husband was wanted for murder. I could not believe it of him and attempted to tell authorities as much when he was arrested.

"No!" I gasped.

"What is it?" Timothy asked.

Mrs. Hodges leaned closer.

I turned away from both and forced myself to keep reading.

Though I vouched that he had been with me during our recent journey from England, I had no ship's log or other documents to prove this.

I regret to tell you that at present he is incarcerated in Portsmouth, on Hampton Road, awaiting trial. I thought you would wish to know and urge you to make all haste to come.

Enclosed, please find sufficient funds for your travel. I am hopeful it may be of some assistance to you in this time of difficulty.

Sincerely,

Captain Edward Shenk

I lifted the letter to view a second paper behind and saw a face I might have once mistaken for my husband's, the notice of his crime written beneath.

Ian. Anger burst within me. Could he not have kept himself from trouble even a short time? *Collin, imprisoned. At the mercy of the English.* My hands trembled on the paper.

"What is it? You look as though you've seen a ghost," Mrs. Hodges said.

Quickly I covered the picture.

"A ghost who sent you a generous sum," she added,

peering over her spectacles at the pound notes that scattered from between the pages as I thrust them together. We knelt to pick them up.

I held the letter close to my heart, not wishing her to see it. She might evict Timothy and me this very minute, on the grounds that Collin had been arrested.

Murder? In Virginia? What had Ian done? I longed for a minute of privacy to closer read the enclosed notice.

"Mrs. Mercer?"

"I am quite well," I said, perhaps a little too quickly and cheer-fully, given Mrs. Hodges' folded arms and the suspect look she bestowed upon me. I stood slowly, then folded the letter and began clearing my papers and pencils from the table. "Though I am afraid my husband is not. I'll need to go to him as soon as possible. I shall see if Mr. Cook is able to help me arrange passage to Virginia."

"You'll have to pay next month's rent before you leave, or I cannot promise you a room upon your return."

"I understand." I also understood perfectly that she would bestow no sympathy upon me, no matter that the accusations against Collin were unjust. Mrs. Hodges was the sort who was friendly enough when it suited her purposes. But when it did not . . . There was no point in asking for help. There was also no point in spending precious funds on a room we would not be here to use, for I felt little hope that Collin's freedom would be readily obtained.

Collin. Imprisoned. How many weeks had he suffered already? Silently I cursed my gift, feeling keenly that it had led me astray. I had been sketching waterfalls while my husband's life was in danger.

I threw my supplies into my basket, tossed the letter on top, and marched from the room. I was angry with myself, the British—the world at large for repeated attacks upon the man I loved.

And, as Alistair Campbell once said, an angry woman is not to be trifled with.

Especially one who is both Campbell and MacDonald.

"Mrs. Mercer, to what do I owe this pleasure?" Mr. Cook crossed the deck toward us, an unreadable expression upon his face, much the same as the one he'd worn the first day of our acquaintance.

"I must admit to being rather surprised at finding you aboard once more. You'd led me to believe you had somewhat of an aversion to ships."

"She doesn't like carriages either," Timothy piped up before I could begin an explanation as to our uninvited and likely unwanted presence.

"Not now, Timothy," I scolded. "Be silent and let me speak." I caught Timothy's scowl but had no time to soothe him now.

I shifted my attention to Mr. Cook. "My apologies for disturbing you when you are preparing to sail, but time is of the essence, and I am in great need of your assistance."

"Of course." He took my elbow with one hand and placed his other on Timothy's shoulder, steering us toward the gangway. "But let us discuss the matter somewhere less conspicuous."

"As you wish." I allowed him to guide us from the ship. We crossed the gangway to the wharf, then walked a piece until there were no ships directly across from us and not much traffic back and forth upon the walk.

Mr. Cook stopped, took another step, giving us a proper amount of separation, then turned to face us. "Now then, what may I do for you?"

"Here. Before I forget." I extended my hand, his rolled map in it. "I did not have time to add all of my latest sketches, but I have included them within this, for you to reference as you please."

He took the parchment. "Thank you. I shall long be indebted to you for sharing your extraordinary talent."

"You are most welcome." I tried to force a smile, but it would not come. "And now I must ask your assistance. I need to find passage to Virginia as soon as possible. I've just today learned that my husband has been mistakenly imprisoned there."

"Mistakenly?" Mr. Cook's brows arched with what I supposed to be curiosity and perhaps disbelief. I remembered that he had never met Collin. If he had I'd no doubt he would know at once, as did I, that the accusations against him had to be false.

"He is wanted for crimes on a ship upon which we did not sail, and in a town which we have not inhabited. I am certain they have mistaken Collin for his twin, Ian. I fear I may be one of the few who will be able to prove this. But—as murder is one of the accusations—time is of the essence. I must leave as soon as possible."

"So you must, if it is murder your husband is to be tried for." Mr. Cook's wide eyes and shocked expression softened into one of compassion, then almost instantly shifted to one of purpose. His brow furrowed as he looked up and down the wharf, scrutinizing the ships at harbor. "I think . . . Yes, I think he might be persuaded." He began walking in the same direction we had first come.

I grabbed Timothy's hand, and we ran alongside him.

"Who may be persuaded?" I asked.

"Are we going on a ship?" Timothy asked excitedly.

"I know of a reputable man, a maritime merchant from Rhode Island, who regularly makes port here. I believe his ship, the *Charming Sally,* came in last week. She may have sailed already, but if not, it is possible he may be of assistance."

"Is Rhode Island close to Virginia?"

"Not particularly. It would be my hope that Nicholas might take you all the way to Virginia. He often trades to the south as well."

"Is it a big ship?" Timothy asked, skipping along beside me.

"What do you think?" Mr. Cook stopped and pointed to a vessel just ahead of us.

"Not as big as *your* ship," Timothy said, but he was bouncing up and down excitedly anyway.

"You forget that I haven't a ship of my own," Mr. Cook said.

"Yet." I spoke without thinking, as a brief glimpse of his future swept through my mind. He would indeed have a ship and command her to great and thrilling adventures. Captain James Cook would become famous for his explorations throughout the world.

He smiled. "I am flattered, Mrs. Mercer. But a mapmaker does not necessarily earn his own vessel."

"You are far more than that, sir," I replied. Our eyes met, and his smile broadened.

"As you are far more than you seem as well."

I gave a brief nod.

"I thank you for trusting me with your unusual abilities. As you requested when we first began our work together, I will tell no one of them."

"Thank you. And now, may we meet the *Charming Sally's* captain?" Collin's life was in danger, and I'd no time for lingering pleasantries—with anyone.

"Of course." Mr. Cook indicated we were to walk ahead of him. "His name is also Cooke, though no relation that either of us are aware of. Nicholas hails from the Colonies and has a rather different view on some matters than do I. But he is a good sailor and a trustworthy man. It is only our politics that I fear may someday see us on opposite ends of a sword."

This rather startled me, though I did not say anything. Instead we followed our Mr. Cook to the ship and waited while the captain was summoned and our plight explained. Mr. Cook insisted on paying our passage himself, allowing me to keep the money from Captain Shenk for later expenses. We were to depart the next morning.

The time came to bid our benefactor farewell. Recalling my irritation with him the first day of our acquaintance, I felt some guilt and told myself I must henceforth show more patience and be less quick to judge.

"Mrs. Mercer, I shall be forever in your debt." Mr. Cook took my hand and kissed the back of it gallantly. Had it not been a parting gesture, I should have been most discomfited.

"The map of Cape Breton shall be the most useful and thorough to date."

"You will make many more," I predicted. "When you sail to both the far off and exotic. Take care on your travels."

"I shall." His smile widened. "And you on yours."

Timothy shook Mr. Cook's hand vigorously; then at last we took our leave of him. At the end of the wharf I paused and looked back, tempted to return and tell him what I had glimpsed of his future. It was to indeed be fraught with danger, and I feared very much his life would be cut short before he had done all he intended.

I shuddered and tried to block the scene from my mind. What-ever I might tell him, however much he might believe me, he was not a man to be dissuaded from his destiny.

"What's the matter, Katie?" Timothy tugged on my hand, eager to pack our belongings. We had been told we might board the ship tonight.

"Sometimes knowing is hard," I said, grateful my little brother would not be burdened with my gift. "As is parting with one who has been a friend."

"Like Mr. Cook?"

"Yes." I swallowed my sorrow.

My thoughts must all be for Collin now. I must concentrate hard on seeing his future—ours together—and what must be done to secure it.

Chapter Forty-two

Portsmouth, Virginia, July 1762

"There's trouble at port." Finlay burst from the trees, having just returned from town. "You!" He pointed a shaking finger at Ian.

"So what if I stirred up a bit of trouble tonight," Ian said, looking up from his place on the ground. "They'll get over it." He'd been hungry, for something other than beans. And thirsty, for something other than water. It wasn't as if he could saunter into a tavern and ask for a drink. He'd borrowed one instead, one measly cup of ale from a night watch sitting on the dock, more concerned with their cards than their cups.

But the man he'd taken it from had noticed his cup was missing sooner rather than later. Still not a problem until he'd traced the drops of ale to the split board in the walk Ian had squeezed it through, and peered beneath it to catch a glimpse of Ian, hurrying away.

It had been a narrow escape, with every half-drunk seaman and Redcoat along the boardwalk joining in the chase. Worst of all, his hiding place below the wharf was forfeit now. He wouldn't be able to go back there to see if the *Ulysses* was in port or anything else.

"He's *in trouble*," Finlay repeated and began digging through his sporran.

"I'm right here." Ian glanced to Alistair to see how he was taking his friend's hallucinations.

"Who is?" Alistair asked, coming nearer as Finlay pulled a folded parchment from his pouch.

He held up the poster Ian had seen around town, the one advertising a reward for his capture. It had a crude sketch of him and stated he was wanted for the murder of Rupert Star, crewman on the *Ulysses*.

"Your abilities are slipping if you're just figuring that out." Ian lay his head back once more and closed his eyes. He heard a shuffling around the camp and low, urgent voices. A minute later he jerked to a sitting position after a toe connected with his side.

"Not you," Finlay said urgently, the paper still held in his hand. "Collin is here, and he's set to hang for your crime."

"Dismantling the gallows was a good idea, but it did not stop them long." In the early light of dawn Alistair stood before a circle of bleary-eyed, grim-faced men and women, some Campbells, some MacDonalds, all people Ian would never have believed he'd see outside of his homeland.

Upon learning of Collin's arrival and capture, Finlay had returned to Norfolk to gather them all the past week while Alistair and Ian had remained behind to do what they could to gain Collin's release, or at the least, to postpone his execution. They'd dismantled the gallows last night.

"The gallows have been rebuilt, and the hanging is scheduled for tomorrow afternoon," Alistair said, looking—for the first time, Ian thought—like the old man he was.

"Should have burned it to the ground." Ian rose from the log he'd been sitting on. "Though that wouldn't have stopped them either. Plenty of trees around here, and when the Redcoats want to hang a Scot, they will."

"Are you saying all is lost?" one of the MacDonald women cried.

"Didn't say that."

"Of course he's not." Alistair's wife, Mary Campbell, stepped into the circle. Though she was an older woman, well past child-bearing years, she held a baby in her arms, bouncing the child as she spoke, while several other small children clustered behind her like ducklings waddling after their mother.

"I have come to know the MacDonalds in the past year, and they do not give up on each other. Ever." Mary's voice was sharp, her gaze fierce as she looked at each in the circle. "In the absence of Collin, our leader and laird, we must give our loyalty to his brother. Ian will direct us in what must be done."

"Thank you." Ian nodded cordially and tried not to feel irritated that a woman, and a Campbell at that, had just pled his case before this people, many of whom were his own. In Collin's absence last year they had shown Ian their loyalty. He believed he still had it now, but the Campbells were likely another story.

My own fault. It could take years to undo all the harm he'd done in the Highlands during his time with the Munros. Though his reputation as a ruthless, cunning thief might prove useful here too—when what he intended to steal was the most precious of all. *Collin.*

Eliza might be lost to him—after weeks of searching he had forced his mind to that conclusion. It brought no end of pain and regret. But there was naught he could do about that now, except to turn his grief and anguish to action, for the person he could still save.

He'd wanted to act sooner. The jailer's home was not overly large or well guarded. Ian felt they could have overpowered the man and freed Collin, but the poet had spoken out against it, insisting they must wait. They must gather everyone first, so all could make their escape together.

Ian hadn't cared so much about that as he cared about freeing his brother—until this morning. Seeing all those who had walked the miles to come to his aid, knowing they had willingly followed Collin across the ocean, Ian felt that same stirring of compassion and the weight of responsibility that had been cropping up since meeting Eliza, and even before. Since reuniting with Collin years earlier.

He'd lived the life of a man looking out for only himself, and it was no life. Better to lose his in the pursuit of others' happiness. It seemed such a contradictory way to fulfillment and peace, yet there it was. And at last, he felt not only resigned to it, but ready to embrace it as well.

Stubborn, their father had always said of him. *Slow to learn. But when you do eventually make your mind up to the way of things, there's not a finer man to be had.* Ian recalled his father's praise as well as his scolding. He remembered the weight of Da's hand upon his shoulder the day he had spoken those words to him. *You are a natural leader, Ian. You will be a great laird. You must only be cautious in the direction you lead those who would follow.*

Let me be careful today. He looked around the circle of faces and felt responsibility for every one of them rest upon him. They needed to rescue Collin, but not at the cost of other lives.

"Many of you remember last year when the MacDonalds came to the Campbell holding. It was Collin leading you then, but I was the one who'd come up with the idea of appearing as more than we were. Women and bairns were made to appear as mighty warriors."

"We are mighty!" a young voice shouted from the back of the circle.

"So you are." Ian raised his cup to the lad who'd spoken. "Common tools were disguised as weapons, and you fanned out in a great circle, with stumps and brooms and rakes between, creating the illusion of a mighty clan."

"I remember," Alistair said. "You scared Brann and his counsel off. But I don't see how that can work here."

"Hear me out," Ian pled. "It will not be quite the same here, though I pray the result will be. Not one drop of blood was shed when the MacDonalds surrounded the Campbell keep. That is my goal today—that not one of you will be harmed in the rescue of my brother."

Grunts of acknowledgment came from the circle.

"How do you propose to accomplish that?" Gordon asked.

Ian answered with a question. "What happens when a man is hanged? Who gathers to see the spectacle?"

"Many do," Mary said softly. "Men and women. Some bring their children."

"Aye. And in a town this size and with much ado that has now been made rebuilding the gallows in the square, there is sure to be a large crowd come to see. What I propose is this: We must—all of us, excepting the very young—spread out amongst them." He'd known the trickery with the gallows in the dark of night would not change or even long delay Collin's sentence. What he had hoped to achieve by that, aside from buying time for all of them to gather in Portsmouth and rally to Collin's defense, was to generate interest within the town. The more who knew of the hanging and anticipated the event, the more crowded it would be the day of.

The more opportunity to create chaos. A square packed with people, a few well-timed and aimed shots, and he'd have a scene of bedlam from which he could more easily reach Collin and spirit him away.

"What good will that do?" a man whose name Ian did not know asked.

"Let him finish," Alistair called as other voices echoed the man's.

Ian raised his hands for quiet. "I have learned that Collin is to be transported to the gallows by a barred carriage. It will enter the square on the south side, where I will be waiting in the crowd, close to the place it will stop for him to be removed. When the door is opened and Collin exits, I will fire into the air—" He raised his pistol for all to see— "to spook the horses and create a distraction."

"It will take more than a distraction," Alistair said. "One of you against several guards, not to mention the hangman. You'll swing beside your brother."

"Not if I have your help," Ian argued. "At the precise moment Collin steps from the carriage, every one of you stationed throughout the crowd will raise the battle cry. We've acquired a half dozen pistols. Those of you in possession of one are to fire into the air. Those nearest the carriage are to help frenzy the horses. If necessary, those of you near the gallows will set it on fire. We don't want to hurt anyone—not even the guards if possible—but we want to create enough of a disturbance that Collin is able to get safely away. Which is precisely what each one of you must do, as soon as you have done your part."

"Safely away to where?" someone asked.

"The wharf." Finlay rose and came to stand beside Ian.

"We haven't arranged for a ship," Ian began but stopped when Alistair held a hand up.

"Let Finlay speak."

Finlay stepped in front of Ian, walking closer to the middle of the circle, where he turned slowly, looking at each, and began to speak with all the poetic animation of a jester at court.

"The small children are charming. To the sea take them now." Finlay's hands swept wide. "*Sally* is awaiting; the captain stands at her bow." He straightened to his full height, hands behind his back, feet spread, eyes staring straight ahead as if he was a captain upon a ship, looking out to sea.

"Brought to us here by the lass we all loved, grown to a woman now, her direction from above." He raised his hands to the heavens, his face angled back as well.

Ian was speechless after this recitation, and not a little confused. They weren't acting. This wasn't time for a play. Yet the poet was apparently well respected. Murmurs flew around the circle, and he heard the name *Katherine* whispered more than a few times. If Finlay had just suggested that she'd brought a ship here to rescue them all, Ian didn't—couldn't—believe it.

"If we go to the wharf we are likely to be trapped there. A better choice would be to leave in groups through the various woods skirting town where—"

"We'll meet at the wharf." Alistair spoke with finality. "Look for a ship named *Sally* and a captain standing as Finlay demonstrated. He knows what he's talking about. We'll trust you with the first part of the plan, Ian, but you have to trust him—trust the Campbells—for the second."

Ian did not like being told what to do; nor did he appreciate that it seemed his entire clan, all the MacDonalds left here with them, so readily agreed with Alistair. What had happened during those months he'd been away?

"All right," he said at last, reluctantly. He and Collin needn't go to the wharf. If the rest of them wanted to get themselves in trouble—

Then I'll be there to get them out of it. He would have to follow them, whether or not he wished to. Ian closed his eyes briefly, not yet comfortable with this new Ian, the one who must think of everyone else before himself.

Chapter Forty-three

Portsmouth, Virginia, July 1762

The boat had scarcely docked when I made my way from it, Timothy's hand clasped tight in mine. I had spent the better part of the last eleven days—record time for our voyage, I'd been told—considering what I must do upon our arrival in Virginia, and whether or not I should have Timothy at my side as I attempted to gain Collin's release.

Though we'd had the acquaintance of Captain Nicholas Cooke less than a fortnight, I judged him to be a good man and would possibly have felt Timothy safe in his company for a few hours, while I first made inquiry about Collin. I feared the condition I might find him in, and worried about frightening Timothy if it was indeed as poor as I suspected. But I could not bear the thought of being parted from my brother and having that additional worry to contend with. I hoped the presence of a child would soften the jailer's heart and that we would be permitted to both see Collin and plead our case.

For while I had pondered and prayed over what I was to do to free Collin, no idea had manifested itself to me. It was with a great deal of faith and false bravado that I marched Timothy from the relative safety of the *Charming Sally* toward town and the Hampton Road mentioned in Captain Shenk's letter.

The wharf was crowded this morning, with a great number of people walking in the opposite direction, their meager possessions clutched in their arms. A ship, or perhaps several ships, must be preparing to leave. I wondered where they might be going. Back to England or on to one of the other Colonies? Our journey down the coast had given me but a glimpse of how vast this new world truly was.

A baby cried nearby, and my head snapped up, matching time with the increased beating of my heart and some instinctual, maternal reaction within. *Lydia?*

I looked that direction, searching, but the cry did not come again, and the wharf was too packed with people to distinguish from whence it had come. Mentally I scolded myself for even a second's distraction.

Collin. I must find Collin. But the cry had shaken me, and the vision I'd had months earlier, while crossing the Atlantic, returned to haunt me. What if Mhairi *had* changed her mind? What if she was here and it was she who would end up with Collin?

"Don't fret so, Katie." Timothy seemed not solemn as he trotted along beside me, but carefree and happy, as a boy should be. Clearly the gravity of Collin's situation had not settled upon him. I felt grateful for this and once more questioned my judgment in bringing him along. Should I not preserve his innocence and spare him from realizing the ugliness of the world as long as possible?

"I've brought my lucky rock," Timothy whispered loudly as he turned out his pocket to show me the treasure from our day at the beach, his grin so hopeful that I could not help but smile myself.

I squeezed his hand appreciatively, though I did not believe a rock or any other such token could provide us the luck we needed. "What an astute boy you are."

Timothy's nose crinkled. "What does that mean?"

"Clever and intelligent—" *Oh.* A young, terribly thin, and dirty Collin appeared before my eyes, the great hall of my grandfather's castle materializing around him. Grandfather was there too, and the words I had just spoken were his—to Collin.

Collin is *clever and intelligent. And so are you.*

I almost turned my head, searching for the voice, though I already knew it was impossible that Grandfather was really there with us, speaking to me. *First Lydia's cry, then Grandfather's voice.* Anyone else might have believed they were going mad. Instead, the brief glimpse of the past brought comfort and bolstered my confidence. We had not come so far to fail. Collin and I both still had much work to do. *Together.*

"Tuck your treasure away and come along." I hastened my steps again, and Timothy kept pace.

Having no notion of where I was or the layout of Portsmouth, I stopped often to ask directions. Though I was inquiring as to the whereabouts of a prison, all I encountered were pleasant enough, and helpful when they could be. I wondered if I would have been so well received had my accent been Scottish brogue instead of English and my dress the rags from our shipwreck. What were the sentiments here toward Scots? Toward the poor?

We had traveled several blocks from the wharf when Timothy tugged at my hand. "I'm thirsty. And hungry too."

My own stomach grumbled. The day was muggy and hot, the sun already well on its way toward noon. I thought of the child I carried and admonished both him and Timothy to be patient. I had money with which to see to our needs, but I could not think of providing for our sustenance until I had proof of Collin's well-being.

"Collin is likely hungry and thirsty too. Let us find him, and then we can all eat together in celebration." If only it could be so simple. Today, at best, I hoped to be permitted to see Collin and perhaps to discover what might be done for his defense.

We crossed two more blocks, Timothy sagging like a wilted flower at my side.

I pulled him along. "Hampton Road should be just around this corner. Look for a building that has bars on the windows."

"I see it!" he exclaimed a moment later, and I nearly cried with relief. The building appeared almost a normal house, save for the barred windows. *Much better than Father's description of the foul prisons in London.*

I straightened my hat as we hurried up the walk and knocked upon the door. A man answered, his large frame filling much of the doorway, though leaving enough of a gap for me to see a woman working at a table behind.

"Yes?" His eyes hastily scanned Timothy and me, then the space behind us before returning to rest on my face.

"We are here to visit a prisoner. Collin MacDonald."

"You his wife?"

"Yes." I nodded. "May we see him, please? We have traveled a great distance and only just arrived—"

"He's not here. You'll find what's left of him at the square." The man began closing the door.

"What do you mean?" I cried as the woman I'd glimpsed nudged her way into the space beside him, blocking his attempt to shut us out.

"Your husband wrote you a letter." She withdrew a folded paper from her apron pocket. With shaking fingers I took it.

"His trial was three days ago," she said solemnly. "They came for him this morning, not ten minutes ago now. If you hurry, you might still be able to see him . . . once more."

"Wha-at do you mean?" I repeated, my attention flitting back and forth between the two, noting the compassion in the woman's expression and the hardness in the man's.

"Convicted of murder," he said. "A crewman from the *Ulysses* recognized him and gave testimony. Sentence would have been carried out yesterday, but there was some problem with the gallows."

"Gallows!" I gasped. "My husband was never on the *Ulysses*. We sailed together on the *Cleopatra*. To Halifax. This is all a terrible mistake."

The man shrugged, and his mouth twisted in such a way

that I knew he didn't believe me. "Mistake or no, you're too late to change it."

The woman pushed past him to join us on the step. "Follow me," she urged. "Hurry."

Chapter Forty-four

Portsmouth, Virginia, July 1762

The problem with keeping one's head low was that it was impossible to scan the crowd. Ian had to trust that those who'd come with him had followed his instructions and were stationed as they should be, near the gallows, around the perimeter, and in the midst of those gathered along the carriage route.

Even with his chin tucked and his hat brim slanted close to his eyes, he couldn't miss the numerous Redcoats surrounding the gallows and standing at attention at the four corners of the square. There had to be close to thirty, all armed. He had but a dozen pistols, most with but one shot each, in the hands of the MacDonalds and Campbells.

No matter, he told himself. Highlanders were used to being outnumbered. What was the saying? *Twelve Highlanders and a bagpipe make a rebellion.* If so, they were about to have one here today—minus the bagpipe.

The tone of the crowd seemed celebratory, with good-humored jostling, drinks in many hands, gossip flying from the lips of those beneath the fanciest bonnets. You'd have thought they were attending a ball, not an execution.

It was all too much like England, and after today he wanted no part of it. If he couldn't return to the Highlands, if there truly was nothing there for him anymore, he'd travel with the others and try out this Nova Scotia they all spoke of with a great deal of hope and yearning. It had better be someplace far from towns like this, from civilization where the people rejoiced in such *un*civilized acts as the hanging of an innocent man. It had better be a place wild and untamed. They would all do well enough in an environment like that, so long as it was free of those who would take it and everything dear to them.

Ian glanced at the sky. It had to be nearly noon. Not long now.

No matter what happened, Collin would walk away from this place today. *Even if it means I do not.* What Ian had not told the others, was that he'd an alternate plan if things went awry. It was the plan he should have followed months ago. If he had turned himself in then, Eliza might still be at the millinery. Her employer, Mrs. Perkins, might be alive and well. *Eliza would be alive and well.*

Even the situation of Mrs. Campbell, Taye, and Aisla might have worked out all right if he had just turned himself in.

Twice now he had made the mistake of walking away, leaving those he loved behind to suffer the consequences. He would not do it again. *Collin, you won't hang for me today.*

Ian looked up at the gallows. It cast hardly any shadow at all beneath the sun. If this was his fate, so be it.

Chapter Forty-five

Portsmouth, Virginia, July 1762

"I'm sorry I can't lend you a horse. My husband wouldn't like it." The jailer's wife hurried us along first one street and then another.

"I knew your husband had to be innocent. He wasn't like most of the other prisoners we get. I could tell he was a good man. Always thanked me for his meals and spoke polite."

This report of Collin's behavior did nothing to ease my terror. Nor Timothy's either, it seemed.

"Katie," he cried in a high, panicked voice. "Are they going to hang Collin? Like that man we saw in England?"

"No," I said emphatically. "We aren't going to let them."

The jailer's wife stopped at the corner, her breath as short as mine. "Take this road four blocks, then two to the left, and you'll see the square. There will probably be a crowd gathered."

"Thank you," I called as Timothy and I began running. My side soon hurt, and twice my foot landed wrong and I nearly toppled forward.

Timothy kept pace. Neither of us spoke. The four blocks seemed to go on forever as we flew past houses, shops, children and adults, horses and carriages, one of which nearly ran us over as we cut across the last street to go left.

The driver stood, shaking an angry fist. "What do you mean by—"

His words were lost as we rounded the corner. Up ahead I could already see the crowd. *Collin!* What was the time? How much longer?

My sides ached, and my chest burned. I dropped Timothy's hand to cradle mine below the swell beneath my gown. *Just a little farther. I'm coming, Collin.*

The jeers and chants of those gathered reached us. They didn't even know my husband, yet they were crying for his death. Timothy surged ahead of me, and I ran faster to keep up. *I should have left him at the ship. If he sees—*

He wouldn't.

We were stopped short by the edge of the tightly packed crowd. I rose up on tiptoe and scanned the many heads and faces for any sign of Collin. My gaze landed on the platform and gallows. *Empty.*

My relief was fleeting. Grasping Timothy's hand once more, I began making my way around the perimeter to get behind the gallows instead of to the side of it, all the while turning my head to and fro, searching.

"I see wheels. There must be a wagon." Timothy tugged at my hand.

"It wouldn't do any good." I pulled him in the opposite direction. "Too many people to drive anywhere." We were here already. *I just need to find—*

"You could stand in it and see better."

His suggestion stopped me.

I allowed him to pull me, trusting that his lower view had really allowed him to glimpse what I had still not seen.

We wended our way unapologetically through the crowd until we were outside it again.

"There." Timothy pointed some distance away, up on a rise on the street behind the gallows.

Not a wagon. My heart leapt at the sight of the barred carriage surrounded by four soldiers on horseback.

We ran toward it, panting heavily as we made our way up the incline. "Collin," I shouted when we were close enough that he might hear. *Let him be inside.*

My shouting caught the attention of one of the men on horse-back. He angled toward me.

"Stop right there."

"I am—his wife," I panted. "Please let me see him."

"You may see him on the gallows, madam. And count yourself blessed to soon be free of marriage to a murderer."

"You have the wrong man."

The Redcoat ignored me and instead gave a nod to his companion. The procession started forward, toward the gallows.

"Collin!" I screamed.

"Let him go!" Timothy cried.

There was no answer from the carriage, no stirring from within or even a muffled cry. *Is he harmed? Unconscious? Already dead?*

My imagination led me to dark, frightening places.

We ran toward the carriage. Shades were pulled low inside the bars, making it impossible to see inside. The man seated next to the driver turned his head to stare as they passed, and his sneer felt somehow victorious, as if he was lording some great achievement over us. His uniform was not that of a British soldier but some other costume, similar to that which Mr. Cook had worn.

"Stay back," the rear guard ordered, swinging his sword our direction.

I shoved Timothy behind me and watched helplessly as they passed.

"Do something," Timothy wailed.

Something. Do. Something. I took a step forward, then another, and began running after the carriage, slipping and sliding down the slope of the street we had just come up. The carriage was faster and reached the bottom before us, pausing for the crowd to clear before it made its way closer to the gallows.

My throat was thick, my body stiff with terror as I stared out over the sea of heads, willing them not to part, not to allow the vehicle through. They did not heed my wish but began to ripple from the center near the carriage outward, much like the ripples when I threw a stone in a loch.

A stone...

"Your lucky rock—give it to me." I didn't wait for Timothy to dig it from his pocket but pulled it free myself, drew my arm back, narrowed my eyes. The driver and his companion's heads bobbed below me, at perfect level. *Strike one of them. Cause a disturbance.*

I took aim and with all my strength sent the stone spinning forward, as if to skip across the surface of the water. Instead it found its mark, striking the driver's companion in the back of the head and toppling him into the crowd.

Chapter Forty-six

Portsmouth, Virginia, July 1762

Millet nearly hit Ian as he fell from the carriage and landed in an unconscious heap on the ground. Ian had no idea what had caused this good fortune but intended to take every advantage of it. He bent swiftly, pulling Millet's weapon from its holster.

Around the carriage chaos erupted, cheers turning to screaming and the mood shifting to panic as one of the Redcoat guards fired his pistol into the air and the horses reared.

For once Ian felt reason to thank the soldiers for their stupidity as their efforts to control the crowd quickly resulted in bedlam. The driver stood, pulling back hard to restrain the stressed team. Ian slashed at the reins with his knife, severing one side while Finlay sawed at the other.

Just as Millet had, the driver toppled suddenly, his body falling forward over the front of the carriage, folding in half on its way down and landing wedged between beasts and carriage. Ian spared no thought for him but finished cutting the second strap, then ran around the side of the carriage. He used the back of Millet's gun to shatter the glass, then thrust his hand through and ripped the black curtain away. Before he could glimpse Collin through the bars, the tip of a rifle pressed into the side of his face.

Ian froze, and the corner of his eye followed the long barrel up to the hand of one of the mounted Redcoats.

"Hands up," the soldier ordered. "Hand me your gun."

Slowly Ian began raising his hands as if in surrender. But when they reached his shoulders he swung wildly, first knocking the barrel away, then jerking it hard, yanking the weapon from the surprised soldier's hands. The butt of the rifle struck the horse's leg on its way down, and the animal kicked in surprise.

"Collin!" Ian directed his shout toward the carriage as he swung the rifle toward the soldier struggling to remain on his horse.

Ian spared a glance toward the barred window and saw the carriage empty. A jagged, gaping hole shone through the other side, as if the door had been chopped away—certainly not by the uniformed man standing there. Ian raised his gun as the man turned toward him. But the face that peered at him through the bars was one he would never harm.

"Eliza?" Ian pointed the pistol skyward and fired another shot, startling the horse even more and throwing its rider. The cries and shouts of the crowd escalated in further confusion as the distraught animal tried to find a way out.

Ian ducked below the carriage and rolled beneath to the other side. *Any day now,* he thought, wondering why the other Campbells and MacDonalds had not yet fired their weapons.

A hand reached down to him, and Ian looked up into Collin's face. Eliza stood beside him, utter astonishment written in her scrunched brow and open mouth. The uniform hung on her, the coat ridiculously large, the knee pants baggy and falling well below her knees.

Ian couldn't help but smile at her.

"Let's go." Collin pulled Ian up.

A man lay at Eliza's feet. Not dead, Ian thought, but definitely unconscious. He must have been the guard riding inside with Collin, as Ian could see both of the other mounted guards busy contending with the clamoring crowd.

Collin moved off toward the back of the carriage.

"Not that way," Ian said. "We'll do better staying in the crowd. We'd be spotted as soon as we're away."

"Katie's back there," Collin said, staying his course.

"We'll find her later." Ian jerked hard on the back of Collin's shirt. "You know how to hide as well as I, and it isn't out in the open."

"Split up, then," Collin said. "We look too much alike not to cause—"

A rousing war cry cut him off, and both brothers' attention snapped outward at the sound. Ian hadn't heard anything like that in years. Not since Culloden.

From every side of the square seemed to come the MacDonald battle cry.

"Creagan an fhithich!"

In unison, Ian, Collin, and Gordon raised their fists and echoed the same. "Creagan an fhithich!"

"Cruachan!" a second cry reverberated around the square, with Finlay's chant seeming the loudest. Gun shots followed the Campbell battle cry, and screams of terror ensued.

Twelve Highlanders without *a bagpipe will work too.* The MacDonald cry came once more, lifting the hairs on the back of his neck and his arms. *Warriors. Wherever we are.*

"Collin!"

Ian whirled around to see Collin's wife running toward them, dragging a small lad along behind her. They both launched themselves at Collin, and he caught them in a great hug, then pulled back almost immediately, still keeping hold of his wife. "Let's get out of here."

"Follow Finlay." Gordon used a piece of the broken carriage to hit a soldier just rousing himself.

"Thanks, Brother." Collin grinned at Ian before guiding his wife and the lad into the swell of people.

Ian's gaze slid to Eliza and noted her eyes following Collin as well.

"Let's go." He grabbed her hand and started pulling her in the opposite direction. Collin would be all right now. Finlay and Gordon had folded in behind him. All but one of the guards who'd accompanied the carriage had been rendered unable to fight, and the other was busy, along with the Redcoats who'd been stationed at the perimeter of the square, trying to control the crowd.

Eliza's hand felt cold in his. Ian glanced at her and noted she was pale and trembling.

"Stay with me," he said, pulling her along as fast as he dared and as much as he could in the throng of people, many of whom were trying to flee themselves.

All the better for our escape.

When they'd moved away from the carriage and the soldiers still contending with others there, Ian stopped abruptly. "Give me your hat and coat." He pulled the tricorn from Eliza's head then helped her shrug out of the coat. He thrust his arms through the sleeves, then swept Eliza into his arms.

"Close your eyes," Ian ordered. "Let your arms hang limp."

She did as he directed, allowing her head to fall back as well. This created an even better ruse, though if anyone looked closely they might find it suspect that she was wearing breeches.

Ian threaded his way through the crowd. "Make way! She's fainted. Move aside!" He carried Eliza with ease, noting how light she was. *How thin.* Wherever she had been hiding these past weeks, she had not had enough to eat.

Twice Ian noted other MacDonalds and Campbells and motioned to each he saw to withdraw as quickly as possible.

After what seemed like an hour they left the square, quite opposite from where they had started near the carriage and gallows.

He allowed himself to stop at last, and for the first time

really took in Eliza's appearance. She was not only thin, but her face was drawn, with dark circles beneath her eyes.

She was no less beautiful to him than she had been before.

He set her gently on the ground and reached for her hand to find it already full—gripping the handle of a small hatchet. It was so small Millet's stolen coat must have slipped over it with ease.

"*You* were the one who hacked the door off the carriage?"

She nodded. "I thought you were inside." Tears brimmed and overflowed.

He gathered her close. "Eliza."

She sobbed harder. "I was so afraid."

"I've been mad with fear myself, not knowing where you were these past weeks. I've been searching everywhere for you."

"I did what you would. I hid. And I became a—a thief." More sobs. "I even stole this." She held up the hatchet.

Ian took it from her and used his free hand to stroke her back, trying to soothe her. "It's only stolen if you don't return it," he said. "Do you remember where it came from?"

Eliza nodded and pointed up a distant street. They started toward it, Ian carrying her once more, so as to avoid question about her attire.

"Might you have a gown stashed somewhere nearby?"

She shook her head. "I traded it—for food."

"No matter," he said. "We'll get you another—anything you need or want." He would, so help him. He'd put his every effort into providing a good life for her.

They returned the hatchet, not to the exact spot she'd taken it from—a stump in the middle of a yard—but just inside the fence, where Ian dropped it casually as he passed.

He hurried his steps now, conscious that this far from the square, passersby were giving them curious looks.

The wharf, he remembered, heading in that general direction, worrying that they'd never make it to a ship named

Sally—if there was one—looking as they did now. Spying clothes hanging on the lines in several yards, Ian began looking for a gown or petticoat that might work for Eliza.

"How and when did you come to hear that Collin—or I—was to be hanged today?" he asked as they walked. There were other questions Ian wanted to ask her, particularly about the fire at the millinery, being accused of murder herself, and the night Millet had visited her room. But he wasn't sure how to ask those. If he started at the end and worked backward perhaps she would be more likely to tell him.

"I overheard talk of it at The Young Devil."

Ian tensed. "What were you doing there?"

"I went as often as I could," she said. "I thought if you returned, that was where you might come."

Ian closed his eyes briefly, imagining her in that place. "I am sorry," he said. "I've been here for weeks—with Alistair and Finlay Campbell—looking for you, but I never thought to go there."

"My uncle is *here*?" Eliza raised her head to look at him.

"Your entire clan is, save the few who sided with your laird. The MacDonalds have come too. They're together, if you can believe it."

This earned him a wan smile, and his heart seemed to quicken with a happy, joyful beat, though he told himself Eliza's smile was not necessarily for him or because of anything he'd done.

"I grew up hearing that very thing foretold by Liam Campbell. A fairytale, many said. But I always believed differently. I thought they would join in Scotland, though, beginning with your brother's marriage."

"Is that why you helped me?" Ian asked. "Why you came after Collin today?"

"I came today because Millet threatened that he would kill you if I didn't do his bidding. I couldn't let that happen."

"So you did as he asked?" Ian's heart sank to the slow thud of regret and then anger. He reminded himself that whatever she had done, it had been with a mind to protect him.

"Of course not. Did you not hear what I just said? If I'd done his bidding, do you think your brother would have been within feet of the gallows?"

"Aye," Ian answered vehemently. "A snake like Millet has no reason to keep his word."

"We'll never know if Millet would have kept his word or not. I gave him even more reason to search you out when I poisoned him and stole his clothes."

"Not just drunk then?" Ian's hunch had been right.

"I put Belladonna in his wine," Eliza confessed. "The same I used on the soldier who threw my father into that burning building—except that I gave that soldier enough to kill him."

"That is what you were referring to when you told me you had killed someone."

Eliza nodded. "I was so angry, but I oughtn't have taken his life."

"But you saved mine. And many others' on the *Ulysses*. Who knows but that you spared someone else from being hurt at that soldier's hand." *If he was vile enough to throw a live man into a burning building.* "How is it you acquired Belladonna?" Ian asked.

"Brann grew it in his poison garden at the Campbell keep. When he showed interest in me, Father began to worry for my safety. It was Father who suggested I take precautions. He snuck into the garden at night and procured the plant."

"And then?" Ian asked, angered she'd had threats from so many. *Little wonder she was frightened to learn my identity.*

"Father and I ground it up, and I carried a little vial sewn into my skirt. When mixed into alcohol it is mostly undetectable. Brann drank heavily, and Father thought poison my best possibility for protection. I never used it on Brann, but it worked quite well to be rid of Officer Millet."

"Remind me to stay on your good side," Ian muttered, the vice on his heart lessening again. *Millet did not hurt her.*

"Where are we going?" she asked when he clipped the corner of the next street and then ducked into an apple orchard, thick with the green leaves and the immature fruit of full summer.

"You've need of other clothes. Stay here. I'll be right back." He left her but a few moments while he exchanged Millet's coat and hat for a dress from someone's wash line.

He held it out to her when he returned. "Put that over your other clothes quickly." He turned away, though she should have no worry of immodesty putting the dress over what she already wore.

"Now I've made you a thief again," she lamented.

Ian shook his head. "The coat and hat I left were more than a fair trade."

He stood quietly while she changed, his mind and heart still racing with all that had happened in the last hour. *Collin and Eliza both safe.* He'd never felt so blessed.

"Ian?" Eliza sounded almost shy as she said his name.

"Aye."

"This isn't going to work."

He turned to see what she meant and met the open front of her gown, cut in a wide arc from hem to waist, revealing most of her breech-clad legs beneath.

"What *happened?*" Perplexed, he studied the fabric closer, unable to fathom why it had been cut such. "It looks— as if a child has discovered scissors and been at work here." He brought a fist to his mouth to hold in laughter.

"I look ridiculous," Eliza declared, her cheeks flushing a pretty pink, so that Ian found he very much wanted to kiss her.

A brief snort of laughter escaped his mouth. "Let me see what else I can find." He strode in the direction he had come.

"A petticoat," Eliza called. "I need a petticoat to wear with this. Nothing is wrong with the dress, it is just incomplete this way. That is the fashion here."

"And here I'd believed Paris risqué." Ian chuckled.

Several minutes later he returned with the remainder of the ensemble, and soon Eliza appeared as any properly clad woman.

He took her hand, taking pleasure in the feeling of it clasped in his. "Let's cut through the orchard. It will be safer. We're to meet at the wharf. There is a ship waiting— supposedly. I'd not believed it before, but I think your relative, Finlay, may have been right. He said Collin's wife would bring it, and there she was today, having appeared out of nowhere." Ian pushed aside a low branch so Eliza could pass. "No one had seen Katherine in the Colonies before today, as she and Collin sailed from England, instead of with the others."

"It appears there is much I have missed." Eliza squeezed his hand.

"None so much as you have missed me, I hope," Ian teased.

"None so much," she confirmed with the smile he remembered.

"Not even your Uncle Alistair?" Ian asked, testing the waters.

Eliza shook her head. "No."

Ian stopped walking quite so fast. Soon enough they would be reunited with the others, and who knew when he would have her to himself again? They were in the middle of the vast orchard, sheltered under the leafy protection of the trees, safe from prying eyes and ears. After the noise and heat and stress at the square, the silence, cool, and peace was welcome. For a long moment neither said anything but just looked at one another. Ian felt his heart race once more.

He wanted to talk of their future, but first, there were a few things he wished to understand about the past weeks.

"The fire at the millinery shop—" Ian said. "Do you think Millet might have started it?"

"I *know* he did," Eliza said. "I wasn't there when it

happened, but away on an errand for Mrs. Perkins. He was awaiting my return and made a big scene of accusing me in front of a great many people. Poor Mrs. Perkins." Eliza's lip trembled. "Thank goodness Aisla was not there that afternoon."

"Aye," Ian agreed, thinking of his recent visit with the lass at the dairy. She was settling in well there, and Mistress Johnston seemed quite taken with her. "What did you do after you got away from Millet? Where have you been?"

"Hiding in the woods, mostly," she said. "If it had been winter, I should have been in trouble. But the weather here is much warmer than at home. I took what money Millet had with him when I left, and I've been able to purchase food here and there, though I've had to be careful where I've spent his coins." She nudged Ian's toe with her own.

"I've stolen food outdoors too," she added sheepishly, her eyes straying to an apple hanging near Ian's head. "They're not very ripe yet," she added, making a face.

He laughed. "They're more tolerable when unripe if you roast them first."

"You speak from experience?"

"Oh yes." Ian glanced up at the trees. "There's not a vegetable, fruit, or animal I've not stolen. I'm not bragging about it," he added hastily. "It's just that for many years, that was the only way to survive."

"I know."

He appreciated the understanding reflected in the depths of her brown eyes.

"What will you do now?" she asked. "Since the MacDonalds are all here?"

"I may return to Norfolk—for a while, at least. If Jannet and her daughter and Aisla wish to go north with the others, I'll need to save up and repay their current employer for the clothing and other things she has provided them. Should they wish to remain in Norfolk, I may delay my departure as well."

"Why?" Eliza asked, seeming surprised by this. "Don't you want to be with your brother?"

"Aye," Ian said, wanting that very badly and even now eager for time alone to talk with Collin. "My employer and my friend Ben have been most kind. It was Ben who journeyed to Portsmouth for me and first alerted me of the fire and your circumstance. Otherwise I would not have known." Ian couldn't think of what might have happened then, the possibility that he might not be standing here alone with Eliza. "Circumstances are as *Aunt Ilona* described in her letters. I can stay on at the cooperage as long as I would like, or need to. It has been good working there, earning an honest wage. What do you wish to do?" he asked quietly.

"Go north with the others," she said quickly, without thought. "It is too hot here, for one thing." She fanned her free hand in front of her face. "I want the chance to live freely, without Brann's control, or fear of a man like Officer Millet."

"Aye." Ian nodded. "Of course." She had not even suggested that she might consider staying here with him. But then, what did he have to offer her right now? Perhaps in a year . . .

"Won't the MacDonalds need a leader?" she asked.

"They've Collin now." *We'll soon be at the wharf.* "Eliza, before you go, I—"

She stopped walking and looked at him expectantly, unblinking, making this even more difficult.

"I want you to know that your being a Campbell no longer matters to me." It was freeing to say it, as if he'd released the last piece of a long-held burden. "I don't care if you're Campbell or English or French or a Colonist. I thought you might be carrying Millet's child—if he had forced himself upon you," Ian added hastily, at her gasp and look of horror. "That didn't matter to me either. You not only saved my life, but you've changed it—changed *me*—in ways Collin strove to but could not." He paused and ran his fingers through his hair in frustration. This wasn't coming out like he had hoped. He'd imagined this opportunity to talk to her so many times, and now he was making a mess of it.

"I've changed your life. You don't care that I'm a Campbell, or even if I'm carrying another man's child." Her summary sounded even worse than when he'd said it. But she was smiling. "Ian MacDonald, are you trying to tell me that you care for me?"

"Aye. That's it exactly." He grinned, relieved that she had under-stood his meaning after all. "I haven't much experience saying—expressing . . ." He couldn't even find the right words to finish his thought. *What a disappointment I must be.* When she'd been so brave and eloquent that night in the lean-to.

Eliza's finger pressed to his lips, silencing his blundering. "Sometimes words aren't the best way to show a person how you feel."

A slow grin lifted his mouth. "The Campbells are good at that."

"I *thought* the MacDonalds were too," she said, staring pointedly at Ian's lips. She sighed dramatically. "I keep hoping that at least one of them will catch on."

"My father always said I was a slow learner." Ian pulled her into his arms. "My father also told me I'd best not kiss a woman unless I intended to marry her."

Eliza lifted her head to his. "Is that a proposal, Ian MacDonald?" Her eyes were suddenly bright.

He nodded, then lowered his head until their lips were close enough to brush as he spoke. "Marry me, Eliza. I promise to show you how grateful I am every day for the rest of our lives."

He kissed her once, then once more, shyly almost, hoping he hadn't imagined what had happened between them before.

"Is that all?" she whispered when he pulled away. Her eyes were still closed. "I'd hoped you'd show a *little* more gratitude than that. I did save your life."

Ian heard a choked noise come from the back of his throat, a kind of strangled joy. His mouth found hers again, this time with no apology or hesitation. His arm slid to wrap around her waist, pulling her closer. Eliza gave a blissful sigh and responded to his kiss, her own *showing* mirroring his, her hand reaching up behind him to pull his head down.

"Eliza, what have you done to me?" he asked breathlessly when they finally parted.

Her answer was smug, though her breathing shallow too. "I believe—I have tamed Ian MacDonald."

Chapter Forty-seven

Portsmouth, Virginia, July 1762

Captain Cooke's crew tied off the last of the ropes, and the *Charming Sally* cast off, the final Campbell—Elizabeth—and the last MacDonald—Ian—having finally boarded. At his brother's appearance, I watched the tension ease from Collin. He had been at the gangway, hat pulled low, a large coat outfitted over him, disguising his thinner frame. He had greeted each and every Campbell and MacDonald alike who came aboard the last hour, while I had been ready on deck, helping to provide water and food for all.

We'd been nearly as shocked as Captain Cooke when we'd arrived earlier, to find a considerable number of Campbells and MacDonalds already on board, having been directed here this morning by Finlay.

Ian's dark head met Collin's. The brothers embraced, and a hush fell over the others on deck.

Thank you. I felt only gratitude for this reunion, in spite of the rocky start Ian and I had shared the previous year.

Collin and Ian had not yet relinquished their grip on one another, and it was accompanied by much slapping of backs and exclamations and grunts.

Scots. Highlanders. MacDonalds. How I adored mine.

At last they broke apart. "What happened to you?" Ian asked. He stared at the scar above Collin's eye before his gaze slid down to Collin's discolored hands.

Collin shrugged. "Played with a bit of fire, is all."

"How? When?" Ian demanded, apparently dissatisfied with Collin's answer.

"When you turned yourself into the Redcoats, I followed and heard one say you weren't long for this world—fool thing that was, getting yourself shot."

Ian gave a good-natured growl. "I wasn't the fool. That Redcoat had a pea for a brain. I was turning myself—as yourself—in. And he was supposed to deliver me to the ship in prime condition. Not half dead."

"You were hurt badly?" Collin asked.

"Nothing a bit of care from Eliza couldn't fix." Ian turned to the woman beside him—Elizabeth, I'd heard Alistair call her—with a look I recognized all too well.

I caught Collin's eye, and we shared conspiratorial smiles. *A Campbell. Who would have guessed?* I wondered if even my grand-father would have seen that coming.

"We were discussing your wounds," Ian reminded Collin.

"Oh, aye." Collin held his scarred hands out. "A few days later I believed I saw the Redcoats throw you into a burning barn. I figured if you were fool enough to be shot for me, I could stand to suffer a burn or two on your behalf. So I went in after."

"But it wasn't Ian. It was my father," Elizabeth exclaimed.

I realized suddenly why she looked familiar. The day Collin had been taken by the English patrol Elizabeth had been among those being sold by Brann. I remembered her, walking slowly to help her crippled father.

"I am sorry," Collin said. "He did not live. His remains are buried in the Campbell kirkyard."

"That is more than I had hoped for. Thank you." Elizabeth's eyes were glistening. Ian seemed to take note and wrapped a comforting arm around her before Alistair, on her other side, was able to.

"At least people will be able to tell us apart now." Ian grinned, something completely uncharacteristic of the man I had known before.

With his good humor at what might be its zenith, I

decided now was a good time to reintroduce myself. Leaving my spot near the water pail, I moved closer to the trio.

"Hello again, Ian," I said, with a slight curtsy and extending my hand for him to take—if he would.

"Hello, Katherine." His touch was light, as if he was unsure the status of our friendship as well.

"Welcome, Elizabeth." I dispensed with formalities and hugged the woman I guessed might soon be my sister-in-law.

"Thank you," she said, still misty eyed. "However did you come to be here? And with this ship?"

I gave a brief description of Captain Shenk's letter but mentioned only that I had secured passage on the next available vessel. There would be time enough later to tell Collin all Timothy and I had learned and done during his absence. I continued my story of our arrival in Portsmouth.

"Then Katie chased the carriage and threw rocks at it," Timothy jumped in just as I finished relaying our unsuccessful visit with the jailer this morning.

Just this morning. It felt as if a month or more had passed since then.

"A rock, that's what it was that knocked Millet from the carriage?" Ian sounded incredulous. "You threw a rock at the back of his head?"

"It was my rock," Timothy piped up. "My *lucky* one."

"Yes, it was." I patted Timothy's shoulder with affection. "I don't know what the man's name is, but yes, I threw a rock at him. I didn't care for the look he gave us when I asked to see Collin, else I would have aimed for the driver first."

Ian laughed out loud. He took up the dipper of water and raised it high. "To my sister-in-law." His eyes, full of respect, met mine over the ladle. "Who did us all a great many good turns today."

"Not the least of which was her arrival in this ship," Finlay added.

"Here. Here." Campbells and MacDonalds alike shouted.

"To Captain Cooke," I said, raising a hand to our captain,

though I was thinking of the explorer and cartographer I'd had the privilege to know.

"Here's to the generous payment from my many unexpected passengers," Nicholas Cooke said good-naturedly.

Alistair had given him a good portion of our remaining funds to see us quickly and safely away.

Collin and Ian resumed their conversation. I left them to their reunion, eager though I was for my own with Collin, and went to lean against the side.

The sun set over Portsmouth behind us. I watched the town fade and felt immensely grateful that Collin and I had first sailed to Halifax instead. For one thing, the summers were much more pleasant there. Though likely that meant winter would be harsh.

No matter. We were Highlanders and would do well. The Mi'kmaq woman had indicated that Cape Breton was largely uninhabited, wild and beautiful. It was exactly what we needed.

Though it was late July, I felt we should go there at once. If we stocked up on supplies in Halifax, and if the land was truly as plentiful as she had shown me with her drawings, I thought we could survive the winter. Quarters would be close. It would not be easy, but if our greatest challenge was nature— not men—I believed we could do it.

"Does it remind you of when we left London?" Collin came up behind me, placing his hands upon my shoulders.

"Perhaps a little," I said. "But not too much. A nice enough place, I suppose," I said, staring at the tree-lined shores. "But not for us."

He moved to stand beside me, and I felt another hand on my shoulder. In unison we looked back to see Finlay standing between us.

"Today's rain is tomorrow's whisky." He broke into hearty laughter, then moved away, shaking his head and wiping at his eyes.

"What was that about?" I asked. It had been some months

since I'd been around Finlay, and I worried that his dangerous journey the previous year had finally come back to haunt him. I hated to think that, to think he might have succumbed to needing alcohol to soothe his wounds, physical or otherwise.

"I don't know," Collin said, his concerned gaze following Finlay. He took a step, as if to follow him, then stopped when Finlay reached Alistair's side and the two began conversing. "I'll find out later. Alistair will look out for him in the meantime."

I turned back to the rail. Collin stood behind me once more, his hands kneading my shoulders and rubbing my arms, as if to melt away the tensions of the day.

"I have much to tell you of our summer." I took Collin's hands and pulled them around me, placing them over the swell beneath my dress.

His hands moved a minute, then stilled suddenly. I turned in his arms to face him. His eyes, wide with wonder, met mine.

"How?"

"A miracle." I smiled through sudden tears.

"Earlier I thought I saw—" Collin broke off, pressing his hand to my stomach, as if he still couldn't believe. "I knew I must be mistaken, but you're saying—What miracle is this, Katie?"

I leaned my head back to better see his face. "I believe it is called a baby—a bairn, if you're Scottish."

"Aye," he said. "But you lost the child. I nearly lost you." His voice was gruff.

I nodded. "I saw Susan Parker about a month ago. She says this happens sometimes. When a woman is carrying twins, one sometimes dies while the other lives."

"*Twins?*" Collin's reaction was much as mine had been. He pulled me close, burying his face in my hair. "Our child. We're to have a child."

I wrapped my arms around him and basked in his joy,

my own as well. "Yes," I said. "In three more months, I believe."

"I love you so, Katie. Let us never part again."

"Never," I agreed. "Where you go, I will too."

"And me." Timothy wiggled his way between us.

"Aye, lad." Collin placed a hand upon his shoulder. "What a braw family I have."

"It's about to become even finer." Thumbs in his jacket, Alistair sauntered up to us, a curious expression on his face. "Forgive my eavesdropping, but expecting a bairn, are ye now?"

"Aye," Collin boasted, not seeming the least annoyed that Alistair had listened to our conversation. "Katie has gone through much for this child already."

Alistair nodded and scrubbed a hand over his auburn beard. "Want a large family, do you?"

"I will be perfectly happy with the lad," Collin squeezed Timothy's shoulder, "and this one." He glanced toward my stomach.

Alistair frowned. "That was not the answer I was after. Mary and I have done our best, but we're old now. We've raised our bairns. And these, one in particular, belong with you." Alistair stepped aside, revealing a procession making its way toward us. Four small children in a row, from shortest to tallest, walked our direction, with Mary Campbell bringing up the rear. A child squirmed in her arms, twisting about until the covering fell away from her face.

"Lydia!" I ran toward her, stopping short, only when the baby looked at me with frightened eyes and leaned her head back against Mary's chest.

Collin grasped my hand. "How—"

"Mhairi changed her mind," I said, glancing about, wondering where she was right now.

"She did," Alistair confirmed. "The children's father drowned his very first day working the kelp. Became entangled and panicked. He wasn't even that far from shore."

I brought my free hand to my mouth, overwhelmed not only by the tragedy and by Lydia's sudden appearance but by the thought that I had seen all this before. I'd seen Mhairi standing on Scotland's distant shore. I'd felt her anguish and regret. Somehow, in the recesses of my mind, I had known this was coming. What was still to come was what terrified me.

What if I died in childbirth? What if she tried to take Collin from me again? What if—

"Would you like to hold Lydia?" Mary held her out to me, but Lydia turned away, unwilling, or at least uncertain about this exchange.

"I don't want to frighten her," I said, disappointed. She'd grown over the past months. She looked more like her older sister, with a headful of curls. I smiled at the children huddled before us.

"Hello." I knelt before the smallest. "Do you remember me?"

She nodded. I held my arms out to her, and she came willingly, returning my embrace, soothing a bit of my hurt at Lydia's rejection.

"Mhairi brought them all back to us," Mary said. "She was too overwhelmed to care for them on her own."

"Of course." Collin sounded sympathetic. I was, too, though I could not entirely forget how she had so cruelly taken Lydia from us. But Collin was holding her now. She still looked uncertain but had allowed him to take her from Mary's arms. My dream, and the sketch I had drawn of him and the children, returned to haunt me.

"Hello. I'm Timothy." My brother gave a proper English bow to the eldest boy, whose own response was somewhat lackluster.

These children have been through so much.

Bravely trying to push away my own anxiety, I stood and moved closer to Collin. "Hello, Lydia." I reached a hand out to touch her curls. "I have missed you so—"

An unexpected flood of tears caught me by surprise, streaming down my cheeks as I turned away, one hand wrapped around my middle, while my other covered my mouth and tried to hold in sobs. I became vaguely aware of Collin handing Lydia back to Mary and his arm around me as he led me from the deck to my room below. He closed the door behind us, then enfolded me in his embrace, letting me cry until my tears were spent.

"Ah, I've missed you, Katie." His mouth lifted in a teasing smile. "No one else knows quite how to soak a man's shirt the way you do."

"You're not amusing." I punched him over the wet spot on his shirt.

"You're right. It's not," he said solemnly. "I'm going to have to build a much bigger house now."

"Oh!" I whirled away from him, a dozen emotions assaulting me all at once. How could he be so casual? Why couldn't he see how frightened I was—of losing him.

"What is it, Katie? Tell me?" Collin wrapped his arms around me from behind and held me tight.

The second tidal wave started. In between sobs I managed to express my fear. "I— saw—" Hiccup. "Mhairi's regret. You holding Lydia. I—wasn't—there. Not me. What if—"

Collin turned me into his embrace, then used one hand to stroke my hair. "Shh. Katie. Everything is going to be all right. *We* will be all right."

"What of Mhairi?" I pulled back to see Collin's reaction to her name.

"What of her?" he said. "She is not my wife. You are. If you knew how deeply I regret last year, not telling you the truth at once when she had figured it out—"

That still cut me to the core. As did the memory of Collin dancing with Mhairi at Hogmanay. I'd forgiven him for that. We had moved past those wounds. We *were* so very happy together. But this frightened me.

I took Collin's hands and held them in my own as I looked up at him, attempting to explain. "She took Lydia so cruelly from us. What if she tries to do the same with you?"

"She won't," Collin said assuredly. "She's—"

"You can't know that," I said. "She's loved you so long she's mad with it." I would remember that last conversation with Mhairi as long as I lived, the ultimatum she'd given me—Collin or Lydia. It had been like tearing my heart out and giving a very fragile piece to her. And now she'd returned and wanted the rest.

"What she feels isn't love," Collin said. "Though madness may be right. When a person loves someone she does not do something as cruel as she did to us. You were not the only one hurt by her actions when she took Lydia."

"I know." I squeezed his hands.

Collin looked deep into my eyes. "Know this, Katie. Mhairi has no power over us. We will never have to see her again."

"What do you mean? If the children are here—"

"She is not," Collin said.

"How do you know? Have you asked Alistair?"

"I don't have to," Collin said. "Before we left the Highlands I gave Alistair and Gordon strict instructions. If Mhairi changed her mind she was not to be permitted to come with them. She was to be given adequate funds to provide for her decently for a time, but she was not—under any circumstances—to be allowed to join with us again."

I gasped. "Gordon agreed to this—banishing his own sister?"

"He did not fight me on it," Collin said. "He understood that I could no longer trust Mhairi, particularly where you are concerned. I would not risk her rejoining us. I would not risk you, Katie. *No one* matters more to me."

I opened my mouth to speak, but no words came. *Not permitted . . .* Collin had chosen me over a longtime friend and member of his own clan. I felt stunned.

Collin gathered me close. I lay my head against his chest, and we stood thus, swaying gently with the rocking of the ship.

The fear that had lodged in my chest eased, and I began to feel I could breathe normally for the first time since Lydia's appearance.

"Lydia—the children—they're ours?"

"Aye. If you want them." Collin leaned back, his mouth quirked in a smile. "Today's rain is tomorrow's whisky."

"What?" I asked, as bemused by his repetition of Finlay's words as I was at his sudden snort of laughter.

Collin hugged me again and kissed me soundly, leaving my head spinning even more. Then he flopped back onto the bed, hands behind his head as he looked up at me.

"It means, Mrs. MacDonald, that we have had quite a bit of rain this past year, more than our fair share I would say— from your near drowning in the river to nearly drowning in the ocean. Assault, treachery, imprisonment. Losing Lydia, losing our own child, nearly losing you. Today's close call with the gallows. It does seem rather improbable we have survived it all. Our first year of marriage has been a veritable tidal wave of rain! Of troubles," he clarified at my blank look.

"Are you asking me to get you some whisky?" I sat beside him on the bed and brought a hand to his brow, worried he had suffered some before-unnoticed harm while imprisoned these past weeks.

Collin captured my hands and pulled me toward him. "We are about to be deluged with it," he predicted merrily.

"I'm going to fetch Mary." I tried standing, but he pulled me back down.

"Deluged with happiness, Katie. With laughter and joy— and peace."

Lydia's cry sounded outside our door, followed by what could only be Timothy's boots clomping at full speed along the passageway. "Well, perhaps not a lot of peace, with all these children about. But *so* much happiness." He wrapped an arm around me. "So much love."

"Rain turned to whisky. Old Scottish proverb?" No wonder Finlay had been laughing. We were about to become the parents of seven children.

Collin nodded. "Highlanders are very wise, you know. Especially when it comes to love."

"Truly?" I scooted next to him on the bed, arms crossed, brows raised with skepticism. "Prove it."

Chapter Forty-eight

Johnston's dairy, Virginia, December 1762

"Well, what do you think?" Ben's sister stood aside, hands planted on her ample hips as she awaited Ian's reaction to the festive touches added throughout the parlor. Evergreen boughs wound up the stairway and swooped over doorways. Red ribbon festooned the corners and banister, and a bell jingled merrily each time one of the doors was opened or shut.

"You ought to do this all year," Ian said. "First time this place doesn't smell like a cow."

She thrust an elbow sharply in his side. "Ian MacDonald, I hope you have better sense than that when your wife is fishing for a compliment."

"She won't need to fish." At the sound of another bell, this one from upstairs, Ian's eyes flickered upward toward the second floor. Female voices drifted down, but he could not discern what they were saying.

"The house looks—perfect," he said, struggling for an appropriate word and settling on one he thought he could not go wrong with. "Truly. It is beautiful. I thank you for providing such a lovely setting for our wedding celebration."

"It's all but ready in the kitchen," said Mrs. Johnston. "Best collect your bride, and we'll all be off to the church."

Ian followed her from the parlor back out to the entryway, where he stood at the base of the stairs, nervously fiddling with an evergreen bough.

"Ian!" Aisla came running down the stairs, Taye right behind.

"Look at you," Ian exclaimed with an appreciative glance toward Mrs. Johnston. The girls each wore new dresses—nicer than any they'd ever owned, he'd wager.

"A wedding is a special occasion," she said with a little shrug of her shoulders. "Of course the girls needed new dresses." Her arm went around Aisla—rather naturally, it seemed to Ian—and she held the lass close, the way a mother would.

Jannet Campbell was next to descend the stairs. She, too, was dressed finely, but Ian couldn't have recalled a thing about her gown, then or later, because right behind her, on the landing, stood the woman he loved.

Her gown was cream, with bits of red ribbon adorning both the sleeves and neckline and hem. Sprigs of tiny red flowers covered the fabric and matched the darker petticoat beneath that fell wide and full and made a satisfactory swishing sound as she walked.

As grand as any lady at a ball in Edinburgh, Ian would tell his children for years to come. Though he would always remember that day in the orchard with fondness, when Eliza's gown had been missing this key piece.

New slippers peeked out from beneath her hem as she descended the stairs, and the sight of her stockinged ankle about did him in. He wished they could dispense with the wedding formalities and he could take her away this very minute.

"I know what you're thinking, Ian MacDonald," she scolded. "Quit looking at my ankles before I change my mind about marrying a scoundrel like you."

"Guilty," Ian admitted. He'd learned long ago there was no point in being anything less than truthful with this woman. The amazing thing was, even knowing his truths, she still loved him.

At the bottom of the stairs he placed the cloak over her shoulders, then turned her around to face him and tied the strings before Mrs. Johnston could speak her objections. After today he looked forward to little pleasures like this all the time. He intended to take every opportunity possible to touch his wife.

He helped her on with Mrs. Johnston's borrowed muff and fur cap.

"My hair," Eliza exclaimed when he'd placed the cap on her head and tied that as well—apparently too tightly. "It will be a sight by the time we get to the church."

"You're a *sight* this very moment," Ian whispered in her ear playfully and received an elbow to his other side.

The sleigh ride was both the longest and shortest of his life. He wanted to remember every single moment of this day forever. Holding Eliza's hand, entwining his fingers with hers—including the one that was soon to have a ring on it— the lasses' giggles as they sat across from him, stealing a kiss when Mrs. Johnston wasn't looking, placing his hands at Eliza's waist as he helped her down. It was all sweet torture that he alternately could not wait to end and hoped would last the rest of this life.

Rogers and his wife, along with Ben and his family, waited inside the church. Notably absent were both Campbells and MacDonalds, all busy laboring for their support far north, on Cape Breton.

Ian wondered briefly, once more, if he and Eliza should have waited to marry until they were reunited with their families. They had discussed it at length but decided against it. Three or more weeks at sea with Eliza—not spent in a dark hold under dismal conditions—seemed like the perfect wedding trip to Ian. They would start their life together on the Atlantic, where their love had first begun. Only this time they would have a cabin of their own, with idle hours to pass together as they pleased. No doubt the opposite awaited them once they rejoined the others.

Collin's letters described the land as one of stark beauty

and harsh conditions. *It will feel like home,* he'd said. *Or home as it used to be, without anyone to bother us.* Ian was certain it would be home, especially with Eliza at his side.

After leaving Eliza at the back of the chapel with Mrs. Johnston, Ian took his place at the front near the priest. Aisla and Taye came up the aisle first, each carrying a bundle of holly and berries, wrapped in ribbon. Taye stopped on the side where Eliza would stand, while Aisla stood beside Ian.

Ben and Eliza were next. Her smile was bright and her eyes all for Ian, never leaving his, as she traveled the short distance between benches.

At the top of the aisle Ben took Eliza's hand and placed it in Ian's.

Ian gave him a nod of thanks, for that and a hundred other things over the past months. Ben had proved himself a worthy friend time and again. *If I can be even half the man that Ben is, half as generous and kind as his sister . . . I will have lived a good life and contributed to many.*

Ian took Eliza's other hand, and they faced each other, perhaps contrary to what the priest would have preferred, but Ian didn't particularly care. He was making vows to her this day and wanted her to see his face as he spoke each of the promises he intended to keep.

Neither of their hands shook. Neither hesitated. Eliza's voice was as angelic as the first time he'd heard it. Ian held onto her tightly, still in awe that it was he to whom she was speaking such beautiful words.

"Above and beyond this, Ian MacDonald—" She added his name, almost as if she knew he was still disbelieving of the miracle of her, and his extreme good fortune—"I will cherish and honor you through this life and into the next." Eliza's brown eyes were moist as she made this promise, and Ian found his own responding accordingly.

He thought suddenly of his parents, long separated, but even longer together now. He thought he understood why his father had never remarried and had only spoken of their mother in the most loving and respectful terms.

Aisla stepped forward, the ring clutched in her small hand.

Ian winked as he took it from her and knew the only sadness of this day, that Aisla would not be making the trip to Nova Scotia with them. Jannet Campbell and the lasses were content here, well provided for and more comfortable than they had been in their lives. Aisla, in particular, had become fast friends with Mrs. Johnston and followed her around like a baby chick might its mother.

They need each other. Mrs. Johnston had never been blessed with a child of her own. Ian liked to think—he had seen—that Aisla had helped fill in some of the lonely corners of Mrs. Johnston's heart. And Mrs. Johnston had done the same for Aisla.

He would miss her, but after almost six months, it was time for him and Eliza to make their way north.

Taking Eliza's hand, he spoke clearly. "I give you my heart at the rising of the moon and the setting of the stars. To love and to honour through all that may come." He slipped the ring onto her finger, then folded her other hand over it.

Mine. All mine.

The priest pronounced them husband and wife, and Ian took Eliza's elbow to turn her toward the small congregation for well-wishes. But she did not turn as he'd expected.

"Aren't you going to thank me first?" she asked, a smirk upon her lips. "I did just marry you, after all."

Aisla leaned around them, stood on tiptoes, then stretched her arm high, mistletoe dangling from her finger-tips. Ian took it from her and raised it the rest of the way, so it was over Eliza's head.

"So you did." Ian took Eliza in his arms and kissed her right there for all to see how very grateful he was.

"Goodbye, goodbye!" Aisla and Taye ran along the dock, waving lace handkerchiefs as the *Charming Sally* left port and started downriver to the Atlantic.

"We'll write," Eliza promised, waving in return. "Thank you for everything!"

Ian kept his hand in the air as well, until Ben, Mrs. Johnston, and the others were mere specks on the shore.

"I'll miss them," Eliza said, looking at him a little teary eyed.

Ian brushed his thumb along her cheek and smiled. "I'll just have to do my best to keep your mind occupied elsewhere." They moved from the rail, making their way carefully across the crowded deck. Though the passengers on this voyage were few, the cargo was considerable, with most of the numerous crates and barrels on board to support the MacDonalds and Campbells in surviving their first, harsh winter in Nova Scotia.

In addition to what Eliza and Ian had been able to purchase with their pooled income of the past six months, Collin had sent all of the clans' collective funds, along with a lengthy list of needed items. Mrs. Johnston, Ben, and even Rogers had helped procure and pack these over the past several weeks. Captain Nicholas Cooke had once more been contracted to make the voyage north, and at last they were under way.

Ian helped Eliza down the short stairwell, eager to retreat to the warmth of their cabin, where a table had been thoughtfully set out. He eyed the bottle and glasses with suspicion. "Not planning to poison me tonight, are you, Mrs. MacDonald?"

Eliza blushed prettily. "I think not—tonight. However, you'd best mind your behavior in the future, Mr. MacDonald, or I may just decide to grow Belladonna in our new High-lands."

"Grow whatever you'd like, and poison me with it, too, just so long as you're the one who takes care of me when I'm ill." Ian caught her around the waist, and they tumbled together onto the bed, where he kissed her soundly for several long minutes.

"Villainous behavior already, I see," she said, breathless, her own eyes dancing with mischief as she reached for his cravat.

"You confuse my intentions," Ian said, turning his mouth down as if hurt. "I am only thanking the lady. My grati-tude overflows."

Eliza laughed as she undid the knot at his throat and began unwinding the cloth. "The time for gratitude is long past. From now on, it is happiness that we must be about."

"I have a few suggestions for that as well." He helped her with the rest of his neck cloth, then flung it aside. "The first involves the removal of all these cumbersome layers of clothing, so we might enjoy this voyage in comfort." He slid to the floor, then knelt before her and proceeded to remove first her slippers, then stockings, all the while wholly enjoying the deepening stain on Eliza's cheeks.

"Ian MacDonald, you are—"

"Aye?" His brow arched as he stood, then pulled her to her feet.

Eliza faced him, her breathing as uneven as his. Their eyes locked. She stepped closer and placed her hands almost shyly on his chest. "My husband." She raised up on tiptoes and kissed him, as she had that night in the lean-to. Only this time Ian did not let her get away.

Mine. His arms wrapped around her waist, pulling her close. *All mine.* He'd never felt more grateful—or happy.

Epilogue

Cape Breton Island, Nova Scotia, September 1763

Katie

The door to the common house flew open, and Timothy barged in. "Katie, Eliza, you may come now."

"What have you done to your breeches this time?"

I frowned as I stared at the torn piece over his right knee, flapping in the breeze.

He shrugged. "Dunno. Tore it on a nail, I think. But come on! You can see the surprise now. Everyone's waiting." Message delivered, he ran out the door again, his bare feet pounding along the dirt path.

"That one will not be content on land forever," Finlay predicted with a shake of his head as he recovered his balance after nearly being run over by Timothy. "Shore to ship, sails in the wind. To the Colonies south, then—back again?"

I didn't care for the question in the last part of his poetic fore-telling of Timothy's future. I'd no doubt my brother would seek the sea at some point, but I didn't like to think of the possibility that he might go far, or encounter danger when he did.

"For now, *thankfully,* he is land bound." I put the worry of Timothy's future aside.

I wasn't certain who the *everyone* Timothy had referred to was, as there were still plenty of us working inside while the sounds of wood being chopped and sawing and hammering carried through the open door. Nevertheless, I set my sewing aside and went to collect Liam from his cradle.

"I'll be right there," Eliza said from her place at the table across the room. "I'm almost finished with this letter to Jannet. I want to send it when Gordon leaves later today."

"No hurry," I called. "If it's *our* surprise, they'll wait for us."

Eliza had become the sister and friend I had yearned for since Anna's rejection years earlier. Ian and Eliza were the perfect complement to Collin and me, and the four of us had wonderful times together, whether on berry-picking outings, searching for the waterfall I had drawn the previous year, or simply sitting together before the fire at night, talking. We shared a corner of a common house—one of the long log cabins built hastily last fall to shelter everyone through the winter.

The structure had done its job. We had survived our first winter in Nova Scotia, though our diet was not worth mentioning, and privacy had been nearly as limited as it had been aboard the *Cleopatra.*

It was with much eagerness that many were now engaged in the process of building their own cabins. Collin and I and the children were to remain in the common house another year at least, along with Eithne and Gavin, and several others. There was too much other work to be done, crops and livestock being more important than a home of our own. I understood but had been disappointed.

However, Collin had been intrigued by my drawing of the narrow boat hollowed from a tree trunk. He had promised that before summer's end we would have one of those. As summer was rapidly drawing to a close, with leaves beginning to turn and night falling earlier and earlier, I anticipated that our surprise today would be the presentation of the boat I believed he had been secretly working on.

Throughout the summer Eliza, the children, and I—excepting Timothy and Jacob, Lydia's oldest brother—had been forbidden from crossing over the hill into the shallow valley below. A great deal of stout trees were to be found on the other side, as well as an inlet that led to the sea. I guessed it to be the perfect place for Collin and Ian to have set about building their tree boats.

"I'm ready." Eliza met me at the door, and we started off, Liam settled on my hip as we walked.

"Does Mary have the other children this morning?" Eliza asked, for the first time seeming to note their absence.

I nodded. "She's taken them to collect the last of the summer berries."

"Even Lydia went?" Eliza sounded as surprised as I had been when Mary had offered.

"I suspect Lydia went because Mary is in on our 'surprise.' Collin must have told her it would be difficult to travel in the tree boat with a toddler running about."

Eliza smiled. "You still think it's a boat they're surprising us with today?"

"What else would it be?"

She shrugged, but the spark of mischief in her eyes told me she believed otherwise.

"Eliza MacDonald, what do you know that I don't?"

In answer she shook her head, gathered the sides of her cream skirt, and hurried ahead of me through the tall, wild grass.

"What do you think of that, Liam?"

He shoved his fist farther in his mouth and drooled in response. I hugged him close, ducked beneath a low branch, and followed Eliza. "Soon enough I suppose we shall both know."

She reached the crest of the hill first, then, with a joyous shout, started running down the other side.

I was still a minute or more off, my arms aching from carrying Liam. Ian liked to tease that we fed him straight cream from the cows Mrs. Johnston had sent. Though that wasn't at all the truth, no one could deny that Liam was of sturdy stock. My illness while carrying him seemed not to have affected his health in the least. Collin and I were grateful and loved him dearly, every roll and dimple included.

By contrast, Lydia had thinned out over the past months, since she'd learned to first walk and then run—running everywhere and keeping me running too, going after her. She and her siblings were a great delight to us as well, especially the youngest two, the way they had taken to calling me "Mama."

"We made it." I set Liam on the ground at the top of the hill and bent to catch my breath a moment. It was then I saw Eliza's surprise. A fine log cabin lay in a direct line below us. As I watched, Ian swept Eliza into his arms and carried her across the threshold.

"No evil spirits for them," I said, smiling as I remembered when Collin had carried me across the threshold of our room in my grand-father's castle.

I scooped Liam up once more and started down the other side of the slope, shielding my eyes from the sun with my free hand.

By the time I reached Ian and Eliza's cabin they were outside again, where Eliza was happily admiring everything from the window shutters to the butter churn on the front porch.

My own anticipation for a boat ride dimmed a little in light of her surprise, but I was happy for them. They had been married less than a year and yearned for privacy as much or more than Collin and I.

Still searching for Collin and supposing him to be near the river, I followed a stream to the narrowest point, then held Liam tight with both hands as I jumped across.

"You could have used the bridge," Ian called. I glanced upstream and saw that he and Eliza were crossing on a fine, sturdy bridge made of hewn logs. Posts had been driven on either side of the stream, with rope strung between them as handles to use when crossing.

"Collin and I built this," Ian said. "So you and Eliza can visit easily, even when the water is high."

I was about to ask why I might wish to visit with her from the other side of the stream, when the sense that I had been here before overtook me. For a few seconds my vision blurred. I was back on the *Cleopatra,* sketchbook in hand, as I worked over a puzzling drawing of Collin. *And our children.* Or, most of them, at least.

Once more my grip on Liam tightened, as simultaneously the breath I'd been holding released. My vision cleared, and Collin stepped into view holding Lydia, the other children clustered around him—exactly as I had seen and drawn over a year earlier.

"Welcome home!" they shouted at once, leaving his side and running toward me.

Liam gurgled and squirmed with happiness as they reached us, each jumping up and down and trying to talk at once.

"Come see! You have to see how lovely it is."

"I want to go in first. May I? We haven't been allowed yet."

"Collin says you must be first. Can we come in too?"

I realized they were talking about the boat, but could only think of what Ian had said about visiting and the children's chants of "welcome home." "You're going to build our home here?" I asked, staring at Collin, still feeling somewhat dazed by the brief vision while also being overwhelmingly happy to have finally realized why I had not seen myself with Collin in that moment, many months ago. It had not been because I'd died in childbirth or any other way, but because I had been on my way to join them, with Liam.

Collin reached over the heads of the others, taking Liam from me with his free hand, so that he had a child in each now. "We are not *going* to build here."

"We already have, Katie!" Timothy grabbed my hand and pulled me forward. Ten steps more, and I saw it between the trees, a cabin as handsome as Ian's, though considerably bigger, to hold our unexpectedly large brood.

"Oh, Collin." I stopped moving, in spite of Timothy's tugging. *Our home.* I wanted a moment to take it all in—everything from the large stone chimneys traveling up both sides of the house to the wide porch, and the empty rocking chair waiting there.

"Collin made that too," Timothy boasted, as if he'd done it himself. "He made everything, and I helped."

I bent to kiss the top of his head. "Thank you. It's beautiful. It's perfect." My eyes watered as they sought Collin.

Ian and Eliza came forward and took the babies from him.

"And now it is this Mrs. MacDonald's turn," Collin said, sweeping me into his arms before I'd quite realized what he was doing. With long strides he crossed the yard, then stepped onto the porch and pushed open the door to our home. Only when we had entered and he had kicked the door shut behind him did he set me down.

"Collin," I scolded, glancing at the closed door. "The children are out there."

"Aye." He leaned forward and pulled in the latch. "And there they'll stay for a minute." He gathered me in his arms and kissed away my frown. "Welcome home, Katie."

I ignored the banging on the door and kissed him back. "I don't know how you managed to get all this done. This is quite the surprise. I thought—I thought you were building a boat."

He laughed and kissed my forehead. "*Timothy* is building the boat. And you shouldn't have been surprised at all. I promised you a home."

"You've been keeping that promise for over two years." I twined my arms around his neck. "Wherever you are, Collin, *that* is my home."

A final note,

Thank you for reading *The Promise of Home*.

I continue to appreciate those who take the time to read my stories and those who post reviews as well. You make it possible for me to continue doing what I love.

If you would like more information about my other books and future releases, please visit:

www.michelepaigeholmes.com.

You can also follow me on Twitter at @MichelePHolmes.

Happy reading!
Michele

About Michele Paige Holmes

Michele Paige Holmes spent her childhood and youth in Arizona and northern California, often curled up with a good book instead of out enjoying the sunshine. She graduated from Brigham Young University with a degree in elementary education and found it an excellent major with which to indulge her love of children's literature.

Her first novel, *Counting Stars*, won the 2007 Whitney Award for Best Romance. Its companion novel, a romantic suspense titled *All the Stars in Heaven*, was a Whitney Award finalist, as was her first historical romance, *Captive Heart*. *My Lucky Stars* completed the Stars series.

In 2014 Michele launched the Hearthfire Historical Romance line, with the debut title, *Saving Grace*. *Loving Helen* is the companion novel, with a third, *Marrying Christopher*, followed by the companion novella *Twelve Days in December*.

When not reading or writing romance, Michele is busy

with her full-time job as a wife and mother. She and her husband live in Utah with their five high-maintenance children, and a Shitzu that resembles a teddy bear, in a house with a wonderful view of the mountains.

You can find Michele on the web:
MichelePaigeHolmes.com
Facebook: Michele Holmes
Twitter: @MichelePHolmes

CPSIA information can be obtained
at www.ICGtesting.com
Printed in the USA
FSHW012213191118
53899FS